Dublin's Girl

EIMEAR LAWLOR

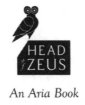

HEAD
ZEUS

An Aria Book

9 7 5 3 1 2 4 6 8

A catalogue record for this book is available from
the British Library.

ISBN (HB): 9781801101479
ISBN (XTPB): 9781801101486
ISBN (E): 9781800249288

Cover design © Cherie Chapman

Typeset by Siliconchips Services Ltd UK

MIX
Paper from
responsible sources
FSC
www.fsc.org
FSC® C020471

Aria
c/o Head of Zeus
5–8 Hardwick Street
London EC1R 4RG
WWW.ARIAFICTION.COM

For my beautiful daughter Ciara
25/08/98 – 09/07/2016

Angel

On a Wednesday in July
We dried our tears and said goodbye
Another Angel gone before her time
But she's still alive in our hearts and minds
And heaven knows when we are old
She will be forever young

(Angel, Kodaline 2017)

The winter of 1916 had been long and harsh,
and the insipid spring of 1917 left little hope of a
promising summer. War raged in Europe, and the Irish
were waging their own war against British occupation
in their country. Since the executions of the leaders of
the Easter Rising the previous year, the Irish people had
rallied together in revolt against the English in their
country. English soldiers frequented many farms in
the Irish countryside looking for rebels and terrorising
people. Real resistance against British Rule in Ireland
started in 1919 in the War of Independence.

1

June 1917 Virginia, Co. Cavan

'Veronica will you hurry with those potatoes?' Her mother sighed. 'I've to make the bread yet, and the men will be here early today. The soldiers shot poor Tommy Brady, and his wake is tonight. I've so much to do,' her mother said as she took the brown bread out of the black Aga stove. She bent to sniff it, which always amused Veronica. She thought, *How can you tell if something is cooked by smelling it?*

A potato slipped from Veronica's hand into the bucket and water splashed everywhere.

'Veronica,' her mother screeched, 'for God's sake, will you watch what you're doing? All you're doing is creating more work for yourself.'

Veronica rolled her eyes and gritted her teeth as she peeled the last potato and dropped it to the mound beside her. Thirty potatoes, three each, enough for the family and the farmhands. The sunshine filled the yard outside the kitchen, weeks of rain had retreated, and the countryside had erupted into an assortment of green hues. The arrival of summer sunshine was no guarantee it would last, and Veronica itched to get outside to go to the lake to fish or swim. As children, she and her brother Eddie had spent many summer days by the lake fishing and exploring the forest, but in their teenage years they spent less and less time together, their time demanded elsewhere. Now Veronica's days in the house involved helping her mother and their cook Mrs Slaney in the kitchen and Eddie helped his father in their grocery shop in the village.

In the yard, there was a squawk and a spray of feathers. Veronica's mother let out an exasperated cry behind her.

'That damn dog is at the chickens again!' Her mother ran to the yard, flapping her maroon apron while screaming at the dog. Veronica held her ribs with laughter. Her mother's nostrils flared like a cow ready to charge to protect her calf from danger. Picking up a broom, she swept the black and white collie dog out of the yard into the field.

Veronica stopped laughing as she glimpsed movement on the other side of the yard – a flash of tweed, a muddied shoe. It was Eddie. Veronica watched him, narrowing her eyes as Eddie stealthily crept along the side of the shed. *What was he up to now?* He had left earlier to help their father at the shop in the village. There was a time Eddie never kept secrets from her, but lately, he disappeared for hours, and when she asked where he had been, he'd mutter, 'Nowhere,' and dismiss her with a scowl.

She stood back from the window and watched as he furtively unlatched the side door of the shed to slip inside before Frankie the farmhand walked past and pushed his wheelbarrow into the nearby pigsty. The chickens had

4

calmed, and her mother was back at the stove, stirring the stew, mumbling about the dog.

The potatoes peeled, Veronica grabbed the bucket with the peel, and shouted to her mother, 'Mammy, I'm giving the skins to the pigs.' She had to see what Eddie was doing.

Her mother continued to stir the pot. 'Don't be late for dinner and close the door after ye.'

But it fell on deaf ears as Veronica left the back door swinging open. She knew he was up to no good; he had probably stolen apples from the orchard and was hiding them in the shed, or maybe a pheasant from the nearby Taylor estate. One time they'd taken a pheasant from the local estate, and they were grounded for two months after the bird was found in the side shed Veronica and Eddie used as their hideout.

Mr Brady, the groundsman from the estate, had arrived to speak to the twins' father saying their groundsman Simon had seen the twins running from the estate. 'They could hardly hold the sack with the animal jumping, frightened for its life,' he said, shaking, his face red ready to erupt.

'Rabbits,' the children had replied in unison. Neither Mr Brady nor their father believed them, and he grounded them for two months. But those days of doing things together were long gone.

Veronica dropped the bucket of potato peel outside the pigsty for Paudie. With one last glance around the yard, she slipped into the shed and stood back in the shadows and squinted. The sun threw rays of light into the gloom which caught the dust particles dancing in mid-air.

There was a cough from the back of the shed, and a silhouette stood on a bale of hay. Slowly and quietly, she inched forward. It was from Eddie.

He stood on his tippy toes, reaching up to the rafters and brushed away cobwebs. Veronica shivered, she hated spiders. Letting her eyes adjust to the darkness, she moved with care, placing one foot in front of the other, trying not to make a sound and moved further into the shed. Eddie was only a few feet away from her, and she stayed in the shadows not daring to breathe. He took a small object from inside his jacket and put it high on to the rafters, but it fell out the other side. She stifled a gasp. *Christ.* It had had a wooden handle and a barrel: it was a small gun.

'Eddie McDermott, what are you doing?'

Eddie jumped down from the bale, his hands quickly covering the gun.

'Jaysus, Veronica, don't creep up on me like that; you nearly gave me a heart attack.'

'What are you doing with that gun?'

'I'm joining the volunteers.'

'Daddy will be the one to have a heart attack if he finds out. You know it's dangerous. The soldiers are everywhere, and James Sheridan's daddy was sent to prison last week, and Mammy said that's what got Tommy Smith killed.'

He held the gun tight to his chest.

'Veronica, we have a chance of freedom. Do ya' not get it? We're suppressed. We're nothing more than puppets. Do ya' think it's right that decisions are made by the eejits in a different country?' He stood as straight as possible, trying to show he was the taller of the two, and at six foot he towered over most people.

He walked toward the door. IA small brown bag fell from inside his jacket, its contents rolling across the flagstones. Ten or twelve coins rolled across the floor only stopping when they got caught in bits of winter turf that littered the back of the shed.

'Eddie, what are you doing with that money?' The money was more of an astonishment than the gun. But the gun was a danger. And danger often meant death.

Eddie continued, unaware of the change in her expression. 'You know we should speak Irish, not English. They forced it on us. We've not just lost our language, we've lost our culture, our education, our opportunity, our right to be Irish.'

'A gun, Eddie. For God's sake, what will that do? And what about Home Rule? And Eddie, that money, where did you get it and what do you want it for?'

'What do you know about Home Rule? Tell me how you think that will make the situation any better? Didn't you hear me say we're puppets? We need total independence to make our own decisions. If we get Home Rule, the power is still with the English.'

Veronica slumped on a bale of hay. 'Does Daddy know? He is in the Gaelic League. That isn't illegal. I heard Daddy say to Mammy they are helping us not to forget we are Irish, but your gun, Eddie, it could get you arrested.' She hesitated. 'Or killed.'

He snorted and spat onto the dusty floor. 'The Irish language won't get us our rights. Rights as Irishmen to govern ourselves. What good can learning a *cupla focail* do? It won't put food on people's tables, won't give them a chance to better themselves. Me and the Sheridan boys are joining up, and that's that. Don't you dare tell Daddy or Mammy. We're having a meeting later at the Sheridans' and if anyone is looking for me, tell them you haven't seen me.'

'What difference does it make who rules us? We're fine. We're not hungry. Don't we have a good life?'

'God, Veronica, sometimes you just don't get it. Don't you realise how privileged you are? We're lucky. Look at the O'Reillys. Twelve of them in a two-roomed cottage owned by an English landlord who doesn't even live in this country.'

Silent, she frowned. The O'Reillys often arrived at school dirty, and more than often didn't come. Eddie interrupted her thoughts.

'The O'Reillys have nothing, and never will. And people experience worse conditions than the O'Reillys. In the west of Ireland, it's worse. They have no work or little food.'

'Well someone should find the landlords and arrest them,' she said with her hands on her hips, her lips pursed. She felt out of her depth but couldn't let him win another argument. It was always the same since they were little, he always talked over her. She stopped talking when she heard Paudie's out-of-tune whistle.

They stood glaring at each other, waiting for Paudie to pass.

'And who do you think would arrest the landlords? The RIC?' Eddie didn't wait for Veronica to answer. 'The landlords are English. The "R" in RIC is Royal – ROYAL Irish Constabulary, get it, Veronica? Believe me just because they have an Irish accent that doesn't mean they are on our side. They work for the Crown – they would hardly arrest people who pay their wages, would they?'

Veronica knew there was little point arguing with him. Eddie said, 'I am warning you – don't mention the gun or money to anyone and forget you even saw them. What I do with them is none of your business.'

She kicked the dirt floor. It hurt her he was friendlier with James Sheridan. He was trouble. She had a bad feeling.

There were footsteps in the yard, coming rapidly towards them.

'Veronica, where are you?' her mother shouted.

She groaned. The last thing she wanted was more chores. At the back of the shed was a window, and she climbed onto a bale of hay and squeezed through it, ripping her skirt on a nail.

'Veronica, where the devil are you?'

Veronica gathered up her skirt and ran down the hill without looking back. Breathless, her heart thumping, she only stopped when she got to the lakeshore. She looked over the lake, beautiful Lough Ramor. She could get lost in the stillness of the water. Thirty-two islands. 'One for each county of Ireland,' her father said. A world inhabited the lake. Not people, but birds and wild animals. Herons, cranes, otters, ducks and swans.

The last of the morning mist swirled over the lake, the remaining cold air of the morning in a battle with the heat from the rising midday sun. She would forget about Eddie. This was her time, that was more important. After checking that she was alone, Veronica stripped down to her undergarments and got into the ice-cold water. Every cell in her body tingled. She closed her eyes, now transported to another world. She was in heaven as the cold water sent a tingle through her, all her senses awakening. It was the only time she felt alive, away from the mundane routine of life in the kitchen.

She got out when her skin stung from the water, her skin pinched and translucent, and retrieved the towel she kept hidden in the boathouse. Veronica lay on the grass, looking up at the blue sky. The sun filtered through the trees, shining on the lake like diamond dust. Seven ducks flew overhead and made a perfect V. She watched as they disappeared into the horizon, wondering where they were going. She envied their freedom, but soon Eddie infiltrated her thoughts. The gun had been a pistol: a shiny one, with a wooden handle. Veronica had once seen a similar one in the drawer of her father's desk. What was he doing with all that money? Where did he get it? She chewed her fingernail, wondering whether he had stolen it. What other explanation could there be?

Veronica sighed, thinking how once they'd known each other's every thought and feeling. They argued, but they had been close. A special bond only twins have with each other. Away at boarding school, they wrote daily, devising escapes from their respective schools, both despising the confines of daily routine and the authority of the clergy. When Eddie stopped writing as often to her, it upset her, but then the sadness turned to anger. James Sheridan had called at their house more often, and if she tried to join them, they dismissed her and went off to the woods or lake without her.

Now the sun was high in the sky. She dressed and went to the woods. She stopped by the bridge over the Blackwater River to inhale the woody incense of the pine trees and then ran to the icehouse. Shrubbery concealed it up on a slope off the main path. The icehouse stored the meats of the Taylor family estate. They were an English family who owned the land around the village, but they lived in England and only came for the summer months to fish and shoot ducks.

Veronica climbed up to the slope, careful not to scratch herself on the thorny briars which concealed the entrance. The icehouse overlooked the stone bridge. Laughter echoed through the trees, and she saw a group of ladies wearing white lace dresses appear on the bridge, their words lost beneath their matching umbrellas. Behind them walked two young men, one of whom she recognised: Seán McCabe, the farm labourer. He spoke to the ladies in the poshest voice she had ever heard him use.

'We're nearly dere, ma ladies.' It did little to disguise his Cavan accent.

Wearing his father's oversized suit, he shifted from one foot to the other.

Veronica sat on a soft mound of moss, watching the ladies and the two servant girls who did everything for them. Every year, ever since she could remember, her younger sister Susan got into a tizzy when the Taylor women arrived from England during the summer, desperate to see their outfits.

But Veronica had no interest in their clothes or their lives, and she thought the dresses they wore looked ridiculous. Still, she watched them until they had passed out of sight and the wood was silent once more.

A twig cracked behind her. She pushed herself into the undergrowth and peered through the bushes and saw James Sheridan. He raised his hand to his eyes to scan the forest before he tightened the twine around his long brown overcoat. She inched forward, careful to keep quiet. He bent to pull at a pile of branches and twigs and tugged at something, and when he rose, he held a long-barrelled hunting rifle. He turned towards her. She pushed herself further into the ground but kept him in sight. His eyes passed over her and continued to scrutinise the rest of the forest. He put the rifle inside his long coat, tying the string tight and leaving hastily. She couldn't believe he was so stupid after the RIC had arrested James's father the previous week for possession of guns.

After a few minutes, she raised her head. James was gone. The sun now filled the forest with light and warmth. She turned to lie on her back, looking up between the branches, the green hue of new leaves filling the sky. It was her favourite time of the year, and Eddie and James had to destroy it. For the second time that day, she forced thoughts of Eddie and James to the back of her mind.

She stood and brushed off the moss from her now damp dress before returning home, trying not to think of the things she had seen.

2

The following morning, after their usual chores, Veronica and Susan sat by the lakeshore, with the sunshine on their backs. The dry spell continued, the grass in the fields had turned brown, and the mud on the farm cracked. Summer heat drained their energy, and the girls welcomed the reprieve from kitchen chores to sit by Lough Ramor. A swan glided on to the lake.

'Susan, do you wish you could do something more exciting?' Veronica asked.

'What do you mean?'

'Work with Father in the shop, or with Mrs Smith in the office. Anything is better than scrubbing and cooking all day. Imagine, Susan, having a proper job.' Veronica's mind drifted to a life she could only dream of.

'Why? What's got into you?' Susan said as she swatted away a buzzing bee.

'Nothing is wrong, but, I mean, are you happy?'

'Veronica, sometimes I don't know what goes on inside your head.'

Veronica sat up and leaned over and grabbed Susan's hands, causing her to drop the daisy chain she was making.

'Would you not like to go to Dublin? You love fashion and clothes – it'd be exciting. Virginia is just so boring.'

'Why on earth would I want to go to Dublin? Did you not see in the paper all the burned buildings and danger? Did you see the pictures of men walking through the streets with rifles slung over their shoulders?'

Veronica swept back a few curls that had escaped from her pinned hair. 'Oh, Susan, I'm sure it's not always like that.'

When Veronica went to the shop with her father, she would sit on the wooden barrel behind the counter talking to customers. But more than anything, she wanted to work in the office above the shop. Mrs Smith, a widow, helped her father in the office, and she arrived to work on her black bicycle, wearing black clothes. Veronica and Susan would giggle that they didn't know where the bicycle began, or Mrs Smith ended.

'And tell me, Veronica, what you would do in Dublin?'

'Mrs Smith told me about the secretarial school she went to; that's how she got the job with Daddy. She learnt to type, and to do shorthand.'

'School. Sure, you got expelled from school.'

'I didn't get expelled. There was an outbreak of measles. That's why I left. Lots of girls got sent home.'

'Veronica, I heard Mammy crying when Daddy said you had to leave school. He told Mammy you brought a dog into the dormitory.'

'Well, it was snowing outside, and I felt sorry for him, his little paws frozen.'

She knew Susan was only interested if her scones or

bread were cooked, or if more sugar would make her jam better. But sometimes Veronica wanted to talk about more.

'Susan, did you ever hear of a man called John Redmond?'

'Who?'

'Apparently, he has told people they should fight for the British. He said the war is our war.'

'What do you mean, Veronica? What's the war got to do with us?' Susan frowned and shook her head.

'Last week when I was with Mrs Smith in the office, Mr Tynan came in to pay a bill. You know the man with one short leg? Anyway, he and Mrs Smith started to talk.' Veronica leaned forward and lowered her voice. 'They forgot I was there. He told her he had been to one of John Redmond's rallies somewhere in the west, Co. Mayo. Anyway, Mr Redmond has urged men to fight for the British in the war. He said if they fight for Britain that they will pass the Bill for Home Rule, and that means we will have our government here in Dublin.'

'Why, but what difference would that make?'

Veronica sighed. 'All our money won't go to England. We could keep the money for ourselves.' Veronica had often heard her father complain about having to pay taxes to England.

Susan huffed and tutted. Most people took this as a sign she was irritated, but Veronica knew she did this when people talked about something she didn't understand. She thought nobody noticed when she suddenly got an itch, or a headache when her brother and father discussed politics.

Susan sat up. 'Since when did you become interested in politics?'

'I've always been interested. Especially since the executions last year.' She wasn't, but Veronica wanted to irritate Susan knowing this was something that wouldn't interest her at all.

The sun was now hot, and the swans moved on the lake with five grey signets following them closely.

'Look, Veronica, aren't they so beautiful?' Susan's attention went elsewhere. 'You know they stay together for life after their swan children are gone?' Susan sat forward and looked dreamily at the swans.

'Signets, Susan, they're called signets.'

'Oh, whatever you call them, it's just so romantic.'

Sometimes their two-year age gap felt like decades. Veronica didn't tell Susan the rest of the conversation she had heard between Mr Tynan and Mrs Smith about how men were joining the Volunteers, the illegal group of rebels against the British, and how a lot of local lads were signing up.

The same afternoon Mr Tynan had come into the office, she had been sitting at the window overlooking the yard and saw a group of men talking, their hands moving feverishly in tandem with their mouths. The men were gathered by the lumber piles, passing packages to one another under their coats. With bent heads and caps low that concealed their faces, distance muffled their words. At the yard entrance, she saw a man take off his cap and frantically wave it when any RIC approached. The men would then scatter, loading grain onto their carts and returning to their idle chat when the RIC man walked into the yard.

'Veronica, sometimes you talk nonsense. C'mon. It's time we went home to help Mrs Slaney make tea. Look if you want to go to secretarial school, ask Daddy.' Susan stood up, the conversation finished. She picked out the dried grass that got caught in the fabric of her tweed skirt.

Veronica had asked her father a few weeks earlier. When she had approached this with him in his study, he hadn't even raised his head. He'd just said, 'No'. And to highlight the conversation was not for further discussion he then said, 'Close the door after you, Veronica.'

The girls neared their home, and Veronica caught sight of Eddie.

'You go on, Susan. I've to ask Eddie something,' Veronica said. She followed him as he made his way to the shed. Veronica's mother was washing the dinner pots at the kitchen sink, so focussed on scrubbing the pot she didn't notice either of them go into the shed.

At the back of the shed, Eddie sat on a bale, and he kicked the floor, raising the dust on the floor with his work boot.

'Eddie,' said Veronica. 'I don't get it, why do you want to get involved with the rebels? You will run the shop with Daddy someday, is that not enough?'

'No, it's not. We are going to get our freedom from the British, and I will help.'

She tried another angle. 'What about the money? Where did you get that?'

His face reddened, he stood up, and grabbed her wrist. 'Don't you dare say anything about the money to anyone.'

She pulled her hand away and shook it. It hurt. This wasn't her brother, her twin, her closest confidant. The person she had shared a womb for nine months. He had changed.

Their father's loud voice filled the shed from outside in the yard. Veronica couldn't understand what he was shouting. She left Eddie to see her father shout at Paudie, who was pushing a wheelbarrow full of potato skins across the yard to the pigsty. Her father's face was red like the Aga when it overheated. He grabbed Paudie and pulled him across the yard by the scruff of his shirt collar as Paudie cried, 'I didn't do it.'

Veronica ran to her father and pulled his arm just as he was about to strike.

'Daddy, what are you doing to Paudie?'

He shook Veronica off like an insect. 'He took thirty shillings. The thief!'

'Daddy, why would he do that?'

'Veronica, let me handle this,' he bellowed. He grabbed Paudie by the scruff of his collar again and dragged him across the yard, Paudie's protestations of innocence now a snivelling whimper. She watched as he threw Paudie out the gate.

'Get out, ye thief, and never come back!'

Susan, now in the yard, gestured to Veronica. 'Quick, come upstairs. I've to tell you something.'

'Not now, Susan.'

'Did you hear? Paudie stole money from Daddy's study.'

Her heart stopped. Paudie was simple, but not a thief, and she had seen Eddie with money... but would he do something like that?

Veronica spotted Eddie now trying to shrink into the shadows of the falling ivy on the walls of the shed, but Susan saw him.

'Eddie, did you hear Paudie stole money?'

Veronica tried to guess whether the look on Eddie's face was one of pretend shock or self-righteousness? Veronica glared Eddie in the eye. He was the mirror image of her. They had the same shade of green eyes, brown hair and olive skin, that always went a shade darker in the summer months. 'Eddie, do you know anything about the money?' she added.

'No, he probably took it. You know he is an imbecile.' He snorted and kicked the ground with his boot, rising dust. 'I'm off.' He shrugged his shoulders. 'I'll leave you girls to discuss the mind of a thief.'

'Can you believe that, Veronica? It's just awful. Veronica, are you listening?'

Paudie wouldn't find a job anywhere else. He had no family. She watched the back of Eddie's head as he walked away. Stealing and letting someone else take the blame was not the Eddie she'd once known. Veronica didn't know what he was up to, and she told herself she didn't care. Her immediate concern was to get away from Virginia. She knew what her future would be if she stayed at home. Married to a man she hardly knew, her own dreams forgotten.

★

In her second year in boarding school, she heard her mother and father discussing Eddie's future.

'Law, maybe he could do law.'

'No, he will work in the shop with me,' her father had replied.

'You're right, Richard, and the girls will be married soon. Mrs Mulvaney's daughter has a lovely home, and her mother said he is a good man from Ballyhaunis. She is expecting her first child.' Veronica had wondered, *where the hell was Ballyhaunis?*

Veronica's uncle had studied law in Dublin. It was rare for a Catholic to go to university, but her mother's parents wanted their son educated, and he had gone to King's Inn in Dublin. She had gone to see him once, and she remembered the large imposing white stone entrance, but the street up to it had barefoot children running around, and washing lines hung from house to house.

She had held her breath and tightened her fists; she was no Elizabeth Bennet.

Now, as she watched Eddie leave her, she thought about her future. Maybe this could be used to her advantage.

3

One Sunday after dinner, the family retired to the sitting room as this was the only day of rest in the busy haymaking season. Veronica's father dozed in his armchair, his glasses resting precariously on the tip of his nose, and with each snore, they inched further down. It was only a matter of time before they fell onto the book on his lap.

Her mother sat in the seat in the bay window, checking her embroidery as the sunlight from the south-facing window filled the room. Veronica scanned the newspaper but kept one eye on Eddie as he shifted in his chair.

He abruptly got up. 'Mammy, I'm going fishing.'

'Em. That's nice, Eddie,' Bernadette said without lifting her head, concentrating on her embroidery. She lifted it to the light of the window and smiled, happy with her needlework. 'Are you going, Veronica, as well?'

'Yes.' Veronica jumped up, her book falling on the floor. 'Eddie, com' on.'

Eddie clenched his teeth and glared at her. Veronica grabbed him by the arm and pulled him out of the room.

Outside he whispered, 'You're not coming.'

'I don't want to know whatever stupid things you are up

to. I want you to do something for me.'

He tugged his arm free and took his cap from the hallstand. 'What now? I'm busy.'

'Eddie, please, ask Daddy to let me go to Dublin to secretarial school?'

He stopped as he opened the front door, his cap in his hand.

'Veronica, just ask him yourself.'

'I did. He said no.'

'Well then, that's your answer.'

'I'll tell Father that I saw you with the money.' He was halfway out the front door but stopped.

He turned and glared at Veronica, his lips tight and white. 'Don't you bloody dare.'

'How could you let Paudie take the blame?'

The dog barked when Hughie the new farmhand passed the front door. 'Whist, would ya, you fool of a dog.' He banged an empty bucket on the gate, a warning to the dog to leave the chickens alone.

She waited until Hughie was gone, 'Eddie, I WILL tell Daddy, I know it was you. You can't tell me it's a coincidence that I saw you with the same sum of money that Paudie apparently stole.' She didn't know how much money Eddie had.

'But... maybe I won't say anything if you say to Daddy you think it's a good idea for me to go to secretarial school. Women do lots of things now. I see it in the newspapers.' It was a lie. All she saw in the newspapers were advertisements for soaps and clothes. 'Mrs Smith went up to Dublin to learn how to type, and she went to secretarial school.'

'Veronica don't be so daft. I'm going now. Forget about that stupid idea.'

She shouted at his back. 'I will tell, I'm serious.' But her words were lost in the wind as he turned the corner of the house.

Later that night while she lay in bed, a continuous rumble of whispered excitement filtered its way upstairs to Veronica's ears. Susan slept soundly in the opposite bed. Veronica tiptoed out of the room and along the landing, knowing which creaking floorboards to avoid. She knelt and tried to listen. She saw the light from the drawing-room creeping beneath the door into the hall. People were arguing in Irish and English. She listened to the people talking, and there was an occasional sound of someone's fist hitting the dining table. The door opened and all talk ceased. People filtered out of the room into the hall, shaking her father's hand as they left. One of them was a woman she had never seen before. She was tall and wore an enormous hat. Veronica moved to the landing window to watch them outside the front of the house. As the woman spoke, the men hung on to her every word. Only when they were all gone did Veronica return to bed. She thought about the woman, about how she would have to think of another plan to get away from Virginia or try again with Eddie. She tossed and turned, sleep evading her when the only prospect of a future was one that demanded the mundane drudgery of a kitchen. Eventually, sleep came.

4

Veronica wiped a cobweb off her face to peer out onto the road from behind the bush, but the person whistling wasn't Eddie. It was James Sheridan. Her pulse quickened. She hadn't seen him since the day in the wood with the rifle, and she stepped back into the scrub for him to pass. When the whistling faded, she stuck her head out again to look at the road leading to the village. In the distance, a figure wearing a flat cap pushed a bicycle. It was Eddie.

She moved back in between the green foliage, and when the click of the wheels grew louder, she jumped out.

'God, Veronica, what are you doing?'

'Eddie, have you said anything to Daddy yet?'

'Veronica, I've other things to worry about than your silly little games.'

'You have to help me.'

'Stop bothering me, I've more important things to do. Why do you want to go to learn to type anyway?' He pushed past her. 'Now, just leave me alone.'

'You took the money, didn't you? I will tell Daddy I know it was you who took the money. He blames Paudie, and he got sacked.' She stared at him. This was a gamble as she wasn't sure if he had taken the money.

She spat her words at him. 'I hope you get caught and sent to prison, and the rats eat you when you lie in bed at night.'

He didn't deny it.

'Christ, Veronica, just go away.' Shaking his head, he started to push the bike up the lane to go home, but Veronica grabbed him by the sleeve.

He shook her arm off him, as if she was an unwanted insect, and got back on his bike.

'Go away. I'm warning you. Just go away, Veronica.'

'Eddie, I'm—'

Their father's voice boomed as he came out of the cowshed. 'Good, Eddie, you're home. I need to show you how to keep a ledger for the shop. You need to understand everything if you are to help me run the businesses.'

'Daddy, I need to speak to you.'

'Not now, Veronica, I want to talk to Eddie.'

He motioned Eddie to follow him inside the house. As Eddie passed Veronica, he hissed, 'I'm warning you. Don't you dare say anything.' His green eyes narrowed, his face red.

Veronica ran into the house and up to her room, and flung herself on her bed, thumping her fists on her pillow as tears of anger flowed. *Bloody James Sheridan.* The more time Eddie spent with him, the more distant she and Eddie had become. She felt he had got Eddie into something more serious than a few guns. Soon, she fell asleep, only waking to her mother shouting for her. 'Veronica, your father wants you in his study.'

She knocked on the study door and entered. Books lined two of the walls. The red carpet, faded by years of sunshine, looked shabby, but her father so far had refused to listen to her mother's pleas to change it. A head of a lion hung over the fireplace. Its eyes were wide, and its jaws open as if to eat anyone who dared to venture too near. She hated it.

Veronica coughed and waited until he looked up from his paperwork from where he sat in his high-backed chair, his large frame obscuring the evening sun.

'Eddie tells me you'd like to go to secretarial school.' He looked down at his papers and shuffled them into another pile. 'Veronica, the only secretarial schools are in Dublin. Your mother thinks that's not a place for young women. I assume you see the papers in the shop, and I talked it over with your mother, and she doesn't want you to go.' He didn't take his eyes off her as he spoke. 'But...' He paused. 'Personally, I think it may be good for you. I have a good friend who has a secretarial school in Dublin, and he'll take you. And you can stay with my sister Betty and her husband, Tom. And your uncle Tom said he would look after you.'

'I'm, I'm...'

'Well, what do you think?'

Her heart raced; her mind whirled.

'Yes, Daddy, I'd love to go, and I'll make you so proud of me.' Veronica said it quickly in case he changed his mind.

'You start the first week of September, and you are to stay with your Uncle Tom and Aunt Betty. They live near St James's Gate, beside the Guinness brewery where Tom works. They've room for you.' He paused. 'Now with Padraig gone.'

Padraig had been their only child. Every summer, Tom and Betty sent Padraig to Virginia for a few weeks to help with the hay. But like many Dubliners, when the war started, he'd joined the Fusiliers to fight in the trenches in France. He had only been gone a few months when Betty got a telegram to say he had been killed at Suvla Bay, Turkey. Apparently, Betty didn't speak for months. At the funeral, she didn't cry, but when the tears came, they fell in a continuous stream.

'Thank you, I won't let you down,' said Veronica. She wanted to run and hug her father, but he always dismissed any affection she tried to show him when she was a young child.

'I need you to give Tom a parcel for me.' He paused. 'And you're not to tell Susan about it or your mother.'

Veronica had no interest to ask him what he meant. She wanted to leave and share her good news with Susan. She was going to Dublin! Nodding and closing the door, she saw Susan in the front garden and knocked at the window, gesturing wildly at her sister to come inside the house. Susan walked towards the house leisurely, humming and picking rhododendrons on the way to replace the withering ones on the hall stand. It began to drizzle, and she shook her head. Like Veronica, she had a mass of unruly uncontrollable curly hair that only pins could tame. A hairpin fell onto the tiles on the porch, and she languorously picked it up to stick it back in her hair.

'Quick, Susan,' Veronica said, impatient with her sister.

'I have something to tell you,' she whispered, signalling her to follow her upstairs. On the landing, Veronica watched Susan stop at the bottom of the stairs to look in the mirror and pushed a rogue blonde strand of hair in place.

'Come on, for God's sake!'

Susan followed Veronica into their bedroom. Veronica grabbed Susan by her hands. 'I'm going to Dublin to learn to be a secretary.'

'What? Why?'

'What do you mean "why"? To learn to type and to learn shorthand, and file. It will be so exciting. They have electricity in the homes in Dublin, and the street lamps are lit by electricity too. There are trams, and cars bringing people to destinations you could never dream of going!'

Virginia had electricity from Eliot's Mill generated by the Blackwater River, but only a few benefited from it.

Thunder rolled in the distance. The blue skies of earlier in the day were now dark with thick clouds. Susan's attention veered back to her loose strands of hair. Veronica didn't have the energy for further conversation with her sister. She may have become her closest confidante, but that was only because of a chance of nature, not by choice; they were worlds apart. She missed Eddie, and sadness enveloped her like the mist on the morning lake, only this would not clear. She opened the door of her mahogany wardrobe, wincing at the overpowering smell of mothballs. Mrs Slaney, the cook and part-time housekeeper, hung Veronica's clothes in colour order. This habit perplexed Veronica. Most of her dresses looked new – she would hardly be home from Sunday Mass when her Sunday shoes and skirt would be swapped for her hobnail boots and old skirt so she could go fishing, or to the woods.

Veronica heard footsteps on the landing, and she knew they were Eddie's. Susan had returned to fixing her hair, and Veronica went out to the landing.

'Eddie,' she whispered to him as he turned to go down the stairs, 'thank you.'

He waved her away but turned back towards her. 'Veronica, I really don't have time for this, I've other things to think about.'

'Things? Like what?'

'Look, Veronica, I don't have time, and "Things" is stuff you don't need to know about.'

He sighed, and took her arms in his hands, looking down at her, so close she saw her reflection in his eyes, and the three brown flecks that distinguished them apart when they were toddlers. 'Veronica, I'll be fine.'

But his words didn't soothe Veronica, remembering her mother's words about how Tommy Brady was shot.

5

Summer passed and on a beautiful morning in late September Veronica was getting ready to leave for her new life in Dublin. Looking out her bedroom window at the Lough Ramor, she breathed in the stunning view of the lake. She would miss it, but more exciting times were ahead of her. She twirled around a few times, hoping that the stiff new skirt would soften soon. When her mother had given her the pale brown skirt, she had hated it at once.

'Mother,' Veronica had said, 'it's awful.'

'Now you are an adult you need to dress like a lady and throw away those hobnail boots and pinafores, and as for dressing in Eddie's trousers, you can forget all about that. You are a lady now, Veronica.'

As a child, Veronica had worn Eddie's trousers and shirts. People could not tell them apart. But as Eddie's hair got shorter, his curls disappeared. Her breasts grew. She hated them. Outside was where she wanted to be, fishing, or in the forest. But as the twins advanced from childhood into adolescence, they filled in the expected roles in the family defined by their gender, Eddie outside helping on the farm and Veronica in the kitchen helping her mother and the cook Mrs Slaney.

'Veronica, are you listening to me?' Her mother glared at her. 'You never listen, how will you cope in the city?'

Now, Veronica looked in the long mirror on her bedroom wall, smothered down her skirt, and pushed her brown curls under her new hat.

She took a yellow primrose from the vase on her chest of drawers and put it in the blue ribbon of her hat, like the ladies at Mass. Maybe she looked nice. She sighed and pulled the flower out and threw it on her bed.

'I don't understand why you want to go,' her mother said, as she stood in the bedroom doorway. 'What gets into you?'

Veronica groaned. This was a conversation they had many times. 'Mother, there's no need to worry. I'll be fine. I'll be back in months. It finishes at the end of January.'

Her mother's eyes watered, and she sniffed.

'Susan is here, and anyway, Mammy, I'll be home for Christmas. It's only a few months away and I'll be able to help Mrs Smith in the office. Please, it's all arranged. Sure, you won't miss me, don't you always tell me how useless I am in the kitchen? I might learn something useful.'

Her mother sighed, twisting her pearl necklace. 'I suppose,' she said and dabbed the corners of her eyes with a white hankie. 'Stand up straight, Veronica.'

This was more like the mother she knew. Veronica knew sometimes her mother felt it was her duty to play the grieving mother. 'And, Veronica, don't forget to write.'

'Yes, Mammy, I promise, every day.' It was a promise she

wouldn't keep. She had taken her blue skirt and matching cardigan out of her case and squeezed in her hobnail boots and a pinafore. The thoughts of wearing dresses with flowers made her shudder; the cardigans she could tolerate but wearing stiff dresses and skirts every day wasn't what she wanted.

Her father shouted from downstairs, 'Are you ready, Veronica?'

She gave her bedroom one last look before she shut the door, whispering, 'Bye, bedroom.' At the bottom of the stairs, she heard a sound like thunder. She went outside, and her father stood beside a black motor car.

'I've borrowed Dr Reynolds's motor car for the day,' he said, rubbing his hand on the bright lamps at the side of the vehicle. 'I might get one someday,' said her father. 'Come on, Veronica, get in. Don't look scared. It's not dangerous.'

It wasn't fear, but the car was part of the reason she wanted freedom. The doctor and her father had been friends since their boarding school days in Terenure College in Dublin.

A bachelor, and Veronica's godfather, he spoiled her, taking her regularly for trips in his car around the drumlins of Cavan. Unknown to her father, Dr Reynolds had shown Veronica how to drive his car on her sixteenth birthday. This was when she had tasted her first real freedom. Veronica's gloved hands had clutched tight around the steering wheel and her body moved with the wheels of the car as it swerved around the corners. The pins in her hair loosened, her curls freed in the wind. It was an exhilaration, a freedom she had never experienced before.

From that day she knew there was more to life than inside the four walls of her home.

Veronica turned. Eddie stood beside their mother, his cap in his hand. She always felt his presence before she saw him. He now had the start of a moustache and was beginning to look like a man.

'Veronica, we'd better leave. It looks like it'll rain, and we must be in time for the train.'

The train station was in Oldcastle in Co. Meath, six miles from Virginia.

She waved to her mother and Eddie, their eyes locking. He gave her a nod, no words needed, and a rough, quick hug.

'Veronica, let's go.' And her father started the car.

On the drive to the station, the fresh September breeze challenging her tightly pinned hair, she closed her eyes, enjoying the wind on her face. On arrival, her father parked the car at the front entrance, careful not to leave it too near the row of bikes.

'You wait on the platform. I'll bring your bags and get your ticket.'

'Are you… are you not coming to Dublin with me?'

'No. The parcel for Tom, it's in your big case, the brown one. And don't let anyone see it, even Betty.'

Veronica heard a whistle before she saw the train snake around the corner.

'Daddy, eh.'

'Come along, Veronica, hurry. You go and wait on the platform. I'll get your ticket at the office. Go on, girl. I'll only be a minute or two.'

Hesitantly, she joined the crowd of passengers. A mother holding a young girl by her hand, her arms pin thin. Farm labourers with rolls of clothes tucked under their arms. Veronica stood beside three girls. They were wearing black and white domestic uniforms. She wondered where everyone was going, trying to imagine what their lives were like.

She jumped at the sound of her father's voice. 'Come on, Veronica,' he said, his voice impatient now. 'You are in the second-class carriage. There are Mrs Lynch and her daughter, follow them.' He looked long and hard at her, his eyes softening. 'Veronica, you will be all right. This is what you want, isn't it?'

Veronica swallowed. 'Yes, Father, I'll make you proud of me.'

The train's whistle blew again.

Her father held her elbow, guiding her through the passengers to an empty carriage. He stood back to hold the door open and then hugged her tight. His breath warm on her ear, he whispered, 'Remember Veronica, don't show the package to anyone, just give it to Tom.'

The conductor shouted, 'All aboard.' He waved Veronica to hurry onto the train. Settled at the window seat, she watched her father through the train windows as he left the station. Doubts were beginning to rise. Was she doing the right thing? She had never been further than Kells.

She shifted uncomfortably on the hard, wooden seat, wishing she had listened to her father's suggestion to take a cushion. Soon the train was rattling across the countryside, flat pastures filled with grazing cows and sheep soon replaced by hills. The full thick black clouds gave in to a build-up of pressure and rain began to fall diagonally on the windows. Veronica drank in the unfamiliar countryside. She hadn't known that continuous rolls of hills could stir such excitement and wanted more.

Her stomach rumbled, and she looked around the carriage to see if anyone had heard. A woman opposite nodded and smiled at her. Veronica laid her sandwiches on the table in front of her. The children opposite her whispered something to their mother, and she shook her head. Veronica tried to ignore the way the children stared at the food. She leaned over and handed them the sandwiches. They snatched them; in one bite, they were gone, before their mother could scold them. The mother smiled a shy thank you.

After lunch, sleep took hold of her. The train whistle blew, jolting her awake as they slowed into Broadstone Station. A flash of sunlight filled the carriage before the platform roof of the station replaced the sky. She stretched, and her stomach somersaulted. The passengers in her carriage were all standing now, buttoning the coats on their children, fixing their hats and smoothing down skirts or trousers crumpled after the long journey.

'Are ye here to work?' a boy asked her, his face like one large red freckle. 'I'm going to work at the docks.'

Veronica nodded, words lost in her throat. She didn't know what the docks were.

Looking out at the crowded station, Veronica had never seen so many different people in one place.

The conductor walked past, telling everyone to hurry and collect their luggage which was piled on the platform.

Suddenly, British soldiers thundered past in unison. Their boots pounded the wooden floorboards, marching with a determination reserved for people who thought they were superior. A path opened, allowing them to pass, rattling guns hanging from their shoulders.

People were standing behind the railings, searching the passengers' faces for loved ones.

Tom sluggishly walked towards her, slower than she remembered the last time she had seen him at her cousin's funeral. Her mother told her once that years of lifting barrels hadn't helped his health. He took off his worn cloth cap to reveal thinning, tobacco-coloured hair.

He shook Veronica's hand then; his grip was firm, and his skin was rougher than her father's. He had aged since the time she had met him at Sheamus's funeral. His lined face emphasised the sadness in his tired eyes.

'Betty is at home and getting the supper ready; she's looking forward to you coming.'

The bustling station was so different from Virginia. The smells, the noise, even the air felt different.

'Come on, Veronica, our dray is outside,' Tom said.

Outside the smell of urine stung her nose. At home on the farm, the farm smells escaped with the wind. Here in the city, it hung in the air, leaving a stale taste in Veronica's mouth.

'Come on, Veronica, climb up. That's a good girl. It's not far to your new home. That's right, hold your case tight, it can be bumpy.' With a flick of the reins, the horse snorted, and they started to move. 'I'm sure you're nervous, but you'll be grand.'

The slow, bumpy journey allowed her to take in her new surroundings. Thick black clouds finally broke, emitting a drizzle of rain diluting the foul infusion of smells of Dublin. Her leg jittered in rhythm with the wheels moving across the cobblestones.

Tom leaned forward, cracking the reins. 'C'mon boy, faster. I borrowed this for the day and have to get it back to the brewery for deliveries later.'

The horse and cart rattled across the cobblestones, past a few children with dirty torn clothes playing in front of three-storey buildings. Women sat on the steps, their shawls pulled tight, and their faces grim. Tom pulled the reins, halting the horse, to allow a group of people on bicycles to pass. A young lad on a bike swerved, grinning. He shouted, 'Sorry, sir.'

'Not long now,' Tom said, waving at the boy.

She wished her heart would slow, it hurt her rib cage. Her mind overloaded with noises and smells. People looked different. It was a lot stranger than she thought it would be.

They crossed a bridge.

'Daddy told me to give you a package,' said Veronica. 'It's in my case.'

'Grand.' Tom was quiet for a few minutes. 'Just keep it in your room, and I'll get it soon from you. Look, Veronica.' He pointed straight ahead. 'Your new home, Thomas St.' He pulled the reins to slow the horse.

Veronica noticed a different smell.

'What's that smell?' She winced as she put her hand quickly to her nose.

'That would be O'Keefe the Knackers. It's where they kill all the cattle. The smell is sometimes people.'

Veronica didn't understand what he meant. They entered a narrow street where the sun fought but failed to light the street between the high buildings. Tom stopped outside one of the red-brick houses.

'Yer new home, Veronica. Come on, love. You'll be fine. I know it's different than the country, but I'm sure you'll get used to it, and Betty could do with the company.'

She wished she could say something to him, but her throat was so dry she just nodded at him. Her new home was in front of her. The red-brick three-storey terraced house had a basement partly hidden with black railings. She wondered whether the servants lived there. The high windows were like her own home, but most of the sashes were pulled tight. At home, they would be open to let in the light and the breeze from the lake, keeping it bright and fresh. Tom helped Veronica off the dray, and her shaky legs carried her up the steps to the black front door. Once inside the building, with the doors closed, the hallway was sparse compared to her home and smelled of musty damp. She heard a baby crying behind one door; she assumed it belonged to one of the staff.

Tom went up a flight of stairs to the door at the top of the stairs, to another hall then into a small room. A modest room. 'Betty, love, Veronica is here,' Tom gently said.

The room was in desperate need of repair but clean, and an over-swept red carpet told of a woman who had too much time on her hands. Veronica realised then that this room was her new home, not the whole house.

Betty got up slowly, and hugged Veronica, her bony arms giving Veronica a fright. Betty's mouth smiled a welcome, but her eyes showed no joy. Betty was smaller than she remembered, her once red hair now speckled with grey, and the bouncing curls had gone.

After a few awkward seconds, Betty said, 'It's not as generous as what you are used to, and we don't have a lot. Tom has a job in the brewery. We get by.' She had a quiet voice and paused for a moment, her eyes distant. 'The war has made everything expensive. It's only the two of us now.' She moved slowly, her face pinched in pain. 'I will show you to your bedroom.'

Her bedroom was a few feet from the sitting room, which also seemed to be the kitchen. Tom poked the fire, moving the embers to let the room fill with heat. Veronica could hear voices below, mixed with the noises from the street. She wondered how she would get used to the new sounds. Betty stood at the bedroom door. Silent. Something invisible had taken hold of her.

She said something, but Veronica had to bend down to hear her.

'This is your room. Assume you're tired.' Pausing, she said, 'How are your mother and father?'

'They are both well, Aunt Betty,' she said as her eyes hovered around her new bedroom.

The light from the lamp fell into a bare room with a bed, a wardrobe, a small desk with a jug and bowl on it for washing.

'You can hang your coat on the hook and put your clothes in the wardrobe, and there's a candle on the desk.'

The wardrobe door was ajar, the sleeve of her dead cousin's jacket poking out.

'I'll leave ye be.'

Alone now, Veronica closed the transparent brown curtains. Fog misted the small window which refused any remaining daylight into the room.

Someone knocked on her bedroom door, and Tom came in.

'Your case, Veronica. I hope you'll feel welcome; Betty is sometimes... well, since Padraig is gone, she can be distant.' After a second, he continued, 'He didn't want to be lifting barrels his whole life. The money in the army was good. He got one pound a day. He said he wanted to do something exciting. And that he liked being with other lads.' Tom paused. 'He wanted to see the world. Recruited in Grafton St, he was, and then he was gone – gone for good.' He sighed and looked around the room. 'Sure, I know it's smaller than you're probably used to. I'll leave you to get settled. Rest for a while and Betty will have supper for you.'

He closed the door tight after him.

Veronica sat on the edge of the bed. It was not as soft as her own but she smiled. This was her room. No more sharing. She could be as messy as she wanted; no more Susan nagging her to be tidy. She would prove to her father he had made the right decision and show Susan how this was more exciting than baking scones. She pushed down the butterflies in her stomach to explore her new room.

She ran her hand across the top dresser and over a stain beside the water jug, before opening the drawers, which thankfully were empty. She laid her clothes on the bed, wondering if they were too lavish. The clothes men and women she had passed on the way to Thomas St had shocked her, especially the dirty, barefoot children. At home, she saw shoeless children, but they didn't have the desperation in their eyes the Dublin children had.

The package her father gave her sat on the bed. Tom hadn't mentioned it again, and her father's words reverberated in her head. *Don't show it to Betty.* It was only about the size of a book wrapped in brown paper tied tight with brown string. But it was heavier than her reading books. She squeezed her index finger under the string, but it held firm. She dropped the package on the bed, her interest gone.

Another small knock and her aunt entered. 'Here,' she said, and handed Veronica a steaming cup of tea and some bread. 'Tom said you'd a long day so you can eat it here and get to sleep early. Tomorrow will be even longer.'

Her aunt's face seemed lined with disappointment that it wasn't her son she was handing a cup of tea to. She nodded at Veronica and turned as a coughing fit took hold of her and she held onto the doorframe.

Betty was right. After tea, Veronica lay on the bed exhausted and watched the lamp's wick flickering, trying to hang onto its last breath. As it drew its last gasp at life, the room went dark, and Veronica was soon asleep.

6

The following morning Veronica woke to a loud, shrill whistle. It took a minute to remember she was in Dublin. Stretching her arms behind her, she wondered how her six-foot cousin had slept in such a small bed. The whistle stopped as suddenly as it had begun. Veronica stretched with excitement at her new life as pinpoints of light crept through the thin curtains. She listened to the new noises. Embers scraped in the fire in the living room and voices drifted in from the street.

In the biting morning air, she washed with the cold water that Betty had left in the porcelain jug on her bedstand beside the framed picture of her family. She put on her cream blouse and best Sunday skirt. She felt stiff, restrained by her Sunday clothes.

She used the new mother of pearl hairbrush to tame her curls before pinning them tight as best she could, but a few refused to be restrained. She put the unused pins in the bottom drawer of her music box and opened it to watch the ballerina twist and turn to the notes. As a small girl, it had fascinated her when she got the music box for Christmas. The ballerina pirouetted to the music, thinking she was free. She smiled and closed the lid. This was the start of her new life.

In the kitchen, Betty poked the fire into life. The frost had arrived early, the warmth of the summer long gone.

Veronica stood in the doorway, waiting for Betty to say something, unsure of what to do. Betty's skeletal frame and her ill-fitting clothes that hung too loosely on her, reminded Veronica of the homesick girls at boarding school. They had hoped starvation would bring their parents to the school to take them home, but Veronica had taken a different approach. In the middle of the night, she'd stolen one of the nuns' bicycles and cycled home from Carrick-on-Suir. Her father had returned her to school as soon as she'd arrived home.

Veronica coughed.

Betty rubbed her back as she stood, the fire now alive. 'Come and sit, eat your breakfast while it's still hot. Did you sleep well?'

A rectangular wooden table with four chairs filled the centre of the room. The kitchen table at home had up to ten chairs, usually filled up with the farm labourers. There was no white linen cloth or covering, unlike on the dining table at home. There were no fresh flowers in the middle of the table either, or any flowers anywhere. The dull silver cutlery matched the dullness of the room.

A large ginger cat rolled around on the rug in front of the fire purring, his tail moving in rhythm with the flames. He jumped on the mantelpiece, expertly rubbing his tail in between the statue of the Virgin Mary and a brass jug.

A small picture of Padraig smiling in his British army uniform was on the centre of the mantelpiece.

Betty placed a steaming bowl of porridge beside a blue and white Delph cup on the table. The table was set for four, and there were crumbs on the table, evidence someone had eaten already. The place setting to her left was untouched.

The sparse kitchen was clean and neat, but bare. The dresser had more blue and white Delph porcelain but not as many pieces as their dresser at home. She thought of what Mrs Slaney would say: 'It lacks soul.' Veronica believed that this was her excuse for not being good at her job, only ever half tidying the kitchen.

Beside the fire, there was a well-worn armchair with a blanket loosely thrown around the back of it, and a pair of knitting needles and wool on the ground. The room felt homely.

The front door creaked, and Tom came into the room backwards dragging a sack. 'Those stairs are getting tougher,' he said while stretching and rubbing the small of his back.

'That's the fuel to keep ye warm for the day, it's going to be a cold one today,' he said. 'I think the winter will be a cold one this year. I'm sure of it, I can feel it in me bones.'

'Tom, wash your hands before you eat your breakfast.'

He shivered as he immersed his hands, a useless task without hot water and soap. The coal was embedded into his fingernails, and only in death would they be scrubbed clean.

'People don't like black nails to deliver their barrels of

the black stuff, but they will have to do,' he said, wiping his hands dry on his trousers and sitting beside Veronica.

Betty put two bowls on the table. Veronica noticed her movements caused her to grimace.

'Rheumatism,' Tom whispered to Veronica. 'It's always worse in the winter. Damp doesn't help us, so we try to keep the place warm, and someone told me copper helps.'

Betty handed him a cup of tea. He thanked her with a softness in his eyes, a look that Veronica had never seen pass between her father and mother. Veronica didn't know if she should talk. At home constant conversation flowed at the breakfast table, from her mother fussing over the list of chores for Susan and Veronica, or the farm hands looking for more tea.

'Well, love, ready for your big day?' Tom said.

Rubbing her knuckles – a habit she had had since she was a young girl – Veronica tried to keep her voice steady. 'It's the biggest thing I've ever done.'

Tom rose, squeezing her arm gently as he stood. 'You'll be grand, love. We'd better be going soon. Remember to walk along the route I'm going to show you. Along the quay, best to keep by the river, the back streets can be dangerous – the pickpockets, and now the rebels.'

'The rebels?'

'Volunteers, and with the English soldiers, you never know what will happen. The soldiers are ruthless when they catch one of the volunteers.'

Eddie's gun drifted into her mind.

Veronica lifted a spoon of porridge to her mouth and then put it down, pushing the bowl away. It was tasteless and watery, unlike the milky porridge Mrs Slaney made with the right amount of salt so that when sugar was added, it tasted perfect.

'I'm not very hungry, Betty.'

Betty nodded and pushed a small brown packet into her hand. 'Your lunch, and I'll have something for you when you return.'

As they left, the smell of soot on Thomas St stung her nostrils and bit her eyes, making them water.

'Com' on, love, up you go,' said Tom. 'I'll do my deliveries on the way back. But remember the way I show you. It's longer but safer as we don't want anything to happen to you. Sometimes the soldiers patrolling the streets can harass young women.' The horse moved at a slower pace than he had the day before, with the heavy barrels strapped tight on the dray. 'I'll show you some of the sights of Dublin. I'm sure it's a lot different than Virginia.'

Veronica nodded. She was still in awe of life in Dublin.

A group of children ran beside the dray as it moved, pushing sticks into the wheels so that it made a rhythmic, clacking sound. Turning from *The Maltings* onto the quays, she took in the new sights and smells. It excited her. This was her chance for a life of her own.

Two barges moved up and down the river to deliver goods and bring the empty barrels of Guinness back to the brewery. To her right, the streets were dark and uninviting. A young boy and girl in torn, dirty clothes ran out in front of them, a man shouting and waving his fist behind them. 'Thieves!' He chased after the children, but they soon disappeared among the laneways.

'Uncle, does everyone in Dublin live like this?'

'Tom, call me Tom. On the other side of the bridge, it's nicer.' Tom gestured to a white bridge in the distance.

'Well, why do they live here? Why don't they move to somewhere nicer and bigger?'

'Ah, where else would they live? Would people in the country move if they wanted something better?'

'I don't know, maybe not.'

'Look, it's the same here in the city; they've little choice in the matter. They have no money; most have little or no work. Rich people moved out to the country and rented out the houses they left behind. They couldn't sell them, so they put loads of families in them. Up to fifteen families can live in one house. The place is filthy, full of diseases, with TB. It's an absolute disgrace if you ask me, expecting people to live like this and children dying, not just from disease, but hunger as well.'

Leaning forward, he said, 'Veronica love, there's little that can be done, some people are just more unfortunate than we are.'

The sun was rising above the buildings as they passed, falling on a group of soldiers marching along the quays on the opposite side of the river. The buildings were showing signs of life as shop doors opened. Haberdasheries, furniture shops with tables and chairs lining the street outside the front. A woman in a once-white apron swept the path outside a bread shop.

'Not long now.' Tom pointed to his left across the river. 'That big street across O'Connell Bridge is Sackville St, and that's Nelson's Pillar.'

On Sackville St, she saw flower sellers at the bottom of Nelson's Pillar. The colourful flowers were a stark contrast to the damaged buildings from the Rising. Buildings that had once stood on either side of the wide main street of the capital lay in ruins. The GPO looked undamaged, but she had read in the papers it had been burnt inside and that the shell of stone was all that remained.

They were passing a large wooden gate. 'Trinity – Protestants,' Tom said with disdain, as they passed along the stone-walled building with the largest wooden doors she had ever seen.

Tom was right. On the other side of the city, it was a different Dublin. 'That's the bank now,' he said, pointing to a white round building whose pillars reached into the sky.

'That was once our parliament.' He gave the reins another flick. 'We'll be at Leinster St in a few minutes.' He slowed, pulling on the horse's reins to bring them to a stop. He turned to her with a smile, and gently squeezed her arm. 'You'll be fine, Veronica. If you're like your father, you won't find this a challenge at all.'

Veronica hesitated. 'The package Daddy told me to give you... I left it under the bed.' It didn't seem right to call it her room, or worse still Padraig's room.

'Later, I'll get it later. Go and start your course.'

Veronica felt her optimism wavering.

'Go on, love, you'll be fine. Don't forget to walk back the way I showed you, and make sure you are back before the curfew.'

As she walked across the road, a bicycle bell tinkled.

'Watch yerself,' a boy screamed at her. She steadied herself as she tripped on the kerb. Holding her lunch tightly, she looked at the sign above the door: *Underwood School of Typing*. Three laughing girls walked past her linking arms as they walked into the building, followed by two more chatting girls. This was it. This was the doorway to her future, but now she was here, she felt suddenly overwhelmed by how alone she was. She turned back to her uncle, but he had gone.

Staring at the sign for a moment, Veronica inhaled deeply. It was now or never. She walked into a bright and airy hall, full of girls standing along the walls. Veronica joined them, trying to appear relaxed, but her heart was pounding. A few of the girls chatted but most looked at the floor or their shoes. She didn't want to stare so she coughed into her hand to look at them. Some wore hats that matched their coats, and their shoes shone so that you could see the reflection of electric light. She looked at her shoes, now regretting not shining them as her mother had told her to do, and smoothed her skirt. She noticed a loose thread at the cuff of her cardigan and pulled the sleeve down. One of the girls in the matching hat and coat put her hand to her mouth and whispered to one of the other girls, and they giggled while looking at Veronica. A door squeaked followed by hurried clipped steps down the stairs to the end of the corridor.

'Girls, this way,' said a short, stout man in a sing-song voice. 'Follow me, and I will show you to Mr Begley's room.'

Veronica had counted twenty-four girls and assumed

they would be split into two groups. They followed him to Mr Begley's room where sunlight fell through four large windows and the nine-feet-high ceilings. Dispersed evenly were four rows of six tables, each with a black typewriter.

'Girls, find a seat,' sang Mr Begley in a similar accent to the first man. He was a stern-looking man with a tall and narrow frame and his nose held high. He looked at them over his round-rimmed spectacles. 'First, I'll do a roll call. When I say your name, say "present, sir," and soon we will begin.'

Mr Begley stood at the head of the room. He was a welcome change to the nuns, but Veronica thought that it was just like school. The girl at the next desk moved her book around the table and put her gloves on top of the lunch and then under it. Veronica's leg jittered, but most of the girls in the room sat rigid in their seats. The girl on her right side leant towards her and whispered, in an accent Veronica now recognised was a Dublin one, 'What's your name?'

'Veronica.'

'Quiet,' Mr Begley squeaked as his gaze wandered over the girls.

'Mine's Bridget,' the small freckled face said quickly before Mr Begley could continue. Her red curls moved as she spoke.

Mr Begley closed the door and continued with the roll call, ticking each girl present, then with a slight cough he said, 'Now, girls, let's begin.'

He talked all morning, showing the girls the ribbon, the

keys, and how to bring the carriage back to type the next line.

'The course will take eight months, and then you will be secretaries.'

Veronica hung onto Mr Begley's every word, repeating every sentence in her head – a memory trick she had used in school. It had kept her mind from wandering in class at the convent where she often thought of fishing at the lake in Cavan, especially during sewing class, and when Sister Lavinia shouted at her to pay attention, she would be forced back to her sewing.

At their lunchtime break, the girls went to the yard. A few of the girls stood sporadically around the wall looking downward as if searching for something on the ground, and some searched for a potential friend. The three girls that had passed Veronica in the street chatted in the middle of the yard, occasionally eying up some of the girls and turning back to each other giggling. Their disparaging eyes fell on Veronica, looking her up and down slowly. She pulled her cardigan around her and looked at the ground, moving her foot as if pushing a piece of dirt. She wished she had listened to her mother and taken more care with her dress. The girls' shoes shone, and their clothes were neat, and not crumpled like her skirt. Their cardigans matched their skirts, and one of the girls had a small black handbag.

She looked up to the blue sky in between the buildings, where swallows swooped. Soon they would leave for warmer climates. She felt very alone.

'Do you come from Dublin?'

Veronica turned around. It was Bridget, the girl that had spoken to her earlier.

Smiling and chewing her bread, she said, 'I live in Drumcondra, at home with my parents. I get the tram every day. My ma said I should learn a skill, she's very independent. Are you from Dublin?'

'No, I'm from Virginia.'

'Eh, where's that?' she laughed. 'And you speak strange.' She lowered her sandwich and her voice. 'I'd say you're better than those girls over there.' She nodded to the girls huddled together in the middle of the yard. 'They think they are something special. Where's that then?' she asked again.

'It's in Cavan, in the country,' Veronica replied.

Bridget chewed on her bread again and shrugged. 'Don't know where that is. Do your ma and da work?'

'We've got a farm, and in the village, we've a shop and a public house. When it's busy, especially during the haymaking, the kitchen work is endless. My brother Eddie helps Daddy, and me and my sister help Mammy and Mrs Slaney, our housekeeper, in the kitchen and around the house.'

'Wow, that's a lot. My ma's sister is a nurse in St Vincent's.' When Bridget spoke, her face never lost its grin, and sometimes she nodded her head in agreement with herself.

'A nurse? Really? That must be so exciting?'

'Ma's sister told me that there are loads of soldiers in the hospital over from France. Some of them are English, not just the Irish lads but English, you' know! It sounds a bit gruesome at times, but the doctors are so handsome.'

Bridget continued, chewing noisily as she spoke. 'Loads of women work now. My ma helps in the Red Cross, and our neighbour knits hats for men on the war front. Well, they used to, I don't think as many signs up anymore. Da says he is glad he doesn't have a son.'

'At home in Cavan a few spinsters work,' said Veronica, thinking of Mrs Smith and Mrs Slaney.

Veronica found out they were the same age, but Bridget looked younger with her bright bushy red hair, blue eyes, and freckles, which amalgamated as if she was always blushing.

A bell rang. 'Girls, back to your room!' Mr Begley stood at the door, the chatter stopped, and one by one, the girls filed back to the classroom.

The afternoon passed quickly, and after class, Veronica strolled with Bridget to O'Connell Bridge, where they parted. On her own now, she quickened her steps as unrest was in the air, and people rushed with their heads low to get back indoors before the curfew. In bed, her head was full of clanking black keys and Bridget.

Every evening Betty welcomed Veronica home with the smell of stew. Tom, Betty, and Veronica would mostly eat in silence, apart from the odd question from Tom as to how she was getting on. After dinner, Tom sat smoking and reading the previous day's *Independent* that he got in one of the pubs on his deliveries, or he would take his cap, throwing it on as he walked out the door.

'I'm off now. I've got a meeting.' He kissed Betty on

the head and squeezed her arm. 'Don't wait up for me, Veronica will keep you company.'

Betty didn't have much to say to Veronica. She sat in her armchair, staring into the flames of the fire. She always had rosary beads in one hand and stroked the cat with the other. Her mouth moved silently as her hand slid from one bead to the next, finding comfort in Hail Marys or Our Fathers. Veronica found it hard to understand how someone could die inside, yet live at the same time. Her home in Virginia had been a busy household of farm labourers, and her mother would be inevitably scolding her for being too slow at her chores or giving orders to her father, which he usually ignored. The silence was deafening, and she would sit at the table to write in her diary, or pen letters to Susan about her new friend Bridget, or the busy streets of Dublin.

Her letter to Eddie was different. *Burned buildings. Sackville St in ruins, menacing English soldiers, unrest in the air, shoeless dirty children playing in the streets.* But as she sat at the table in her bedroom rereading the letter in the flickering candlelight, its shadow falling on the page like flames of the fires that burnt Dublin, she crumpled it up. These were not the images she wanted to share with Eddie. Closing her eyes, she could see her mother waving the letter in her hand, reinforcing her fears of life in Dublin, demanding her father bring Veronica home.

7

Veronica washed and dried the dishes after Sunday dinner to the soothing rhythmic breathing of Tom and Betty in a deep sleep resting in their armchairs by the fire, glowing red from the turf her father often sent down from Cavan along with food parcels from the shop. After she swept the floor, she tiptoed to her bedroom to read for the afternoon so as not to wake Betty and Tom. Betty's lined face softened as she slept. A crocheted blanket slipped from her knees, and Veronica carefully picked it up to cover Betty who stirred but went back to sleep. Tom sat up, arching his back in a stretch. Veronica motioned she was going to her bedroom to read.

Veronica tried to get lost in her book in Massachusetts with Jo March and her family, but she threw it to her side, sighing and wondering what Susan and Eddie were doing. A knock at her bedroom door was followed by Tom. 'Veronica, you have a package from your father for me.'

Veronica had forgotten about it. She groaned, hoping it wasn't food as it would be spoiled and probably smelly.

Tom limped into the room, closing the door softly.

'Betty is asleep. Best she does not know I'm here.' He sat

on the chair, careful not to lean back and crease her dress hanging on it. Rubbing his leg, he said, 'The package, it's for a man, a Captain Smith at the docks, and I can't go. My leg.' He paused. 'I slipped during the week, and with arthritis and cold weather, it's mighty sore. I'll ask one of the lads at the brewery to bring it to him, during the week.'

She nodded.

'Leave it under your bed so I can get it without Betty knowing. She worries about me that I might get arrested leaving the meetings.'

This was the first time he made any reference to the meetings. Veronica thought he must be involved in the fight for freedom and wanted to ask if it was in the Gaelic League like her father.

A delicate snore came from the living room. The cat wailed, and a tin pan crashed to the floor.

'God damn cat, he'll have woken Betty,' Tom cursed, leaving the room. Veronica lay back on her bed with the sounds of families in the other rooms in the house, trying them. Babies cried, doors banged, and laughing children ran up and down the stairs. Betty and Tom kept to themselves. Veronica didn't know if it had always been like that. It seemed Betty's grief was all the company they needed.

The following morning Veronica entered the kitchen to see Betty struggling to lift the bubbling pot of porridge from the fire onto the hearth. Veronica moved to help her, but Betty jumped hearing a knock at the front door. The pot dropped onto the floor. The cat ran to it, licking the porridge cautiously. Tom's forehead furrowed as he got up from the table. Betty's pale complexion went even paler, and her eyes were full of panic. Veronica guessed the last time someone had knocked unexpectedly was to give a telegram from the war office.

Veronica strained her ears to hear what the muffled voices said. After a few minutes, doors banged shut and Tom stuck his head into the room, his cap already on his head. 'It's nothing to worry about, love, but I've to go now. Some of the lads have been arrested.'

He put on his brown work coat. 'Veronica, make your way to Leinster St by yourself.'

Bridget was not at the school again and Veronica's day passed slowly. She tried to fill her head with black lettered keys. The squiggles of shorthand were finally making sense, and she could now write a sentence or two. At lunchtime, the girls gathered in their groups forged from day one. Alone she ate in the corner of the yard watching the pretty girls with matching cardigans and skirts huddle together, laughing loudly and then whispering with their hands over their mouths as they glanced in Veronica's direction. She missed Bridget. On her walk home, she thought maybe she would write a letter to Susan in shorthand. She could imagine her face! But she dismissed that thought as she wasn't well practised yet. Maybe she would try knitting. Betty had wool and needles. She shuddered, remembering Sr Jacinta's disparaging remarks about her attempt of knitting mittens in the third year of school.

Resigning herself to an evening of reading *Little Women*, Veronica lit the candle on her bedside locker. The electric lights were too weak. If this were going to be her life for a few months, she would have to get used to it.

There was a gentle knock on her bedroom door. It was her uncle. 'It's only me.'

He sat beside her on the bed. 'Veronica, I hate to ask you this, but maybe you can help! The lads arrested this morning were the O'Mahony boys who work with me. They help with a lot of errands, and it's crucial that Captain Smith gets that package soon. I thought it could wait, but he leaves again on Thursday, and we need to get to him before that. I hate to ask this of you, but it's essential.' He paused, then whispered, 'Would you go?'

'But I don't know where to go,' she said. 'I'm sorry, Uncle, I don't think I can.' She was getting butterflies just thinking about it.

He stood slowly, his face blanching with pain.

Oh, Christ. 'Yes, of course, I'll help.' She was glad she said it as the pain in his face changed to relief.

'Sunday, you will deliver it on Sunday. Captain Smith was delayed and won't dock now till Friday.'

Bridget didn't return to school for the rest of the week, but Veronica didn't mind. Her thoughts were on the delivery of the parcel.

After Sunday dinner, Tom motioned Veronica to follow him upstairs and into her bedroom.

'Go, before it gets dark. The October fog can make the evenings even more dangerous.' He rubbed his leg, his face in pain. 'And if anyone stops you, say you are going to see a sick aunt. You should get the tram; it's easy to get lost, so get it from Nelson's Pillar in Sackville St to Ringsend. Walk down Brunswick St and take the second right to Grand Canal Quay.'

Veronica removed the package from its hiding place in the wardrobe.

He took it and turned it over. 'Get your coat and scarf and meet me outside,' he said. 'Hide the package inside your coat. Don't look so worried. You'll be grand. It's just a few papers.'

She stuffed the parcel into the large inside pocket of her winter coat. She shook her head at the nonsense of hiding a few papers.

'Be careful of the crowds,' Tom said. 'It'll be lively out there. De Valera has just been elected the president of Sinn Féin. He's giving people hope. Veronica, be careful. It can be dangerous. Don't look worried, keep your head down and avoid looking at the soldiers or Dublin Metropolitan Police.'

She had read in the newspaper about a man called Éamon De Valera, the growing support for Sinn Féin and how most people now wanted a united Ireland. Veronica nodded, her hand on the package in her coat. Her stomach dropped, maybe Eddie was right. But the gun would only lead to trouble.

As Veronica left the house the autumn evening was drawing in, so she quickened her step, fearing it would soon be dark. She wanted to return home before the promised autumn fog immersed the city. Along the docks, twilight softened the outline of the ships tied to the quays for the night. To her right were rows of dark empty warehouses which seemed to increase in size with every step she took as if they would rise and engulf her.

She shivered and pulled her scarf tight around her neck. A group of four or five men loomed out of the fog. Keeping her head down, she quickened her pace, but couldn't stop giving them a surreptitious glance. Their faces were as dirty as their clothes.

The tenements near her uncle's house had once frightened her, but now she knew where to avoid the danger. Here, it was different. There were no screaming children, no smells of life except the familiar stench of the river Liffey.

In the distance, a lonely foghorn echoed. The fog had drifted across the city, the gas lights shimmering to a dull glow. Willing her legs to walk faster, her eyes watchful of unwanted visitors who might lurk in the shadows, she asked herself, *What am I doing? What would Susan think? Would Eddie be proud, or mad?* The constant chatter in her head gave her comfort, a sort of courage.

When she crossed O'Connell Bridge onto Sackville St, Veronica took the tram to Ringsend. Ringsend was the last stop. She replayed her uncle's instructions. 'Look for the pile of coal at the end of the pier, and take the second right onto Hanover Quay. You'll see a small red shed. Captain Smith will be expecting you.'

Her heart raced when a black cat ran in front of her and screeched like a banshee. *Damn*, she thought. She'd always scorned the men in the yard at home for cursing;

now it eased her mind. The warehouses screamed silently at her to go home, to be somewhere safer. Not one of the three-storey-high windows had a shine of comforting light escaping. Her eyes moved from left to right.

She was relieved when light fell onto the path once again, and that it came from a small red shed. She tapped at the door. A bearded man opened it, his frame blocking most of the light. He passed his eyes slowly over her. She shuddered. He stood aside.

'Quick, girl, inside.

'You must be Veronica,' the bearded man said gruffly in an unfamiliar accent. He was built like a bull, with a brown, weather-beaten face that held a hard expression that only a man of his years could have.

'I'm Captain Smith.' He wore a sort of uniform. Dirty, baggy trousers tucked into heavy worn boots, and a once-white shirt, black with streaks of coal.

'Tom said you've got a package?' His voice was hoarse, and he grunted as he sat at a desk in the middle of the shed.

She swallowed the knot of fear in her stomach and took the package out from her coat. He glanced at it, muttering as he nodded, then slipped it into the desk drawer. Without taking his eyes off her, he took out a smaller parcel and gave it to Veronica. As he did so, he leaned towards her, and she winced at the pungent smell of beer on his breath. When he spoke, his voice suggested a threat rather than an instruction.

'Take this package. Don't show it to anyone, or your life will be in danger. And keep it hidden.' He handed her a small waxy brown parcel. But when she went to take it from his rough hands, his grip held firm. 'Don't show it to anyone.'

She gasped. 'What am I to do with it?'

'Weren't you told? The Cumann women would know what to do.'

This startled Veronica. The Cumann na mBán. was the women's branch of the Volunteers, the group of freedom fighters Eddie had joined.

'I'm not one of them,' she stammered. 'I was only helping Tom out.'

Captain Smith gave her a long look.

'No?' he said at last. He raised his eyebrows and snorted. 'Well, then do your part, everyone has to. Give it to Joseph Connellan at 6 Henrietta St.'

'Me?'

Captain Smith gave her another hard stare.

'Yes, you. You are up for it, aren't you?'

Despite her panic, a voice in the back of her mind said, *Yes, you are.* She nodded to the captain, but he had already turned his back on her and was looking at the ledgers on his desk.

She needed to leave; the smell of paraffin was making her nauseous. Unbuttoning her coat, she put the small brown parcel tightly in her skirt band. She was now thankful darkness had fallen and hoped it would be easier to avoid the soldiers or Dublin Metropolitan Police.

She was still fumbling with her buttons when the captain spoke.

'Take the bike outside the door. Don't bother with the tram. It's a long walk to Thomas St from Nelson's Pillar.

Just keep cycling straight along the quay until you know where you are.'

She gladly took the bicycle. The night air was now thick with fog. Her hair was damp and her hands slippery, but she pedalled as if her life depended on it. In the distance before O'Connell Bridge, a man shouted, 'Stop!' She pedalled harder, afraid she would get lost if she didn't get to the familiar streets. Soon she was past O'Connell Bridge, and cycling along Merchant's Quay. She stayed at the same speed until she got to The Maltings. Only then did she breathe normally again, but her throat still burned with each breath.

Fear, mixed with adrenaline, raced through her body. The cold air stung her nostrils, and her hands were now numb, but that didn't stop her pedalling. When she finally reached her uncle's house, she hopped off the bike, letting it fall against the railings before running upstairs.

Her aunt still sat in her armchair, in a deep sleep while the cat purred on her lap. She spent her evenings staring into the flames, only moving to refresh the embers. Tom sat on the chair in front of the fire.

'Everything all right, Veronica? You gave him the package then?' he whispered, glancing over Betty.

'Yes,' she whispered, 'and he gave me another. He told me to deliver it to Henrietta St.'

Nodding, Tom said, 'I'm sure my leg will be better, and I'll take it. But would you keep it in your room? Betty might see it, and you know, it'll give her unnecessary concern.'

'Of course, and I won't say anything to her.'

Later, Veronica sat on her bed and her muscles finally

relaxed. She thought about what she had just done. It felt good, satisfying. She needed to hide the package, but her room didn't offer many options. The wardrobe was an ideal hiding place, but shuddered as she thought about Betty, and what the wardrobe meant to her. A few weeks previously on a Saturday afternoon, she had found Betty standing motionless in front of it. There were markings etched on the side of the wardrobe, similar to the markings on her bedroom wall from when she had shared it with Eddie. Height markings. She didn't know how old her cousin had been when the first marking was etched on the side of the wardrobe, but there was at least a four-foot difference between that and the last. Only when Veronica had coughed had Betty turned to look at her, 'Sorry,' she had mumbled, turning to leave.

'Betty,' Veronica mirrored sympathies she heard her father say at funerals, 'I'm sorry for your loss,' but that sounded too formal and adding, 'about Padraig.'

Betty had nodded to leave, but stopped and took Veronica's hand. 'Thank you, Veronica, that means a lot.' She left Veronica to look for a hiding place.

She tried to move the dresser, but it was too heavy. As she walked back to her bed, the floor underneath the rug creaked. And that only meant one thing. She pulled back the rug to reveal a broken floorboard. The loose floorboard easily lifted, showing a space big enough to hide the package. She replaced the rug and fell into bed. At once, sleep grabbed her. Her dreams were filled with faces of bearded men and brown packages that turned into a large parcel that she couldn't carry.

*

In the morning, the whistle screeches from the factory jolted Veronica awake, but she was still tired from her unsettled sleep. Her first thought was the new package.

In her desire to get away from Virginia to be an independent woman, she had dismissed the fight her fellow countrymen were having for their independence. Now she was being drawn into it. Dublin was not what she had thought it would be. The poverty she saw disturbed her. She didn't know who she'd delivered the parcel to, but she guessed it had something to do with the opposition to British rule in Ireland.

The smell of frying bread brought her back to the present. The light filtering in through the flimsy curtains warned her she would be late for school if she didn't get up and she dressed hastily.

In the kitchen, Betty put the sizzling bacon on plates. 'Your father sent a few food parcels from the farm, and I'm afraid it will go off if we don't eat it soon.'

The front door opened, and Tom groaned as he pushed it with his back. 'I've two buckets of coal for ye, Betty,' he said, huffing with relief as he dropped the buckets. A few coals fell out of the buckets.

He fell into his worn armchair beside the fire. 'Only the start of the day and I'm tired already.'

After a few minutes, he sat beside Veronica at the table. He leaned into her, watching Betty in the kitchen with one eye and whispered, 'Did you hide it?'

She nodded.

He winked at her with a smile.

8

The church bells from St James's seemed to ring louder on Sundays, reminding everyone it was a day of rest and to worship God. The booming bells' vibrations rattled Veronica's windowpane. This was her cue to get up, and she stretched. She wrapped the blanket closer, knowing the cold morning would greet her with goosebumps as soon as she got out of bed. She wanted to linger in the bed a few extra minutes, as it would be hours before she could have any food.

Every Sunday since Veronica could remember her mother said to her and Susan, 'Girls, isn't it wonderful to receive the Body of Christ? You should be honoured.' And she would clasp her hands, holding them tight to her chest, her eyes glazed as if the priest was in front of her with the host in his hands.

Veronica had always held her tongue, wanting to say, 'Wouldn't it be just the same if we had breakfast?' The one time she had said this to her mother, it had driven her into a verbal frenzy. While Veronica's family were upstairs washing and dressing for Mass, she would go into the larder and eat a few of Mrs Slaney's scones.

Veronica thought she had better get up when the front door slammed shut.

Tom shouted, 'Betty, more coal for after Mass.'

Now dressed, Veronica put on her hat, the yellow primroses and bright-blue ribbon a welcome burst of colour. The autumnal days were rapidly being replaced by the dark, dreary winter.

A Sunday routine of words had ensued over the weeks.

Veronica's offer to help Betty to prepare the breakfast on their return from Mass always yielded the same response.

'Veronica, you have enough to do with your secretarial school. You rest yourself. It's a day of rest for you,' Betty would say, the lines of her face softening over the weeks.

Tom sat in his armchair beside the fire. He was scrubbed clean and wore a crisp white shirt. He spat on his shoes, rubbing them shiny. Veronica sat at the kitchen table, looking at him and wondered if he hoped his sins bounced off the shiny shoes like a light. *What sins would he have?*

Tom glanced into the kitchen before going to Veronica, and whispering, 'The parcel.'

'Do you want it now? I'll get it.'

Tom nodded and followed her to her room, closing the door behind him.

'You're a good girl, Veronica, and I hope you are enjoying the typing. I know your father wasn't too pushed that you wanted to go to Dublin, but Eddie thought it was a great idea.'

She sat up straight. Eddie had thought it would be good for her!

'Eddie said it would be a good excuse for your father to

come to Thomas St. They think people are watching, so it gives your father an excuse to come to Dublin.'

Watching him. Did her father know about Eddie? Was her father involved?

Tom stared into the middle of the room, pushing himself up with one hand on the bed frame, and the other holding his hip.

'Christ, this damned hip isn't getting any better. I'll ask one of the young lads from the Brewery to go.'

From the kitchen, Betty screamed, and a saucepan crashed to the floor. 'Shoo! Tom, the cat, brought in a mouse! Quick, Tom!'

'I'm on my way.' Tom chuckled. 'What harm can a mouse do?'

'I'll go.'

'What?' Tom had reached the door. 'You can't go, your father wouldn't allow it, and I shouldn't have asked you before, but we needed it to get to Captain Smith. Your father was very annoyed.'

'He doesn't need to know. I'll go today. After dinner.'

She'd said it without thinking, but for the first time in a while, she felt excited. The monotony of her pen and diary for nightly company was getting to her, along with the loneliness she had not expected.

'No, you can't, and that'll be the end of it. I'll think of something. Your father expects Betty and me to look after you, not to put you in danger.' He looked directly at Veronica, his eyes teary. 'I can't put you in danger, Betty would never forgive me. Your arrival has cheered her up no end. She feels she has a purpose now.'

When Tom left, Veronica sighed in guilt that Betty appreciated her presence, but all she felt was boredom, and that was replaced by frustration. She wanted to do something other than sit at home on her own every night. She wanted to do something, anything and threw herself back on the bed and thumped her fists on her blankets. She retrieved the package and turned it over in her hands. The tightly wrapped brown paper was the same as the last package, but this was slightly heavier. She was more interested in this package now she knew what it might hold.

'Veronica, come on, we'll be late for Mass.'

'Coming, Betty,' Veronica muttered, as she restored the package to its hiding place. She needed to think carefully. How would she find where Henrietta St was?

Tom winked at her as she got her Sunday coat and he took his cap from the hook in the hall stand and patted his coat pocket for his cigarettes. Betty joined them with her brown Sunday coat fastened and her lank hair pinned back, ready for their Sunday prayer.

The following morning after breakfast Veronica was thankful to go to secretarial school to break the monotony. As she sat beside her uncle on the day, she shuddered as soldiers marched passed them to the Royal Barracks on the quays, and her scalp prickled.

'Veronica, don't let them bother you; ignore them, and they will ignore you, and there's not as many soldiers on the streets, love, they've all been shipped off to France. The Somme and some to a place called Vers in Belgium.'

Tom didn't mention Suvla Bay, where her cousin had died.

Bridget returned to school. Her return was a relief for Veronica as she'd missed her company.

At lunchtime, Veronica and Bridget sat together in the shelter of the yard.

'Bridget, I'm glad you're back. It's been so boring without you; the other girls don't talk to me. You look, well, thin but you don't look sick.'

Bridget looked at Veronica, her blue eyes deep in thought. 'Actually, to tell you the truth, I wasn't sick, my sister had a baby.'

'But I thought you said she wasn't married.'

Bridget sighed. The sun caught the worry that lined her face. 'She's not. The fella ran a mile – he promised to marry her, but packed his bags and went straight for the boat. Da was angry, kicked a hole in the wall. He wanted to kill the fella. The priest called saying he would arrange for the baby to go to the nuns. Da wanted to run the priest as he hasn't much time for the church, but Ma insisted on Maura to go, saying the neighbours would never let her live it down. She couldn't bear the whispers of the women when buying their bread and the sorts, looking at her, she said life was hard enough to keep four mouths fed without having another, and that was the end of Maura.' Bridget sniffed. 'Life doesn't always turn out the way we want.' She smiled. 'But, you and me, Veronica, we're bettering ourselves.'

Veronica was speechless. She had secretly thought it was just another way of the church keeping women down. One of the girls at her school had gotten pregnant, and the nuns beat her, but an old nun had come to her rescue and contacted the girl's parents. The old nun helped the girl and arranged for her to go to England to her sister.

'I'd die if that happened to me, between the mother and baby home, or having to go to England, and my mother would kill me. The priest is a regular visitor for tea to our house.'

Bridget frowned. 'Veronica, are you all right? You're quiet, and you're also looking tired.'

'I'm fine,' she replied, pausing for a minute. 'Bridget, the soldiers, there's quite a few on the streets. Do they make you nervous at all?'

'Look, Veronica, ignore them. If you ever meet one, go the other way and don't talk to him.'

Veronica remained silent for a minute. 'Bridget, would you be in favour of Home Rule? Or our independence?'

'Don't care either way. My Da has a good job; he is a mechanic, and sometimes the British send him their cars to fix. We need the money. Anyway, I think we will need it more now that we have an extra mouth to feed. I'm used to the British, just stay out of their way, and no harm will come to you.' She put down her bread and jam sandwich. 'I've more news. I met a lad from Henrietta St. Mammy is afraid I'll end up the same as my sister. Henrietta St, it's not a nice place. Well, she put a stop to that soon enough. No prospects, Mammy said. He was good looking, but his daddy was drunk all the time.'

Veronica tried to sound casual. 'Henrietta St. Where exactly is that?'

'You wouldn't want to go there, it's the opposite to where those girls are from.' She nodded to the four girls huddled together. 'Veronica, he wrote a lovely letter to me.' Her eyes lit up. 'I think I'll write to him. Charlie, that's his name.'

'Sorry, where did you say he lived?'

'Henrietta St, it's near King's Inn, the place where all the solicitors go, you know just off Parnell St at the top of Sackville St.'

Veronica frowned. *Should she chance another delivery?* 'Come on. We better get inside, it looks like rain, and you know Mr Begley will have our guts for garters!'

Two girls, who had ignored Veronica at lunchtimes, overheard Bridget. They looked at each other and scoffed in disapproval at such common language.

Veronica took Bridget's arm and laughed, skipping inside the building. Bridget liked to shock.

9

On Sunday after Mass, her aunt and uncle didn't linger outside the church to talk to neighbours or listen to the weekly gossip, eager to get home to their breakfast. Afterwards, Betty sat in front of the blazing fire with knitting needles and the wool placed on the small wooden table beside her. The cat lay on his back, his paws rolling back and forth teasing the string of the yarn that dangled from the table. Veronica watched Tom chip away on a long piece of wood. 'A whistle, I'm making the young lad across the street a whistle. Something I used to do for Padraig.' He rubbed his leg, and muttered, 'Damn leg.'

Veronica's heart beat fast. She was going to go to Henrietta St with the parcel before her uncle asked for it. She would prove she was as good as any man.

Veronica told Betty and Tom she was going for a walk. Betty got up and stretched, bent to her knitting box, 'Veronica take this scarf, I knitted it last year, but it didn't get much use. I don't like to go out much,' she explained as she wrapped it around Veronica's neck.

Tom smiled at Betty. 'And Veronica don't forget to bring

your coat, love. It's nippy out there, don't be fooled by the sun, frost will be on its way,' he said.

Veronica slipped back into her room to get the parcel. With the brown package in her hand, her curiosity became too great to ignore, and she carefully peeled back the paper to reveal another layer of brown paper. She stared and persevered to pull back to the next layer. Her fingers fell on cold metal. Her heart quickened, and she hastily pulled back more of the paper. Her heart stopped. It was a gun, a small one like the one she saw Eddie with. Veronica exhaled a long slow breath, quickly wrapped the gun back in the paper and tucked the parcel into her skirt band.

Christ, she thought. Blood flowed quickly around her body. Her mind whirled. *What had she got herself into?* She needed air and rushed out onto Thomas St past a family on a Sunday stroll and out to the quays.

She needed air and inhaled deeply, and kept her head high, walking fast, concentrating on every step, trying to remember the way. At Nelson's Pillar, she heard the bell of an approaching tram. Maybe she should take the tram. It felt safer, even though it was only a few stops to King's Inn. On the tram, she fell into a seat, the package stuck to her skin. Two soldiers got on. When they reached the stairs, she wished for them to go to the upper deck, but they continued towards her. They nodded at Veronica before they sat two seats in front of her. A bead of perspiration dripped into her eyes. Watching the back of their heads, she secured the parcel in the band of her skirt.

When the conductor shouted, 'King's Inn Road', she pulled the overhead rope running down the middle of

the tram and willed her legs to stop shaking as she walked
steadily past the soldiers.

She thanked the conductor, surprised at the steadiness
of her voice.

He said, 'Wrap up well, I smell the rain coming.'

The driver rang the bell to announce the tram was
leaving, and when it was out of sight, she slowly let out
a breath. Soon she was at Henrietta St, its cobbled street
like all the others. It had the same red-brick Georgian
buildings, three storeys high with lattice windows, but
somehow it felt different. These tenements were some
of the worst in Dublin, with over a hundred people to a
house. As she looked at these beautiful buildings, it was
beyond her imagination how so many lived in one house.
The stench of sewage coming from them was worse than
O'Keefe's.

Above the chimneys, the sun escaped through the thin
November clouds, sprinkling the street with warmth and
offering rays of hope. The sunshine may have been a
pleasant reprieve from the conditions families lived in, but
Veronica felt it was also teasing them. It would be gone,
and they would return to their dismal lives. The grand
Georgian houses had once been home to the gentry. Now
poor women sat wearily on the steps, their threadbare
shawls pulled tight as they watched their children run,
playing chase on the streets. Veronica thought they looked
battered by the poverty of life.

Men stood at the street corner, waiting for something
to happen, talking and spitting out black chewed tobacco.
Veronica walked by the railings on the footpath, counting

the numbers on the houses. Number seven was near the end of the street. A white marble arch spanned the width of the street with the words *King's Inn*. It was the entrance to a life few would have the privilege to enter – a place for educating people in the law profession.

On many of the houses, newspaper replaced windowpane glass. Every second or third window a washing line of torn, dirty-looking clothes stretched across to a window on the house on the opposite side of the street. Number seven was no different from the other houses. The glass over the door was missing. The door was ajar. Veronica entered a dark hall, and the stench was nauseating, a mixture of the musty smell of years of neglect and human waste. There were four doors downstairs, some with a letter etched in the wooden frame. She couldn't see *D*. As a small shoeless boy ran past her, she shouted, 'Do you know where Joseph Connellan lives?'

He stopped to stare at her, the whites of his eyes shining out from the dirtiest face she had ever seen.

He pointed to the end of the corridor before turning and running out the front door.

'Thank you,' she said, but he was gone. Veronica went to the end of the corridor, passing an open door. There was desperation in the faces of children, desperation you wouldn't wish on farm animals. *D* was scratched into the split wooden door. She knocked, and the door opened to a room full of people.

Veronica, trying to keep her voice steady, said, 'Is Joseph here?'

'Come in,' said a woman with a husky voice, rushing

her inside, 'Have you the package?' Her gummy mouth was wrinkled, and wispy grey hair fell to her shoulders.

A sheet hung from the ceiling, separating the room into a bedroom and a mattress on the floor. The bare room was home to many children. At least ten sat huddled in a corner for warmth. Eight of the children sat around the table in the middle of the room, two sitting on each of the four chairs. Others lay at all angles on the mattress. The fire burning in the hearth gave enough heat for the pot hanging above it but left the room cold. The once blue and white wallpaper hung in pieces from the wall. The smell of the lavatory on the landing outside snaked across the room. Another dishevelled woman sat in an armchair rocking back and forth, the rhythmic squeak of the chair putting the small child on her lap to sleep. A little girl with a grey smock sang to herself on the large bed.

One of the children said to Veronica, 'What d' ya' want with our da?'

From the corner of the room, a man coughed. He rose from a seat revealing a small bundle of life under his arm. It stirred as he got up, letting out a little whimper. He said hoarsely, 'I'm Joseph.' He handed the bundle to what Veronica presumed was his wife, who looked as thin as her children.

Veronica whispered shakily, 'I've got a parcel for you.' She handed it over.

Joseph bent under the chair and pulled out another parcel, handing it to Veronica. 'Keep it closed at all times. Here, take it.' He coughed as he thrust it into her hands. 'Tell Tom to take it on one of his deliveries.'

She moved back at the smell of his breath. He grabbed her arm and pulled her to him. 'Tell him to give it to Pa O'Driscoll in Davy Byrne's pub on Duke St,' he said and pushed her away. 'Go on, and remember to tell him, Pa needs these papers as soon as possible.' He waved his hand at her while holding his stomach with the other, coughing. 'Go!' he bellowed at her as he coughed uncontrollably again.

She ran out the door into the hallway and to the street, which was now full of children. The girls wore similar pinafores to the girl in Joseph's room, hardly enough threads to give any protection from the morning cold.

'*Ring a Ring o' Roses*,' they sang, dancing in circles.

'Miss, give us a shilling.'

'Look at ya, don't ya look lovely.'

Veronica kept her head down, not looking at the children. It was heart-breaking to see the conditions people lived in and compare it to her own. Tom and Betty's house was a home of grandeur compared to Henrietta St. Anger bubbled – anger for the people, anger for Betty's loss. After years of not giving other people's lives a thought, Veronica felt guilty. Her life had been so insular, so selfish. Now she saw how privileged she was. The streets were quieter now as the Sunday strollers had returned home for their dinner. Finally, she arrived home full of adrenaline. Betty was asleep in her chair with the cat purring on her lap. The room was warm and clean. Tom put his newspaper down and nodded to her. 'Did you have a nice walk?'

She nodded back, unsure of herself now. 'Eh, I went to Henrietta St. The place. It smells, it's awful, and the children look desperate. How do people live like that? Why do they live like that?'

Tom sat up, dropping the newspaper. His face blanched, then turned red. 'I told you not to go. Did anyone follow you?'

'I don't think so,' she said, but she hesitated, not too sure.

The fire crackled, and a wet log hissed. Tom kicked the log, turning it over to the dry side.

'I know, but look at your leg, you couldn't go and who would follow me? A lady out for a stroll.'

'Your father told me not to involve you. Don't say anything to him. Did Joseph give you anything?'

'Yes, and he told me to tell you to bring this package to Davy Byrne's pub.'

Tom didn't say anything for a minute. 'Veronica, this is dangerous. It's not silly games, people are shot for less. Don't dare do anything like that again.'

Blood returned to his face as he shook his head and lowered his voice while keeping an eye on Betty. He took Veronica's hand and squeezed it. 'Thanks, Veronica. Will you hide it for me, and I'll ask the lads at work to take it to Davy Byrne's.' He stood to stretch his leg, nodding his head towards the fireplace. 'Rest yourself, you look exhausted. There's tea on the hearth there, and bread on the table.'

She shook her head. 'I'm not hungry.' How could she eat after seeing the conditions the children lived in?

She pulled the bedroom door tight behind her, pulled back the worn carpet and placed the package under the security of the floorboard. Exhausted, she eased into a restless sleep of guns, old men with pipes and hungry children.

10

Veronica arranged to meet Bridget on Saturday where she helped at her aunt and uncle's small grocery shop on Abbey St. Her uncle had been struck with the Spanish flu and never fully recovered. Veronica arranged to meet Bridget on her lunch break in a teashop opposite her aunt and uncle's shop.

On her walk along the quay to O'Connell Bridge, her thoughts returned to the parcel. She noticed more soldiers on the streets and the way people sidestepped them and kept their heads low when they passed.

Dublin was turning out different from her reassuring words to her mother. *'I won't get into any danger.'*

She crossed O'Connell Bridge, with the white Customs House to her left. The morning mist was gone, and the seagulls swooped and dived at the barges. This was what she'd imagined her life in Dublin would be like, going to meet a friend for afternoon tea and being independent, but was she? At Sackville St, the ruined buildings were a stark reminder of the reality of the situation in Ireland. The street was clear from the rubble, but the glass had not been replaced on many of the buildings. On Abbey St, she stopped outside Wynn's Hotel to look at the damage. A workman nodded to her as he pushed a wheelbarrow of stones from the hotel; the repair work had begun in the hotel.

Veronica reached the tearoom as a church clock bell rang once; it was one o'clock. She knew Bridget only had an hour for lunch, and as she hurriedly pushed the door to the tearoom, the bell tinkled to announce her arrival. Bridget was sat nestled in the bay window. She waved and, with her usual beaming smile, pushed a chair out for Veronica. Bridget had cut her hair into a modern short style like the ones Veronica envied in magazines.

Veronica sat down, placing her handbag on the pink and white tablecloth and exclaiming, 'God look at you, who did that for you? It's lovely and that dress, ya would turn any fella's eye.'

'Mary, my sister, did it last night. I wasn't sure. Ma said, "You will attract unsuitable attention," and give the wrong impression, especially when I wear red lipstick.' Bridget reached into her brown bag and took out a small cylinder shape. She twisted it to reveal a long red barrel and handed it to Veronica. 'Here, try it.'

Veronica giggled, 'God no,' and looked around the tearoom first before she took Bridget's ivory mirror and carefully and slowly put on some lipstick. The red of the lipstick, coupled with her dark skin, accentuated her green eyes.

'You are gorgeous. Go on, you keep it. I can get more from ma sister.'

A waitress arrived with a pot of tea. Her eyes were red as if she had been crying.

'I ordered for you when I came in. I can only stay for an hour.'

'How is your uncle?'

'He's on the mend, but it's a while yet.' She lowered her voice. 'You know I never told you, but my aunt is a Protestant!'

Veronica's eyes widened, and she sat forward, leaning her elbows on the table. 'Really! One of them? How'd they meet?' she asked quietly.

In an equally hushed voice, Bridget replied, 'My Uncle Brendan worked in the shipyard in Belfast, and he met my Aunt Lizzy while working there. It was love at first sight. They got married in Belfast, and when he came home, everyone thought she was a Catholic.'

'A Protestant? How do you know?'

'She told me,' Bridget said, her chair scraping on the floor as she moved in closer to Veronica. 'She swore me to secrecy, and sure, who am I gonna tell? They've been married years.'

'Gosh, that's dangerous. Your aunt must trust you if she confided in you. What about their children?'

'Well, they never had children, so religion was never an issue.'

'What about Mass on Sundays?'

'Neither goes to Mass!'

'Really? Don't people think that's odd?'

'Maybe in the city, it's different.'

The clock chimed two.

'I'd better go, Veronica. I'll see you on Monday.'

Veronica strolled home with time to reflect on her new life, comparing it to the lazy sunny summer days at home by the shores of Lough Ramor. She tried to imagine what the shelled buildings had looked like before the few days over Easter that changed everyone's lives.

A group of young boys shouted to Veronica, 'Miss, got a tuppence?'

This was how life in Dublin should be. Typing and meeting a friend for tea, not delivering parcels. At O'Connell Bridge she waited for a group of bicycles to pass before crossing the road. A man on a bicycle slowed as he passed, leaning into her. 'Tell Tom to bring the parcel to Pa O'Driscoll in Davy Byrne's pub this Sunday night. Third booth on the right.'

Veronica's heart jolted. She stood rooted to the spot. Her eyes followed the group of cyclists, searching for the man, but he was lost among them. Nondescript, all dressed the same, white shirts and flat caps. She had no idea of what he looked like and wanted to get home as quickly as possible. *Were people watching her?*

Finally, she was home. Betty stood at the sink washing the last of the dinner plates. She asked Betty if Tom was at home.

'No, he'd a few deliveries. Is it important?' Wiping her hands on her apron, she nodded towards the oven. 'I've kept you a few spuds hot. Tom will be back soon, Saturdays are quiet.'

'I'm not hungry, and I've got a headache. I think I'll lie down for a while.'

In her bedroom, she got the parcel and sat on the edge of her bed, rolling it in her hands. Soon the front door banged, and she immediately opened her bedroom door, gesturing Tom inside.

He leaned against the doorframe, still in a lot of pain. He limped over to the chair, rubbing his leg. 'Dammed weather, sorry, sometimes it gets to me. Padraig should be helping me lift the barrels.' He paused and gathered his emotions. 'Go on then, love, you wanted something?'

'A man passed me on a bicycle and told me to tell you to deliver the parcel Saturday night to Pa O'Driscoll in Davy Byrne's pub.' She inhaled and handed the parcel to Tom. Her hands shook a little. 'How did he know who I was?'

'Veronica, everyone is watching everyone. Sure, the English have spies everywhere. I always say, "Don't trust anyone. Everyone is capable of being a spy".'

He was silent for a few minutes. His head bent. Slowly, he lifted his head. 'Saturday night? I was hoping to do it during the day on one of my delivery rounds. I can't deliver Guinness at night. I'll think of something.'

Later in bed, Veronica twisted and turned in a battle with sleep, and just as she was about to win the battle, she sat up. It was so simple. Lighting the lamp on her bedside table, she got out of bed careful of the squeaky floorboard beside her bed. She opened the wardrobe. Her cousin's clothes hung, untouched, smelling of mothballs. Everything was there. Men's trousers, a white shirt and waistcoat. It would be weird wearing her cousin's clothes. The shoes would be a problem, but in defiance to her mother, she had brought her boots. She stood back and felt a thrill inside her stomach. Would her uncle agree?

11

During the week Veronica mulled over her plan, Mr Begley often berating her lack of typing due to daydreaming.

On Saturday, Veronica helped Betty clean the house; she needed to keep her hands busy to quell her racing mind and so offered to scrub the floors. She thought about Davy Byrne's pub and imagined walking through the dark streets to there. *Would she even make it to the pub? She might be attacked. When she got there, would the men laugh at her?* So many questions.

Earlier, she had suggested to her uncle that she would go to the pub and wear Padraig's clothes.

First, he had said, 'No.' His face had blanched, replaced by a distant sadness.

He rubbed his chin, staring into space, and sighed. 'Maybe, just maybe it will work. These are desperate times. All the lads have gone to Cork to hear Michael Collins speak at a rally. He's a great way with words, and he stirs up fire in the belly of many a young lad; they hang on to every word.' Tom was silent for a minute. 'It's risky, but what choice do I have? But, please, Veronica, don't let Betty know. You'll have to be careful. Keep your head down but be watchful, be careful.' He gave Veronica the directions. 'Veronica, remember. Not a word to Betty.'

Veronica didn't stop scrubbing the floor when Betty called her name. Kneeling in front of the fire hearth, she dipped a cloth into the tin bucket again and didn't notice she had splashed water on her dress.

'Veronica, are you, all right?' asked Betty. 'You've been rubbing the same spot for ages and look, you're bleeding. You've scraped your knuckles. Here let me get you a cloth to wrap around your hand.'

'I'm fine, just thinking about some typing I have to do.'

'Are you sure that's all it is? You're not in trouble or anything with Mr Begley, or fighting with Bridget?'

'No, nothing at all. That bacon smells lovely.' The smell of the sizzling bacon usually sparked Veronica's appetite, but not today.

At tea, Veronica forced herself to eat the bacon and bread, hoping Betty would stop asking her if she felt fine. After tea, she told Betty she was tired after the day's chores so that she would have an early night.

Betty yawned and stretched, opening the drawer in the side cupboard where she stored the delph. She had a notebook in her hand. 'I think I'll have an early night as well. Your uncle said he'd be late; he has to get the barrels ready for tomorrow.' She lifted the darned sock to the candle flame. Satisfied with her needlework, she placed it on top of the three other patched socks. When she stood, she rubbed the small of her back. 'Would you put the cat out before you go to bed?' She left, but turned to Veronica, looking at her for a minute. 'Do you know, Veronica, I'm really glad you're here.' She said no more and went to bed.

Guilt swept over Veronica. She waited for Betty to settle, until she heard a small snore from Betty and Tom's bedroom, and then she went to her bedroom and put her plan into action. Outside a British patrol vehicle passed, its lights bouncing off the walls. She took the folded pile of clothes from the wardrobe – trousers, shoes, shirt and braces – whispered *Sorry, Padraig* and put on his clothes, shuddering. If Betty saw her in his clothes, it would be the death of her. After rolling up the trousers, she tiptoed past Betty's bedroom and put her ear to the door, and the deep breathing of Betty's sleep reassured Veronica.

The noises of life she rarely saw filtered through the walls of the hall. A drunk husband shouted profanities at his wife, and a baby cried, looking for food or comfort. This was not her concern, and so she silently opened the front door to check nobody was in the street. Silently cursing her curly hair, she tucked it tight under the cap, wishing she had done it upstairs in front of the mirror. The parcel was safely concealed in the inside pocket of the jacket. When ready, she got the bike Tom had left outside for her. With one last check on the street, she cycled towards Davy Byrne's. The night was dead and dark.

She cycled with her heart pounding, and though the air was bitterly cold, beads of sweat rolled down her forehead. She thought about the women who went to pubs. At home in her father's pub, they sometimes ventured in on payday when anger overpowered them. In a weekly rage, they would drag their husbands out of the pubs hoping to rescue a few shillings. Her uncle had told her Jim Larkin, a union man, had tried to stop men receiving their wages in pubs in the hope it might stop them from spending their few hard-earned pennies on liquor. This deterrent was like attempting to stop a mother giving her baby milk. The men's desire for the hard stuff had no relevance where they received their wages.

Soon she arrived at the pub. She dropped the bike amongst a pile of bikes on the pub wall and stood in the shadows for a few minutes, allowing her breathing to slow to an even pace. She wiped away the sweat on her forehead, which could be mistaken for damp as the fog descended on the streets. Veronica kept her head steady as she walked to the entrance of the pub and stepped inside after two men. The only pub she had ever been in had been her father's, and he had never allowed her into the bar, only into the lounge. The familiar smell of sawdust and smoke greeted her as the door opened, reminding her of her father's pub. She pulled the cap low over her eyes, keeping her head high enough to take in the bar, but low enough to conceal her gender.

A fiddler and an accordion player sat on three-legged wooden stools beside the fire. Its flames were dancing to the music filling the pub. Men sat around them, tapping their feet and smoking pipes. Her eyes adjusted to the smoky light. At the bar, there was a woman who sat on a barstool. Her legs hung loosely, swaying to the music, or beer. She tried to conceal her years with heavy makeup and red lipstick. Her bosom left little to the imagination. She hung unsteadily onto a man's arms, laughing too loud, nodding drunkenly to anything any of the men said.

Veronica hoped that with her oversized jacket, and baggy trousers that gathered around her shoes, she was just like any other Dublin lad wearing their older brother's hand-me-downs. When she walked, her shoes dragged, sending sawdust into the air. However, the men who sat at the bar counter paid no attention to her. She looked for the third booth to the left from the door. Two men looked at her as she sat down to them and whispered, 'Pa O'Driscoll? I was told to give this to him.'

The light was dim, and the shadows covered the men's faces.

'Give it to me.'

Veronica took the parcel out of her jacket. He grabbed her hand, squeezing it hard and twisting it to pull her towards him. He looked at her in the eyes.

'I'm Pa, I've never met ya before, take your cap off so we can see ye.'

She kept her eyes down, not moving, but wished she could get up and run. He pushed her hand back, saying, 'Leave quickly. Go back to Thomas St along the quays this time.'

Veronica turned to leave, but he took hold of her arm and pulled her back, and laughed, smelling of beer and cigarette smoke. 'Where are you going? I've something for you to give to Tom.'

Before she could answer the door opened, and four DMP policemen entered. All chat stopped. The fiddle and accordion stopped too.

Pa O'Driscoll pulled Veronica down beside him and pushed a tankard of stout in front of her.

Three soldiers, one of whom was not much older than
Eddie, slowly moved around the pub, stopping to stare
at the men. They stopped to talk to a grey-haired man
who stood at the bar counter. Veronica kept her eyes low,
lifted the tankard and took her first taste of stout. It tasted
vile and wanted to spit it out, but out of fear of being
caught, she swallowed, trying not to grimace. Glancing up
slightly, she saw the soldiers walk to the door and leave.

Pa O'Driscoll pushed Veronica. 'Quick go, now. I'll get
it to him, tell your uncle to collect it here on his deliveries
on Monday. Go,' he said, throwing her out of the pew.

Outside the pub, she grabbed a bicycle, hoping it was
her uncle's. For a second time, she cycled at speed with the
wind in her face. The damp fog stuck to her hair, and it
dripped into her eyes but she ignored it. She just wanted
to get home and peddled hard. Her hair came loose and
fanned in the wind like drowning arms crying for help.
Her legs burned, her throat raw with each breath, but she
didn't stop until she got to Thomas St.

Tom stepped out of the shadows. 'Did you give it to Pa?'

'Yes, but soldiers came in, and I had to leave before…
Pa told me to leave, and he had something for you, but he
didn't give it to me, and—'

'Slow down, Veronica, take a deep breath. You're safe,
nothing happened. Did it?'

'I know, I'm all right now, I just got a fright.'

A cat shrieked in the darkness, and Veronica jumped.

'Veronica, go on to bed now. Ye've had enough
excitement for one night.'

As she lay in bed, watching the moon shadow on the

wall grow smaller as she succumbed to sleep, her last thought was she had had enough excitement to last her a lifetime. She'd come to Dublin to learn to be a secretary, and that's what she would do.

12

A snowy December replaced damp November. In the
few months since her arrival so much had happened
that she didn't notice Christmas creep up on her. The week
before Christmas she began to look forward to going home
to Cavan. A twinge of guilt snuck over her. Christmas
would be hard for Betty and Tom without Padraig, but
she had to go home to her family. On the morning of her
departure, after checking everything was in her case for
her break, she left a present for Betty under the Christmas
tree. She imagined Betty's face when she opened it. One of
joy she hoped. One evening on her way home from work
she got the idea to make the present while getting lost
in glittering Christmas decorations in Switzer's window.
She had bought a silver and a red ribbon, and red felt in
a haberdashery shop on Earl St. She had tied the silver
ribbon into a bow and flattened it, and cut the red felt into
the shape of a cone, doubling it and sewing the bowed
ribbon to it. She looped the red ribbon, tying it to the cone
and dangled it, the silver ribbon glittering in tendrils of
moonlight as it spun. She hoped Betty would hang the
angel decoration on the tree and think of Padraig.

The front door slammed shut, and Tom came into the living room. 'Veronica, your father is coming to the capital today to collect goods. So, you can return home on the train with him. Wrap up well; it's a cold one.'

Relief flooded through her that she wasn't travelling alone. Stories hadn't escaped her of soldiers harassing passengers on the train while they searched for rebels. Bridget had told her soldiers on a train had found a boy hiding in the luggage compartment. When the boy tried to escape, a soldier had shot him in the back, the bullets narrowly missing the other passengers on the train.

Tom moved quickly in front of the fire, rubbing his hands and stamping the snow off his boots. 'Sorry, Betty, for dragging the snow in, but it's so damned cold outside. I needed to warm myself first.'

She gave him a disapproving look, and he apologised for cursing.

Veronica was smiling at their exchange when a knock came at the front door.

'I'll get that, Betty. Veronica, it's probably your father.'

'Richard, you're early, come in and warm yourself. Give me your coat.' Tom shook the coat and snow tumbled onto the tiles, but Betty didn't give her brother the same disapproving look. The weave on her father's coat was tightly bound, unlike the loose-knit on her uncle's threadbare jacket. Her uncle's Sunday coat looked inferior to her father's day coat.

Richard dropped three packages on the table, all wrapped in brown paper. One opened and pudding, bread, and butter wrapped in waxed paper fell onto the table.

The two other packages stayed closed, the brown string on them pulled tight. Veronica thought of the package she had delivered to the captain, but these were a lot bigger.

'Betty, some bacon and eggs from the farm and a few things from the shop, not much, though. Things are in short supply. Rationing.' He clapped his hands together in front of the fire. 'It's cold, all right.'

'Oh, I do look forward to the eggs. Everything is a help, Richard, thank you. Sit, I'll put the pot on, I'll get you a cup of tea.'

Tom pulled the chair by the fire and put Richard's coat on it to dry.

'I'll just have a quick cup. I've to meet someone in half an hour.'

After tea and a few words, her father put on his now dry coat. 'Veronica, I won't be long, and then we'll go.' He pulled his coat collar up high and gestured to Tom to follow him into the hall where they had a few quiet words.

For as long as she could remember, her father was always going somewhere. It was then she noticed the two parcels on the table were gone.

Betty hummed as she put the food away. The cat jumped up on Veronica's lap, and she stroked him absentmindedly; his rhythmic purr was soothing. After a while, Veronica's head started to fall, and she didn't fight it. She woke in a cold room, Betty asleep in the chair on the opposite side of the fire and Tom gone. She gently pushed the cat from her lap and put coal and tinder on the fire, poking it to life. The crackling wood woke Betty.

'Betty, you stay where you are, I'll make tea for us. I

don't know when I'm going.' Sighing, she poured the kettle into the teapot with one hand while spooning tea leaves in with the other. She had hoped to be home before it was dark, but it looked unlikely.

Veronica put the kettle on the fire as the cat rubbed her legs in the hope of a few scraps. Tom came back just as the kettle boiled shivering with cold as she smothered butter on a few slices of bread.

'I'm glad to be out of that,' he said, 'it hasn't snowed all afternoon, but it's cold. Richard is here as well.'

Betty poured tea, feeling her brother's hand. 'Are you cold? Warm yourself first.'

'No, I'm grand. We were inside and got a cab back.'

When they had finished eating, her father said, 'Veronica, go off to bed. We'll wait until morning.'

In bed, Veronica tossed and turned listening to her uncle and her father talk past midnight. Eventually, she succumbed to slumber.

With the stars and moon still high, her father knocked on her door. 'We'll need to leave before sunrise. The train will be packed, everyone going home for Christmas.'

At breakfast, Betty cut fresh bread and, putting it in a small paper bag, said, 'Something small for your journey.' The beginnings of tears were in her eyes, and she hugged Veronica.

'Don't be upset, I'll be back after Christmas, and there's a small present under the tree for you.' She hugged Betty.

Her father said goodbye to his sister while Tom carried her case downstairs and hugged her, whispering, 'You have helped Betty. Thank you.'

Tom brought them to the train station in the dray. The station was full of people returning home for Christmas, and her father was right, there were few spare seats. Veronica and her father had to sit separately unlike their previous journey to the capital. Soon the whistle sounded, and steam filled the platform as it pulled away from the station. A group of carol singers gathered on the platform to sing for the travellers on their journey back home. People stood in every available space possible, using each other's bodies for support as the train rattled and thundered across the countryside. The journey was not interrupted by soldiers as Veronica had feared. There was no room on the train for unnecessary passengers.

Veronica sat nestled in between two young women, housemaids who were not required in their houses over Christmas. The fields were covered in snow and looked peaceful. She sat back in the seat and closed her eyes, her head filled with thoughts different than her first journey three months previously. She woke to her father's gentle shake as the train stopped at Oldcastle.

Eddie waved to Veronica as they disembarked and took Veronica's case. 'We should hurry, there is little daylight left, and the clouds look full of snow.'

There was little chat on the journey. It was cold, and the fields were white from the frost, but no snow had arrived.

When Eddie pulled the horse's reins in front of the house, the heavy clouds emptied their burden, the first snowflakes of Christmas. Veronica turned up to the sky; the tumbling flakes shimmered as they floated past the candles in the windows, the cold snowflakes melting as they landed on her face. Their house was the same as every other house in Ireland, each window of the house had a lit candle to guide Mary and Joseph to a place of refuge. When Veronica stepped across the threshold of her front door she was greeted with the warm smell of Christmas. The hallway stand was lined with cuttings of pine and red holly. But best of all was Mrs Slaney's Christmas pudding of soaked fruit, that hung in muslin in the pantry waiting to be covered with whisky and lit on Christmas night. She was home.

'Eddie, will you bring the case up to Veronica's room? Veronica, I want a word with you.'

After Eddie had disappeared up the stairs, her father turned to her and said, 'I won't keep you long. I want to thank you for all your help.'

'It's-it's fine. Really. I see women marching in Dublin, I know it's the right thing for the country.' She leaned in, putting her hand on his arm. 'Daddy I promise you I'll make you proud.'

'You concentrate on your typing as well. And your mother worries so, especially about Eddie.'

'Why?'

He patted her arm. 'We'd better go inside, your mother is looking forward to seeing you safe and sound.'

She ran to the house covering her hat with her hand as heavy snowflakes floated down shimmering in the light from the candles in the windows. Her mother pushed open the front door, her arms wide open, and the smell of Christmas greeted her.

'Quick Veronica, close the door, keep the heat in,' said her mum and welcomed her with a tight hug.

She took off her coat, welcoming the warmth of home as it wrapped around her. The snow that fell from her coat melted as soon as it landed on the tiled hallway.

She was glad to be home as the smells of cooked ham, and soaked fruit surrounded her, inviting her in. Only now did she realise that in Betty and Tom's home there had been no smell of Christmas, no cakes or pudding for the holiday.

Sprigs of red-berried holly sat on the inside of the windowsills surrounded by coloured pine cones. Every autumn, Susan went into the woods to collect pine cones, and after weeks of drying in the pantry, she painted them ruby red and yellow.

Susan ran down the stairs, flinging her arms around Veronica. 'Tell me all about Dublin! Are the shops full of Christmas? Have you been to any parties?'

Susan seemed oblivious to the fact that there was a war on; even though it was in Europe, it affected people in Ireland. Veronica's head was full of brown-papered packages and hungry children. She couldn't tell Susan the initial days of being in awe of Dublin had soon been replaced by pity and fear for the people. She was embroiled in something she couldn't discuss with her sister.

'It's fantastic, Susan. The ladies look magnificent, out for their daily walks in the city. And the shop windows are full of the latest fashion.' She didn't tell her about the shops and buildings that lay in ruins, or the Volunteers who marched the streets.

'Where's Eddie?'

Ignoring her, Susan said, 'I bet you can't wait to return?'

Susan was right, but it felt so good to be home. On the landing outside their bedroom, she heard footsteps.

That night Veronica lay in bed watching the large snowflakes stick to the windowpane. Pulling the duck-down eiderdown tight around her neck, she thought about all that had happened the last few months. Even if she had not been delivering parcels, her life in Dublin was so different. The ruins and soldiers patrolling the streets... Dublin was in turmoil.

The following morning the kitchen, warm with the smells of Christmas, was busy. Veronica was surprised how she relished in the business of housework; the quietness in Thomas St sometimes compounded Veronica's loneliness.

'Veronica, would you pass me the lard?' her mother asked.

Mrs Slaney had prepared the turkey for the family before leaving to spend Christmas with her sister in Dublin. Her brother Tommy collected her for their annual visit. Mrs Slaney's husband had passed away when she was only married a year, and since then she and her bachelor brother spent every Christmas with their sister in Dublin.

'I can't see where Mrs Slaney put it. I'll check the pantry.'

'Oh, where is your mind, Veronica? It's there beside the stove. I'd think you were trying to avoid me.'

She groaned at the thought of another conversation about the dangers in Dublin.

'No, Mammy, I just like to keep busy.' She knew her mother wouldn't see through her lies.

'You used to hate kitchen work. Maybe you are maturing.'

They continued preparing the Christmas dinner, her mother staying up late to put it in the cooker overnight.

The following morning the family gathered around the Christmas tree to open their presents. Susan squealed with delight at her purple scarf and matching gloves and her mother made approving sounds at her new wool coat. Veronica thought of Betty and Tom opening their presents, just the two of them. She hoped Betty liked her gift.

'Veronica, check the turkey and Eddie, get more wood. I don't know what's got into the two of you. You've hardly spoken since you got home.' Her mother didn't waste long mulling over the presents. There was too much to be done to get the dinner ready.

When they reached the kitchen, Veronica pulled Eddie's arm as he walked past. 'Eddie, please talk to me. I was never going to tell Daddy about the money. You have to understand I'm mad at you as well, you...'

'Ah God, Veronica, I'm not angry with you, it's... it's nothing. Why are you mad at me?'

'The gun, Eddie, the money.'

'Look, it's just different now.' He looked at the kitchen door, voices and laughter from the parlour trickled into the kitchen. He moved from foot to foot before nodding at her to follow him, taking her by the arm to the far side of the kitchen to the pantry. The wafting smell of turkey stopped the conversation. Their mother had entered the kitchen, and the door of the cooker was open as the turkey sizzled and spat.

'It's ready. Veronica, check the potatoes and put the apple pie in the oven to warm. Eddie, go get the wood.'

Eddie winked as he passed Veronica and she whispered, 'Please be careful. I don't know what you're up to – well I do, I think I do. Just be careful, Eddie.' She was deciding whether to confide in him about the parcels, when their mother's voice boomed, 'Children. Dinner.' When she called the young adults children, that meant they had to do what they were told.

13

January 1918

Christmas passed in a haze of warm family contentment with Mrs Slaney's tasty dinners, and family card games at night. After two weeks, on the morning of Veronica's return, she again reassured her mother she would come to no harm in Dublin.

During her train journey, she had to bite her lip to stop the tears, but her homesickness retreated as the train approached Broadstone Station, as she looked forward to seeing Betty and smiling as she thought of going back to Underwood to see Bridget's wide grin.

Tom collected her from the station. 'Good to see you, Veronica. Betty will be delighted too. Is everyone good at home?'

'They're good.' She told him about her Christmas, as the wheels of the dray dragged through the sludge as the snow melted.

Soldiers ran past them down a side street in an English accent shouting, 'Stop, you bloody Fienen,' and fired shots that hit the wall of a house, as the boy they had chased ran down an alleyway.

The horse jolted and Tom pulled the reins. 'Easy boy.'

One of the wheels hit a rock of frozen snow, and she lurched from her seat. She pulled the case tight against her legs. Tom calmed the horse with soothing words and flicked the reins.

Tom shuddered. 'I'm glad this snow will be gone soon. It's bitter. Betty didn't go out at all.'

The snow kept people indoors; few children were on the streets, and no bicycles passed. They approached the river, which was black and angry from the melting snow coming down from the mountains. A surge of excitement filled her as they went down the Maltings to Thomas St.

Betty greeted her with a timid hug, and the house was warm. 'I've soup and bread for you.'

Veronica handed Betty a parcel of food. 'Are they all well at home? Your mother and father, are they well? Eddie?'

'Eddie is fine.' It was great to hear Betty chat, but she didn't want to talk about Eddie. 'Betty, I'm not hungry, I think I'll go to bed.'

'Veronica, before you go,' she took Veronica's hands, 'thank you for the lovely present. I'll leave ye be and rest easy.'

The following day Veronica walked to Leinster St, careful as the pavements were slippery. As she walked the temperature rose, and the snow melted. The streets of the beautiful white city were slowly transformed into a slow-moving river of melted snow, the sludge grey and black. It was not a day for observing her surroundings or watching the soldiers on the street corners. Finally, at school, her stockings soaked and her feet cold, she met Bridget as she entered the building. Bridget's face broke into a broad smile when she saw Veronica and she took her arm affectionately. 'Isn't it great to be back? I enjoyed Christmas, but I love it here.'

'True, just a few more months, and we'll be qualified in shorthand and typing.'

Mr Begley coughed as the girls sat down, ready to begin his monologue on secretarial etiquette. Just as he opened his mouth, there was a knock at the door, and a thin, tall priest entered. The men shook hands over a few quiet words.

The priest looked at the girls, and each one stared back at him. He removed his black hat to reveal his wispy hair.

He cleared his throat. 'Veronica. Veronica McDermott.'

Veronica didn't answer him, her mouth dry. *Why did a priest want to speak to her?*

He repeated her name.

'Yes, Father, I'm here,' she said, stiffening in her seat. She straightened her skirt as she stood. She didn't like to be singled out. Her mind whirled. *Had Mr Begley called him to report her for something she did?*

When he spoke, his bones moved with his narrow face. 'Hello, Veronica. My name is Fr O'Flanagan. I need someone to take shorthand for me a few days a week, and Mr Begley has recommended you.'

Mr Begley walked past Veronica, his hands behind his back, and said in a hushed voice, 'Well done, Veronica.' At the top of the classroom, the two men had quiet words, and they shook hands warmly before the priest left.

Veronica didn't know what to think. She glanced at Bridget, who mouthed to her, 'Well done.'

She tried to control her shaking hands. She glanced around the room at the other girls. Some of them stared at her with envy and others with curiosity.

She'd got a job without looking, a real job. Job – the word reverberated inside her head.

'Veronica, come to me at the end of class, and I'll tell you how to get there,' Mr Begley said and continued with the lesson.

Veronica's stomach fluttered. This was the reason she'd left Virginia.

At the end of class, Mr Begley stopped her on her way out. 'Tomorrow, Veronica, you start tomorrow.'

'Pardon?'

'You start tomorrow, Veronica. It's 42 Pembroke Road. Your uncle will show you how to get there. And don't be late.'

She was about to ask how her uncle would know the address, but Mr Begley then told her more details about her work, and that she would get paid for the two days at the end of each month.

On her way home, Bridget walked with Veronica. The girls linked arms and stopped at O'Connell Bridge.

'Veronica, I'll miss you at school. You know what the other girls are like, so snobby and full of themselves.'

Veronica laughed, 'Bridget. I only go there two days a week, and then I come back here for the other three.

There's no typewriter in the priest's house, and I've to go back to the school to type the letters. Anyway, he's a priest – how many letters does he need typing?'

'Imagine! You'll be a working woman. Did he say how much you will be paid?'

Veronica shook her head, 'I don't know. Does a priest have money? I never thought of that.'

With one last hug, the girls parted to go to their homes. Veronica loved this time of year. The few minutes of extra daylight in the evening promised spring was around the corner. The chill of winter was still present though, and Veronica walked briskly to get to the warmth of her home.

Over dinner, she shared the good news with Tom and Betty. Tom nodded in between mouthfuls of stew and said he would take her to Pembroke Road.

'It's nice there, and quieter as well.'

'Oh, do you know Fr O'Flanagan?'

Tom stopped eating but didn't look at her. 'I've heard of him. He's involved in politics here in the city, and up the country.'

She ate in silence, trying to digest her new job and practising her shorthand in her head.

Betty said, 'Veronica, I've made bread and butter pudding – your mother sent it to me.'

Veronica smacked her lips. That was a real treat as Betty hadn't made anything sweet since her arrival. Betty opened the oven, and the waft of sweet raisins teased her taste buds.

'That smells lovely,' Tom said as he winked at Veronica.

Suddenly, there was a loud bang from the kitchen. Tom ran over to Betty who was leaning over the basin of dirty water.

'Love, what's wrong?'

'I'm fine. It's nothing. I'm just a bit lightheaded.'

Veronica got up and cleaned the contents of the saucepan from the floor. The cat was already licking the stew on the ground, disappointed with the lack of meat, a valuable commodity to everyone.

'Come on, love, you go to bed. Veronica will clean up.'

The small kitchen didn't take long to clean. Veronica scrubbed the few plates in a couple of minutes. Nobody had left any of the thin watery stew on their plates. She placed the pan of bread and butter pudding on the sideboard; they could eat it with tomorrow's dinner. On the table beside Betty's chair lay the notebook she had seen Betty use before. Sticking out was a bit of silver ribbon, an angel wing. Veronica put her fingers lightly on the notebook, wanting to open it, but something held her back.

After the usual breakfast of tasteless, watery porridge, Veronica got her coat and her hat, fixing the blue ribbon and pulling it tight so the yellow bow didn't come loose. She wanted to look her best. This was probably the most important thing she had ever done.

'Good luck, Veronica, an' here's some lunch. Wrap up warm.' Betty looked down at the grey tiles and murmured as Veronica was leaving, 'I'm glad you're back.' She returned to her usual silence to wash the dishes.

The morning was grey and still. The light from the gas lamps on the street had receded to a yellow glow.

'It's further than Leinster St, so I can't delay as I've to do the daily deliveries, so we'll make a start. We'll go the back way to Leinster St. It's quicker, but don't go this way on your own, walk on the quays.'

A young boy in bare feet ran after a squealing pig, waving a stick. A girl ran after him holding her once-white dress so that she wouldn't trip on it. The pig ran into a corner. Soon the pig was surrounded by a ring of children so that it couldn't escape; two of the boys carried it by its squirming hooves into a nearby house.

Tom looked at Veronica and said, 'I know you think it strange the way city people live, but as I said they have no choice. Pigs and cows. They have nowhere else to keep them, so they keep them in the backyard. For meat and milk.'

They passed many men idly dragging the last puff from cigarettes on the street corners. Tom nodded over to them. 'The women sometimes earn more money than the men. Some women sell fish, others sell flowers every day, or you will see them on the side of the streets selling bags or even small homewares they made themselves.'

'The church, would they not help?' Veronica said with a sense of despair.

Tom shrugged, giving the horse a flick of the reins. 'Not a chance.' He added, 'Country people make money from the war. It's been good for them, selling food and the like, but here it's hard. And some women, they… well, it's not for you to understand.'

Veronica knew what Tom meant. Bridget had pointed these ladies out to her, calling them 'Ladies from The Monty,' and had lowered her voice. 'You know, the women who entertain the soldiers for money.'

Veronica blushed, her face mottling thinking about what Bridget had said. The cold air swept over her face as the dray gathered pace, and the streets became wider when they reached Trinity College.

She thought about the two sides of Dublin life. Trinity College, with its wide entrance, had a commanding presence. The students who entered every day, men dressed in suits carrying books, rushed to gain knowledge that promoted them to a position in society that only Protestants could attain. But the new Catholic University gave Catholics a chance to better themselves, a chance once denied to them by their birth, the university that her parents hoped Eddie might go to.

As they passed Merrion Square, a different way of life now emerged – the stench of the Liffey gone, as well as the smell of humans. Here everything was calmer, the air quieter, not spoiled with noise. Women in black and grey clothes pushed prams bringing babies out for the day to get fresh air. Nannies were an uncommon sight near Thomas St, and certainly in Virginia.

Veronica remembered the street names. They passed the Shelbourne Hotel onto Baggot St and reached Pembroke Road, a wide tree-lined street. Number 42, her new place of employment. She clutched her lunch bag tighter, her breath caught in her throat. As she climbed down from the dray, Tom took her hand. 'You'll be fine, love.'

Her heart raced as she rapped the shiny brass knocker. Veronica turned to give her uncle a wave, but he was already busy on his way.

14

The door opened. A girl stood in front of her, about the same age as Veronica, and she wore a dull brown dress the same colour as her hair. 'Can I help?'

'I'm Veronica McDermott.'

She stared at Veronica with a blank expression. Veronica thought she had the wrong address, or worse still Fr O'Flanagan had changed his mind, but the girl stood aside, gesturing for her to enter. 'Mrs Brown is expecting you.'

The hallway spoke of a house with a lot more money than her aunt and uncle's home. Small things like the vase of snowdrops on the hall stand, and a crimson red runner in the hall where her aunt and uncle's house had bare floorboards. Veronica had no idea who Mrs Brown was. The girl brought Veronica into a warm room packed with logs and turf. The smell of turf was rare in Dublin. It reminded her of home where there was an abundance of bogs. A tall, middle-aged woman stood in front of the three book-lined walls. Her cream dress hung elegantly on her, highlighting her slender frame.

She stuck out her slender hand to Veronica, 'Welcome. You must be Veronica? I'm Mrs Margaret Brown.'

Veronica nodded.

'Right, dear, follow me, and I'll show you what you have to do.'

Mrs Brown explained that she was the sister of a doctor, who was a good friend of Fr O'Flanagan. She added that Veronica would have to type replies to letters, and that Fr O'Flanagan was involved in elections. All her words ran together, and Veronica tried to take it all in, nodding as Mrs Brown spoke, afraid to ask questions.

'A good friend of Fr O'Flanagan,' Mrs Brown repeated. 'Now, dear, we need a good shorthand and typist. Fr O'Flanagan has lots of letters to answer and wants you to put them into order first, and then into a topic category. Don't look so puzzled, dear. It's easy. Some people may just be offering him support, or favours to get some land. He is in Sinn Féin. Some people don't like that he is involved in politics as he is a priest, and sure you know who that is...

'The bishop,' said Mrs Brown nodding her head.

Veronica followed Mrs Brown through a door at the opposite side of the room into a dark corridor, and downstairs to a basement. There were no windows, but three lamps and a fire. In one corner, there was a large mahogany desk with stacks of papers on it, and Veronica could see the long task she had. 'Fr O'Flanagan won't be here for a while. If you sort out the paperwork, he'll be back at some point for you to take shorthand. So, for the moment file the letters by date and separate into piles. The ones that require an answer Fr O'Flanagan will deal with first.'

Alone, Veronica immediately set to work. She had no idea which letters needed an answer; this was a responsibility she never imagined would be bestowed on her, but after reading a couple of letters, it was easy.

My son needs a letter from a priest to say he can sit the scholarship exam.

My brother needs to get help to keep his farm as he has no money, and the landlord wants him gone.

My neighbour stole my pig.

She thought it was a policeman he needed, not a priest. The letters with Fr O'Flanagan's signature had something scribbled beside his name. She squinted and pored over it but had to hold it to the lamp for light. It read *Vice President. Sinn Féin*.

She couldn't believe she was now working for Sinn Féin, let alone the vice president. In her own small way, she was helping the country to remove Ireland from the clutches of British rule, of British suppression. She knew who Sinn Féin were. They opposed Home Rule and organised marches and protest rallies in Dublin and other counties around the country. Life for people in Dublin was affected by British occupation. Hunger, poverty, no future; that was the destiny for many people in Dublin, and she knew it was the same in most of the country folk as well. One difference was some country people could have a small farm, and even with that, they would still go hungry. She now realised she had had a sheltered childhood because her father had land and business.

Fr O'Flanagan's handwriting was neat and elegant. As she read his letters, she could see him writing sermons to stand on his pulpit, sharing his eulogies with his congregation.

After a few hours, the door opened. 'I've got a drop of soup for you, dear,' said Mrs Brown entering with a tray of a steaming bowl of soup and buttered bread. 'It's stuffy. Can you concentrate? I sometimes get a headache when it's too hot. A good brisk walk in the fresh air usually sorts me out.'

Mrs Brown spoke without waiting for an answer. The heat from the fire did fill the room, but Veronica had no problem concentrating. She had gotten lost in the pleasurable world of filing and organising the letters. Mrs Brown placed the tray on the small dark wooden table.

'I'll just have a cup of tea with you,' Mrs Brown said and then asked Veronica about her family and her course.

'It's great more women are involved.' She paused and spoke with a far-distant look in her eyes. 'Maybe someday we'll... Well, enough of that, eat up, and later, before you go, I'll introduce you to the other staff.'

A warm feeling went through her when she was called staff. Finally, she was achieving something, and Mrs Brown seemed to think women were worth more than just being wives or housekeepers to their husbands.

After lunch, the day passed quickly. In the evening, Mrs Brown came back.

'Well, Veronica, all done?' she said, 'I hope you didn't find the work too hard.'

'It was no problem at all. I enjoyed it.' And she meant it; never in her life had Veronica felt so satisfied doing any task.

'Grand dear, it's late. Come back on Thursday morning at nine, and Fr O'Flanagan will be here. He'll dictate shorthand to you then.' She looked in the mirror to fix a loose strand of hair. 'I thought he'd be here today, but he must have been held up at a meeting. He's a very busy man with the elections and everything.' Mrs Brown talked as she walked up to the stairs. Veronica grabbed her coat following her to the front door. Before she could open it, Fr O'Flanagan entered, shaking his umbrella.

'I've had to come back early, Mrs Brown.' He extended his hand, shaking Veronica's hand with vigour as if shaking the hand of an old friend. 'Ah, you must be Veronica. You know, I know your father well. He does great work in the Gaelic League, and so does your brother, Eddie. Good people, excellent people.'

Veronica nodded, thinking that people from all parts throughout the country seemed to know each other.

'Come back again on Thursday. That's every Tuesday and Thursday. I'll have some filing for you to do, and you'll take shorthand, which you will take back to Leinster St to type.'

Veronica left Pembroke Road, feeling like a real worker, a woman with a job. On the way home, she saw Bridget outside Joyce's hairdressers talking to a tall man in a suit. His hat was pulled low over his face. The man moved closer to Bridget, but she pulled away quickly and turned and rushed at a pace which Veronica found impossible to equal. The heavens opened again, and people ran for shelter, or to their destination. Veronica called out to Bridget, but she didn't hear. Soon the distance between them increased, and Veronica lost sight of her friend.

When she reached Thomas St, she met Tom on the front steps, 'Well, love, how was it? Did you meet Fr O'Flanagan?'

'It was great, and yes, I met him. I've to go back again on Thursday.'

'That's great.' Tom put on his cap. 'I'm off to a meeting. Betty's inside waiting for you.'

Veronica rushed up the stairs wondering which of her day to share with Betty first, and she was starving. For once, she looked forward to Betty's dinner.

In the kitchen, Betty spooned out stew onto the blue and white plates. 'There's a letter for you,' she said nodding towards the mantelpiece above the smouldering fire.

A white envelope rested against the statue of the Virgin Mary. She removed the letter, careful not to knock the rosary beads, which Betty held every night with the small picture of Padraig while she sat staring into the flames of the fire. The neat handwriting was Eddie's. The postmark said Belfast. Tearing open the letter, shock replaced her initial excitement when she read the address:

Crumlin Road Prison,   17 January 1918
Belfast

My dearest Veronica,

It is with great regret I must tell you this. You were right when you said the gun would come to no good.

I was made the captain of the Volunteers in Lurgan, and during a foot drill, I was captured by the British. My sentence is eighteen months in prison.

'Are you all right, Veronica?'

Speechless for a minute the reply struggled to reach her throat, 'Eddie is in jail.' She handed the letter to Betty, her hands shaking.

'I know. Your father wrote to me last month. He didn't want to worry you.'

Betty put the pot of stew down on the table and wrapped her arms around Veronica, but the warmth of Betty's arms didn't console her.

After a few minutes, Betty said, 'Sit down, leave the stew, and I'll make us some tea.'

Veronica watched the letters smudge as the ink ran into each other as her tears fell onto the page. She wished she had told her father about the gun. It was all her fault.

Betty scalded the teapot. 'Don't take it too hard,' she said.

'I know,' she said, drying her eyes with her handkerchief, 'but it's all my fault. I found the gun and should've told Father. He would've taken it away. Instead, I told him if he didn't ask Daddy to send me to learn to type I would tell.' She placed her head in her hands. 'Oh, God I could have stopped him.'

'Here, pet, drink your tea.' Betty stood beside Veronica holding the teapot in one hand and the other hand on her hip. 'I can tell you now it would've done no good. If it's on a boy's mind to do something, he'll do it.'

This statement brought Veronica back to reality. Eddie was in jail, alive, and Betty's only child was dead. She took Betty's small skeletal hand in hers. 'You're right. It would have done no good.' But she didn't believe her words; she felt she could have stopped him.

Betty sat in her armchair. 'Write to him, writing is good, it helps heal. I write to him all the time.'

'Eddie?'

Betty slowly shook her head. She held the brown leather notebook with the angel decoration Veronica had made placed between its pages. She knew who Betty meant.

'Padraig?'

Betty nodded. 'I write and tell him how Tom, his father is. Initially, it was to write my pain, how taking a breath would hurt, how my heart was ripped in two, I felt I was splitting in two.'

Betty stopped talking, her cheeks wet. 'Then you came, and I would tell him what you did and how I think of him when I look at the angel you made.'

Veronica knelt beside her and rubbed her hands, the way her mother did when she was upset when she was a child. 'Betty, I know it's hard, but I'm glad you can talk to me.'

'I sometimes open the window in the spring breeze and close my eyes and feel his arms wrap around me, and hear his voice whispering my name in the wind. And this,' she pulled the angel from her notebook, 'Thank you, Veronica,' she said, her voice full of tears. Betty closed the notebook and stood. 'Let's get some sleep, pet, I'm sure Eddie will be fine.'

★

The next morning started the same as every other day. The warmth of the kitchen greeted her as soon as Veronica walked in and sat at the breakfast table. She eyed the usual neat empty place setting with the empty, clean bowl and shiny spoon and thought of Eddie, his seat at the table at home in Cavan also vacant.

15

Veronica settled into her new routine attending many meetings at Pembroke Road, taking notes in shorthand, typing them later in the school. Her two-day week soon turned to three days. The cosy basement equalled the warmth she received from Fr O'Flanagan and Mrs Brown. She liked the mixture of working in Pembroke Road and returning to the secretarial course, especially to see Bridget.

Words like *rebellion, retaliation, Irish rights*, were a constant in the letters she typed. Initially, the words meant nothing to her, but slowly she wondered if there could be a connection between her father's midnight meetings and what they wrote in the letters. She knew her father had an interest in politics.

Fr O'Flanagan met men in his drawing-room, men of means. They wore expensive suits, white shirts and ties, unlike her uncle in his grey shirt and work boots. One day, Fr O'Flanagan called her into his office.

'Veronica, I want you to take some shorthand for me. *Dear Eoghan, now we have enough money to buy more guns, I would like...*'

Veronica stopped writing and felt her cheeks heat.

'Don't look so shocked, Veronica. We have to help the people of Ireland get their independence – by whatever means. They're my people. I took a commitment to serve God, but, I also think it's my commitment to look after the people of Ireland as well. Because I am a priest, some people think it's wrong. I think the living are equally as important.' Pausing he continued, 'Sometimes their help often requires more than a prayer.'

Some days, Fr O'Flanagan would join Veronica for soup. After the soup, he would lean back in his armchair, smoking his pipe and listen to her as she told him about her life in Cavan and how it differed in Dublin. She was unsure if she should confide in the priest that Padraig had been in the British army. He could be sympathetic because he was a priest, or unsympathetic because of his involvement against the English. She took a deep breath and blurted, 'My cousin Padraig, Uncle Tom's son, was killed in Turkey two years ago. My Aunt Betty is lost without him.'

He pulled on his pipe. 'I know, dear; it's terrible to lose a child, but a lot of young lads were urged to their deaths with promises of money. They thought we would get Home Rule, that would be good for us. But it isn't really, Catholics can't get employment, most pay rent. Home Rule means all our taxes still go to England, leaving our people with no means to even have food on their table. It's cruel. Your uncle and aunt must be so sad, and he was their only child. They're lucky they have you now.'

A knock on the door and Mrs Brown entered with the

welcome smell of two bowls of vegetable soup, and a plate of thick bread spread generously with butter.

'Veronica, you should have your lunch here every day,' she said.

Veronica welcomed the suggestion as the thick soup had more vegetables than Betty's stew. She still let Betty continue to make the bread and butter every day, but she gave her lunch away to the children she met on her walk to work. There were so many children running the streets.

The work was demanding, and her days passed quickly, especially on the two days at her secretarial course when she had to type the letters at great haste before class. The course was to finish soon, and now she was well practised, she wondered about getting a full-time job. One Friday evening in February as she was leaving the house, and dusk was setting in, Mrs Brown called her back. 'Fr O'Flanagan wants to see you. He's in his study.'

The door of his study was slightly open, and she coughed. He sat behind his desk. His head bent, and from the speed he was scribbling, she knew he was adding his signature to letters. She could see his scalp. The few thin wisps of fair hair remaining on his head would soon be gone.

'Ah, Veronica, good. Come in, close the door behind you and sit.' He stretched his back before he spoke. 'I've to go away for a few weeks, so I'd like you to go to the Sinn Féin offices in Harcourt St to type from now on. Harcourt St, it's near St Stephen's Green. You'll go there every day, and you'll start next week.'

Her heart missed a beat, and she twisted her hands. 'My course finishes soon.'

'It's fine, Veronica. Mr Begley said you can go back to take the exams, and he's confident you'll pass.

'They need a good typist and someone to do shorthand. Let me explain what we are doing. Sinn Féin is a party and in opposition to John Redmond's Irish Parliamentary Party. They promised the British that if we agree to conscription and let our men fight for them, they will give us Home Rule. But we're not going to let that happen. For starters, we want to have an Irish government here, and they can get their own killed. They can fight their war.'

The following day at school, during lunch break the girls took their usual seats in the yard. Bridget stretched her legs out, trying to catch the weak February sun. 'I love this time of year, but imagine, we'll be finished soon!'

Veronica gulped and gushed, 'Bridget. I've got a job, a real job, and I start next Monday. In five days!'

Bridget sat up, spilling her can of milky tea over the flagstones. 'Veronica, where? How? That's brilliant.'

A flash of sadness crossed Bridget's face, but with her usual optimism, Bridget hugged her saying, 'That's wonderful, you're so lucky.'

She told Bridget how she was going to work for Sinn Féin. It was the only time Bridget was speechless, but not for long.

'That's a big job! Imagine! You'll meet the people everyone is talking about.' Sighing, she said, 'I'll help my aunt in her shop for another while; my uncle never recovered fully from the flu. And I think she likes the company. It gives me a chance to do something waiting for something to come up.'

'Bridge, don't worry. We'll still see each other and keep in touch. I'll write often.'

'Your parents will be so proud of you.' Bridget hugged her again, her eyes wet. 'We'll write and arrange to meet. Oh, I'm so excited for you.'

Veronica thought back to the pride on her uncle's face the night she told him. 'Veronica, I'm delighted and proud of you and so is your father.' Later that evening in her bedroom, she remembered her uncle's words and thought it must have been a mistake. How could her father be already proud of her since she only just found out?

16

February 1918

On Monday morning Veronica woke groggily after another night of unrest on the streets. Her sleep broken from the patrolling vehicles and shouting soldiers, she didn't welcome the morning light trying to penetrate the flimsy curtains. The smell of fresh bread from the kitchen next door told her it was time to get up. Betty managed to make edible bread from the meagre food parcels of flour and eggs her brother sent to them from the farm.

Even though she hadn't slept well, she was alert to start her new job. She put on her clothes she'd laid out the night before on the chest of drawers in the corner of her room. She was glad her mother had insisted she brought the brown skirt and cream wool cardigan. The heat of the fire had not yet replaced the crisp air in the kitchen. Her morning ritual of splashing ice-cold water onto her face and flattening her curls was interrupted with a shout from the kitchen.

'Veronica, your uncle is leaving soon. He'll take you, but you've to eat first.'

'Coming.' She rechecked herself in the mirror.

Betty was checking the clothes drying over the fire. 'Morning, are you all set for your day?'

Veronica detected a small change in her voice, something positive.

Her aunt looked closely at her. 'You look pale, are you ill?'

'I couldn't sleep. God, I'm sick with nerves,' she said and sat at the table tugging her fingers. 'I feel this job is more important than typing for Fr O'Flanagan.'

'Why?'

'There are always people in to see Fr O'Flanagan and they usually meet in the drawing-room. When I arrive in the morning, men are leaving, and they pull their collars up, pull down their hats to cover their faces, their clothes crumpled as if they have been up all night. I hear some of them say to Fr O'Flanagan I'll drop that letter, or whatever into number six. That's where I'll be working, 6 Harcourt St is on so many of the letters I typed.'

'Veronica, you're overthinking it. Get some breakfast into you. It'll be all right. I know it's more responsibility. You've only to type letters and take shorthand.'

Veronica stared at her porridge, forcing herself to put some on a spoon. 'I know I have worked for Fr O'Flanagan, but the Sinn Féin headquarters. I read about them all the time in the papers and the work they do. I never thought I'd work for them. Fr O'Flanagan said it's important work.'

'Go on. You'll be fine, girl. Now don't delay, your uncle is waiting outside.'

Veronica pushed her bowl away. 'I'm not hungry at all.

I don't know if I'll be any good at this job. It's just they are so important. I don't want to let myself down.'

Betty smiled, giving her an unexpected hug. 'Go, you don't want to be late.' Veronica went downstairs to her waiting uncle, who had the dray ready. She looked up at Betty, who stood in the window above, and waved to her as they moved off.

Veronica shifted on the seat on the dray trying to get as comfortable as possible. Her leg jittered, and she wrapped her scarf close to her neck. As they left Thomas St towards the quays, her uncle looked at her jittering leg and put his hand over her gloved hands.

'You'll be fine, Veronica.'

'I know, but this is a real office with real people.'

'Fr O'Flanagan is a real person, isn't he?'

'Yes, but he is a priest. And I worked in his house. Now I am a ... what is it Bridget called it? A professional working woman.'

He laughed, but Veronica didn't notice. The morning was breaking and, in the distance, fingers of light appeared in the sky above O'Connell Bridge. Outside Trinity, a group of soldiers gathered in conversation with the DMP.

Tom continued down Grafton St. A motor car crossed in front of them beeping, causing the docile horse to jump. Tom pulled the reins to calm him. The car turned left and stopped in front of a large grand pristine building. The driver got out to open the door of the car for its passengers.

Tom stopped and pointed to a white building with large polished windows, the sun bouncing off the brass name. A doorman in hat and tails stood outside. 'That's the Shelbourne Hotel. For the English and posh people. It's not for our kind.' He flicked the reins. 'We're nearly there.'

Tom soon stopped outside a four-storey brown brick building, Veronica's new place of work. 6 Harcourt St. To the left of the white arched doorway, there was a large sign, *Sinn Féin Bank*. A stream of men walked up the steps, some turning left into the bank and others going straight into the building.

Tom squeezed her arm as she got down from the dray. 'Go on, love, you'll be fine. Take a deep breath. It'll be grand.'

When Veronica entered the building, she immediately noticed how different it was to Pembroke Road. To her left, she saw silhouettes of men through a frosted glass window. A phone rang followed by loud talking but she couldn't quite catch what they were saying. Another phone rang. Few places had a phone, but to have two in the same building was something she could never have imagined. The bright hall was alive with a continuous stream of people going up and down the wide staircase in front of her.

A man rushed past her but turned back. 'Can I help you?' he said in a similar accent to Mr Begley.

'I've to meet Mrs O'Reilly. Fr O'Flanagan sent me.'

The large handsome man pointed upstairs. 'She is on the first floor, and the door is straight in front of you.'

People moved in and out of the building like a steadily flowing river. On the landing, a group of men gathered deep in discussion, shuffling through their papers comparing notes. She excused herself past them and followed to the half-open door, hearing the familiar click-click of a typewriter. She hesitated outside the brown door and politely knocked. Nobody answered. Her heart pounded louder. She took a deep breath and formed a fist to knock harder. Finally, a voice shouted, 'Come in.' Veronica couldn't decide if it was a woman or a man.

When she opened the door, light flooded onto her from the two large windows in front of her and a fire burned at the back of the room. The heat mixed with the smell of cigarette smoke and leather reminded her of her father's study. Beside the fireplace were large piles of papers stacked neatly against the wall. A rounded, wrinkled woman sat at a large desk and squinted over her glasses, looking Veronica up and down.

'Can I help you, dear?' she said in a husky voice.

'Fr O'Flanagan sent me.'

The silver-haired lady stood, her hips full with a waist to match. 'Dear, you are welcome. You must be Veronica. You're a sweet thing, aren't you?'

She shook Veronica's hand, her plump fingers soft and warm.

'Come on, dear, I'll show you what you've to type.'

Veronica's heart thumped so hard that it hurt her chest, and she was sure Mrs O'Reilly could hear it.

Doors slammed, and there was continuous shouting up to the top floor. Heavy boots on the wooden floors reverberated through the building. There was a strange noise; a faint whirring from the top floor. The chaos was welcome.

'I'd say it's a lot busier than Fr O'Flanagan's,' Mrs

O'Reilly said with a slight throaty laugh. 'He comes here, but like everyone else, he is always on the go.'

A soft voice behind Veronica said, 'And who are you, dear?'

'Mrs Moore, this is Veronica. She's here to help to take shorthand and type,' said Mrs O'Reilly. Mrs Moore had beautiful cream coloured skin and not a line on her face. Her hair showed few signs of her age.

'Veronica, such a lovely name. Here to work and help with our cause? I work upstairs, but I like to come down for a chat – it's all men up there, and they don't appreciate a good chat. Isn't that right, a good cup of tea before we start the day?' Mrs Moore said, opening a few buttons of her blue coat that was the same colour as her shoes. Veronica had never seen blue shoes before.

'Yes... yes.' Veronica wasn't too sure how she was involved with the cause now she didn't deliver any more parcels.

'Good girl. Mrs O'Reilly, I was delayed. Soldiers were questioning and arresting some young lads, and they took one of them away. They found he had a small pistol.'

'God, did they stop you?' Mrs O'Reilly said.

'No, no. I'm just a lady out for a stroll enjoying the morning. Thankfully, I got the letters posted for Michael. He wants to organise a rally in Sligo.'

Mrs Moore looked like the women in magazines with her styled hair and the golden embroidery on her blue cardigan matched the design on her matching skirt. Veronica made a mental note not to wear her purple dress anymore. She had to look more grown-up. She had seen a lovely red cardigan in the window of Arnott's department store, and now she was earning money she would save up for it.

'Veronica, can you type these letters and drop them up to Mrs Moore's office? You'll also have to cash cheques at the bank in the office below. It can be hectic there at times. They give out loans to people, but also they collect donations for our party,' said Mrs O'Reilly.

Veronica sat at her desk and started to type words that were repeated continuously like *'rally, support and independence'* in the same tone as the letters she had typed for Fr O'Flanagan.

Veronica typed furiously through the morning. She had never bothered with politics, mainly because her family didn't want for anything. All her siblings had gotten a chance to receive an education. In Dublin, she saw a different side to life, one that had initially shocked her, and now Eddie was in jail. She was angry that he had got into this situation and hoped he was treated well. She thought back to her train journey. Now she knew why the farm labourers had looked glum. They had no choice. She thought of the few privileged ones. They were mostly English people so removed from the hardship of people in the city and the country.

'Conscription, they want to introduce conscription.' Mrs O'Reilly slammed a piece of paper on her desk. 'It's not our war, why should we fight for them? Michael will never give into conscription. Anyway, we want our independence to rule ourselves, not Home Rule. We need to get rid of the English altogether. I lost a family of cousins

in Co Mayo in the last famine, they starve, while any corn
the farmers here grew was sent to England, leaving people
to starve, like wild animals to scavenge.' She sniffed and
patted her nose with a white handkerchief. 'That's why
we need our parliament here, with our own men as our
leaders; all Home Rule will do is let them let us have
our parliament here, but we will still be their servant. Isn't
that right, dear?'

Veronica nodded, though she didn't know who Michael
was. A constant stream of men came to the office and left
documents on Mrs O'Reilly's desk, and she passed them
onto Veronica.

After work as she walked home to Thomas St, Veronica
wanted to pinch herself. *She was a working woman.* As
soon as she entered her home, she saw the emptiness had
returned to Betty's eyes. She wanted to hug her and tell her
'Time is a great healer,' but she imagined it wouldn't do
any good.

'How was your day?' Betty asked.

'It was demanding, and people came in and out all day.'

Betty nodded and continued to stir the already stirred
pot of stew.

'It is different than working in Fr O'Flanagan's. At the
new place, it's so noisy and much busier. They are shouting
and arguing. It's like a war zone.'

Veronica froze. A dark shadow crossed Betty's face, and
she knew her remark had made Betty think about her
son. She studied Betty as the light flickered from the fire
along the lines of sadness etched on her face. She stood,
slightly crooked.

'I'm sorry, Betty, I don't want to bring memories of Padraig up.'

'It's fine, it is a burden I drag with me every day, sometimes it's worse. Grief plays hide and seek with me, some days it's worse than others. Com' on, sit and eat. The stew is ready and Tom will be home soon.'

Veronica pushed the potatoes in the watery stew longing for some of Mrs Slaney's steak and kidney pie.

Outside the whistle blew at the brewery to tell the workers to go home for another day. Soon Tom's work boots dragged up the wooden stairs, and the front door squeaked open. The door was stiff from years of waiting for repair, but Veronica knew that was never going to happen.

Tom fell into the chair beside the fire and kicked off his boots, sighing loudly. 'Another day over. Well, Veronica, how was it?'

'Come on, Tom, sit yourself at the table, and we'll hear all about her day.'

'Someone called Michael is mentioned a lot. I'm not too sure who he is, but he sounds important.'

'That's probably Michael Collins. I told you about him, he's the fella from Cork. He is doing great things for us, he's a great speaker, organising rallies and protest marches. He and Eámon De Valera are great men.'

Now Veronica knew who they were. They had been involved in the 1916 Easter Rising, some of the few leaders that had escaped executions in Kilmainham Jail. She told them about the Sinn Féin Bank and the letters she had to type.

Tom nodded every so often, scraping up the last of the stew with a crust of bread.

'It's a great honour, Veronica. You're in the heart of helping the cause.'

For the second time that day, she had been told she was helping the cause. Veronica wanted to say, 'Not really, I'm just doing a job,' and that's all she wanted to do.

When dinner was over Betty took their plates, which only needed a splash of water to clean them. She also put the clean, untouched plate back in the cupboard until the next meal. Veronica wondered when Betty would stop setting the table for her dead cousin: did she live in hope? Was it a habit? Did she find comfort in it?

Later that evening, Veronica sat on her bed and wrote to Bridget. Susan wouldn't understand her excitement, but Bridget would. She sealed the letter with the hope they would meet soon. She pulled the eiderdown tight and closed her eyes, but sleep didn't come. The lights from the patrol vehicles crawled across her bedroom wall.

17

Over the next few weeks, Veronica found her job exciting, meeting many new people. Soon she could put faces to the names of people she read about in the newspapers, Éamon De Valera, Arthur Griffith, Ernest Blythe, Liam and Barney Mellows. Mrs O'Reilly would briefly introduce Veronica to them as the new typist. They would nod and move on, but she was in awe of these men; they all seemed so sophisticated in their suits and ties.

On Friday at the end of her first week, a large man entered the office with confidence and a twinkle in his eyes that set him apart from the other men. It was the man who had directed her upstairs on her first day. His broad square face commanded authority. He stood in the doorway, chatting easily to Liam Mellows and smoking, oozing a confidence few men possessed.

'That's Michael Collins,' Mrs O'Reilly mouthed across to Veronica.

Veronica was glad to put a face to the name.

She was never bored at work, letters and speeches had to be typed, some with more urgency than others. Letters to inform people of upcoming Sinn Féin rallies to gain support for protestations against the English were always typed and posted with haste. Mrs O'Reilly told Veronica that the frequent visits and raids of the DMP meant that any evidence of an upcoming rally would have to be hidden. The building was alive with people. Doors banged constantly, and there was a relentless flow of footsteps up and down the stairs.

On arrival home, at the end of her working day, she asked Betty the same question, 'Any news? I know I am mad at him, but he's my brother, my twin.'

Her aunt shook her head. 'Sorry, no letter for you. Why don't you write to him?'

'I have written a few letters, but he hasn't written back.'

'But,' Betty hesitated, 'maybe he isn't allowed. It is tough for them in there, and Tom has asked his friend who works in the docks in Belfast to go to see him.'

Veronica was surprised. Gone was the hurt and anger she felt at Eddie, replaced by relief that she would soon find out how he was.

'When will Tom know?'

Betty shrugged her shoulders and Veronica saw her aunt's bones through her thin cardigan. A pitiful sight. Betty returned to the stove, spooning out potatoes and soup just as Tom came home from work.

He slumped in his armchair. 'I'm too old for this lark,' he said, rubbing his knuckles. 'I'm glad spring is nearly here so I can get some heat into these old bones.' He lay back in his armchair and closed his eyes.

'Tom, dinner is ready, come on to the table before it gets cold. I told Veronica your friend went to see Eddie.'

Veronica's heart leapt. She had misunderstood Betty, she thought she said he would see him on another day, not that he had already been.

Tom didn't speak as he was eating his dinner and stopped for a minute, 'Love, it's not great news, but not all bad.' He paused and looked at Veronica, his eyes full of sympathy. 'When my friend went to see him, Eddie had to be carried out to him. His two friends had to help him, he had two black eyes, and he couldn't walk.'

'Of course, if he couldn't walk, he would have to be carried.' She gasped, putting her hand to her mouth. 'I'm sorry, Uncle, I didn't mean to snap. It's shock, or relief he's alive, I don't know.'

'He could talk well, and he said he wasn't in too much pain and that it looked worse than it was.' He paused, looking at her gently. 'Eddie asked after you, and said to tell you he couldn't write back to you because he broke his hand.'

'What happened? Why did he get beaten up?'

Betty sat beside Veronica and lightly stroked her hand.

'He wouldn't tell the guards the name of a Volunteer who shot an RIC man while they were questioning him. But,' he leaned across the table to take her other hand, 'Veronica, he is all right. A good lad who wouldn't snitch on anyone.'

'He's still alive,' Betty said quietly. 'This is our war.'

Veronica knew she was right.

Eddie was alive, and Veronica knew that she should be grateful, but Betty was right; it was a war.

★

After three weeks working in Harcourt St, Veronica was pleased with herself as her typing was as fast as Mrs O'Reilly's.

'Veronica, could you take these letters to Fr O'Flanagan in Pembroke Road, for signing?'

Mrs O'Reilly stood and rubbed her back before walking to Veronica's desk. 'God, sometimes sitting for hours I'd swear is not good for your back.' She gave Veronica a large pile of letters. 'Don't let anyone see them, and I don't mean just the soldiers, there are many spies. They are important anti-conscription letters for the trade unions. We need to get as many rallies organised to stop conscription and to get people on our side. It's not our fault the English have no men to fight their war. The English are losing men at a fast pace.'

Veronica looked forward to getting out to the breezes of spring morning. As she walked towards St Stephen's Green, men rushed to work holding onto their caps. Women stayed in the doorways in the hope the westerly wind would soon pass. She kept her head down, but not out of fear of the British soldiers constantly around the Green; they were like a chronic illness that wouldn't go away. When she passed a group of soldiers, she stuck her head up high and walked with brisk confidence that was only on the outside. She held her breath until she passed them. Suddenly, a gust of wind snatched her papers out of her hand, propelling them into a doorway.

'God, Miss, I am sorry. I didn't see you there. Here, let me help you with your letters.'

An English accent. She forgot about her hair; her hat had blown away, her hair escaping around her face and shoulders. She ran to the steps of the door and gathered up the letters, quickly stuffing some of them into her bag.

'I am so sorry. Did you get all your paperwork?'

Why is he apologising again, he didn't do it? Frantically she scanned the near-empty street for any rogue letters. She felt numb, glancing at the man in a brown army uniform. He was as tall as her father, who was over six foot, but that was where the similarity ended. This man had no beard and tufts of ash brown hair stuck out under his peaked hat, as it was not cropped close like the soldiers patrolling the streets, and he wore a tidy jacket.

It took a moment to find her voice. 'No. I am fine. Thank you,' she said, the calmness in her voice not reflecting her inner confusion, and snatched a letter from his right hand. Her mind spun. *Had any of the letters opened? Did she get them all?*

'Again, thank you, sir,' Veronica straightened her coat, her hands cradling the bag stuffed with letters and ran without stopping until she reached Fr O'Flanagan's house and pressed the doorbell twice in quick succession.

Mrs Brown opened the door, leaves catching in a gust of wind entering the hallway.

'Come in quick, Veronica, keep the cold out. Are you all right? You're so pale.' She took the bag with the letters from Veronica and, with the other hand, guided her to the fire in the drawing-room.

Fr O'Flanagan sat at his mahogany writing desk.

'Margaret, hand me that blanket from my armchair.'
He put it around Veronica's shaking shoulders.

'I'm fine, Father. It was cold. I ran the whole way because
of it. There were a lot of soldiers around the Green. One
did try to stop me, but I just carried on my journey.'

'Margaret, would you bring Veronica a cup of tea,
please?'

Veronica welcomed the steaming hot sweet tea, and the
colour slowly filled her cheeks.

Fr O'Flanagan signed the letters but kept an eye on
Veronica. 'Here you are. They're all signed. I'll walk back
to Harcourt St with you.'

Outside the wind had calmed, and the sun was high in
the sky. Veronica and Fr O'Flanagan walked at a leisurely
pace. She relaxed with the sound of birds chirping, flying
from tree to tree, looking for the best one to build a nest
for their imminent young.

'We can take our time. My train is not due until six
o'clock. I'm going to Roscommon for a few days. How are
you finding your new job?'

'It's great, Father. It's so busy,' she stopped, 'but I'm not
complaining.'

'Do the soldiers intimidate you when they come to the
office?'

Veronica tensed at the thought of her recent meeting.
'Not really, Father, we have had a few visits at the office, and
soldiers are always outside on the streets. The DMP have
come in a few times. They just walk around the office and
look at what we are typing. We try to hide any paperwork

that might give them an idea where any meetings or rallies are going to be. Mrs O'Reilly said to ignore them.'

On arrival at Merrion Square, Fr O'Flanagan said, 'I'll leave you, and it was good to see you, Veronica. Take care of yourself. I've to meet someone first before the train.' He fixed his hat. 'I'll see you in a few weeks.'

Soon she was back at Harcourt St and before she started to type the pile of documents on her desk, the office door opened.

Veronica looked at Michael standing at the door, his large frame filling the doorway. 'Ladies.' He took long confident strides to Mrs O'Reilly's desk.

She took her fingers off the keys on the typewriter to give him her full attention.

Eoin O'Malley, a Galway man with a lisp who worked in the bank, put his head around the door. He pushed his shock of black hair back from his equally dark eyes. 'Is Michael there?' Nobody answered; all eyes were on Michael. 'Nice girls. I'm being ignored now.'

He grinned and walked across the office to Michael, handing him some documents. 'Read this letter, it's interesting!' Eoin looked at his watch. 'I've to be off. Christ, I'm late.'

Michael took the papers, nodding to Eoin as he left the room. He spoke to Mrs O'Reilly, mumbling a few quiet words first before he handed her some papers. 'Would you type these speeches for me?'

'Veronica will do it for you. She typed for Fr O'Flanagan and started to work here while you were away.'

'Veronica, lovely to meet you,' Michael said in an energetic accent.

She now knew his accent was from Cork. She wondered whether everyone from Cork worked in Dublin.

'Ladies, I'll leave you,' he said, lighting another cigarette. He exited the room with the same energy as he had entered.

'God, he is lovely,' Mrs O'Reilly said dreamily. 'I'm so glad he's back. That's his office next door, Veronica. Do you know he spent many years in England?' She leaned towards her. 'He knows how the English tick. That's why he's the best person to deal with them.'

Veronica agreed and shuddered, thinking again about the mild spoken soldier she had met at St Stephen's Green.

18

Any doubts Veronica had had about her ability to type for such a prestigious organisation soon diminished over the following weeks. By the end of February, she typed speeches and letters for Michael Collins, and Mrs O'Reilly gave her the occasional speech to type for Éamon De Valera. Most days she rarely had time to think, let alone relax, and was glad to see the pile of typing down to the last page.

Mrs O'Reilly smiled and looked over the gold rim of her glasses. 'It will be a slow day now. Thank God, I'm exhausted,' she said as she pulled on her cigarette. 'I think everyone is away at meetings. Veronica, since it's so quiet will you go and collect the typing from Fr O'Flanagan's house?' She stretched over to the other side of the desk, saying, 'Give these papers to him. He came back from Roscommon this morning. And do be careful, the streets seem to have more soldiers than usual. There's definitely not as many since the war started, but it's still dangerous.'

Mrs O'Reilly's face suddenly turned red. 'They stole our lads from us to fight in France. They have stopped signing up for the British army since the rebellion.'

Veronica stiffened. She had never shared with Mrs O'Reilly her cousin's death in France.

'That's why we've to stop that daft Redmond,' Mrs O'Reilly huffed as she stubbed out her cigarette and gave a bundle of papers to Veronica.

'Hurry back with the typing. Éamon came in earlier, and he said we have to get the letters posted as soon as possible.'

The day was still damp. Veronica pulled the scarf tight around her face and neck. Her hair was now cut short like Bridget's, so it was easier to tame, but it still had to be pinned down. With the early morning deliveries finished, the streets were empty, save for a few men on bicycles on their way home from the docks. Few dockers lived this side of the river, but a few lived on Crumlin Road. She kept her head down as she passed the soldiers who stood around St Stephen's Green with their rifles in a threatening position. When Veronica approached them, their chat stopped as she passed, and her scalp prickled at their eyes on the back of her head. Ahead, more soldiers stood in front of the Shelbourne. Holding her bag with the papers tight, Veronica tried to blend in with the crowd rushing to their destinations to quickly escape the damp cold. She walked faster as a group of soldiers walked towards her, and the soldier she had seen a few weeks ago walked in front of them. He had a slight limp in his left leg, but this didn't slow his long strides.

Her heart raced. She looked straight ahead so as not to make eye contact. Veronica didn't know why she didn't slow or pretend to look in a shop window. She walked in his direction, her breath quickening as she neared him. Her scarf partially hid her face. She pulled at it, but it fell away, exposing her face just as he was about to pass her. His eyes caught hers, and his mouth moved to a smile of acknowledgement.

'Hello again.'

Veronica stopped and gripped her bag. She waited for him to question her, to demand to empty the contents of her bag. He was alone now as the rest of the soldiers had gone ahead.

'It's awfully cold, out for a stroll?'

Her mouth dried and any reply stuck in her throat. This was it, she would be arrested and shot. 'Yes, eh, I am on my way to visit my aunt on Pembroke Road.' She silently cursed; she had said too much. Her bones trembled, and she tried to steady not only her voice but her body as well.

'I am waiting for my car. My men have gone back to the barracks. I can drive you to your aunt's.'

With petrol scarcity due to the war, only the army and the dreaded patrols could now drive freely around Dublin.

Veronica shook her head. 'No. It's fine. I love the fresh air.' It was time to leave.

He offered her his hand. 'I'm Harry. Major Fairfax.'

Veronica automatically took it. His grip was firm, and his hand was soft. 'Veronica. Veronica McDermott.' Her head spun, and a small bead of sweat dripped down her forehead.

She snatched her hand away. Was he laughing at her? She clenched her fist, careful not to drop the papers. 'I've to go.'

He nodded and walked to his waiting car, but then stopped, and shook his left leg which slightly tailed as he walked back to her.

Christ. She inhaled, and broke into a cold sweat, getting ready to run.

He took off his cap, his brown hair glistening with oil. 'Would you like to come for tea next week? Shelbourne Hotel on Saturday at four?'

Veronica stepped back, her hat falling to the ground. The thought disgusted her. Not only had she never met a man for tea, but he was an Englishman.

He picked it up and handed it to her. 'Sorry, did I startle you?'

She grabbed her hat from him. 'No.' Eddie's beaten face flashed in her mind.

A car tooted. The major lifted his hand to the driver of the car and took off his hat in a salute to Veronica. '4 p.m. on Saturday at the Shelbourne.'

She opened her mouth to reply to him, but he was already walking to the waiting car. He stopped to talk to a group of dirty children with torn clothes. They laughed. He put his hand in his pocket and gave them something. It could have been sweets or money. Grabbing the contents out of his hand like wild hungry cats, they laughed again and ran away.

Mrs O'Reilly's words, *we want our freedom from the English; they have suppressed us long enough; there has been nothing but poverty and death; we have to get our own parliament,* reverberated inside Veronica's head as she rushed to Pembroke Road. Thoughts whirred through her head as she ran, and her hair came loose. When she entered Fr O'Flanagan's, Mrs Brown said, 'God, dear, you look a mess. What happened now? Did the soldiers bother you again?'

'No, it was freezing, and I ran.' She didn't know why she didn't tell Mrs Brown the truth.

'Come in, you poor thing. Wait in the drawing-room.'

As Veronica sat and investigated the dancing flames, a plan began to form.

Mrs Brown returned, and she followed her into the study. Fr O'Flanagan sat in front of the roaring fire, the small desk beside him covered in papers. He sat back, rubbing his eyes.

'Good, I was hoping you would get here soon. It's getting late. Did you have any problems on the way?'

'No.' She didn't want to talk about the encounter with the soldier. 'Sorry, Father, what did you say?'

'I said you had better go. It looks like rain is on the way. Are you sure you're all right? You do look a bit flushed. I'll take you back.'

'No, it's fine, Father. I'll walk.'

Her walk would give her time to think. The soldier was undoubtedly handsome, and he did possess politeness that seemed contradictory to his reason for being in Ireland. Even though the encounter was brief, it angered her that he would assume that he had the authority to ask her for tea as if she would obey him.

At home later, as Betty cooked dinner, she put vegetable skins in the bin. Veronica knew Betty would have scraped the vegetable peel, so nothing edible was left to waste.

Food was a precious commodity, and even more so now as a lot of food farmed in Ireland was sent to England. The farms in England had lost many of their working men due to conscription.

'Well, dear, how was your day?'

'It was fine, Aunt Betty.' She couldn't talk to her aunt about the English soldiers she saw every day for fear it would only stir the painful memory of what she had lost. Veronica found it confusing that her uncle had not stopped Padraig from joining the British army. It was clear from the people she had met when delivering the parcels that Tom was involved in trying to get Ireland independence.

A rare parcel of food from the farm had arrived. The smell of soup with fresh vegetables from the farm in Cavan brought her back to the present. Sometimes she missed home.

19

On Friday Mrs O'Reilly stopped typing with a big sigh. 'All done and dusted. Are you doing anything nice for the weekend, Veronica?' She looked at her over the rim of her glasses, but didn't wait for a reply. 'We can all go home now and have a well-deserved sleep.'

Veronica stopped tidying up her desk. She remembered the soldier's words – 4 p.m. at the Shelbourne – and shrugged the memory away with a shudder. 'No, I've got a few letters to write, and I might try to get my aunt out for a walk. She's so stiff, but I think it would do her good.'

Mrs O'Reilly nodded and pinned down her hat. 'It's still a bit blustery outside,' she said, and pulled on her coat. 'I've to rush as I've to bake a few tarts as my sister is coming up from the country tomorrow.'

Michael Collins entered as Mrs O'Reilly was leaving, and tilted his hat. 'Have a good weekend, Mrs O'Reilly. I want a word with Veronica.'

'You just caught us, she's just about to leave as well.'

He nodded to her. 'Veronica, will you come into my office for a minute before you go?'

Michael Collins rarely spoke to her; he gave the typing

to Mrs O'Reilly, and he spent a lot of time in his office next door writing speeches, or having a meeting with other Sinn Féin members.

In his office, he stood looking out the long window behind his oak desk, dark with age. His paperwork was neater than her desk.

'Tell me about the soldier, the major you met the other day.'

Veronica's breath quickened. The room suddenly felt hot even though the window was open. She had told no one about talking to the major. And now she was going to be fired for talking to an English soldier and sent home to Cavan in disgrace.

'I'm told he wanted to meet you?'

'Eh, yes.' *How did he know that?* 'I said no.'

'We have people in The Castle willing to get us information, but we need to know how they know about our rallies. We do get some information from Dublin Castle, their headquarters, but soldiers turn up disrupting the meetings too often, stopping us getting our message across to the people that Home Rule is just an empty promise. The major you bumped into is not long in the country, and we need to find out what he is doing here.' Michael sat behind his desk, the window behind him blowing a gust of fresh air into the room. Veronica opened the top button of her blouse, wishing she could fan herself. Had talking to the soldier been a treacherous act?

'I was caught off guard and... I'm not going to meet him.' The words were tumbling out.

'Why would you not meet him?'

Indignant, she said, 'Because he is English, and...' she hesitated, '... Eddie, my brother, is in prison. I have seen the squalor people live in, and their landlords went back to England. They don't care about anyone here. And the work we are doing here, trying so hard to get independence, all your meetings and the anti-conscription campaign—'

He raised his hand to stop her. 'Go and meet him in the Shelbourne as he asked.'

'But how did you know?'

'We are watching him. He is not long here. He will be at the hotel. He goes there for tea every Saturday. The major works in Dublin Castle and we need to get information, like what their plans are for conscription. Our spies there are being watched.'

Her face paled. *Did he want her to spy?*

'Your uncle told me about the parcel deliveries,' he said, tapping his foot on the wooden floor. 'He said you were brave and could hold your nerve.'

This was not something she had ever considered doing. *Would she do it? Could she do it?*

'Veronica, we need all the help we can get. We need to know what the English know about the volunteers and if they have any names of our lads. We are recruiting more volunteers, and we are trying to get more guns and keep the ones we have. Ambushes are happening all over the country. Eddie was one of the best volunteers we had in Cavan. Now he is gone it's a bit of a mess, and we can't let that happen anywhere else. We also need to know what they know about our anti-conscription rallies.'

'Any news of Eddie?'

'Veronica, don't worry, we are doing our best. We are looking after him. There's talk of being able to get him out.'

She didn't know, but could she refuse? It was something she wouldn't have considered a few months ago, but things were different now. She was different.

'Yes,' she said quickly, in case she changed her mind.

'Go home, don't tell anyone. Tell your aunt you're meeting a friend tomorrow, or going for a walk. And Veronica don't say where you work, it would only arouse his suspicions.'

It was a bright, crisp day, the fresh air diluting the smell of the Liffey. She walked briskly, her thoughts on the soldier. Not only had she never met an Englishman before, he was a different class. How would she sit, what would she talk about? Would she sit and listen? The loud bell of an oncoming tram brought her back to the present. She was not far from the hotel, and soon she stood outside it.

SHELBOURNE HOTEL was engraved ominously over the door, inviting to a few, but like a warning to others saying, 'this is our place, and only a select few can enter'. The building was impressive; the bronze ladies on either side of the entrance told a person this was for the privileged. The bay windows were surrounded by black railings with flower boxes and the sun shone directly inside. She was glad her mother had packed her good skirt and blouses now. Even still she was underdressed compared to the women here. They looked like the women from the Taylor Estate in Virginia.

In the foyer, the reality of what she was doing engulfed Veronica. She had never seen such grandeur before. The shiny white marble floors sparkled, and the stairs shone like gold. She had been in Wynn's Hotel, and she had thought it magnificent with its red soft carpets and doorman, but the Shelbourne magnificence was something she had only imagined in books. Veronica held her head high as she walked through the foyer with false confidence, trying not to look like she shouldn't be there.

At the front desk stood a poker-faced man with deep-set eyes. He was the strangest looking man Veronica had ever seen. Trying to slow her breathing, she stood in front of him. His head lowered to scan over his books.

After a few seconds, he looked up and sighed. 'Yes, can I help you, madam?'

'Excuse me, where are the tearooms?' Veronica asked, her words running into one another.

Lifting his finger high, he snootily pointed to the left; a sign with tearooms on it directed her to a bright and colourful room. The afternoon sun mixed with the gold curtains and the blue wallpaper made a kaleidoscope of colours that bounced around the room. Under her feet, the soft carpet was like walking on the moist moss in the forest.

A man in his mid-fifties wearing a black-and-white striped waistcoat approached her. 'Can I help you, madam?'

She opened her mouth, but no words came. A voice

from behind her said, 'She is with me. We've got a table over there by the bay window.'

Her stomach somersaulted when she turned and saw the major standing beside her. Was it fear or excitement that she was a spy? Still speechless, she tried to stop her legs from shaking and followed Harry to the table set for two. He pulled out a chair for her.

'Her coat. Murphy, will you take it please?'

A man appeared behind her to take her coat. His face was motionless with a neat black moustache.

Veronica stood still but shook on the inside. She opened her coat slowly and carefully concentrated on each button. *What was she doing?*

Major Fairfax's limp didn't detract from his erect posture or his broad shoulders. As he sat down smiling, he moved to block the sun from shining into her eyes.

'Murphy will bring the tea and scones over to us. Would you like some jam and cream with your scone?'

Veronica nodded. She wasn't hungry, but the cream was a real treat that she couldn't refuse. She had entered a different world. At home on the farm, cream and milk were plentiful, but here in Dublin, everything was in short supply due to rationing.

'I know some of the kitchen staff, and they always keep me some cream. They're kind.'

Kind was not a word she would have expected an English soldier to use to describe an Irish person, and a kitchen porter at that.

'It is a beautiful day, isn't it?' said the major. 'I love springtime, don't you?'

She had heard no one speak like him before, so smooth and quiet. The soldiers that came into the office spoke loud, harsh gruff words. She thought he spoke a little too fast... or did he always speak like that? His leg jerked up and down, and the quicker his leg moved, the faster the words flowed out of his mouth.

Veronica nodded and glanced around the room. To her left, there was a family with two boys dressed neatly in perfectly ironed shirts under their coats. She felt everyone was staring at her, judging her.

Two grey-haired ladies, who Veronica assumed were sisters, whispered conspiratorially to each other under large hats nestled sideways on their hair. They stared at her. Their eyes met, and they gave her a slight nod which Veronica could either take as an acknowledgement, or *we know who you are and everything you stand for*. Her face reddened. Michael hadn't told her what to say if he asked her about her work. She couldn't disclose she worked for Sinn Féin.

She looked at the women again, but they were lost in conversation, their heads moving in unison. Their silver hair caught by the sun at the edge of their hats glistened in the sunlight, and Veronica relaxed when she saw the women's shoulders relax.

Veronica gripped her handbag on her lap, thinking what to say. With a rattle of cups, the waiter placed a shiny silver tray on the white linen cloth. He put pink flowery cups with matching saucers on the table. Steam rose from the scones, but Veronica had no appetite.

'Thank you, Murphy, that's fine. I'll pour the lady her tea.'

'My pleasure, sir.' Murphy smiled at Harry, who nodded and smiled back. Harry poured her tea first, offering her milk and sugar. Veronica's throat was dry, but when she lifted her cup, her palms were moist, and she put it back as she feared it would slip from her hand. Her stomach somersaulted, twisting and turning. The sun shone in through the large bay window, lighting up the room. Veronica could see his face. He was handsome. His skin was unmarked from childhood diseases, unlike a lot of the people in the city or even the soldiers. He had no scars of war or lines of worry or despair. His relaxed posture had a calmness about it, not the aggression of the soldiers she saw marching through the streets or the soldiers who were always coming into the office.

'Veronica, you're not from Dublin, are you?'

She swallowed her nervousness. 'No, I'm from Cavan. My aunt is from Dublin.'

'Cavan, is that near Cork? I was in Cork briefly, but I came back up to Dublin.'

Clouds now covered the sun, and she could not hide behind the rays anymore. She took the pink teacup to her lips. Veronica's mind raced, willing him to talk.

'Veronica... it's a lovely name,' Harry said.

Veronica replied with more confidence than she felt. 'My father named us. I know it is unusual for a man, as mothers usually choose names, but my father named my siblings, too.' The words all ran into each other, but she didn't know what else to say.

'So, there are more of you?'

'Eh, yes, I have a brother.' She froze; she didn't want

to encourage him to ask about Eddie. She added quickly, 'And a sister, Susan. We live in the country.'

Veronica put her cup down and rubbed her hands together. Seeing her teacup empty, Harry poured her more tea.

'That must be exciting. I am an only child.'

'How long have you been in Ireland?' Veronica asked.

'Three months now. I was in France but got wounded. So, the army sent me over here. I was lucky. A lot of the wounded never made it home...' He trailed off, a faraway look in his eyes. Veronica had heard horrible stories about the conditions in which some men died, and she assumed that these memories were better forgotten.

'Why are you in Dublin?' Harry asked.

Again, her head spun. She couldn't say she worked for Sinn Féin and had to think quickly.

'I work in a shop, on Abbey St. Sullivan's shop. I do the accounts. I live with my aunt and uncle. Their son was killed in Turkey.' His face changed; was it pity?

'Was he with the Fusiliers?'

'Yes, he was shot in Suvla Bay,' she said, more relaxed now she didn't have to lie. 'He was my aunt and uncle's only child.'

'Oh, that's awful, that must be hard for his parents.'

'It must be hard for your parents that you are away.'

'No, I was always away, boarding school since I was six years old.'

'Really? That's very young.' Veronica couldn't believe a child would be wrenched away at such a young age.

He told her about his school days, and talked easily about the bond of friendship from the boys at school.

'Initially, I felt betrayed by my parents. I was very close to my mother, but my father said I needed to grow up and it would make a man out of me,' laughing at the memory, 'I was only six.'

He poured her more tea and nodded to two gentlemen who were leaving the room. She stole a glance at them. They were not army men and were dressed in expensive black suits with crisp white shirts.

He saw her look at them. 'Men who work with me.'

'Oh, where do you work?' This was a bold question, and she took a scone to butter it, hoping to give the impression she was not too concerned.

'At Dublin Castle, nothing too important. Tell me, do you like Dublin?'

Her pulse quickened. 'It must be different to work in Dublin, than in the war – it must be calmer? Quieter?' She tried to keep her gaze steady.

His eyes deepened to a mahogany brown. 'It is different, it's busy but I'm learning. Do you like Dublin?' he asked her again.

And that was the end of the conversation about his work. They chatted for another half an hour before he looked at the grandfather clock at the entrance. 'I have to go. Thank you for the tea, it was lovely, Veronica. Maybe we can do this again?'

She answered without a second thought. 'Yes, Harry, that would be nice.'

Murphy brought her coat, and she rushed from the hotel to walk home. As she left, the major called her name. Her cover had been blown, she thought immediately, and she ran almost instinctively up Grafton St, past Trinity across O'Connell Bridge and to Abbey St.

Her adrenaline flowed, but she needed a distraction, someone to calm her. She decided to call to see Bridget in her aunt's shop in Abbey St. The wooden sign painted with the word 'Sullivan' swung as Veronica pushed the door open, and the bell chimed as she entered. The shop was empty; Bridget wasn't behind the counter. It was much smaller than her father's shop. Rows of glass jars full of butter-toffee and boiled sweets lined the walls behind the counter, away from prying hands. On the shelves under the jars were packets of Waverley cigarettes, Sweet Afton and matches. Fresh bread sat beside the weighing scales on the counter, waiting for a housewife's visit.

A small door at the left of the shop opened.

'Yes, dear. Can I help you?' said a silver-haired lady with tight curls. Her voice was clear and clipped, but the accent was unlike any she had ever heard.

'Hello, eh. I'm Veronica. Is Bridget here? I was at the secretarial school with her. She said she helped you some Saturdays.'

'Oh, Veronica, I've been told all about you. No, Mr Sullivan is feeling a lot better, so she only comes to visit now. I'm her aunt, Mrs Sullivan.' She stood on her tiptoes and stuck out a tiny, translucent hand. Veronica shook it with care thinking it might break in her hand.

The bell behind her rang as the door opened, and a young soldier entered, his uniform hanging from his thin frame. 'A packet of Waverley please and a quarter of toffees.'

He shifted from foot to foot. It was either nerves or the cold. He didn't look at Veronica. Mrs Sullivan got the little wooden stool to take a jar high on the shelf.

She weighed the toffee into a bag, twisting it tight for him. 'Here you go, love. Tuppence please, for the two.'

As he put them in his coat pocket, he turned, catching Veronica looking at him. She quickly let her eyes drop.

The bell rang again as he departed, and Veronica lifted her head.

'Lots of soldiers call,' Mrs Sullivan said. 'I serve them with a smile. I don't judge them. Some are only boys, children really, and in a foreign land as well. You know I'm from Belfast.'

Mrs Sullivan continued to chat with Veronica. It was lovely to listen to her Belfast lilt, and the conversation was a welcome reprieve from the silence at home. Veronica knew Betty meant no malice, but sometimes the silence was painful to her ears. Mrs Sullivan questioned her about her family and her work.

'Bridget said you got a job. That's exciting, isn't it?'

Veronica's stomach dropped, remembering the lie she'd told the soldier about working in the shop. She had wanted to confide in Bridget, but that was not to be.

'Yes, I'd better go, it's getting late. Tell Bridget I called.'

Veronica pushed the door, but stopped and opened her bag. She took out a paper and pen and scribbled a note for Bridget saying that she would love to meet soon. 'Would you mind giving this to Bridget when you see her?'

On Monday morning, at the office a pile of letters that needed typing greeted Veronica. She knew Michael wouldn't be in until Wednesday, and worried he would be disappointed she hadn't been able to get more information from the major.

20

6 March 1918

On Wednesday morning, as Veronica started to type her first letter, Ernest from the Sinn Féin Bank burst into the office. 'Redmond has died,' he said, holding his side. 'I'm out of breath. I've to sit down for a minute.'

'Good God.' Mrs O'Reilly stood up, pale. 'Sit down, Ernest,' she said and gave him her chair, before pouring him some water. She turned to Veronica. 'Tell Arthur and the men upstairs that John Redmond is dead.'

'Was he murdered?' Veronica asked. Nine months ago, Veronica would not have asked that question, let alone think it, but now it seemed a natural question.

'I don't know. Does it matter? Go on quick and tell the men in the office upstairs.'

Veronica ran upstairs to the third floor, taking two steps at a time. The whirl of Arthur Griffith's printing press where he printed the *Nationalist* newspaper mixed with the click-clack of typewriters. She knocked on the door, but there was no answer. *They probably can't hear me*. Veronica clenched her fist and banged on the door.

'God, what is all the racket?'

The office upstairs was smaller than her own – there was only enough room for the chairs behind the desks. Like her own office, its fire blazed, but it lacked a woman's touch. There were no flowers on the desks, ashtrays overflowed, and a pile of papers had fallen from the desk into a mess on the floor.

She blurted, 'John Redmond is dead.'

'What?' said Arthur.

She started to shake. 'John Redmond is dead.'

'God, girl, how? What happened?'

'I don't know.'

'Let me think.' He paced up and down the room for a few minutes. 'Go back downstairs. I've got to get word to Michael and Éamon. I'll get everyone to meet in your office.'

Veronica returned downstairs.

'I know it's wrong to speak ill of the dead,' Mrs O'Reilly was saying, 'but now, hopefully, this nonsense of Home Rule will stop.'

She said it with an intensity Veronica had never heard before.

'Paddy and my two boys off somewhere, hiding in some godforsaken place, for what, I ask you?'

But before Veronica could think of a reply, Mrs O'Reilly continued. 'All they wanted was to protect our country, and the bloody soldiers call them rebels. Twins just turned sixteen – hardly had their front teeth and they took off.'

Veronica shivered. The office had turned cold; the fire had been unattended with the news of Redmond's death, and the whole building was eerily quiet. Even the printing press upstairs had stopped.

'You might as well go home early,' Mrs O'Reilly said, composing herself. 'They are having a meeting upstairs, and it might go on for some time.' She paused for a few minutes; her frown lines always became more prominent when she was deep in thought. 'Do you know, Veronica, this will be a good thing for Sinn Féin. John Dillon, who is probably going to be the new leader, isn't as good as John was with the people. It might give us a better chance in the by-elections now in June. We need to win as many seats in the elections to oppose the British. Go on home, Veronica, not much more for you to do today.'

Veronica grabbed her coat, thankful the spring days were lengthening with the promise of warmer days. When she reached O'Connell Bridge, she turned left onto Sackville St. The bell rang as she pushed the door open.

'Veronica, lovely to see you.' Mrs Sullivan's face broke into a smile. She bent down below the counter to retrieve something. 'Bridget called to see me yesterday and will be here for the next few Saturdays. Mr Sullivan has taken a turn for the worse again.' She handed Veronica an envelope. 'Here you go, this was left for you.'

Veronica tore open the envelope with her name beautifully scripted on it. Her heart missed a beat when she started to read, and she steadied her hand. She frowned. The note wasn't from Bridget.

Veronica,

Would you like to go for a walk on Sunday the 24th? I will meet you at O'Connell Bridge at 2 p.m.

Harry (Major Fairfax)

'When the handsome officer came in looking for you, Veronica, I didn't know what to say. He handed me a note and asked if you were working. I told him you weren't, and he asked me to give this to you.' Mrs Sullivan smiled. 'Don't worry, your secret is safe with me.'

Veronica was surprised he remembered where she had said she worked. It was a perfect opportunity, and she hoped the excitement about John Redmond dying had eased so she could speak to Michael. She sighed with relief. Now she had something positive from her meeting with Major Fairfax. She didn't stay long with Mrs Sullivan, asking her to tell Bridget she had called, and that she would write to her soon.

All week Veronica anxiously waited for Michael to come into the office.

On Friday as it neared six o'clock, Mrs O'Reilly was wrapping a green scarf around her neck. 'Do you like it, Veronica? My sister in London gave it to me for my birthday. What's eating you? You've been fidgeting all day, are you coming down with something? That damned flu still hasn't gone.' Mrs O'Reilly looked worriedly at her.

'No, honestly I'm fine, it's just been a hectic week with everything that has happened.' She yawned to show that she was tired. 'Do you think Michael will be in before we go?'

'But dear, he has gone to Cork.' Mrs O'Reilly bent down to pick up her bag and didn't notice Veronica's crestfallen face. 'I've to lock up for the weekend. We'd better go, I'll walk a bit with you.'

They left the silent building behind them, Grafton St now bustling with people going home from work. At St Stephen's Green two soldiers were talking to a young boy, questioning him.

'Why don't they stop terrorising innocent people? Look he is just a young lad,' said Mrs O'Reilly. 'What do you think, Veronica?'

Veronica didn't say anything, but as they poked the boy in the stomach, anger bubbled like water sprouting from a broken pipe. The boy doubled over holding his stomach, his face creased with pain. In that moment, she decided she would meet the major on Sunday and do her duty for Ireland.

21

Veronica didn't sleep well and found it hard to concentrate on the priest at Sunday Mass thinking of her day ahead. After Mass they ate breakfast. Tom spoke between mouthfuls of fried bread. 'Mass always makes me hungry; you'd think we'd be used to fasting before Communion, but by God, it works up an appetite.'

'Don't overeat, Richard sent up a lovely bit of beef as well for our Sunday dinner.' Betty put down her fork on the table, 'Veronica, are you feeling ill? You're not eating.'

'No, I'm fine. I'm just not hungry, Aunt Betty.' She wasn't lying; even the smell of the sizzling Sunday roast in the stove didn't make her hungry. 'I'm meeting Bridget later for a walk.'

Veronica forced herself to eat, not just to suppress any further questions from Betty, but also not to waste food, as so many people living around her had none. She could hear her mother, 'It is a sin to waste food – not a mortal sin, but a sin, nonetheless.'

After washing the breakfast dishes, she tried not to let her voice quaver as she said, 'I'm off to meet Bridget. I won't be late.'

'All right, dear. It's a lovely day for a walk but take your coat. It's good the sickness has passed,' Betty said.

Tom had stretched out in front of the fire, had succumbed to his Sunday afternoon sleep, steam from the drying clothes in front of the fire spiralling upwards.

Before she left, Veronica checked herself in the small mirror in the hall, coaxing her curls to stay in place with the pins, and tightened the top button of her blue Sunday coat, making sure to wear her matching hat. The note at the bottom of her coat pocket burned through to her skin.

The shops were closed as it was Sunday, but a few people were out, taking a stroll. Four soldiers walked in the middle of the road causing the bikes to swerve to avoid them. Not wanting to catch any of the soldiers' attention, Veronica walked steadily with her eyes ahead. The earlier rain had stopped, and the weak sun broke through the clouds with the promise of a lovely day. Harry stood waiting on the corner of Abbey St. He shifted from foot to foot, holding a small bunch of yellow daffodils.

He smiled when he saw her. She felt her cheeks heat as he gave her the flowers. If anyone saw her! Now she wished she had talked to Michael. Why hadn't she spoken to her uncle? The incessant chatter in her head made her stomach churn. It took all of Veronica's strength to smile at him. She looked at his face to see if he could hear how fast and hard her heart was beating. But all she saw was his smile, a pleasant smile. He had long eyelashes that made his brown eyes darker.

'Veronica, it's lovely to see you. I was afraid you might not come. I ran after you when you left the Shelbourne, but you were gone. I hope you don't think I was presumptuous calling at the shop?' He waited for a reply, smiling, but Veronica's response stuck in her throat, so she replied with a nod. It didn't seem a good idea to see him on her own. How could she pull this act off if she couldn't even speak? 'No, I'm glad you wrote,' she replied, eventually. They walked towards Merrion Square. She relaxed the further they got from Harcourt St.

'I know you told me, but where did you say your family were from?'

'Cavan.' She stuttered and rambled, 'they were originally from Scotland.' She was telling the truth; the McDermott's were originally from Scotland, some were Presbyterian, but some were Catholic. The knot in her stomach was getting tighter thinking about Eddie. She had to do this for him.

He didn't respond for a moment, but nodded at a gentleman and his wife, taking in the first days of spring.

'I remember my father's regiments were going to go to Scotland, but then he was posted to India for years.'

Veronica thought briefly about whether she should drop the flowers and run but then glanced at his face. It was interesting, his nose was perfect and his hair slightly curled sticking out under his cap, but it was his eyes that grabbed her attention. They were the darkest eyes she had ever seen, a deep chocolate brown.

She relaxed a little, telling him about the lake at home, the forest and how she loved to read there. She hoped that if she kept talking, he would ask fewer questions. There was something about the way he listened to her, so intently, that made her face warm.

'What about your family, Major?'

'Harry. Call me Harry. My mother and father are in Shropshire, and, as I already told you, I am an only child.'

His accent differed from those of the soldiers who came into Harcourt St. She wanted to be repulsed by him, she wanted to hate him, but she felt herself becoming comfortable in his company.

He stopped walking and turned to look her straight in the eye, 'Veronica, I...'

She waited for him to say the rest of the sentence.

'I am so glad you came, I feared you wouldn't,' he said quickly. 'I don't care what religion you are. I won't even ask.' He paused. 'I am half Catholic. My mother is a French Catholic. That's why my father never did well in the army. I know my superiors will frown upon our meeting – the soldiers do meet Dublin girls, but for men of my rank, it's frowned upon. I know we are two very different people. I don't know what your politics or beliefs are, but I'm not really cut out for this job.'

He went to take her hand but stopped at her stricken expression.

She had never held a man's hand before. This was not what she had expected.

'Sorry, I'm sorry, I don't know what came over me.' He dropped his hand by his side.

The sun shone down, but she saw rain in the distance, and a rainbow appeared over the rooftops. She stopped as they turned onto Pembroke Road. She hadn't realised they had walked so far from St Stephen's Green. Mrs Brown's house was at the top of the road. Her heart began to beat wildly. This was too much for her; her breathing became short and shallow.

'You look pale. Are you all right? I'll see if we can get a cab.' He looked up and down the street. 'I think there is rain on the way. Getting a cab will be hard. Maybe we should keep going before the rain comes.' She started to walk ahead when the sounds of hooves, rubble and the grating of wheels came up behind them. She prayed it was a cab, and it was. Harry raised his hand to stop it.

In the distance, she saw a lone figure dressed in black approaching them. It was Fr O'Flanagan. She silently prayed the cab would stop before he spotted her; she couldn't talk to him. The hooves slowed.

Harry spoke with the driver, they climbed in, and she sank back into the soft seat as the figure in black walked past. Sitting side by side in the cab, she was intensely aware of Harry. She had never sat this close to a man who wasn't a relative. His arm touched her arm. She fought the urge to pull it away – what he stood for repulsed her.

'Are you all right? I'll ask the driver to bring you home.'

She could see the trees of St Stephen's Green to her left. The threatening rain had not arrived, but the sun was low. She looked out the window of the stopped cab and saw the doorman of the Shelbourne holding the door open for a group of ladies and gentlemen entering the hotel.

'No, I'm feeling much better,' she said truthfully.

'Shall I take you home? It's getting dark.'

'No, it's fine. I'll walk. It's not far from here to my uncle's house, and it isn't raining.'

He leaned over and brushed something from her shoulder, and she flinched.

'Sorry,' he said, moving back. 'It was a small feather. Would you like to go to Kingstown someday? Spring is here, and I hear it's a lovely place to spend a day in the sun.'

He stared at her face as if memorising every feature. Gazing back, she unwillingly noticed his chiselled chin, his clear skin slightly darker than most Irishmen. *What does he want? I don't know if I can do this.*

'I'm not sure...' she said, trying to buy time.

He took her hand before she got out of the cab and said, 'Veronica, I've had a wonderful day.'

Veronica's chest was tight. *How could you have had a wonderful day when you've only just met me?* she wanted to shout at him. What about her brother in prison, was he having a wonderful day?

'Kingstown. Will you come to Kingstown with me? I've heard it is beautiful, and the seaside has so many pleasant memories for me. My mother and I went to Dorset every summer for the month of August.' She was taken aback by his gentle expression. Usually, the soldiers she saw were aggressive and angry. This would make her job easier.

'Yes,' she said with a lot more composure than she felt. She was suddenly not as angry as she should have been, and this unsettled her.

22

The following morning Veronica was refreshed and ready for her week's work. Glad of the warmer days, the dull, damp winter was soon forgotten. Mrs O'Reilly told Veronica how the freshness of spring would be short-lived if it were a hot summer. The smells of the city would circulate the houses, like the tentacles of a trapped monster, until the fresh autumn breeze carried them away.

Tom had just finished his cup of tea when Veronica sat at the table for breakfast. He threw his cap on and said, 'Suppose I'd better go. Start the day as you mean to go on.'

Veronica smiled. That was her father's favourite saying. He was an early riser and got up when the fingers of dawn spread across the morning sky.

Tom kissed Betty goodbye on her cheek. 'Veronica, I'll drop you to work. I've to go and get the dray from the yard so come down when you are ready.'

After combing and pinning her hair, she put a little of the lipstick Bridget had given her on her lips. She looked at herself in the mirror. The girl who had come to Dublin only months ago seemed to have been replaced by a young woman.

She shouted to Betty in the kitchen, 'I'm going now. I'll see you this evening.' Downstairs her uncle puffed on his cigarette as he put the halter on the horse, the plume of cigarette smoke gently spiralling upwards to meet the smoke from the house fires that were lit for the day. He stretched and rubbed the small of his back as she approached. 'Com' on, love. You don't want to be late.'

'I'm sorry.' Her easy-going uncle just nodded, but the impatient horse snorted as she climbed in beside her uncle, stamping his feet in anticipation.

Tom gave a slight wave to a man on the opposite side of the street who was entering the gates of the brewery.

'You're looking much better than the other day. Me and Betty thought ye might be getting the flu or something. Poor Hubert there,' he said, nodding in the direction of the man he had waved to, 'his wife died from the flu just a few days ago. Nine children and no mother. His only saving grace is he has a job. The eldest is thirteen, so at least she can help.'

As they pulled away Veronica looked back at Hubert. Her heart broke as she watched him almost drag himself into the brewery, carrying a sadness similar to Betty's. They sat in comfortable silence for a few streets with the morning sunshine on their backs.

'This nonsense of Redmond trying to get Irish lads to fight in the English war... I'm glad he is dead, though I know you shouldn't speak ill of the dead.'

It was the first time Tom had mentioned the war since Veronica's arrival seven months ago.

'Padraig joined the Fusiliers out of his own free will. It

is a tragedy me and Betty must bear although we'll never get over it. We thought God would never bless us with a child, and when Padraig came, it filled a gap in our lives. But now that gap is bigger than before.' Tom's knuckles whitened as he held the reins tight.

His hunched shoulders dragged him lower towards the horse. 'I didn't want Padraig to go, you know, didn't support his decision. I told him he would get a job in the brewery. But he was stubborn, so bloody stubborn. I hope nobody must go through what me and Betty have. The pain of the loss of a child... I know people say, "Time is a great healer" but,' he turned to look at Veronica, his eyes wet, 'but it's not really.'

'Daddy told me how hard it was, I'm really sorry, it must be so awful for ye both.' It was the longest she had heard him speak about Padraig.

Tom nodded, sighed, 'Life can be cruel, but Betty and I have each other...' he paused and looked at Veronica, 'and now we have you.'

Tom and Veronica passed the corner of Grafton St. A group of men walked to the Shelbourne wearing shirts of pure white, their suits pressed stiff. More soldiers than usual were on the streets. The men stopped outside, meeting another group coming from the opposite direction. Paperwork in hand, their heads were stuck together, their hands moving quickly as they talked. Seven or eight men she recognised from the office came from Harcourt St chanting, 'No conscription!'

'Who are those men?' Tom nodded towards the group in suits.

'It's General Maxwell. I heard Michael tell Mrs O'Reilly yesterday. I think he told her the general commanded the British Expeditionary Force in France, and that he's staying at the Shelbourne. The trade unions have organised a rally in front of the hotel. That's them now.'

Memories of her meeting with the major surfaced. It made her uncomfortable to think she had been in the same building as General Maxwell.

'As if he'd bloody well listen,' Tom said, giving the reins a slight flick to move forward. 'Look, you've visitors.'

Tom stopped the dray as the soldiers filed one by one into the Harcourt St office.

'God, I'd wish they would leave us alone to get on with our work,' she said and laughed. 'Ah, well, all in a day's work. I'll walk from here.'

As Veronica climbed to get off the dray, the horse jumped, startled by a shout from a group of men behind them, and she fell. She winced at the sharp pain in her knee, and a red stain grew through her stockings. She watched the swelling crowd filling the streets around the green, the chants of 'no conscription' getting louder.

Tom jumped off the dray beside her. "Ere, love, get back up beside me, I'll drop you the few yards. God, they're making an awful racket.'

'I'm fine, really, it's only a graze and isn't painful at all,' she lied. 'I'm late. I'll get a bandage from Mrs Moore upstairs.'

Veronica limped up the steps to her office. She passed the soldiers to her left in the Sinn Féin Bank. Fear rose in her gut. What if the major was with them? She pushed the thought to the back of her mind. When she reached the office, she made her way slowly to her desk.

'Veronica, are you all right? What happened?'

'I'm fine, Mrs O'Reilly, just a small graze.' Heavy boots thundered up the stairs and she sat at her desk, quickly taking off her coat. She put a piece of paper in the typewriter.

Mrs O'Reilly hissed, 'Veronica, keep your head down and keep typing, just ignore them. They'll be here in a minute. They are only trying to intimidate us.'

The footsteps stopped outside in the corridor on the landing. 'Whose office is that?'

Veronica's fingers stopped cold. She recognised the voice. It was the major. She held her breath and kept her head low, her eyes fixed on the keys of the typewriter. She pictured Harry standing at the doorway, his frame filling the door, staring at her, shouting 'Arrest that Fenian'.

Mrs O'Reilly replied haughtily, 'It's Frank Smith's office. Excuse me, but I have these to type, so if you don't mind, I'd like to get on with my work.'

But before he could enter a soldier shouted from the ground floor, 'Sir, we've to go now. General Maxwell is leaving the Shelbourne, and there is a mob of Fenians outside.'

Harry called the soldiers that were upstairs in Arthur Griffith's office to come down and the uniform thud of boots down the stairs faded as they left the offices for the Shelbourne. Mrs O'Reilly sighed as she sat back in her chair. Loud shouts on the street below and an engine roared to life, the soldiers now gone. Only when they left did Veronica breathe easy.

Mrs O'Reilly stubbed out her cigarette. 'It's never-ending. These raids are so pointless. At least it's positive they see us as a threat to them.' She sat forward, squinted at Veronica, 'Dear, you poor thing. You look so flushed. Open a window.'

Veronica pulled up the sash allowing the flow of cold air to sweep across her face. She inhaled deeply.

'When is Michael back?'

'Not for a couple of weeks, I think he has gone to England,' Mrs O'Reilly replied. 'Why?'

'Nothing.' Veronica said with slight relief that she wouldn't have to meet the major again, as it had been more unnerving than she thought it would be.

'He left you a note,' said Mrs O'Reilly.

'Who?'

'God, Veronica, what's got into you? Michael, who else? He left this for you this morning.'

Mrs O'Reilly handed Veronica a neatly folded note. She opened it feeling slight trepidation.

Veronica,

I am gone to England.

We need you to develop your relationship with the major and find out if the British know where we are holding our rallies. We must be one step ahead of them, and we need as much information as we can get. You

*know how important it is that they don't take our men,
we need them here for our own fight. We need to get our
FREEDOM.*

Michael.

'Veronica, are you all right? You're very quiet.'
'Fine, I'm fine, Mrs O'Reilly. I just have to do something
for Michael,' said Veronica grimly. She needed to think.
Would she be able to do it?

23

April arrived with the usual promise of sun in the morning, and by the afternoon the winds rose with torrential rain showers that retreated as quickly as they started.

After Veronica's morning ritual of opening her curtains, she often wondered why she closed them. The flimsy material offered little opposition to the morning light, and the brightness often woke her before her aunt rose to make breakfast. Now she would sleep through the noisy night patrols. She splashed cold water on her face, and made her bed before looking out the window again to see what the day offered. The sun shone, and she looked forward to her walk to work now the winter chill had left the air. Even though Veronica had been in Dublin for seven months, she couldn't bring herself to like the taste of the watery porridge, no matter how hungry she was. As usual, Betty sat at the table beside the empty setting for her cousin, her eyes downcast and eating little, but Tom always scraped his bowl clean.

'I'll take you to work, Veronica,' Tom said as he gulped

his last mouthful of tea and Betty handed over both bread and butter wrapped in brown paper.

On the dray, Tom didn't speak until they turned onto Merchant's Quay along the river. The quays were filling with men who walked or cycled to work.

'I met Michael last night. Have you arranged when to meet this soldier again?'

'He said he wants to go to Kingstown.'

'We need to find out if he knows anything about General Maxwell. He's the biggest threat to us and the anti-conscription rallies.' He flicked the reins of the dray. 'Our support for the opposition of conscription is building every day. But we need to know what they know about the rallies we are trying to organise. How do you contact the soldier?'

'Bridget's aunt's shop in Abbey St, he left a note there for me once. He asked if I would go to Kingstown with him but didn't say when. I don't know how to contact him.'

'Go on, ya English scum.' A hunched woman with a tightly wrapped black shawl waved her walking stick at passing soldiers. She was like the haggard, gaunt women Veronica saw in Henrietta St when she delivered the parcel. She pulled something from the inside of her shawl and threw it at the soldiers; it was a stone, but it hit Tom's dray. Neighing loudly in fright, the horse jolted, but the heavy wooden harness prevented him from jumping as he shook his head in anger.

'Whoa, boy, it's all right. Will you watch it?' Tom shouted to the woman, but she was dragged screaming down the street by the two soldiers.

'Look, Veronica, meet this soldier and get as much information as you can. We can't have our boys and men going to fight, we have lost enough men already. We need to keep them here to fight for us.'

She nodded, but her uncle didn't see her. Instead, his eyes bore into the soldiers' backs.

'Now, Veronica, you see how important it is you try to meet the soldier. What did you say his name was?'

'Harry. Major Harry Fairfax.'

'We need all the help we can get. Write to the Royal Barracks. I'm sure there can't be that many Major Fairfax's around.'

Veronica nodded her head, moving with the flutters in her stomach.

When she was at home that evening, she wrote to Harry and posted the letter the following day.

Veronica called to Mrs Sullivan's shop most evenings.

Mrs Sullivan looked up when she heard the bell and smiled. 'I was hoping you'd call. I've something for your uncle and aunt.' She tied a knot on a brown paper bag and handed it to Veronica. 'Give these hard-boiled sweets to your uncle, and there are a few chocolates in there as well. Just a little treat for you and your aunt.' She didn't raise her eyes as she tied the bag.

'He came in, you know, the soldier, and asked if you were working? I was just about to close. He left you this.' She gave Veronica a note. 'He didn't say too much, and I said you'd gone home. He is handsome, isn't he?'

Veronica tore open the note.

11 Feb 1918

Veronica,

I am sorry to have missed you. It would give me great pleasure if you came to Kingstown. 23 March, Saturday at 11 a.m. I'll wait for you at O'Connell Bridge.

Yours,

Harry

'Are you all right, dear?'

'Eh, I'm fine, Mrs Sullivan.'

The bell chimed behind her.

'Mrs Ryan, I've kept some bread for you.'

Mrs Ryan nodded at Veronica.

'This is Veronica, my niece's friend. They went to secretarial school together.'

'Well, that's something, isn't it?' Nodding in agreement with herself and clutching the bread tight, her eyes swept Veronica up and down.

'Isn't it great women work now? What is it you said you do?'

'I didn't say.' Veronica had no interest in talking to the woman. She had met her type many times before in her father's shop in Virginia and knew that gossip was their currency.

'I'd better be off. Frank will be home from work soon, so I'd better have his dinner ready.'

When she left, Mrs Sullivan closed the till. 'Work my eye, her husband has never worked a day in his life. Work, she means when he comes home from the pub. And another thing, her youngest Hughie is in the English army, sending money home every week. Some people talk from the side of their mouths.'

A fit of coughing came from upstairs.

'He – Sammy – never fully recovered from the flu. I'd better go up to him.' Mrs Sullivan gave one more squeeze of Veronica's hand. 'Be careful, dear.' The coughing intensified. 'I'd better see if Sammy is all right.'

She turned to leave.

'Veronica, I know girls meet the soldiers, but it's more than religion that divides you – it's his allegiance to the Crown. I know I let that not bother me when I met Sammy. He was the most handsome man in Belfast, and taller then.' She laughed, her eyes sparkling with the memory. 'I saw him at my aunt's funeral. He called to her house to pay his respects. Even though he worked on the docks, he always smelled of soap. I knew he was the man for me. Belfast was different then, but these are different times, so be careful.' She looked at Veronica steadfastly. 'I mean, careful.'

Veronica wanted to tell Mrs Sullivan it was all right, that she was doing it for her country, but she understood that the fewer people who knew, the better. She didn't want to involve Mrs Sullivan more than she already had.

Upstairs there was a fit of uncontrollable coughing and Sammy banged on the ceiling.

'Oh dear, I've really got to go. Before you go, dear, would you turn the sign around to *Closed* on the door?'

★

'Uncle, he left a note,' Veronica whispered to Tom over the dinner table as Betty went to the kitchen to get more potatoes.

He nodded as he took the note from her and said nothing.

When dinner was over Tom said, 'Betty, I'm going to a meeting. Veronica, I'll take you to work tomorrow.'

Veronica made the excuse she was tired to go to bed early, leaving Betty sitting in her armchair knitting.

She fought with sleep thinking about the note and her task, but it won and she woke to a dark room, the wick of the candle glowing orange. She hadn't been asleep too long. Something had woken her, and she stared into the darkness, listening. A light knock on the door, and Tom softly said her name. She opened the door, and he wordlessly entered.

'Veronica, you meet with the soldier, and see if you can get some information.' He rubbed his fingers through his thinning hair. 'We haven't spoken to your father about this, but this is an opportunity we have to take. I'll get one of the lads to follow you from a safe distance, and we'll send word to our lads in Kingstown. Don't worry about being seen with him, we'll keep you safe.'

24

On Saturday morning Veronica got out of bed as daylight dappled the floorboards of her bedroom. The pit-pat of rain on the roof had intermittently woken her during the night, its rhythmic sound reminding her of the rhythm of a train. The train she was to take to Kingstown in the morning. In her dreams, her uncle didn't have a spy follow her. She was captured by a young group of Irish rebels, tied to a stake in her home village of Virginia, and stoned by local women and children. She woke in a pool of sweat and stayed awake, listening to the birds sing as the rain retreated to the morning sun.

After breakfast, she told Betty she was going to meet Bridget.

'I haven't seen her in ages, so we are going to Kingstown.'

'That will be lovely. I've never been to the seaside, but I heard it's beautiful. I'll give you a slice of tart to take with you.' She stood back and looked Veronica up and down. 'You look nice but try to get some sun, you are so pale. Take a cardigan, though, it may not be as warm beside the sea.'

Veronica had chosen a jade green skirt and her cream

blouse. The cream usually complimented her olive skin, but today there was no contrast; her face was as pale as her blouse.

Betty smiled at Veronica as she cleared the breakfast table. 'Cheer up, Veronica, you might catch the eye of some young man.'

Veronica felt her face heat. She had spent a little more time on her appearance than she usually would.

Veronica hurried towards O'Connell Bridge, as she didn't like to be late for anything. As she approached the bridge, there was a man with a matching hat watching the seagulls. It was Harry. Relief rushed through her veins when she saw he was wearing a striped plaid tweed jacket with matching trousers, his collared shirt crisp white. Yet, though he was out of uniform, the finery of his suit set him apart from other gentlemen. She would still be uneasy.

A distant steam whistle echoed through the air.

'Quick, Veronica, that's our train. I bought the tickets earlier, at the station in Westland Row.'

They ran to the station to wait on the platform with passengers. The D&KR was like the train she had taken from Oldcastle, but the passengers were different. Most were families, mothers or nannies taking children to the sea for a trip to enjoy the first days of summer. There were one or two couples, laughing and giggling as they discussed the day ahead. When the train stopped, Harry stood aside to let her onto the train, and only then was she aware that he had his hand on her elbow, and he had been linking her arm while they had run.

Veronica tried to control her breathing as they sat side

by side. It was a day that held so many promises for many of the couples, but for her, it was all a lie.

'Are you all right, Veronica? You're very quiet,' Harry asked, his voice soft and full of concern.

'I'm fine,' she said, and she tried to relax. 'I've never been to the sea before, so I keep trying to imagine what it's like.'

The houses soon turned to green fields. To Veronica's delight, the sea horizon came to view stretching out to the unknown, and soon they were at Kingstown. When they disembarked the train, she could taste the sea, as Tom had said, the sting of salt on her lips.

They followed the line of people to the pier. Coloured yachts in the harbour surrounded by seagulls were pictures-que compared to the squealing seagulls on the Liffey. The gulls at Kingstown gracefully glided over the sea with a sense of freedom, riding the waves of wind with ease.

'Do you like it, Veronica? It's really quite lovely, isn't it?' Veronica followed Harry's gaze. He appeared to be drinking in the surroundings, before he closed his eyes and inhaled deeply. As she looked at the vast sea, the lake at home paled into insignificance.

'Veronica look,' Harry said, pointing ahead. 'It's a seat. Let's sit for a minute and close your eyes. Listen to the seagulls.'

She didn't want to sit too close to him but equally didn't want to run away. It was calm. It was magnificent.

After a few minutes, he said, 'God, I'd love to stay here all day.'

He sat back, stretching out his legs and turned to look at her. His eyes held hers for a moment, his gaze warm, but she pulled away to look at the sea. She stiffened and swallowed; she had a job to do.

'Shall we walk?' she said.

He linked her arm. His touch sent a shiver pulsating through her veins as she felt the heat of his body.

'Let's enjoy the day, Veronica, and not think about the turmoil in the city. I know that we are something that can never be, but let's not think about that today.'

'It's a pity there is no beach. I do love to walk barefoot in the sand. When I was a boy, I would sometimes do that on the grass on the lawns at home, feeling the morning dew between my toes. Mother thought it was very uncivilised, but somehow, it made me feel free.'

Veronica laughed. 'My mother would get so cross with me when I used to run barefoot in the fields at home, or climbed trees in the forest with Eddie.'

She didn't tell him about her swimming in her undergarments, that was real freedom.

'My mother would shout, "Veronica, it's not very ladylike".'

He stopped to gaze at her, 'Oh, I think you are very ladylike.'

Veronica's cheeks burned, and she ignored his remark. 'What made you join the army?'

'My father was a major in the army, and so naturally, I joined too. I wanted to serve my country.' Harry paused. 'But France – it wasn't right. Men sent to no-man's land. I made friends with a Dublin Fusilier called Paddy Hennessy;

he was from Dublin.' Harry stopped talking, his eyes far away.

Veronica didn't rush him, just let him talk.

'I inquired about him to my superiors after I got injured and left the hospital, but nobody had heard of him. He was a nobody, in no-man's land. I suspect it was because he was Irish. He told me about the conditions he lived in, in Dublin. How the British – how we ruled him and his class. At night he read poetry to the boys and me. I tried to contact his family when I was sent to Dublin, but I didn't know where to start.'

She looked at him; his face had changed. The contours and lines of his face were more profound and looked darker in the light, like the grooves in the mud in the newspapers' pictures she had seen of no-man's land.

'My cousin Padraig was injured in Suvla Bay, he died.'

Harry stopped. 'That's awful.' His face blanched. 'Some injured men suffered more when they came back.'

Bridget had told her that some of the men who came home were changed, their minds broken beyond repair. And the conditions the Irish Fusiliers had endured: rats, bombs, now gas that damaged their minds.

Not only had Harry opened up about his family, but also, she felt his raw emotion. His experience in France was something she guessed men would find it difficult to share. She looked at Harry. He wasn't supposed to feel sorry for Irishmen or give sweets to children.

'I can't imagine what that must have been like for you,' she said honestly. She pulled her cardigan tight as the wind grew cooler.

'Are you cold?' said Harry, immediately taking his jacket off and putting it around Veronica's shoulder. His touch lingered on her shoulders, and her cheeks burned, another new emotion that confused her.

Veronica couldn't find the words to thank him, and his good manners unnerved her, confused her. She was rooted and the only movement in her body was the pulsing vein in her neck.

Three children ran past, pulling a kite behind them.

'Isn't it lovely the way it circles and moves with the children?' Harry said. 'Have you any nephews or nieces?'

She felt uncomfortable talking about family, but she didn't know what else to talk about. 'No, nobody in the family is married. My younger sister Susan spends her days dreaming of some man sweeping her off her feet.'

'Like a Mr Darcy.'

Veronica surprised herself as she laughed. 'Exactly like that, she has read *Pride and Prejudice* so many times. I think if you asked her what happens on, say, page 106, she'd know. When we were little, she used to dress Eddie in his best suit and make him marry her, over and over. That was only short-lived, as Eddie doesn't tolerate games.'

'Eddie, is he your brother?' Harry didn't wait for a reply. 'You're so lucky to have siblings. As I told you the boys at my boarding school were like brothers, but at Christmas and summer, it was only me at home.'

She was only partly listening to him; she hadn't wanted to mention Eddie. She needed him to talk about his work. Seizing her opportunity as he opened up about his life, she pressed him about being in the military.

'I do miss my family, and am often lonely. I'm sure you miss your family, but I imagine being in the army is like having lots of brothers?'

'Yes, and no. We are under a lot of pressure.'

'Why?'

'Orders from London, but I'm sure that's nothing that would interest you.' He turned to look at the horizon, silent for a few minutes. 'Let's talk about something else.'

He spoke softly, nothing like the loud swearing soldiers who frequented Harcourt St. He was polite, and – she couldn't think of the word and thought for a moment – he seemed vulnerable, as if about to break.

He abruptly turned to her and took her hand, the intimacy of the gesture shocking her. Veronica couldn't move. 'Let's go for a walk,' he said, 'it's getting cold.'

As they stood, something fell from his coat. Harry quickly bent to retrieve the small brown leather notebook, picking it up and putting it in his inner coat pocket.

Time had passed quickly, and the sun moved west. A few day-trippers were gathering up their towels and umbrellas.

'Tea. How about some tea before we go? Gilligan's tearooms aren't far from here. The friend I met in France told me about it.' He looked around. 'I think it's near the end of the promenade.'

When they arrived at Gilligan's, a girl in a black-and-white uniform turned the closed sign, and shouted through the glass door, 'Sorry all the milk and scones are gone.' She gave Harry a thunderous look as if blaming him.

'Terrible, this war in Europe. When is it going to end?' Harry mused a rhetorical question nobody could answer.

She bit her tongue, wanting again to shout at him. Ireland was at war with England.

Harry looked at his wristwatch. 'I hadn't realised the time, we'd better leave. I've to get back for a meeting.' He took her hand lightly, looking directly into her eyes.

He was so close she saw her reflection in his brown eyes. He had a fleck of hazel in his right eye. Veronica wanted to back away, but she needed him on her side.

'Let's go. I wish things were different, but I would really like to continue seeing you.' Harry emphasised the 'would', politely asking Veronica for her thoughts.

It was perfect, and Veronica held her nerve steady to answer. She was shaking as if on fire on the inside but calmly said, 'That would be lovely. I've enjoyed myself today.'

The train return journey home was quiet, with few words passing between them.

Harry lay back in the seat opposite her, closing his eyes, his long legs stretched so that every so often they nudged Veronica's. She studied him. Not talking, he looked perfect. It was when he spoke that his accent and polished manner divided them. The train slowed as it entered Westland Row station and stopped with a jolt that woke Harry. Exhausted families and couples alighted, going back to lives from which they had escaped for the day.

'Veronica, when will I see you again?'

She held her breath. It was a lot easier than she'd thought it would be.

'It's difficult for me, I'm still military, and I don't know what my duties are most of the time, they're constantly changing.'

Frowning she said, 'I thought you were a major? In charge, like a boss.' She didn't want to sound like she knew what a major's duties were, and held his gaze as if she was learning something new. She had to admit he was handsome with his thick black hair, and strong jaw.

His gaze was intense. 'Yes, but I'm still under orders from General Maxwell, and,' he paused, 'I don't know if this is a good idea.'

When Veronica heard the general's name, she adopted a look of indifference, her heart racing. 'Who?' she asked, trying to keep him talking. 'Is he in charge of you?' she tried again.

Abruptly, he gathered his coat. 'This is a bad idea.'

'No,' she said, her voice a little higher than normal. 'I'd love to see you again.' He looked up, surprised, even hopeful. 'I don't work at my aunt's shop every day, so just leave a note for me.' At least now if he called, she thought, he wouldn't be surprised when she wasn't there.

Before he could ask when she was working, the distant church bells rang six times. 'I've to return to the barracks.' He smiled, looking at her for a moment. Something flickered across his face but was gone in an instant. 'I'll try to call at the shop,' he said and hurried along the quays toward the Royal Barracks.

When she arrived home to Thomas St, her uncle motioned her into her room and shut the bedroom door behind them.

He sat beside her on the bed. 'Well, were you all right?

I spoke to Michael today, and he will talk to you at work next week. He has a plan.' The smell of fried bread filtered into the bedroom.

'Tom, your tea is ready, and did I hear the front door? Is Veronica home?' shouted Betty.

'Yes, love, we'll be there in a minute.'

Tom nodded at Veronica and turned to leave. With his back to her, he said, 'I'm not comfortable with this if anything were to happen to you. Me and Betty would die.'

She whispered, 'Don't worry, I'll be careful. I think it will be easy to gain his trust.' And she told Tom about the day before they went to join Betty for tea.

25

Veronica couldn't believe seven weeks had passed since she had met the major. It was near the end of April, and each day was becoming warmer and longer.

When Michael came back from England, Veronica told him about her meeting with the major, and that she was waiting for him to contact her. Most evenings on her way home from work she called to Mrs Sullivan's, but there were no more notes.

On Thursday after work, Veronica strolled towards Mrs Sullivan's shop once more. She enjoyed the constant chatter from Mrs Sullivan with her soft Belfast lilt. It was calming and warming in the increasing turbulence of Dublin. The previous day on her way to work, Veronica had seen a group of soldiers on the opposite side of O'Connell Bridge stop a young man for questioning. The soldiers were little older than the boy they stopped, who was no more than twenty. They questioned him for a minute before they pushed him forward with their guns to the bridge towards the other side of the river. Veronica knew they were taking him to Dublin Castle for questioning.

When she reached Mrs Sullivan's shop, the lights were

on. She pushed the door, and the ringing bell signalled her arrival. A grey balding head appeared from behind a stack of brown cardboard boxes. It was Mr Sullivan. He was a man of few words, and Mrs Sullivan made up for that. The few occasions Veronica had met him he just gave Veronica a slight nod as he puffed on his pipe.

'You must be Veronica. I'm Mr Sullivan. I met you once or twice with Bridget. I'm afraid Mrs Sullivan is in bed. She told me to give this to you if you called.' He bent to retrieve a note with Harry's writing. His bushy eyebrows met in the middle like one grey mottled caterpillar. 'I'm not one to cast judgment but be cautious. Unfortunately, the way things are going, the city is getting more unsafe.'

She took the note. 'Thank you.' Her hands shook as she opened it, first looking at the carefully scripted V.

Veronica,

I am truly sorry I have not been in contact. I long to meet again. Can we meet on Friday at 1 p.m. at Bewley's Tearooms?

Harry.

Tomorrow! *I long to meet you.* She slowly reread the note. She should have been uncomfortable with him 'longing to meet her' and yet...

The Pro-Cathedral bells rang 6.30.

'I'd better go, it's getting late. Thank you.'

He nodded and dropped a pile of newspapers on the

floor beside the shop door, and the string broke. A few papers spilt out on the floor. *Soldier wounded in an ambush* screamed one headline.

Veronica's heart dropped. It was dangerous, but she was doing something important. On her way home, she watched the world and wondered what Dublin would look like without the presence of British soldiers. A Dublin where people weren't on guard ready for an arrest or an ambush of the soldiers, or for a bloody battle to ensue.

The following day at work, Veronica anxiously looked at the office door every time it opened. She needed to speak to Michael.

'Girl, sometimes I don't know what gets into you. You are miles away,' said Mrs O'Reilly as she sat at her desk, her glasses low on her nose. She looked up as the door squeaked open.

'Michael, good to see you. How can we help?'

'It's Veronica I'm after. And Mrs O'Reilly would you mind getting someone to fix that door?' Michael nodded to Veronica. 'Would you come to my office? I've got a few letters to dictate to you.'

In Michael's office, before she sat down, she said, 'I've news, he left a note.'

'I guessed. He was seen going into Sullivan's shop a few days ago. That's why I want to talk to you. Where and when?'

He sat back into his chair and listened, and when she had finished, chewing his cigarette for a minute or two.

Standing up and pushing the window open, he stared out over the rooftops for a few minutes.

It was the longest few minutes of her life. It was nearly as bad as the soldiers in Davy Byrne's pub.

Michael looked at the door, as one knock turned into three, and he shouted, 'Come back in a while.' He stared at Veronica. 'Meet him, will you do that?' Without waiting for a reply, he went to the open window and closed it. 'He clearly wants more than just friendship, are you comfortable with that?'

Veronica looked down at the wooden floor and exhaled slowly. 'But why? Sorry, I don't mean to be impertinent, but what can I do?'

'Meet him, flirt with him. If he wanted to meet you, he must be keen, lots of soldiers meet girls at the dances, but they'd be of a lower rank.' He picked up another cigarette from his desk but didn't light it. 'I'll have men there to see who he is, or how he can be of help to us. Leave at 12.45 and get to Bewley's early to sit somewhere private.'

Veronica's mind raced, her senses heightened.

'Don't worry, Veronica. We'll watch your back all the time. The British are really trying to disrupt our opposition, but the big question is how they will do it? Every time we have a rally to gather the support of the workers, the soldiers appear and disrupt us. They're trying to infiltrate our trade unions, who are all organising strikes. There is the talk of the bishops coming on our side, and if they do that will be a huge benefit. We have to keep opposing them, and anything you can learn will help us.'

'Michael I'm not worried,' but the truth held a twinge of guilt. 'I know how important this is, and I am only glad

I can help.' The major was also not the worst company in the world.

The grandmother clock in the office's corner chimed 12.45.

'Mrs O'Reilly, Michael wants me to post a few letters, and I need to get them in the lunchtime post.'

It was a short walk from Harcourt St to Bewley's on Grafton St. Veronica kept her hat low and collar up. The newspapers were full of violence daily.

A scruffy young boy screamed, 'Get yer paper! "Attack on Kevin St".'

She bought the paper; scanning it she read that local people from the tenements had attacked the police station, setting it alight, and had shot a middle-aged man from the DMP. She threw the paper into a bin on the street before entering Bewley's.

Veronica stood inside the door, waiting to be seated, shielding her eyes from the sun. A rush of excitement rushed through her as she reminded herself she was helping the Irish cause. There were few vacant seats in Bewley's. Dubliners were having a cup of tea away from the threat of violence on the streets.

A waiter approached her. 'Yes, madam, are you waiting for someone, or shall I show you to a table?'

'Could I sit at the back, please? I like the quietness.'

With his nose in the air, trying to make his diminutive figure taller, he gestured for her to follow him. The waiter's grey speckled hair, darkened with Brylcreem, matched his v-shaped moustache. He brought her to a table in the back where the sunlight didn't reach, and the lighting was dim.

'Thank you,' she said to the waiter. 'I'll wait for my companion.'

She sat across the booth and sank into the shadows, trying to relax, but the previous night's events she had read in the *Irish Independent* were on her mind. The paper leaned towards the fight for freedom and was kind in their reporting, whereas *The Times* always favoured the English.

She saw Harry out of the corner of her eye. Her heart missed a beat and she composed herself. She wasn't too sure how to flirt, and thought with a pang that Susan would know how to. The waiter grunted as if he knew she was a Catholic meeting a British soldier. She disregarded his look. Harry smiled at the waiter, but he ignored Harry, trying to extend his height so that his black trousers didn't gather around his ankles.

'It's so good to see you. How are you?' Harry said, sitting opposite her and taking off his hat. His dark hair glistened under the weak light bulb.

Veronica loosened her jacket. 'I'm fine, Harry.' Now was her chance. 'I thought you weren't coming back. Were you in England?'

'Let's not talk about that. I meant it when I wrote I longed to see you.'

An impatient cough from the side of the table.

'Sorry, I didn't see you there.'

The waiter stood expressionless beside the table.

'Shall I order?'

Veronica nodded. To her left, a group of soldiers entered and went straight to a table where three men sat. They spoke to them, and then pulled one of them, pushing him roughly on the floor. Two of the soldiers grabbed an arm each, pulled him up and marched him out. Veronica lowered her eyes, wondering whether these were the men that were watching out for her.

Harry inclined his head towards hers. 'I know I shouldn't say this, but I wonder what we are doing here?'

'Who?'

'Us. The British. Irish people should rule themselves from their own country.' He spoke quietly but deliberately. 'My mother was Catholic, but we were brought up Church of England. I have to say she sometimes had funny beliefs,' he said. He looked at her for a few long moments. 'You're beautiful, Veronica. Sorry, I didn't mean to startle you.' He reached over the table to take her hand, and she pulled away, knocking over the empty teacup.

'I'm fine,' she said quickly with a smile, trying not to deflect his advances. She still couldn't believe what he had said about the British.

When the tea and scones arrived, the air was fraught with disapproval from the waiter. He poured the tea into the small delicate porcelain cups. Veronica tried to drink it like a Protestant to dispel any opinions the waiter had. Maybe if he thought she was Protestant, he wouldn't be so judgemental. His disapproval unnerved her. She stirred the milk in her tea three times like the women in the Shelbourne, and her little finger pointed out the way the women had.

'Thank you, I do love the scones here, and cream is a real treat.'

'Do your aunt and uncle never have any?'

That simple question revealed how different their worlds were. 'No,' she said, controlling her anger and keeping her voice level. 'Times are hard for a lot of Irish. Not only do most not have cream, but they don't have milk. We have nothing. Most don't own their own home.'

He sat silent for a few minutes. 'I know. My friend, the one I met in the trenches, told me stories of how hard it was for him and his family. He sent all his wages back to Dublin. I wondered how they coped after his death.'

He was silent for a moment, a vacant look in his eyes before a slight grimace broke the trance. Veronica guessed maybe his memory had taken him back to France for a minute. 'I sent them money,' he said absently.

'Who?'

'His family. Not much, but hopefully they got it. I gave it to his commanding officer to give it to them, but I don't know if he sent it on.'

Harry was such a contradiction to Veronica.

Harry took her hand and said, 'Veronica. I need... I have to tell you...' he stopped.

'What's wrong?' she asked.

'Would you like more tea?'

Veronica had not noticed the waiter until he was refilling her teacup. A small bit of tea splashed onto the exposed wood of the table, just missing the crisp white tablecloth. 'Sorry,' he said, and leaned down to dab the tea. As he raised his head, he winked at Veronica.

She knew then this was one of her men. She was surprised that it unnerved rather than comforted her. She wondered guiltily if she looked too comfortable in the major's company.

'Sorry, Harry, you were saying?' She put her elbow on the table, tilting her smiling face at him.

'Nothing. I want to see you again soon, but I will have to go back to England for a while. My mother is sick, and the general said I could have a few days off.'

'Your general, is he in Dublin?' she asked casually. 'Some people might not welcome him, you know, after the executions in 1916.' She held her breath.

'He is only here for a short visit; he'll be gone before we know it.'

'Why?'

He held her gaze, sighing, and he said, 'I know, but let's not talk about politics.'

She wanted to snatch her gaze from his intense brown eyes. General Maxwell had overseen the executions of the leaders of the 1916 Easter Rising, and he left shortly after them. The killings had galvanised momentum in Ireland for all the people to come together to rebel against the British occupation.

Her mind whirled so fast she thought he would hear it ticking over the questions to ask. 'Do you not have work here?'

'No. No, I have to make a short visit.' He took her hand, and she let it fall limply in his. 'I promise I'll write to you.'

The waiter dropped a tray, causing a baby to wail, and another started to cry.

'Don't be sad, Veronica, I'll be back as soon as I can

after I see my mother. I know this is forward of me, but you are always on my mind.'

She looked at the grandfather clock by the door, uncomfortable with the openness of his feelings.

'Harry, that is, I feel the same.' This was her opportunity, 'I see in the papers soldiers going to rallies, or meetings about something or other, and soldiers get hurt.'

He leaned into her, taking her by surprise. 'I'll be fine, it's not that bad, we often get word from the RIC how many are expected.'

That's it. That's how they knew.

He looked at the clock on the wall behind her. 'Veronica, I must get back.'

'Me too, Mrs O'Reilly will wonder where I am. I only get an hour for lunch.'

'Mrs O'Reilly?'

Realising her mistake, she explained, 'Mrs O'Reilly is working in the shop as Mrs Sullivan is sick. She's her neighbour.'

She stopped herself saying anything more, as to not encourage questions. Harry got up and they parted ways at the entrance.

Abruptly he turned away from her and left.

She stood for a minute, watching him walking away, and then back. She had to tell Michael that General Maxwell was in the country.

Michael was waiting for her when she arrived back at Harcourt St.

'Well, did he say anything?'

She inhaled deeply, wondering where to start.

'Well, he is going to England for a few days, he says his mother is sick. And General Maxwell is here, but only for a few days.'

'What? That bastard? What is he doing here?'

'I don't know. I asked but he didn't say. But he mentioned someone in the RIC is informing them about upcoming rallies.'

Michael shook his head. 'No, he just wanted to let you know he was going.' And raised an eyebrow. 'He must be keen on you!'

He tapped a Waverley cigarette into his hand before lighting it. 'Good work, Veronica.'

The room shook with shouts mixed with a woman's screams, and the bookcase rocked. 'Christ, what was that?'

Veronica followed Michael downstairs and outside the building. On the street, a boy lay in a pool of blood. Women screamed and a woman beside the boy was wailing, rocking back and forth.

'My Johnny, my Johnny,' she wailed, 'he's only a child. You bastards shot him.'

Soldiers no older than the boy and white as ghosts pushed the crowd back with their guns. 'Go! Move!'

'Ye've no heart, what did he do?' sobbed the woman Veronica assumed was his mother.

Across the road from Harcourt St entrance an army vehicle burned.

Veronica watched the scene numbly, any sympathy she had felt for Harry draining away.

26

A quiet office made the week slower for Veronica. The paperwork about the anti-conscription rallies had been sent to the trade unions. Veronica was laying back, resting in her chair with her eyes half-closed, when men shouted and barged their way into the offices below. Mrs O'Reilly jumped out of her chair, knocking over the vase of flowers on her desk, water spilling onto the floor.

'Quick, Veronica, it's another raid. I'm sick of the soldiers coming in here whenever they want to.' She stubbed out her cigarette, looked around her desk and put some papers in the drawer, locking it and putting the key in her cardigan pocket.

'Give me those anti-conscription letters that weren't posted. I'll put them in the safe in Michael's room.' Veronica snatched the letters from Mrs O'Reilly and sprinted up the stairs. Frank O'Malley, a clerk who often helped Michael, stood in front of an open cabinet filing paperwork, humming a rendition of 'A Nation Once Again'.

'Frank, it's a raid, and I've anti-conscription letters here for the unions which we were going to post in the afternoon. We should put them in Michael's safe. It's hidden behind the bookcase, help me move it back a bit so that I can open the safe.'

'What, Christ!' Frank dropped his papers and helped her push the bookcase back, revealing the hidden safe Michael had installed. Frank grabbed the letters from her. He was breathing heavily as he bent to open the safe and shoved the letters inside. He spun the handle on the safe to shut it, and while it was still spinning, they tried to push the bookcase back in front of the safe. Veronica put her back against the bookshelf and shoved hard. Grunting they heaved the bookshelf and it slid in front of the safe as footsteps reached the top of the stairs. Frank took a book off the shelf and Veronica stared, absorbed in it. But it wasn't the DMP or soldiers on the landing. It was Timmy, one of the Sinn Féin bank clerks, speaking fast to Mrs O'Reilly.

'Dev has been arrested and loads of others have been arrested as well.' Breathless, Timmy held onto the doorframe with his hand and slightly bent over.

'Who was arrested?' Frank had dropped the book and run to Timmy.

'Dev,' he stopped, and took a deep breath. 'Dev and a few others – in fact, a lot of the Sinn Féin men.'

'What? How? Sweet mother of Jesus,' said Mrs O'Reilly blessing herself.

The office filled with people from the other offices all asking questions, 'Who's been arrested? Why have they been arrested?'

'I don't know much else. Michael hasn't been arrested, he sent word to us, and he is on his way here from his home,' Timmy said in a much more even voice. He pulled a chair out and stood on a desk, waving his arms to silence the crowd. He opened his mouth to speak, but before he could, Michael Collins pushed through the crowd.

'I bloody well told them all there were going to be arrests,' Michael said. 'The DMP had the names and addresses of all the Sinn Féin people, but no,' and he shook his head, his face red. 'They, he, De Valera decided not to believe me. They didn't think it would happen.'

Michael stomped from one side of the room to the other and didn't stop for a breath. 'They said they had enough evidence, claimed we were collaborating with the bloody Germans. The Germans, for Christ's sake, the Germans.' Michael paced the room, continuing to talk at a pace. Veronica found it difficult to catch everything he was saying.

'Disaster, this is a bloody disaster,' he went on. 'I told them. They knew about the arrests. The Brits think it will stop our anti-conscription rallies.'

'Michael, sorry to interrupt, but on what grounds? They can't walk up and arrest people for no reason,' Frank said.

'A few weeks ago, the RIC captured someone called Joseph Dowling drifting in a boat off the West Coast. He is a former prisoner of war with the Casement Brigade.'

Veronica pushed a little forward in between the shoulders of men who crammed into the office so she could hear clearly.

Michael continued, 'The British said the RIC captured him after the submarine he was in came ashore. Apparently, the RIC found a message he had in code. It was the

Germans saying they wished they had taken the rising in 1916 more seriously, and now they wanted to offer arms to the IRB for another rising.'

Timmy whispered to Mrs O'Reilly and Veronica, 'They arrested up to eighty people. They even went to Henrietta St and raided some of the pubs as well.'

'Listen, folks, we'll talk about this tomorrow,' Michael shouted. 'I'll think of something. Go back to your desks.'

When Veronica hurried home from work that evening, the streets were full of palpable unrest. Soldiers hung threateningly around Harcourt St. Veronica pulled her coat tight rushing past the soldiers. It may have been her imagination, but there didn't seem to be as many soldiers on the streets as a few months ago. It only meant one thing. The English were going to push for conscription in Ireland as there was a shortage of soldiers. Ireland would lose young men to the Crown fighting for them instead of against them. As she hurried along the quays, soldiers on the other side of the quay were marching back to The Royal Barracks.

When she entered Thomas St, she saw a package had arrived from her father's farm. Veronica viewed the regular arrival of parcels with caution, often wondering if there was a parcel for her to deliver again?

Betty still set a place at the table for Padraig, but the setting didn't have the same care as when she had first arrived. The once ruler-straight knife might be a bit crooked, or the teacup was forgotten. In the last few weeks, Betty seemed to have more life and this, Veronica presumed, was either the arrival of the warmer weather, or maybe Tom was wrong, and time the healer was working its sorcery on Betty.

'How was your day?' Betty asked, wiping her hands on her apron as she took the Delph from the side cupboard. 'Your grandmother gave these to me – they are very grand for our humble home,' she said as she traced her finger around the gold embossed cup rim. 'Your grandmother was well off. At first, they didn't approve of Tom, but then...' Her stew hissed, and Betty pulled it off the fire. She pushed her lank hair off her face. 'Sit down and eat it while it's hot.'

Veronica had never heard Betty talk with as much enthusiasm.

'Was it good?' Betty asked.

'Excuse me, but was what good?'

'Your day.'

Glad to be able to talk about it she said, 'Oh, Aunt Betty, De Valera, and others were arrested by the English,' and continued to tell Betty what happened that afternoon. 'Michael said they might be sent to a prison in Wales with all the other Irish prisoners.'

Betty sat beside her, putting her arm around Veronica.

'Go on, love. Eat your dinner, pushing it around the plate won't solve the problem. There's nothing you can do. When you go to work tomorrow, you'll see they'll have everything sorted. They can't keep them locked up.'

Not long later, Tom arrived home and threw the newspaper on the table, its headline *Flu Kills Thousands in the Tenements*.

'Look at that. You'd think we had enough to worry

about.' He slumped on his armchair, pulling off his boots. He walked over to the women in his socks that were more a patchwork of different darns of wool than a pair of knitted socks. They all stood to read the paper.

Betty sighed. 'Sure, look at their conditions. They are filthy. What hope do they have?'

Tom rubbed the stubble on his chin. 'Sure they've no food. Everyone needs good food when ill.'

It seemed that with poverty, the people couldn't hide from the reaper.

'Sit down at the table. Tom, Veronica has something to tell you. Just eat your dinner as she tells you.'

Veronica told him the events of the day. When she had finished speaking the cuckoo clock struck six o'clock. Tom reached for his cigarette, undid his waistcoat and inhaled hard on his cigarette to get as much nicotine as he could, as cigarettes were not immune to rationing. He looked at his yellow fingers and said, 'It'll be all right. I'm sure they will let them go. I know we are making progress and we have this bloody flu to worry about as well.'

'Tea, Tom, let's eat and not think about this or the flu, and let's be thankful Veronica is here.'

Tom nodded thanks to Betty as she put bread and tea in front of him. When she went back to the stove to get her tea, Tom leaned over the table and whispered to Veronica, 'Please be careful, keep along the quays the way I showed.'

The empty place setting on the table bore into Veronica like a hot ironmonger's rod.

Tom stirred his tea four times in a clockwise direction. With care, he spread the butter on his bread, making sure it was even and thin to every corner covering the brown crust.

'What are you two talking about?'

Veronica jumped at the sound of Betty's voice; she hadn't heard her come back into the room.

'Nothing, love, Veronica was telling me about her friend Bridget and how she is going to write to her later tonight.'

That night she wrote two letters, the first to Bridget and the second to Harry.

27

On the second Saturday of June, Veronica took the train to Kingstown to meet Harry in Gilligan's tearooms. When she had sent the message to him at the barracks suggesting another day out, she wasn't too sure if he would get it. Every evening she'd called to Mrs Sullivan's shop to see if there was a reply. The response was quick. He'd accepted and suggested they meet at Gilligan's tearooms in Kingstown. Veronica had looked forward to the train journey on her own, she blended in with the day-trippers. A mother and son sat opposite her. He wore pristine blue shorts and white socks, a far cry from the clothes worn by the starving children she saw running in the streets of Dublin. When the train arrived at Kingstown, the woman nodded goodbye to Veronica as she gathered up her bonnet and coat. During the short walk to Gilligan's from the station, she watched the boats bob on the choppy sea, and seagulls swoop and dive, gliding in the wind.

Gilligan's was quiet. Veronica sat at a window seat. The sea was the colour of treacle under the dark clouds. It wasn't a day for mothers and prams. As she stared at her reflection in the window, she thought she was looking at a different person. Her hair was pinned neat, and the red lipstick made her look mature. Behind her, the door swung open with a gust of wind, followed by a mother pushing a pram with a crying baby. The wind howled outside. Veronica thought how disappointed the mother and boy she had seen on the train must be as it wasn't a day for the seaside. The young mother pushed her pram near the fire, shaking the wet from her coat before sitting down to coo at the baby.

'Do you want a cup of tea, love?'

The waitress startled Veronica. 'No, thank you,' she said.

Harry passed the window, and he had a notebook in his hand to shield himself from the wind and spray of water from the sea as it crashed onto the pier. Veronica recognised it as the notebook that had fallen from his coat pocket when they were last there. When he entered the waitress eyed him with suspicion or disdain. But Harry didn't seem to notice and walked to Veronica's table, his limp not as pronounced. His brown smiling eyes spoke that he was glad to see her. 'How was your journey? I hope you hadn't any trouble on the train,' he said. He took off his cap and rubbed his hands through his thick brown hair. 'I was visiting a friend here and took the earlier train.' He placed the notebook on the table. It was like the tan leather Amity notebook Veronica's father kept in his study. Her father's had a small lock on it, but Harry's didn't.

Veronica rubbed her hand. 'No, it was fine,' she said and looked down. 'Well, there were soldiers on the train, and they searched a few young men. They were younger than me. I admit it was scary. It was like they were looking for something.' She held her breath to watch him, hoping he would say something about the soldiers and their work.

'Let's not talk about those things. I ...' Harry stopped and looked at her. He took her hands in his. 'I've thought of you every day since the first time we met.'

His hands were soft, warm and clean; she thought of her uncle's dirty, hard-skinned arthritic hands and struggled not to pull away. She would have to try another approach.

'If only things were different,' she said, composing herself to look directly at him. She saw an emotion in his eyes, an emotion she wasn't familiar with, something profound, and it disturbed her.

'We'll have tea,' he said after a moment. 'I think it's safe here, and I've longed to spend the day away from everything.'

'What do you mean, safe here?' *Safe from whom? What did he mean by 'everything'?*

Ignoring her, he waved at the waitress. 'Could we order? The baking smells wonderful.'

'Yes, sir.'

'Could we have a pot of tea?'

The girl left, and the baby cried from the opposite side of the room as the mother rocked the pram waiting for her tea to arrive. A rattle of cups interrupted Veronica as the girl put the blue-flowered cups on the table. There was a small crease in the tablecloth which she smoothed out before placing the matching blue sugar and milk jug on the table.

She had to do something fast; she was gaining his trust now.

He lifted her chin and withdrew his hand quickly before removing a loose strand of hair from her face. She thought he had been about to lean over the table to kiss her. She shook away, her pounding heart unsteady.

'Sorry, did I startle you? I didn't mean to overstep my boundaries.'

He spoke softly, his voice caressing her body. She was shocked, shocked that she didn't feel repulsed, and confused. Something stirred inside her.

The waitress coughed. 'Sorry, sir and madam. It's extremely windy, so we're closing early.' She didn't look at Harry as she spoke but pointed to the door. It was more of a command than a statement.

Veronica watched Harry tuck his notebook safely inside his coat pocket.

'I'll walk you to the train station. It's a shame our outing was cut short like this. I'm really sorry, but I can't give you a lift back,' Harry said, and he reached to fix the collar on her coat. 'I've come with a driver, and I have some business on the way back to Dublin.'

A squeal of laughter came from behind them. 'Quick, the train is coming.' A young couple ran past, holding hands to the station.

Veronica said, 'I'm sure it'll be all right.' She had to find out what he'd meant earlier about it not being safe. Did he know what the soldiers had been looking for?

'Veronica, I hear the train. I've to take the car.' He leaned into her to kiss her on the cheek but stopped when a man coughed and said, 'Sir.'

A soldier stood beside them. 'Sir, we have what you

were looking for.' As he glanced at Veronica, a shiver ran through her body.

His English accent was harsh compared to Harry's, and his face was equally as rough, as if he hadn't shaved in days.

Harry nodded, turning to Veronica, and said, 'I must go, Veronica. I'll write.'

'Please do, Harry,' she said, and then took a chance. 'It must be important if they sent a car out here for you?'

Harry cocked his head and smiled at her. 'You are a funny thing, Veronica, why would you wonder about those things?' The soldier coughed again.

Harry looked at him before turning back to Veronica. He said, 'I've really got to go.'

'Sir, please hurry, General Maxwell said it's important. Do you have the paperwork he wanted?'

The soldier walked to a waiting army car to open the passenger door for Harry. As he got in, a piece of paper dropped from his pocket. When the car was a safe distance, she ran to retrieve it before the wind took it out to sea.

It was a torn piece of paper, the top half gone.

Rallies Cork, Sligo

Fr Flanagan

That's all she could make out. On her way back to Dublin on the train, she thought about the notebook. She needed to see Michael as soon as possible.

On Monday morning, she knocked on Michael's door and entered, not waiting for an answer. Michael sat at his desk.

'Here, Michael,' she said and handed him the note. 'I

met the major in Kingstown, but a soldier came to pick him up. He said General Maxwell wanted to see him and asked whether he had "the papers" ready. And this fell from his pocket.'

Michael studied it for a moment. 'They must know about the rallies we are organising in Cork and Sligo next weekend.' He sat back in the chair. 'But I don't know why they have Fr O'Flanagan's name.' He picked up the phone, and while he waited for the operator to answer, Veronica told him about the notebook.

Michael put the phone down, and thought for a minute. 'Veronica, I'll get back to you in a while. I've to speak to Fr O'Flanagan first.'

As Veronica left the office, Michael said, 'Wait, Veronica – thanks. I know it's hard, with Eddie still in prison, but you're doing a great job, and we really appreciate it.'

Three days later an unexpected visitor called to the office. Veronica hadn't seen Fr O'Flanagan for months.

His clothes were a little looser and his hair sparser.

'I was asking Mrs O'Reilly the other day if she could spare you for a few weeks. I need some help with shorthand and typing.'

'I'd gladly help. I enjoyed my time with you and Mrs Brown.'

'It's in Roscommon,' said Fr O'Flanagan.

'Eh, how long, Father? It's not that I'm—'

'It's only for a few weeks, maybe a month, and we'll leave at the end of the week. What do you think? Michael didn't want me to take you, but I need your help. We have a few anti-conscription rallies, and I need letters typed and help to deliver the posters. The bishops and priests are going to tell their congregation to resist conscription.'

'I didn't mean to be ungrateful, Father. I'd love to help.'

'Good girl.'

When Fr O'Flanagan left, the smell of his cigar smoke lingered in the office long after he was gone.

Roscommon was a place she had never been to, and the more she thought about it, a few weeks away from the capital would be good. As her father always said, 'A change is as good as a rest.' She went to Michael's office.

'Yes, Veronica, how can I help you?'

'Fr O'Flanagan wants me to go to Roscommon with him, but what about Major Fairfax? I forgot to say the major mentioned that "things have not been as safe as they were", and when I was going home, a soldier came over to him at the train station. I said to him, it must be important for a soldier to come in a car to pick him up, but he ignored me. But I thought he looked troubled.'

'Write to him. Keep him sweet. Don't tell him you are going to Roscommon. Tell him your mother is sick and you're going home for a few weeks. We'll keep an eye on him. We have to stop the bastards with their conscription madness.' He thumped his fist on the desk. 'Write him a note and post it to the barracks, and put the return address as Mrs Sullivan's shop.'

Veronica nodded and thought about the major on the way home. Her day in Kingstown with him drinking tea like it was normal. At home, Veronica packed her suitcase while Betty fussed, making some bread for Veronica to take to Roscommon.

As the train moved across the countryside from Broadstone to Roscommon, Veronica relaxed into the soft seat, so different from her travel on the trains before. Fr O'Flanagan had met her at Broadstone to give her a first-class ticket, telling her the directions to Sacred Heart Church and that Fr Carney would take her on to Murray's, a public house that had lodgings.

When Veronica arrived in Roscommon, the evening sun was still warm. She carried her small suitcase on the two-minute walk to the Sacred Heart Church. There were few people on the streets, and the air smelled clean. No menacing soldiers were patrolling, and there weren't any children chasing each other. She relaxed in the quietness. It was good to stroll the streets without having to keep a watchful eye out for trouble. She looked at the piece of paper Fr O'Flanagan had given her. He had drawn a little map for her: right, right again and then left for two hundred yards down Abbey St to the church to meet Fr Carney.

The Presbytery house was a large square grey stone building, home to Fr Carney, and his housekeeper Mrs Long.

Fr Carney greeted Veronica with the warmth of an old friend. 'You'll like it here, Veronica, the summer has been kind to us. Fr O'Flanagan isn't arriving for a few days so rest yourself and take a walk around our castle.'

Later Fr Carney took Veronica to Murray's pub. For the few free days before Fr O'Flanagan's arrival, she enjoyed the tranquillity of Roscommon, but that was soon to change.

28

After her first day typing for Fr O'Flanagan in the rectory, Veronica walked back to Murray's. She tucked the letters inside her coat to post on her way home. He had said, 'Be careful, Veronica, the RIC are following me everywhere. If anyone tries to stop you, just nod and politely excuse yourself.'

He stopped to inhale his pipe, but the tobacco had gone out, and he struck a match. Before he lit the tobacco, he said, 'I'm going to Athlone now to a meeting in Hayes hotel. And Veronica, remember, they don't care that you're a woman, they will treat you just the same as if you were a man.'

As Veronica walked across the square to the public house, she slowed and narrowed her eyes as in the distance three RIC men approached. To her right, a cottage's front door was open, and she ran in hoping they hadn't seen her. She was in the living room with an old woman sat in a wooden rocking chair, staring into a blazing fire used for cooking. The woman's face was lined with wrinkles that spoke of hardship only a woman of her years could have.

She nodded at Veronica and lifted her thin bony finger to her lips with a knowing smile.

Silent, Veronica looked out the small window as the RIC men passed, the guns hanging from their belts rattling as they moved with determination. Veronica watched them pass, inhaling slow, silent breaths. The old woman went back to staring into the fire. Veronica left the cottage and moved down Abbey St back to Murray's pub, pulling her coat tight around her. Adrenaline rushing through her veins, she ran up Castle St to Murray's, careful to keep her distance but close enough so she could see them ahead. They went into the police station. Gathering pace, she ran past the station, lifting her long skirt; her coat opened, flapping as she ran. She entered the pub, and the men at the bar gave her a brief, fleeting look. They were still in their work clothes, not wanting anything to distract their drinking time before they set off home. Running upstairs, she took two steps at a time.

In her room, Veronica slumped on a chair beside the unlit fire, taking a minute to breathe normally again. She sat for a few minutes, wondering how she would contact Fr O'Flanagan. He was still at his meeting in Athlone. She reached for her matches to light the lamp, but before she could strike a match, there was a loud banging on the door.

'Open up,' said a man, his accent rough.

She didn't move, breathing quietly.

'Open up, I said. God damn it, bitch, open up.'

The RIC must have followed her here from the station. Veronica walked to the other side of her room. Taking a deep breath and composing herself, she opened the door.

'What do you want?' she asked with false bravado, to a red-faced RIC man.

He pushed her back into her room. She hoped her sparse room held little interest to him.

'Are you Fr O'Flanagan's secretary?'

Veronica didn't answer him, just looked at him coldly.

He snorted. 'No need to answer, we know you are. Com' on, you are to come with us. Move.'

Slowly, Veronica stepped across the hall, the flicker of light falling ominously on the floor. Walking down the dark narrow hallway, an impatient soldier pushed the barrel of his gun into her back, quickening her step. In the pub, the men sitting on the stools along the bar were silent, all drinking ceased. Outside Murray's pub on Castle St, two green-uniformed RIC men were waiting. One clutched her arm tight, forcing her to walk fast. They crossed the square, not saying a word. They walked down Castle St onto Abbey St towards the Sacred Heart Church. Curtains twitched as they passed. Men stood in doorways with supportive eyes that followed her down the street. They went towards the church, breaking the wooden gate as they entered the garden behind the parish house. Without knocking, they walked into the rectory, confronting an open-mouthed Fr Carney in the living room.

'Take us to Fr O'Flanagan's room.'

He dropped his newspaper and scuttled down the hall. The RIC barged past him into Fr O'Flanagan's room.

Veronica stood in the corner silently, watching them. One soldier emptied the contents of a cupboard while the other read Fr O'Flanagan's paperwork, discarding some and putting others in a separate pile. They ripped the curtains from the window rail over his writing desk, and light flooded the room, but it was still hard to see.

One man shouted out of the room, 'Send the housekeeper up.'

Mrs Long, the housekeeper, appeared trembling at the door, tears falling down her face.

'Light some candles.'

Mrs Long didn't move.

'Now!'

She ran to the small hallstand on the landing, taking the matches, her shaking hands failing to strike the match the first time. She finally lit the lamps in the room, and the RIC could now scrutinise the paperwork. They picked up page after page, dropping each one when they had finished looking at it.

'Look at these,' one said and threw some documents at the other, believing them to be important.

'What are you smirking at?' barked one at Veronica.

Veronica shrugged her shoulders and didn't answer. They were the ordnance survey maps Fr O'Flanagan had bought at an auction of a priest who had died. Fr O'Flanagan had an interest in Irish place-names, and he studied maps. Bookshelves were cleared, the books left lying on the wooden floor, and drawers turned upside down scattering their contents. Veronica watched, saying nothing, as the younger of the RIC investigated a jug she knew Fr O'Flanagan kept money in. Finding five pounds, he put it in his pocket. The youngest of the RIC men objected, but nobody listened. As the men were leaving, one of them saw Fr O'Flanagan's suitcase.

'Bring it to the barracks and open it there when we have him,' the older man said, but his suggestion was ignored, and the suitcase was opened and emptied, Fr O'Flanagan's vestments thrown on the floor.

'Take that typewriter over there on the desk. We will look at the ribbon to see if we can get any information from it.'

A large hand gripped Veronica's arm. 'Where is the priest?' the older RIC man barked.

'I don't know,' she said in as measured a tone as she could manage.

The man stared down at her. His breath smelled of beer and tobacco. He'd probably helped himself to some beer when he was in Murray's.

'Leave town now. Just because you are a woman, it will not save you being put up against a wall and shot.'

With that warning, the men left. The house shuddered as they slammed the front door after them. Fr Carney came into the room white and shaken. 'Oh my, are you hurt, dear?'

Veronica said, 'I'm taking the car,' and ran to the kitchen, not noticing the smell of burning bread or steaming kettle on the stove.

Fr Carney followed her. 'Veronica, you can't take the car, surely you can't drive.'

She saw what she was looking for near the back door: the keys to the parish car. Veronica ignored Fr Carney, grabbed the keys and ran to the car. It was a Ford Model R similar to Dr Reynolds's car. She fumbled with the keys, and to her relief, the car started. Veronica was thankful. Dr Reynolds had let her drive his car on her birthday. Now it was a necessity to save a man's life. The full moon bathed the road in silver light guiding her along the roads as she didn't get time to light the oil lamps on the outside of the car.

She finally reached Athlone. It was easy to spot Hayes. She stopped the car in front of the hotel trying to catch her breath, as she felt she hadn't taken a breath on the forty-minute drive since leaving Roscommon. She knew she looked a sight running into the hotel, her hair windswept and her face flushed; she ignored the stares from guests. Assuming the meeting was in the bar, she followed the signs and stood in the doorway surveying the room. As usual, it was occupied only by men, but not the type of men who were in Murray's pub. Their clothes were new, cleaner, and they all had concentrated looks upon their faces.

Fr O'Flanagan sat at the end of the bar with four men. He saw her and excused himself from the men.

'Veronica, why are you here? What happened?'

'The RIC came,' Veronica blurted, dropping into the nearest armchair. 'They went through your documents and ransacked your room. Fr Carney was very shaken; I came to you straight away. They also threatened me.' It was only then that Veronica started to shake.

'Get this lady a glass of water,' he said, slow and measured, to the waiter hovering nearby. He paced the room, puffing on his pipe.

'Right, we'll return to Roscommon.'

It was late when they returned to Roscommon. Fr O'Flanagan didn't speak as he checked his room to see what was missing. He looked in the jug lying on the ground among his vestments thrown in a heap.

He threw the mug on the ground, and the fine china shattered into pieces on the floorboards.

Veronica gasped at his anger.

He grabbed his coat and hat. 'I'm going to Sgt Mulvaney now – let's see what he has to say about his thugs taking my money. Come on, Veronica.'

Within minutes Fr O'Flanagan thumped on the station door and entered without invitation. The sparse room with only a chair and table was filled with heat. Sgt Mulvaney sat in a chair in front of a fire, his socks lying beside his unlaced shoes as he warmed his feet. He jumped when Fr O'Flanagan thumped on the desk, 'Your men terrified my secretary, and stole my money.'

Sgt Mulvaney put on his shoes with no socks. 'Well, I'd hardly say they terrified your secretary! She doesn't look too frightened.'

She shivered as he cast his eye up and down her.

Fr O'Flanagan leaned on the table, his face red, 'And they took my money.'

'Can you prove that?' He now buttoned his black jacket, and pointed to his stripes on his sleeve. 'See these, I'm in charge.' He eyeballed Fr O'Flanagan. 'Now, be off with ye, before I arrest ye both.' He stood a few inches in front of Fr O'Flanagan, their noses practically touching, 'I'm in charge,' he said again and laughed. 'Go on be off with ye, you've no power. I'm the law.'

Fr O'Flanagan did not flinch, but nodded to Veronica to follow him. Outside, the mottled grey sky of morning seeped across the sky as they walked in silence to the rectory.

'Veronica take my bed and rest. I've work to do.'

'Father, I know I will find it hard to sleep.'

'No, lie down, I will go into my study, I need to think.'

Veronica woke as daylight flooded the room, surprised she had slept. Voices filtered into her room. Straining her ears, she heard Fr O'Flanagan talking to a boy. She had not undressed and standing she smoothed her wrinkled skirt to look for them. It was a young man who spoke with a lisp.

She followed the voices into Fr O'Flanagan's room. 'Veronica, come in. This is Thomas Moore. Continue, Thomas, this is Veronica, my secretary. Sit down, Veronica. Thomas was telling me that some RIC men called to his home very early this morning to talk to his brother, who is in the RIC. They went out to the yard to chat. Thomas followed them outside but made sure he was hidden, and he said they talked about the stolen money.'

Thomas interrupted Fr O'Flanagan. 'Father, sorry but there is more. Mickey Brady, also in the RIC said he was in the barracks and overheard someone say that the soldiers want to shoot you. They – the soldiers and my brother

– think if you are shot then the anti-conscription rallies will stop.'

She looked to see Fr O'Flanagan's reaction, but he calmly puffed on his pipe, his face impassive, not giving anything away.

Thomas put his cap on. 'I've to go. I'll be missed. It's mart day, and I've to bring a bull to the mart.'

'Yes, son, you go, don't worry about me. I'll figure something out. Let me think about it. Veronica, you go as well.'

Veronica returned to her room in Murray's Pub and lay on the bed, fully clothed, closing her eyes. Before sleep took hold, there was a knock at her door.

She sat up searching for something to defend herself with. She grabbed the poker.

'Veronica,' said Fr O'Flanagan.

She dropped the poker by her side as he entered. 'Are you going to kill me with that?' he asked, smiling. He tapped his pipe on his hand and threw the burnt tobacco into the fire, looking at it as if expecting it to ignite, but it remained lifeless. After a moment he said, 'We'll return to Dublin. Michael sent word that he wants us back. You'll be glad to know he got word from London that they think the English are going to stop this conscription nonsense.'

Veronica closed her eyes, relief flooding her. Roscommon was more dangerous than Dublin.

'How was your trip, Veronica? I hope you're not too

shaken. Fr O'Flanagan was here a few minutes ago and told us what happened,' said Mrs O'Reilly.

'I'm fine now. It seems many people are in worse situations around the country. I thought it was only in Dublin. But honestly, I'm fine, Mrs O'Reilly.'

Veronica's life had changed so much. She looked at Mrs O'Reilly. *Did she have a simple life outside the work they did?*

Michael walked into the office, nodded to Veronica and put a pile of scribbled notes on Mrs O'Reilly's desk.

'Would you and Veronica type these for me? When you're finished, Veronica, please bring them into my office to sign.'

The letters didn't take long to type, and Veronica brought them into Michael, who furiously scribbled his signature. He had no sooner scribbled his name, and he was signing the next document. His ability to scan the text so quickly for mistakes amazed Veronica, and many times he would say, 'Look, a missing capital letter', or 'that is spelled wrong'.

He signed the last letter giving it one last scan before sitting back in his leather chair and looking pensively at Veronica.

'I heard you got a fright in Roscommon.'

'It was scary, but we didn't stay long after that. And I had to look after my aunt for a bit when we got back because she thought she was getting the flu, even though it is one of the hottest summers I can remember. Aunt Betty is quite fragile.'

Michael nodded. 'I heard. I've news on the major

– General Maxwell had sent him back to London for a bit, but I don't know what for, nor if he is coming back.'

Veronica nodded, her face impassive, hoping it didn't betray the sinking feeling in her stomach at this news.

29

November 1918

Summer passed, and autumn was mild, so nobody was prepared when November surprised everyone with an early scattering of snow. Luckily it didn't last, but the cold of winter was to stay. Veronica blew on her fingers, hoping they would stop hurting. She put them as near to the flames in the fire as she dared without burning them. The weather had determined that her lunchtime walk was shorter than usual. It was cold and wet, but she was fed up stuck inside as the gloomy winter days were so short. After twenty minutes outside, Veronica could not stand the cold anymore and returned to work.

'Veronica, did you hear?' Mrs O'Reilly came into the office shaking the rain from her hat and dislodging a dried, withered oak leaf. 'It's so blustery out there. Dear, did you hear?'

'Hear what?'

'The war, I think the war is over,' said Mrs O'Reilly as she slumped in her chair and loosened her coat.

'I was wondering why there were so many people on the

236

streets. I saw a few groups of men chatting loudly, but the rain was so bad I didn't linger to see what the excitement was about.' Veronica thought of Harry. Maybe he had been sent back to France and killed. A sadness overcame her. He had not been a bad person. She had seen that from the way he spoke about the men in the trenches, and how he gave sweets to the children on the streets. That was in the past, she reminded herself.

'Thank God for that. I hope it's a good thing for us. We've got to keep up our fight. We did so well in the by-elections in the summer, we've to be ready for the next election. But God knows when that will be,' Mrs O'Reilly said, getting up from her desk. 'Can you hear that, Veronica? Quick, open the window.'

The two women looked out of the open window. Crowds of men, women and children in the street ran towards St Stephen's Green waving the Union Jack, cheering and clapping. A few men stood aside, watching the celebrations silently with disdainful looks on their faces.

Mrs O'Reilly closed the window. 'Right Veronica, back to work.' She shuddered, pulling the cardigan tight. 'Do you know there will be some trouble. I can feel it in my bones.'

Mrs Moore ran into the room, stopping to catch her breath. 'Did you hear, the war is over, and they're upon Sackville St singing "Rule Britannia". Thank God, at last, our boys will come home. Too many have come home in coffins, or not at all.'

Veronica nodded. 'That's so true, at least we never gave into conscription.' She briefly thought of Harry again.

His letter was still in the bottom of her music box in her bedroom. He had written to her from England. Shropshire. She never wrote back. He'd said he had to stay to mind his sick mother, and she told Michael. But she never told Michael his other words, *I miss you, even though we've only known each other a short while. I was so comfortable in your silence.* She thought it strange, *in your silence*, but she took it as a compliment. Secretly she wished she could have seen more of him, but she never shared this with anyone. Harry had drawn a seagull at the bottom of the page and a yacht, a sweet reference to their time in Kingstown.

'Veronica, did you hear me?' said Mrs O'Reilly, 'I'm going upstairs to see what they are saying about the news.' She left the office humming a rendition of *Silent Night*.

The phone rang continuously in Michael's office next door, but he was out on business.

Veronica was glad they had no phone to disturb her thoughts. News of the end of the war was on everyone's lips and minds.

'Veronica, Liam asked me to get you to type these,' said Mrs Moore. 'I've to leave work early, and he wants them done.' She gave Veronica the letters, but before Mrs Moore could finish, Liam himself ran into the office shouting, 'Students from Trinity,' he stopped for breath, 'the students are planning an attack.'

'Attack where?'

'Mrs O'Reilly, they plan to attack these offices. Here, these offices,' he shouted as he threw his arms around.

'Seriously, Liam, where did you hear such nonsense?'

'My friend called me at lunchtime, and I didn't believe

him. He works in a restaurant and often he'll hear things and pass them onto me. He is a waiter in the vegetarian restaurant on College St, the one where all the Trinity students go, and he heard a group of students saying they will attack because they fear Catholics are getting too strong. They said Protestants would lose their power. He heard them say this at lunchtime when the war was declared over. They think today is the right time.'

'What are they going to do? Throw books at us?' asked Mrs Moore.

Liam sat on the chair in front of the fire. 'Look, all I know is, they have recruited officers in the British training corps to help them, and some of them are experienced grenade throwers. We'll wait, nothing else we can do. On the way here, I heard a mob celebrating, singing "Rule Britannia"! Bloody song. Sorry, ladies, but it makes my blood boil.'

Mrs O'Reilly coughed behind Veronica. 'Michael told me to tell you all to wait here. Nobody goes home. He said it's too dangerous on the streets. People are drunk, and there may be a fight between the Jackeens and the anti-British side.'

'Well, what can we do? Veronica, be a dear and make tea for everyone and ask upstairs if anyone else wants some?' said Mrs O'Reilly. 'I think I have some biscuits in my drawer. Sure really, what can a bunch of students do?'

The day darkened. Lights were switched on, and everyone waited.

'I think all of this is unnecessary,' whispered Mrs O'Reilly to Veronica as the clock on the wall chimed

7 p.m. Suddenly the window shattered, and a stone landed near Veronica's feet, sending glass all over the office floor. Loud shouts came from the street below with sounds of glass shattering in the offices above and below them. Sticks and bits of timber came through the windows.

Eibhlin ran into the office, shaking and white. Veronica and Eibhlin moved back to the wall in between the filing cabinets.

Men from the bank downstairs came into the room. 'It's safer here,' a banker said. 'All the windows below are broken, and some lads are kicking the front door. We've moved all the furniture from the bank in front of it, so it should be secure.'

Veronica's heart was beating uncontrollably. The shouting outside was deafening. Another window shattered, and she ducked as some glass flew past, missing her face by inches. Trembling, she jumped behind an upturned desk.

Michael strode into the room.

'Michael, thank God you are here!'

He threw his coat on the ground. 'I came as soon as I heard. Tell me, Liam, what do you know and has anyone been hurt?'

Nobody answered him.

He shouted orders to move furniture while pushing a bookcase to the windows, books and files falling on the ground.

'Turn off the damned lights!'

'Move the furniture!'

'Keep the women covered.'

A composite of orders reverberated in the office.

A grenade flew through the window, landing at Veronica's feet.

When it didn't explode, Veronica picked it up without thinking and threw it out the nearest window.

Michael shouted at her, 'That was bloody dangerous.'

She hadn't thought of the consequences of handling a grenade. Sweat dripped down her face and she found it hard to catch her breath.

The office shook with a loud bang, followed by a plume of smoke outside the window. Trembling, Veronica helped Eibhlin to move the other filing cabinet in front of the window. It was impossible to distinguish where the screams came from.

Barney, from the bank, said, 'I've been on the phone to a contact in Dublin Castle, and they won't do anything to stop them. We'll have to sort this ourselves.' He grabbed a chair to block the window as the relentless flying stones and wood came through the window. Men helped to turn a table upside down, knocking papers to the ground. Typewriters broke upon hitting the floor.

Veronica hid behind a desk, not just out of fear, but also for protection from the flying glass. The attack lasted for about an hour, and then the room went quiet.

'Do you think they are gone?' Mrs O'Reilly whispered. The room was dark.

Nobody answered her.

'Veronica?' Mrs O'Reilly said a little louder, concern in her voice.

Michael answered, 'She's here beside me. I'll look and see if they are gone.'

Michael lit a match, and the shouts began, and missiles flew in through the window landing on the shattered glass.

'Jesus Christ, have the fools no homes to go to?!'

'They are leaving,' Barney shouted over the noise of celebrations coming from St Stephen's Green.

As they started to lift the office furniture away from the exits and doors, Barney said, 'Jesus, wait, more people are coming down the street.'

Crowds of people on the streets sang 'Rule Britannia', waving the Union Jack harder in defiance as they passed their offices. They approached the entrance, but the locked door was enough to keep them out.

Everything went quiet. Then, one person below flung a stone at the building; another followed this and then another. As a stone hurtled past Veronica, she pressed hard into the wooden floor.

A voice boomed from the building across the street, 'Go on, yer British bastards.'

By eight o'clock, the last few hours began to affect people. 'Listen, will ye stop, for God's sake, everyone be quiet,' said Liam, jumping to his feet.

Michael and Liam looked out the window, 'Shh everybody. Michael, hear that?'

The only sound was from Liam walking on the broken glass. He looked out through the shattered glass. 'They could be back, but I can't see anything. They broke the lamps on the street.'

'Don't turn on the lights for a while. We'll wait,' suggested one man from the bank.

Ambulance sirens whirred past.

'Turn on the lights now,' commanded Michael.

The office was a mess, there were bits of wood from chairs, and every window shattered.

'Is anyone hurt?' Michael asked.

'No, I'm fine,' came a chorus of answers.

The clock chimed nine o'clock. Veronica couldn't believe that so much damage and chaos had ensued in such a short space of time.

'Bloody travesty,' Liam said.

Women and men sat on any remaining furniture, exhausted, confused, and outraged.

A man tapped Veronica on the shoulder. 'It's late. I'll walk you home. I've my bike, but I'll walk with you.'

'God, James, I didn't see you there.' It was James Sheridan, who she hadn't seen since the day in the woods with the gun. She was unsure how she felt about him. 'It's... I suppose it's good to see a familiar face. What are you doing here?'

'I meant to call on you. Eddie said you were here. It was your father who got me the job at the bank. Jesus, I'm only here for three days.' He laughed. 'It beats Virginia.'

'Is Eddie out of jail? I wrote to him, but I've got no replies, and don't know if he is well or, worse, even dead.' Her voice lowered to a whisper, and she felt the blood drain from her face.

'Veronica, he is alive, but it's an awful place. He broke his hand. A silly accident, he fell down the metal stairs and landed on his hand the wrong way. It has mended well, and Veronica don't look so worried, he's fine. Before

I came to Dublin, I went to see him. He said you had been writing to him, and he did reply, but the prison guards take the letters to see if there is anything in them that might pass on information and I don't think they post them anyway. I told him I was coming to Dublin and he gave me this without any of the prison guards seeing it.' He gave Veronica a crumpled piece of paper.

She grabbed it from James with shaking hands.

'I can hardly see any of the words.'

She held it under a light.

Dearest Veronica,

I hope you are well and enjoying Dublin. Sorry I couldn't write back as I broke my hand in a silly fall. I've met lots of young men my age, but there are some younger, as young as fifteen! I did get your letters, but a lot of what you wrote had been blacked out, so it is hard to get the mood from them. It is tough here, but that is to be expected, I've met good friends, and we help each other out. One of the prison guards let us have a sing-song and a dance at Christmas, so it's not all bad.

Love

Eddie.

Veronica reread the letter looking for a hidden message, anything at all.

'Come on, Veronica, I'll walk you home. There's nothing

you can do,' James said, putting on a long black coat. 'My ma got me this when I told her I was going to work in a bank. She was delighted when I got such a decent job. God if she only knew!'

30

The following day, Westminster announced a general election for 14 December, 1918. Repairs in the Sinn Féin offices started without delay, and campaigning began with a feverish pace and accelerated with the news that more people had a chance to vote. For the first time in Britain and Ireland, women over thirty could vote. Also, the rule that men had to own a property to cast a vote was removed, so men over the age of twenty-one also had the right to vote. The days and weeks before the election, the staff at Harcourt St worked late every night. Posters and leaflets were printed, and speeches typed with haste. Nobody complained about the extra hours.

When the election was announced, Michael called a meeting for everyone working in Harcourt St including the bank workers, the secretaries and all of Sinn Féin.

When Michael had everyone's attention, he said, 'Listen, people, we have to win as many seats as we can. We can do this. Our independence from the crown is becoming a reality. We need to get as many men elected as MPs as we can. This is our country. We are Irishmen, not English, so if we can keep going like we have been and gather votes, you never know what will happen. I know the papers say we will never beat out the Irish Parliamentary Party, but our freedom depends on this election. The people of Ireland deserve our best efforts.'

With those words, Veronica and Mrs O'Reilly worked steadily for the next few weeks. On Friday evening in the first week of December, the women were exhausted.

'I can't wait for Christmas to get back to Cavan,' Veronica said, hoping Eddie might be there.

Mrs O'Reilly leaned forward and frowned as if looking at her for the first time. 'I don't know why you don't have a beau. You have lovely cheekbones and don't look like you have been working incessantly for three weeks now. You are so pretty, but I have never seen you with anyone. Are you not sweet on anyone?'

Veronica's cheeks burned. Memories flooded back to the night James Sheridan had walked her home from Harcourt St. Her initial relief of meeting a familiar face in all the mayhem of the attack by Trinity students had soon returned to the usual hostility towards him. James's arrogance and resentment towards Veronica, in turn, also returned. They had walked in an uncomfortable silence most of the way to Thomas St, interrupted by the clatter of his wonky bicycle wheel on the cobbled streets. At Thomas St, she had offered her hand in thanks.

She closed her eyes, remembering how he had taken her hand and pulled her towards him. He'd brushed his lips against hers, and she had slapped him. He had jumped back, laughing, and said, 'You're a feisty one,' before he hopped onto his bicycle and rode into the night. Her hand had stung, but her pride was hurt more. She had run inside, slamming the door behind her.

'Veronica, are you all right?' Mrs O'Reilly asked. Veronica blushed, returning to the present with a jolt.

'It's nothing, Mrs O'Reilly, nothing really. We'd better get off, I think it will rain, and I feel I may be getting a cold,' she said, hoping that explained her flushed cheeks. 'I feel a bit hot so want to get home as quickly as possible.'

After work, Veronica called at Mrs Sullivan's shop, and the bell tinkled as she pushed the door. Mrs Sullivan put her cup of tea down.

'Veronica, good to see you, love. I've just had tea, would you like a cup?' She chatted as she got an extra cup for her and poured the tea. 'I never thought I'd miss Bridget so much.' She sighed, looking upstairs. 'You know me and Mr Sullivan never had children. It just didn't happen.' She lowered her voice, 'I've some lovely mince pies and I'll put a few in a bag for Tom and Betty. But I've put the rest away until Christmas. Mr Sullivan said I'm eating too many.' She patted her widening stomach. 'Will you have a mince pie now?'

'No, I'm fine. Betty will have dinner ready. I just called for a chat.' But then, at the thought of Betty's poor attempt at dinner, she changed her mind.

'Here, dear, sit down behind the counter, drink your tea, and I'll get a wee mince pie.' She pushed the stool to Veronica. 'And I've something for you.'

She handed her a note with her name on it.

20 November, 1918

Veronica,

I am so sorry that I haven't been in touch but my mother is much better now. I will be back in Dublin at Christmas. Can we meet? Please.

I look forward to hearing from you. Send your reply to The Barracks, Benburb St, Arbour Hill, Dublin.

Yours,

Harry F.

This was unexpected. The letter didn't say much, but more surprising was how her heart fluttered as she read the note. The bell chimed as the shop door opened, followed by a gust of wind that swept the floor. Dust landed on her shoes, and she shook it off, trying to think. She didn't know if she should meet him again, but she couldn't refuse.

'Oh good, you're still open. Have you any bread?' said a woman, shuffling through the doorway. The woman loosened her headscarf, looked at Veronica and leaned into Mrs Sullivan, whispering loudly, 'Everything all right?'

'I'm fine, Mrs Broderick, just having tea with a friend. I'm closing in a few minutes.'

Mrs Broderick nodded at Mrs Sullivan, and before leaving, looked Veronica up and down.

'That Mrs Broderick is so nosey; she'll be in the shop first thing tomorrow morning asking all about you. You had better go home, love. The curfew will soon be in effect. Here, wrap your coat up tight.'

'How is Bridget? She hasn't written at all.'

'Oh, Veronica, she is grand. I was visiting her last Sunday, and she was writing to tell you the good news. I can't say what it is, but it's grand.'

'I bet it's something to do with Charlie. She told me about him. Is she getting married?'

Mrs Sullivan only smiled. 'She wrote you a letter, so you should get it soon.'

She pulled Veronica's collar up for her like a mother. 'Go now, I hear the patrol trucks,' she said as she turned off the light. 'Wait until they pass and then go.'

The trucks slowly moved down the street, their searchlights bouncing off the walls of the surrounding houses and illuminating the street ahead. When the noise of the vehicles was at a safe distance, Veronica stood to go but turned and gave Mrs Sullivan a tight hug first.

Mrs Sullivan held her at arm's length and looked her directly in the eye, then pulled her into a hug. 'You're like a daughter to me. You and the major, I hope you make the right decision.'

The following Monday morning at work, Veronica knocked on Michael's door, entering when he answered.

The room was thick with smoke, and Michael thumped the window. 'Blasted thing is stuck.' Finally, it opened, and a blast of cold air diluted the smell of tobacco and burning turf. 'Who's that?'

'Veronica,' she said, her voice muffled as she covered her nose with her hanky.

'Wait a minute till the smoke clears.'

The cold December air soon cleared the room of smoke.

'Come in. What can I do for you?'

'Michael, I got a note,' she said, and showed it to him as he sat down in his office chair to read it, drumming his fingers on his desk.

'We actually don't know a lot, but what we know of him, he was injured in France, and got sent here. Yes, he works in The Castle. I know our contact said he knows General Maxwell well and has had dinner with him and his wife.' He was silent for a few minutes. 'So why do they want him back? Right, meet him, try to get him to talk about the work he does and see why he is back. I think there is someone passing information onto the boys in the castle. I need to know how they know where we keep our weapons, and how they knew to raid one of our meetings last week in Rathmines.' He banged his fist on the desk. 'Bastards, Veronica, that's what they are. Do you know young Davy Doyle? Davy, my sister-in-law's – a tiny slip of a lad, he was only ten years of age last month. He was shot last week giving out leaflets for the upcoming election. He was left for dead, but a young doctor was passing by and saved his life.'

He paused before continuing, 'Our concern now is to win as many seats as possible so we can have our government. I think The Castle has a mole. The soldiers arrive to break up any of our meetings or rallies before we have even started most of them, no matter what part of the country they occur.'

Veronica weighed up her responsibility. She nodded. 'I'm really proud to be involved, Michael. This is beyond any dreams I ever had.'

'Great. Veronica, with the elections and now we don't have this war in Europe anymore, we must concentrate on pushing forward to getting the British out of our country. You're a great help. Try to use your charm, you're a good-looking girl. He is definitely keen on you, so pretend to like him. Do what you have to do.'

Was this worse than delivering the parcels? 'I will try to get a note to him.'

'Good girl, write to him in the barracks. Tell him you'd love to meet him, maybe a walk, and we'll follow you. The election is in a few days.'

The words weighed heavily on her as she walked home after work. That night in her bedroom, she sat at her small desk and looked at the paper lying in front of her, composing herself before penning a short note.

8 December, 1918

Dear Harry,

How lovely to hear from you, I was hoping you would return. I thought you may have gone back to England for good. I'd love to meet for a walk. I'm free on Sundays.

Veronica.

She posted it to The Barracks the next day and put Mrs Sullivan's shop as a return address.

Election day finally arrived, and the excitement in Dublin was palpable. At Thomas St, doors in the building slammed with loud hurried footsteps on the steps as people left to vote, many voting for the first time.

Betty was up early as usual, but she wore her Sunday best. 'Veronica, imagine me being able to vote. I never thought I'd see the day. We are so proud of you helping in the work you do,' said Betty.

'I did nothing, just typed a few letters.'

'Veronica, you did more than that. You know you did,' Tom said.

Veronica knew he was talking about the parcels, and she wanted to tell him about Harry's return, but couldn't say anything in front of Betty.

'We'd better go, Betty. Veronica, are you going into the office today?'

'Yes, I'll walk. You've to go in the other direction as I'm going to Harcourt St for a while, so you go ahead and vote.'

'Come on, love, and I'll clean the table when I get back.'

Veronica smiled. Betty had spent the last three years cleaning away her grief. Now, for once, she was thinking of something else, especially as their worst day of the year was approaching. It was good to see Betty wearing her blue Sunday coat, her hair pinned neat. Tom was scrubbed clean, and his hair greased shiny, proud to take part in the future of Ireland. They stepped outside into the weak morning sunshine, the sky the usual pale blue after a hard frost. The frosty air bit Veronica's cheeks. Betty's cheeks coloured a little, and she smiled at Tom as he took her hand, helping her up onto the waiting dray. Veronica hoped that it would be a good day, and all their efforts at work would have been worth it.

Outside the front entrance, they went their separate ways. Veronica pulled her coat tight in the morning chill. The streets were alive with people going to the polling stations. First, the men went to vote and then the women left their homes when children were fed and the fires lit. The dogs sniffed the air as if they could smell change.

'God, I hope we do well,' Mrs O'Reilly said. 'I stopped by the church and lit a candle on the way here.' The women brought their chairs to the windows to watch the rows of people in the street below, passing on their way to vote. The office filled up with who had voted, all chatting.

'Do you know who all these people are?' Veronica looked at the swelling of men and women eating and drinking tea.

Mrs O'Reilly shook her head. 'Voters, our supporters I suppose. There's an awful lot of them, aren't there? But isn't it awfully exciting?'

There was a delay with the results of the election, so everyone was tense when the day finally arrived for the announcement of the results. Veronica rushed to Harcourt St with trepidation. When she arrived at work, the bank was closed, but Veronica heard the murmur of men inside pacing up and down. Paperwork was absent from desks, and in its place there were teacups and plates of buttered bread placed randomly on the desks. The kettle was on a continuous boil refilling the teapots once emptied. Veronica poured tea for the men who chatted animatedly with each other.

The office door opened, and Veronica welcomed the cold breeze as the smoke-filled room had made her nauseous. The office was not only filled with Sinn Féin people, Veronica didn't recognise a lot of the people who tried to enter.

They waited for Michael to come from the Castle with the results. Men wrung their caps in their hands, and people walked away from their conversations mid-sentence. Mrs O'Reilly got up and sat down. 'Oh, Veronica, this is more than I can bear. Maybe I'll just go for a walk.'

'Make room,' a small bald man shouted, 'Michael's back, people make way for him. Quick, he's coming up the stairs.' A hush descended upon the crowd as Michael entered, his serious face giving nothing away. Nobody moved or spoke. They waited for him to speak.

Suddenly, everybody in the office cheered and hugged each other. Mrs O'Reilly's round body was squashed between two men. Veronica mouthed over to her, 'What did he say?' But she couldn't understand her. A man stood beside Veronica and shook a woman's hand on his other side. She tugged his sleeve. 'What did he say?'

'We won. Seventy-five seats.'

Another cheer.

Out of one hundred and five seats, Sinn Féin won by a comfortable majority.

'We won't go to Westminster. We're Irish, not pawns to make rules somewhere else. We will set up our own parliament here in Dublin, and rule ourselves,' Michael said.

The men nodded.

There were nods of agreement. Home Rule was dead and gone and with that it was decided Sinn Féin would set up an Irish parliament: Dáil Eireann. To extract themselves entirely from the English parliament the elected MPs refused to call themselves MPs and adopted the name Teachta Dala, or TD. It was also a great day for women. Constance Markiewicz was the first woman TD for Ireland.

Over the next few days after work, Veronica called into Mrs Sullivan's regularly, but there was no note from Harry. Christmas was nearly upon them, and the day before she left to go to Cavan, Veronica called into Mrs Sullivan's shop to give her a small present. The smell of simmering Christmas pudding wafted down from the rooms over the shop. It made her long for the comfort of her own home.

'Hello, dear, are you all set for Christmas? I've put some holly up in the shop. This morning I took the bus to the Phoenix Park and took a few bits. Oh, I've to get something in the back of the shop for you.' After a few minutes, she returned, holding a parcel of red paper.

'And here is a small present for you, it's just a way of saying thank you.' Veronica handed Mrs Sullivan an embroidered handkerchief tied in a purple ribbon.

'Ah, dear, there was no need.'

'Of course, there is. I enjoy our chats,' she said, and that was the truth. 'Embroidery is not my strong point. Just a way of saying thank you,' Veronica said.

'It is lovely, dear. And look,' Mrs Sullivan bent to the shelves below the counter arching her back into a stretch as she got back up. 'I'm so damned stiff sitting here all day. Here you go, love.'

The pale-yellow envelope had Harry's writing on it, a beautiful curve to the V.

Veronica,

I am so sorry. I had hoped to see you even for a few minutes, but I had to return to Shropshire. I will return to Dublin in January and hope to see you.

Harry.

Mrs Sullivan lifted the lid on the shop counter. 'Here, love, he also left this for you.' Mrs Sullivan gave her a package she had stored in the back, a yellow ribbon tied around it with a perfect bow. 'He told me to tell you to open it on Christmas Day and said he would think of you. Go on, now, love.'

Veronica took the parcel and letter, putting them in her coat pocket. She didn't know what to think about the present; the only man that had ever given her a gift before was her father. She felt she should offer some explanation to Mrs Sullivan, but before she could speak Mrs Sullivan said, 'You had better go, love, the curfew is soon.'

Veronica ran back to Thomas St, ignoring the shouts from the soldiers yelling at her to stop, running as fast as she could in case they fired at her. This wasn't supposed to happen; he wasn't supposed to give her presents. She threw the parcel on the bed. Letters were fine, but gifts were different. The package sat ominously on her bed. She sat and traced her finger around the edge of it. Her anger that he was English evaporated; he was so different than James Sheridan, who had mockingly laughed at her.

The next day, Veronica finalised her journey back to Cavan for Christmas. Before she left Thomas St, Betty grabbed her hand. 'Veronica, I'm so glad you came to us. Even though Padraig has gone, and I feel I have lived in a vacuum the last couple of years, you've helped me wake up. The capital has a new future, and us as well.'

They hugged, and Tom brought her to Broadstone train station to return home for Christmas. People on the train were full of chat. She disembarked at Oldcastle to meet her waiting father on the crowded platform.

'Veronica, isn't it a great time for Ireland?' he said. 'And you helped, I'm so proud of you. We'd better move, it looks like rain, and I've had to bring the pony and trap. Petrol for a motor car is too expensive. The war may be over, but we still have to be frugal,' he said, handing her a blanket. 'Here, wrap this around you.'

'Will we go to see Eddie?'

With that question, her father appeared to age about ten years.

'No,' he said quietly. 'He isn't allowed visitors over

Christmas. And don't mention him to your mother, she will only start crying.'

There was no snow this year, and the birds' nests were low in the trees, which meant stormy weather was on the way.

Once home, her mother greeted her at the front door. 'Veronica, you look awful, you're so thin. You must rest. If I'd known Dublin would be so hard on you…' Her mother went on and on, but Veronica didn't listen.

'I'm fine, Mother. In fact, everything is great.'

'But what about all that violence I am reading about in the newspapers?'

'Mammy it's very safe in Dublin,' Veronica lied. 'I'm going up to unpack.'

In her bedroom, she unpacked her suitcase. In amongst the pile lay the present Harry had left for her. Sitting on the bed, she picked it up to examine it more closely and shoved it under her pillow when Susan stomped into the room. 'Veronica, you're home! Thank God, I'm sick of housework.'

Veronica threw her eyes upwards and smiled, enveloping her sister in a hug. 'Lovely to see you as well.'

'Come and help me. We have so much to do. Mrs Slaney will unpack for you.'

Christmas Day. Veronica lay in bed listening to her mother in the kitchen banging pots and pans starting to get the food ready for the family for the day. Her mother would have put the turkey on at 6 a.m. They would eat Christmas breakfast after Mass.

Veronica pulled Harry's present from under her pillow.

Wrapped with soft blue paper, and yellow bow tied perfectly – her favourite colours.

Susan stirred. 'Is that you, Veronica?' she asked, her voice full of sleep, and pulled her blankets up to sleep a little longer.

Veronica held the present for a few moments, and carefully undid the ribbon, watching Susan in case she woke again. It was a book. *Pride and Prejudice.* Her favourite book. Staring at it for a moment, she slid it under her pillow, and lay back in bed thinking of Harry, wondering what he was doing at this exact moment. Her thoughts were warm before guilt consumed her, thinking of Eddie in a cold cell.

31

Jan 1919

After the Christmas break, Veronica returned to Dublin. From the minute she stepped off the train in Broadstone, she sensed a change. This was a new Dublin, one of hope. Maybe she imagined it, but the people on the streets walked with new vigour and confidence. There was going to be a change, and she had been part of it. The last of the Fusiliers were coming back from the war.

Two events happened on 21 January 1919 in the Mansion House. The Fusiliers went there to be celebrated for their efforts in the war and, as they were leaving, the newly elected, Sinn Féin MPs entered. And so, the first parliament called the Dáil, sat in Ireland.

The morning of the meeting of the Dáil, Veronica helped to prepare the Irish speeches for Fr O'Flanagan. When she was done, she handed it to Mrs O'Reilly, saying, 'I do wish I had been better at Irish in school, the nuns made it so boring.'

Mrs O'Reilly laughed. 'I know what you mean. I'd

better get going, a big crowd is expected. It's a great day, Veronica. You do know that? We've waited for this day a long time.' Mrs O'Reilly stood in front of the window using the reflection as a mirror and straightened her matching blue hat. 'Are you not coming, dear? There will be lots of young men there. Surely it would be nice to have some company, and I'd love an excuse for a day out,' she said with a twinkle in her eye.

Veronica laughed, 'I'm fine on my own, Mrs O'Reilly. I need a rest from men.'

Mrs O'Reilly frowned. 'Tired of men, I never saw you with anyone!'

'Don't worry, I'm meeting Bridget – you know my friend from secretarial school – and we'll go to the Mansion House together. I'm really looking forward to seeing her. We haven't met for ages; in fact, I can't remember when I last saw her.'

The door opened, and Mrs O'Reilly said, 'Ah, that must be Mrs Moore, we're going together.'

But it wasn't Mrs Moore. It was James Sheridan. Veronica turned away from him, her blood boiling. She hadn't seen him since he had tried to kiss her.

'Michael wants a word,' he said in a mocking voice, and he motioned her to follow him.

Veronica tightened her fist. Everything about James annoyed her. Michael's office was as usual thick with the smell of cigarettes. She handed him Fr O'Flanagan's speech.

'Thanks, I've only a few minutes, Veronica. I'm late. Has the soldier been in contact with you?'

'He was. I got a letter just before Christmas, and he said he was in Shropshire.'

'Well I got word he is back, so contact him again, make up some excuse. I hope today goes calmly.' He took his pocket watch from his waistcoat, grabbed his jacket from the coat stand and hurried to the door. 'Contact him as soon as possible, I don't know what will happen after today.'

Veronica nodded, thinking about the book Harry had given her. She went back to the office, thankful James had left with Michael.

Bridget had written to Veronica asking to meet her at ten o'clock.

'That's that, Veronica, all finished. Will you clear everything up?' Mrs O'Reilly threw a log onto the fire. 'We could be gone for a long time, so it'll be nice to have the place warm when we get back.'

Veronica quickly put away the paper and tidied up the office before she left to join the people on the streets, making their way to watch the speeches at the Mansion House.

At ten, she spotted Bridget standing at the main gates to St Stephen's Green. 'Bridget, over here,' Veronica waved and shouted.

They hugged and linked arms, holding on to their hats in the blustery January wind.

'Bridget, you look so happy. Have you news?'

'I got a job at Clerys in the office. There are five secretaries. It's so lovely to have a real job finally.'

'No more news?'

'Look, Veronica, come on, the crowd is moving.'

They moved with the people towards the Mansion House. The crowd swelled as a continuous stream of people poured from the houses onto the streets. They pushed, shoved and laughed, all united in a new hope, all striding forward in a common purpose.

A paperboy in a flat cap shouted at the passing crowd, 'Two RIC policemen shot dead in Tipperary by Volunteers.' Veronica paid little attention to the news the boy shouted as he waved his paper in the air, her only thought was he should go home and put on a coat. Few wanted newspapers today. People wanted to witness history as Sinn Féin and the Lord Mayor made speeches initiating the Dáil, the new Irish government.

Even though it was dry, the cold still bit their cheeks as they turned the corner onto Dawson St, and they welcomed the sight of the Mansion House.

When they neared the Mansion House, Bridget whispered to Veronica, 'Those men are so brave, refusing to go to Britain and making a stand to have our parliament here. You are so lucky to be involved with them. I am only working in Clerys.'

'Bridget, that's a responsible position. Isn't it great that women are working now?'

Bridget laughed, the infectious laugh that had drawn Veronica to Bridget on the first day in the secretarial school.

A hush suddenly descended upon the crowd. Veronica

and Bridget squeezed each other's arms, standing on their tiptoes to peer over the sea of heads while the Lord Mayor spoke on a stage surrounded by men with serious faces, clapping and nodding as they hung on to his every word. Distance prevented the girls from hearing most of his words, but when people clapped, they joined in.

'Who's that man, Veronica?' Bridget asked, pointing to a slim man clean-shaven, much younger than the rest of the men beside the Lord Mayor.

Veronica stood tall peering over the heads of the crowd. 'I think that's Terence MacSwiney. He's from Cork.'

Terence MacSwiney spoke next. The tall man's voice boomed over the crowd. 'This is our first step to our own governance. We will get our country back. Our new Dáil President Eámon De Valera sent word from prison that Ireland is a new republic.'

The crowd cheered and clapped.

Bridget tugged Veronica's coat. 'Can you hear what they are saying? This is so exciting, but I can't hear with all the noise.'

'I think they are reading out the Proclamation.' She put her hand to her ear and leaned forward, straining to hear over mumbles of people passing the speech onto the people behind them. 'He is saying something now about a "Message to the Free Nations".' Her hand flew to her mouth. 'Bridget, did you hear that? He said, "we are now at war with England".'

'What? Sure, aren't we already? In our way, we are. How many lads do you know involved in the Volunteers?'

Tears came to Veronica's eyes, and her heart dropped,

wondering when Eddie would ever get out.

'Look, Veronica, how can anything change?'

When the speeches were over, the crowd started to disperse. The girls walked with the crowd, but Bridget stopped and took hold of Veronica's hand. 'Veronica, I've to tell you something. I've met someone.' Her blue eyes glistened.

Veronica waited for more.

'A man.'

'I assumed you meant a man! So that's why I haven't seen you at Mrs Sullivan's. Where did you meet him? What is he like?'

Bridget's smile widened, her blue eyes dancing. 'He is two years older than me; he is an apprentice mechanic. Oh, Veronica, he is lovely. You'd like him.'

Veronica hugged Bridget.

'But Mammy doesn't like him. His daddy is a drunk, and his mother is no better, so me and Sam have been keeping it a secret. I'm meeting him in a few hours. Do you mind if I don't spend the rest of the afternoon with you?'

Veronica threw her head back to laugh, and her hat got caught in a gust of wind and flew, falling a few feet away from the girls' feet. 'God, no, not at all,' she said as she retrieved her hat before it was carried away again by the wind. She was happy for Bridget.

'Bridget, we've to meet again soon. Now you are in Clerys I can meet you at lunchtime.'

'Veronica, why have you not met someone?' Bridget's face was now serious.

'I'm busy at work.'

'Go to the dances and meet someone, you don't want to end up an old spinster like my Aunty Mary.'

Bridget and Veronica hugged one more time, Bridget promising she would meet soon and tell her all about Sam.

Veronica watched Bridget weave through the dwindling crowd, disappointed to be alone, and slightly dejected.

When Veronica arrived back at Harcourt St, people were filtering in and out of the building, some she knew, and others strangers. She knew this was a momentous day for Ireland. If the elected Sinn Féin TDs were effective as the new Dáil Eireann, maybe Ireland could finally get its freedom.

Mrs O'Reilly back in the office smiled at Veronica when she entered and took off her coat. 'I'm glad you left the fire on,' she said as she stood in front of the flames rubbing the cold from her hands.

'With the election success, you know there will be more people working here.'

'But where? The building is full as it is, it's not big enough,' Veronica said.

'Michael said yesterday he is to move down the street to number seventy-six. Did you hear he will be appointed the Minister of Finance?'

'No, I was with Bridget, and we were too far away to hear all the speeches. Well, that's great. Finally, we are getting somewhere. The English will have to sit up and listen to us now – maybe even leave us alone.'

'I don't think so, Veronica, they are sending more soldiers

over. They will try their best to prevent us ruling ourselves. They have been here too long to let us go without a fight, and Michael is their biggest threat now, since Éamon and his men are still in prison in England.'

'So just because Michael is at a different address, it won't stop the soldiers annoying him?'

Mrs O'Reilly nodded, sighed and sipped her tea, then opened the top button on her blouse. 'I'm exhausted, the excitement is too much for me,' she said as she fanned herself with a piece of paper.

'I was thinking, won't Éamon be let go? I mean they have no reason to keep him in Wales.'

'Veronica, he's not in Wales anymore; they sent him to Lincoln's prison in Lincolnshire.' Mrs O'Reilly stood up now she had got her second wind. 'Do you know Ernie Reilly? He is one of the new young men who work in the bank. You must have noticed him? Very handsome? He comes here on a Friday to collect the wages.'

A knock on the door and a young man with red hair and freckles entered the room.

'Speak of the devil. I was just talking about you, Ernie. Your ears must have been burning,' Mrs O'Reilly said with a laugh.

'Veronica, Michael's here. Could you come into his office for a minute? Bring a pen and paper. And Veronica, wear something warm. He's got the windows open.'

In Michael's office, the fire blazed. The flames flickered as the wind blew in. Michael's brush with death with the flu before Christmas meant that he had not only given up cigarettes but also insisted that there would be a steady flow of fresh air in his office.

'Any word?' Michael asked.

There was no need to ask what he meant; Veronica shook her head.

'I'll let you know as soon as I get any word, but maybe he's not coming back. I may not hear from him again.'

Veronica returned to her desk with letters Michael needed typing, and she rubbed her arms. 'It's so cold in there. Not a bad thing there is talk of him moving. Even the landing is freezing.'

Mrs O'Reilly stopped typing. 'Do you know I hate these dark evenings. Everything is so dismal and dreary. It'll be nice to see the first buds of spring. When I was first married, we often went to Kingstown for the day to walk along the promenade. But when the boys came along, our day trips stopped. Now they are men. You really should make a trip someday; you look so glum lately. You need some cheering up.'

The door of Michael's office banged.

'We'd better stop this chit-chat and do some work. Veronica, you can leave once you have typed that for Michael.'

She left the office gladly as darkness had descended. On the street, lights flowed out of the doors of shops. She ran between the shadows, her footsteps light. At the corner of Abbey St, she slowed to catch her breath before she called in to Mrs Sullivan to tell her about the speeches and the Dáil.

When she entered the shop, Mrs Sullivan looked up

from her newspaper as the bell chimed.

'Come in quick, dear. It's a cold one. I've a note, and I'd a chat with him. He is very polite, for a soldier that is, so different from the thugs parading around the streets as if they owned them.' And she whispered even though no one else was in the shop, 'And, so handsome. It's a pity he is English, though.'

Mrs Sullivan handed the note to her, and Veronica tore it open, her body tense. She didn't know what to expect.

1 Feb, 1919

Veronica,

Again my sincerest apologies for not seeing you before Christmas. Will you go to the moving pictures with me Saturday, 15 February?

Yours, Harry

'Well?'

'He wants to go to the moving picture house.'

The bell chimed behind her.

'I must go,' Veronica said and stuffed the note into her bag.

She nodded hello to the silver-haired woman who entered as she walked out. Veronica pulled her coat tight, trying to forget the danger on the streets.

★

Michael clasped his hands together. 'Great news. I'll get James to follow you.'

'No, not James,' she blurted out. His name alone infuriated her; she didn't want to see him.

'What do you mean, not James?'

'Sorry, I didn't mean it like that.'

'Anyway, it doesn't matter who goes, reply to him as quickly as you can. Westminster are not happy about our new parliament, and they will intensify their attacks on our offices and do everything to prevent us from getting any more power. We will have to get more guns and counter-attack as many of the militia and government officials as we can.' He stared ahead and drummed his fingers on the desk. 'I don't know how they are always prepared for every one of our raids on their army barracks, or on the RIC station, but we need more guns. Veronica, remember, use your womanly traits with him, get him to like you, get his guard down.'

Veronica had never been to the cinema. They were nights out for lovers. The papers were full of posters advertising the new picture houses that were popping up all over the city. Even the Gaiety Theatre had converted to a picture house. Ireland was changing with the times. A knock on the door was followed by Eibhlin who brought in a tray with tea and biscuits. Veronica hadn't seen Eibhlin for a while; after her husband had got the flu the previous spring, he had never recovered to full health and had passed away in the autumn.

'There's tea for the two of ye.' She smiled at Veronica.

Eibhlin had lost so much weight that her face was gaunt, her eyes sunk, lost in a pool of sorrow.

Eibhlin had left the door open, and a breeze blew in from the landing as the windows had been left open. Veronica shivered, wondering if there would be an end to this chill.

32

A guerrilla war ensued in Ireland against the British army and RIC in Ireland to weaken them into retreating forever from Ireland. The unity in the country was palpable.

On the second Saturday in February Veronica told Betty that she was meeting Bridget to go to the picture house.

'She's such a nice girl. You go and enjoy yourselves.'

'Thanks.' Veronica tried to shake away her guilt for deceiving Betty.

Veronica handed Betty her breakfast bowl with the porridge uneaten. Betty put her hand on Veronica's forehead. 'Are you coming down with something? You're looking flushed. Are you sure you can meet Bridget?'

'No, I'm fine, absolutely fine.'

Michael's words reverberated in her head. *Act interested, try to look relaxed, get him comfortable with you, and maybe he'll tell you something, or even better try to get an invite inside the Castle. We don't know how they know where our volunteers are, but they keep attacking us. We need to keep all the guns we have, and we must keep attacking the RIC stations to weaken them.*

'Sorry, Betty, what did you say?'

'Do you know, it's very dark, there's no moon tonight. Your uncle will drop you to the picture house and collect you.'

'No. No, it's grand. Bridget's brother will bring me home.'

Tom stood to put on his boots. 'Come on, love. We'll go. I could spend the evening asleep in front of the fire, but I'll only be stiff in the morning if I don't move a bit before bed. That peat your father sends up would put anyone to sleep.'

'Bridget's brother! Is he going as well? I didn't know she had a brother.' Betty smiled and raised her eyebrows.

'No, it's not like that,' Veronica said, not wanting to talk about Bridget or her brother.

The dray stood patiently under the streetlamp, the steam from the horse's warm breath mingling with the cold air like two boxers, each trying to conquer the other and neither winning.

Tom flicked the reins. 'I think it's colder than last year.'

Veronica nodded and picked a white speck off her coat, wishing she had worn the new purple coat, a Christmas present from her mother and father. Instead, she wore her old cream coat that had seen better days, so Betty wouldn't question her why she was getting dressed up for Bridget. She ran her hand across her pinned hair to put any escaped curls back in place.

'James will be there.'

'Pardon.'

Tom looked at her. 'I said James will be there to keep

an eye on you because if the major is in uniform, you may get some hostility from people. He'll be there in case you need him.'

She snapped, 'I'll be fine, and I don't need James Sheridan looking out for me.'

'Don't sound so annoyed. It really is for your own good.'

Tom stopped at the corner of Mary St. A steady stream of people walked towards the picture house.

'Are you all right, love? You've hardly said a word.'

'I'm fine, Uncle, don't worry about me,' she said, jumping down from the dray. 'And thanks.'

'Veronica,' Tom said. 'It'll be all right. Look, there are lots of young people and couples.'

A few couples that were familiar with each other were linking arms and laughing, but she could tell the couples that were only starting their journey of romance, the ones who were keeping their distance, making sure they didn't touch. She doubted any of them had to do what she had to do, and if they did then surely, they would be terrified.

Tom looked at her, his eyes gentle. 'Veronica, don't think about it, just be your charming self.'

She had to try for Eddie and her cousin Padraig, and she fell behind the walking crowd moving towards the picture house. Harry stood at the corner in a brown tweed jacket and a trilby, which was not typical apparel for a young Dublin man. He held his head high above most of the other men, his handsome face scanning the crowd. He smiled at her approach. 'Veronica, you look breath-taking.'

'Thank you,' she replied, now more comfortable with his compliments.

'I'm sorry I couldn't see you before Christmas, I wanted to.'

She couldn't deny she was pleased to hear him say that. He placed his hand lightly on her elbow, barely touching it, but guiding her in the queue. To others, they would appear like an average couple. In the queue to their right, a girl stared at Harry then at her. As she searched the crowd for James Sheridan, the girl whispered to her friend, they giggled, and both smiled at Harry. He didn't notice. Veronica had feared the girls recognised Harry and would shout into the crowd that an English soldier was amongst them, but the girls' flirty looks dispelled her anxiety. She took in his calm, good looks, and sighed. *If only things were different.*

'They are showing a Charlie Chaplin film. Have you seen him before?'

'No, I've never been to a picture house,' she answered.

Squeezing her arm, he laughed. 'Actually, neither have I.' His eyes danced as he looked at her. 'Veronica, it's so good to see you; I'm sorry I haven't been in touch, but I had to go back to England. I didn't think I would be sent back. We are so busy. You must be angry I didn't contact you. Things are, well, they are complicated.'

She kept her head low for a minute. 'No, Harry I'm not angry,' she said, and that was the truth. She should have been angry, but not for the reasons he thought; she should have been angry at him because he was a soldier, and Eddie was still in prison.

Now was her chance. 'I worry it is getting dangerous for you, Harry, there seems to be a lot of fighting.' She held her breath steady. 'The newspapers report the attacks on RIC stations around the country, so I worry that you may get shot.'

Harry shifted, and leaned into her so no one could hear. 'Veronica, I'll be fine, now the war is over, we are recruiting more men to help us.'

She straightened, rechecking her hair, and trying to sound nonchalant. 'Really, more men, wouldn't that be more work for you?'

Harry looked ahead. 'Are you ready? I've already bought the tickets, and the queue is moving.' She looked at him. As the street gaslight fell on him, she was sure she saw a flash of pain cross his face.

Three young men stood in front of them. When they moved with the queue, they shuffled, and war-weary faces told their own story. A few Irishmen wore the English uniform. The reality of life was they had needed a job. A wage to send home to feed their family from their part in the war in Europe.

The cinema was dark, and the smell of smoke lingered in the air. A lady took their tickets and directed them to seats in the back row. It wasn't an ideal setting for a chat. A motor started behind them, and a long bright beam lit up a screen at the top of the room, wisps of smoke swirling in the glow of light. From time to time, their knees touched, and she pulled back. She had to concentrate on the moving picture, knowing Betty would want to know what it was like. Veronica forgot about the fighting on the streets, about the two policemen killed in Tipperary, about the reason she was there. Mesmerised by the moving images on the screen, she was transported to another world, and it was remarkable. As the film ended, she stole a glance at Harry, and he caught the glimpse and smiled back.

She stopped to offer her hand before they parted, but he bent close to her. His soft lips brushed her cheek. One of his hands lingered lightly on her waist. She let it rest for a minute before she pulled it back. Something stirred inside – she was half thrilled, half repelled. She hadn't thought it through. Her pulse beat to a deafening thunder in her temples. She closed her eyes. His slightly parted lips were now on her neck, his breath hot and the velvet touch of his lips trailing on her neck. With the other hand, he held the back of her head firmly. His lips gently found hers.

St Mary's church chiming ten o'clock echoed through the still night. Hearing laughter behind them, she pulled away from him, her eyes wide.

'I've to go,' she said, her heart beating painfully fast.

'I'll walk with you, but I'm not too sure when I can meet you again, my men will be here in the next few weeks.'

Flirt with him, get him to like you.

Veronica stopped, only able to take sips of breath, 'Surely you won't be that busy, there must be an awful lot more soldiers coming.'

The shadows fell across his face. Her body, on heightened awareness, felt the heat of his body as he moved closer.

Flirt with him, get him to like you. It had sounded so formal, but this was new to her and the feeling she had in the picture house confused her.

He brushed away a loose strand of her hair. His steady gaze should have unsettled her, but she moved closer to him and held her breath. Keeping her eyes fixed firmly on his face, she couldn't do anything to stop the hunger of desire that was building in her.

He moved closer, his warm lips on the nape of her neck. His hand slipped down to her hips, and as his fingertips pressed lightly on her clothing, her skin tingled. Not in disgust, but pleasure.

But he stood back, took her gloved hand and kissed it. 'I'll call at the shop. I don't know when I'll get time off as the soldiers may not arrive for weeks. We are so undermanned, and...' He rubbed his temples, a stress line on his forehead.

This was great news for Michael. 'Yes,' she said, encouraging him to keep talking, trying not to think about his soft lips on her hand.

'I've to go, Veronica.' He tilted his cap and left.

She stood back in the shadows to watch him turn onto Bachelors Walk back towards the barracks. After a few minutes, she walked briskly home towards Thomas St. The streets were empty. In the distance, a patrol vehicle rumbled – the curfew. As she quickened her steps, she was pulled sideways. She lurched forward, but before she could work out what was happening, a hand covered her mouth, rough and calloused, and she was dragged away. Her shoes scraped against the alley's cobbles. Before she could scream, she heard a familiar voice.

'Veronica, shh, it's me, Eddie.'

'Eddie! Oh, my God.' She hugged him, falling into him, running her hands over him and checking to make sure he was in one piece. 'It's so good to see you. I can't believe it's you! I thought you were in prison.'

The rumble of an army vehicle on patrol pushed them further back into the alley. The passing patrol lights reached down the alley, but they crouched down low so the lights passed over them before moving back to the street.

'How did you get out? Why are you hiding?'

Eddie didn't answer and pulled Veronica through a door to a musty smelling house. They entered a small dark room off the hallway. The flickering candle in the corner on a small wooden table offered little light. When Eddie moved to a table with two chairs, it was only then she noticed the bandaged hand.

Veronica jumped at a man's voice behind her. 'I'll be off, Eddie, pull the door shut after you.'

Eddie dropped into the chair, rubbing his hand. Veronica saw a shot of pain in his face.

'Eddie, are you hurt?'

The look of pain was gone as soon as he spoke. 'Veronica, Jesus, what are you doing with that bastard? You kissed him! You're not supposed to get that close to him.'

The candlelight flickered across his face, and there was a black look of hatred in his eyes.

'Eddie, I'm meeting him for Sinn Féin, I'm supposed to get information from him. I think he is complex. He said he is half Catholic. He thinks the English shouldn't be here. And Michael said to flirt with him, make him like me.'

'Jesus, Veronica, you're so naive. He only wants one thing. They are all the same.'

'He's kind. I don't know, Eddie, he is...'

'He's fuckin' English, the enemy. I know what Michael said. It just felt different when I saw it with my own eyes.'

'Look, Eddie, forget about it, God it's so good to see you.' She inhaled and said, 'I saw James Sheridan. I thought that it was him who was following me.'

A movement in the corner. Veronica pulled her coat in tighter. Rats were everywhere.

'Eddie, I don't know what to ask him.'

'Ask about his work, but don't get too close,' he growled in reply and grabbed her hand, looking at her ferociously. 'Look at what the Cumann women are doing. Are you making a mockery of them?'

She pulled her hand from him. She didn't know what had got into him. Eddie continued to rant but fell back onto the chair. A dark patch seeped through his thigh trouser leg. Veronica moved quickly to Eddie. She tore his trousers and saw a red bandage filling with blood and took it off. Pulling hard at the trousers, glad they were old and tore with no resistance, Veronica tied the torn trouser material tight around his leg. He winced but said nothing, his face covered in sweat. She pulled the bandage tighter and the blood stopped seeping into the trouser leg. When she sat on the filthy floor, only then did she notice how cold the room was.

'Can you sit for a minute?' She put his coat around his shoulders, dismayed how his once tight-fitting coat now hung loosely from his shoulders.

'Eddie, rest and close your eyes.' She rubbed his hand like their mother used to do when they were ill. 'Get some sleep now.'

Veronica sat on the cold dirty floor beside him, holding him so he wouldn't fall. She had to get back to Thomas St to get Tom's help, but she was afraid if she left him, the rats might attack him, or worse, he might die.

Eddie stirred after some time. It was impossible to tell how long they had been in the room, but as the clouds moved across the sky, the moon shadow had shifted. The damp wall glistened.

Eddie moaned and opened his eyes.

'Eddie, I have to go, Tom and Betty will wonder where I am.'

'It's fine. Tell Tom you were with me.'

It shocked her that Tom knew Eddie had escaped and said nothing. She realised there were many things others knew that she didn't.

'You go home, Veronica.' He caught his breath. 'Tell Tom I'm going to Cork for a while to stay with a friend. Go before the patrol comes around again. James will be here soon; he'll look after me.'

'Why?' she said, exasperated at the thought of him leaving again so suddenly. 'And your hand, Eddie, what's wrong with that?'

'It's nothing really.'

Veronica winced, taking Eddie's hand, turning it over and rubbing her fingers over his displaced knuckle. 'Eddie, it's swollen.'

'It's fine, I've no pain, maybe a wee bit crooked.' He paused for breath. 'Veronica, it's the least of my worries. It's been arranged for me to leave Dublin before sunrise. I'll stay with some friends. I need to keep away from the authorities.'

Veronica shook her head. 'I don't understand.'

'I escaped, Veronica. Mammy doesn't know. There is a warrant out for my arrest. If they find me, I will be shot.'

Veronica's eyes went wide. 'Surely they wouldn't!'

'Two other lads who escaped with me but weren't so lucky and got shot. Veronica, I have to go. Tell Tom I've gone to Cork.'

A knock at the door and James Sheridan entered. 'James, take Veronica home, and we'll be off when you get back.'

'Eddie...'

'Go, Veronica, the patrol might be back soon.'

They hugged, and she left with James.

Veronica refused to talk to James as he took her quickly through the back streets to Thomas St. She didn't even thank him when she arrived home, just ran up the steps, slamming the door behind her.

33

That night Veronica tossed and turned worrying about Eddie. She woke early to speak to Tom, but her aunt told her he had gone to his cousin's funeral in Co Meath. He didn't return until late Sunday night.

On Monday morning after breakfast, her uncle said he would take her to work.

'I've to do deliveries. I don't mind taking a long way around.' Tom rose slower than usual, his face wincing with every movement. He looked over to Betty and whispered to Veronica, 'This unforgiving dampness makes it worse. I'll be OK when I get moving. At least some spring heat is on its way.' He half-smiled at Veronica. 'Love, don't look so worried, sure, you have yourself to fret about.'

On their journey, Veronica said, 'Uncle, you can't keep going like this. Your hands are crippled, let me take the reins. Haven't I watched you often enough? Anyway, you know I have driven a car!'

'Really! I suppose times are different. Women do things now they didn't do a few years ago,' he admitted, and half flicked the reins.

Veronica leant over taking the reins from his hands. 'Sit back and rest.' They travelled in silence for a while, only broken by her uncle's coughing. The streets got busier as they passed O'Connell Bridge.

'Veronica, I know you met Eddie.'

'He looked awful, I'm just concerned. He isn't well, and he has gone off again, I'm beside myself with worry, what if something happens to him and—'

'Veronica, love, he has had a tough time, but he'll be fine. He's with James, and they have each other's back. Don't you worry about him, they are going to Cork and they will be safe there. Try to get on with things as normal as you can.'

She sighed. 'But I can't help it. Eddie said Mammy doesn't know he has escaped, and if they catch him, he could be...' she stopped to inhale and slowly said, '... he could be shot.'

'He'll be fine, and good men are looking out for him. No more talk, Veronica, you'll be late for work. We're nearly there, I'll manage now.' Veronica handed the reins back to Tom with concern in her eyes.

'I'll be fine, my hands are OK,' he said and wiggled his fingers, but they were stiff. Veronica rubbed her numb fingers and blew her breath on them and imagined how much pain the cold caused her uncle.

Tom dropped Veronica to Harcourt St and left to continue his deliveries of Guinness.

As she entered the office, the smoke made her eyes water. Now that Michael spent most of his time at his new office, nobody bothered to open the windows in the building.

At her desk, a note had been left for her to type.

6 Harcourt St,

A, Chari,

To carry effect the Dáil decree, whereby it was decreed that the police forces maintained by the English government in Ireland be ostracised socially by the people of Ireland, you are requested to bring the following to the notice of your Cumann.

a) *Avoid all intercourse with such persons unless where purely business matters make it necessary*
b) *Do not salute or reply to their salutations*
c) *Do not take part in any social entertainments where they are expected to be guests*
d) *Should not be allowed to attend any social entertainments such as dances etc.*
e) *Avoid all places they are known to visit such as public houses*

In the term 'Police forces', we include all members of the RIC, DMP, both officers and men, detectives and spies where they devote their whole time to detective rules and spying, or disguise themselves in engaging in some ordinary civil occupation.

Members report to their club on persons who are seen in any social intercourse.

T Kelly

H Sheehy Skeffington

Veronica had to read the letter twice.

'What are you blushing at, dear?' Mrs O'Reilly asked Veronica.

'Here read this. It's a letter to be sent to all the Cumann na mBán.'

Mrs O'Reilly read the letter, colour rising from her neck to her face. Her eyes moved across the letter a second time.

'Well, dear, it had to be said. I heard they wanted the priests to go to the parents of people involved with members of the police and army and tell them to warn their offspring to leave. However, they felt this too risky for the priests.' Mrs O'Reilly nodded. 'It could have an effect.' She handed the letter back to Veronica to continue with her task.

A familiar voice came into the office. 'Is Arthur here?'

'He's upstairs, Michael. It's great to see you. You're doing fantastic work,' said Mrs O'Reilly.

'Open a window to let fresh air into the room. I'm going upstairs to see Arthur,' he said to Mrs O'Reilly, signalling Veronica to follow him.

Michael waited for Veronica on the landing. 'Well, any news?'

'He said they are undermanned and hoping to recruit new men, now the war is over. Also said he would call at the shop; we didn't have time to talk much after the picture.' She hesitated. It embarrassed her, not because he kissed her, but because she had responded unexpectedly.

'All right,' he sighed and placed his hands behind his back. He took a cigarette from his coat pocket but didn't light it and looked at Veronica. 'Habit,' he said. 'You know they didn't think we'd get this far and wouldn't take our Dáil seriously, but now they are listening to us. We'll get our freedom, Veronica, at any cost. Meet him again. Maybe you could get a few names from him; I know you probably don't want to, but can you do it, it would be of help to your fellow countrymen?'

'Of course, Michael.' It was a difficult decision.

Michael pensively said, 'Veronica, I hope he doesn't get suspicious that you are never at the shop when he calls, but we do need you here.'

'He's right, it's stuffy in here.' Mrs O'Reilly opened the window and stuck her head out to inhale some fresh air. 'Quick, Veronica, run upstairs and tell Michael I can see soldiers on their way here. Give me any documents you want to put into the safe.'

Veronica took two steps at a time and found Michael on the landing talking to Eibhlin, 'Michael there're soldiers on their way here.'

He dropped the paperwork and grabbed the ladder leaning against the wall that people used to get up to the skylight. 'Here, Veronica, hold this and take it away when I am up.'

Shouts rose up the stairs, and loud heavy hobnail boots followed. 'Where's Michael Collins?'

The steps on the stairs neared, and Veronica whispered, 'Hurry, Michael, I can hear them.'

He was nearly at the top of the ladder and pushed the skylight open, but his foot slipped, and he fell back.

'Michael, hurry.'

He steadied himself on the ladder, then was up and out of the skylight. Eibhlin and Ernest Blythe appeared by Veronica's side, and Veronica handed the ladder to Ernest. He put the ladder into the hidden cupboard near the toilet, pushing the filing cabinet in front of the door just as the soldiers arrived.

'Where's the bastard?'

'Who?' said Ernest, trying to walk past them.

'Michael bloody Collins.'

'Michael who?'

'Don't be a smartarse with me, if you know what's good for ye,' the soldier snarled.

A sergeant pushed through the soldiers. 'If ye had moved quicker, we might have caught him.' He looked at them. 'Right, Smith, get everyone's names and details.' He glanced at the wall clock. 'Right, make it snappy.' He handed the soldier a black notebook and pencil.

'What's your name?' he asked Veronica.

'Veronica.'

'Veronica who?'

'Veronica McDermott.'

Writing it down in the notebook, he said, 'How old are ye?' He wasn't as rough as the younger soldiers.

'Nineteen.'

He asked everyone their names. He wrote them in the notebook, and then he clapped it closed and said, 'Lads, downstairs, now.'

Everybody stood silently on the landing, listening to the soldiers on the floor below in Michael's old office. A bookcase crashed to the floor, books pulled from the shelves and thrown against the walls. They opened drawers, relieving them of their contents. Mrs O'Reilly's face was now red, looking like she would explode with anger at any minute. Veronica silently moved to the stairs to see if they had found Michael's safe.

As she passed Eibhlin, they gave each other's hands a small squeeze. A bead of sweat formed on Eibhlin's forehead. Their eyes locked, trying to communicate with each other. Veronica knew the safe was where Michael kept his files on the DMP and the activities of the English. He had many spies in Dublin Castle who passed information to him regularly.

'Veronica, you go and see if they found his safe,' Ernest whispered and gave her a gentle shove. 'Tell them you want to go to your desk or something.'

She walked soundlessly back down to her office. A few unposted letters she had typed to the Cumann lay on the floor. Mrs O'Reilly's flowers had been trampled, the blue vase in smithereens.

On Veronica's desk lay the pile of letters for the Cumann na mBán.

'Nothing in here, lads, search the other office,' said a soldier in Michael's office.

Veronica walked to her desk.

'Stop! What are you doing?' a soldier shouted.

'Sorry, what did you say?' Veronica turned to look at him. The soldier had three stripes on his arm, a sergeant.

Suddenly there was a thud, and Veronica looked round. Mrs O'Reilly had come into the office and fallen to the floor. A trickle of blood flowed from her forehead.

'Quick help!'

'Are ye all right?' said a young soldier, handing her a handkerchief and picking her up to sit her on her chair.

The sergeant said gruffly, 'She's grand, leave the Fenian alone.'

Veronica caught Mrs O'Reilly's eye, who winked at her. In the commotion, Veronica stuffed the letters to the Cumann under her skirt.

'Come on, lads. There's nothing here.' And the soldiers retreated.

Veronica's hatred of the English soldiers was increasing daily. She and others left the office to go out to the landing, papers thrown everywhere.

'Right, listen, everybody,' Ernest said, with remarkable calm. 'Everything's fine. Michael escaped through the skylight.

When are they going to learn, he always is one step ahead of them?'

Mrs O'Reilly nodded. 'You're right, Ernest.' She started to pick up the papers. 'It's late, we'll go home when we're done.'

34

Each Tuesday morning, farmers, shop owners, and business people lodged money in the Sinn Féin Bank. The air in Dublin was thick with hope, but also thick with gunfire. The streets were now full of dangers for people waiting to attack British soldiers. People had developed unity and more insidious methods to fight the British. It was said by many that every man, woman and child concealed a gun. Veronica had arrived in Dublin an innocent young girl, and now she was a woman who had experienced more than she ever thought possible.

More people than ever were joining the Volunteers, and people in the Sinn Féin offices were on high alert as the raids intensified from the soldiers and the DMP.

On her way home, a familiar voice called out, 'Veronica, how are you?'

It was Harry. He looked pale. His once tight uniform now hung a bit looser on him.

'It's good to see you, Veronica. That purple colour of your coat suits you.' He hesitated. 'You look beautiful.'

Her cheeks burned.

'I'm so glad to have bumped into you. Please accept my

apologies for not contacting you, but we are under a lot of pressure. The streets are not the same. My men are under constant attack. The other day some were walking down Dawson St, and a woman pulled a gun out of her pram. Luckily, when she pulled the trigger, it didn't work.'

She had to keep him talking. 'That's hard,' she said, thinking fast. 'How do you feel about the new Dáil? I read about it in the papers. It must be hard especially with the continued attacks on anyone English.' She carefully watched his face, finding herself wishing he wasn't wearing that tell-tale uniform.

'I wish it were different. We are so different, our birth, our accents, but yet I feel we're not. Don't worry, Veronica, we have our surveillance on people that we expect trouble from.'

She shivered as she stared into his eyes, but held her resolve, which turned out to be easy, staring at him.

'Do you know what would be lovely, Veronica? Tea in the Shelbourne. Unfortunately, I don't have another day off until the last Saturday of the month. Will you meet me? At 4 p.m. Please.'

She nodded, smiling up at him, and he stroked her face. This time she didn't flinch.

A young woman, no older than Susan, walked past them in the middle of the road, pushing a black pram and hissed, 'English scum.'

An army vehicle tooted its horn behind her. She tried to lift the pram onto the path out of their way but struggled under the weight of her children.

Without a word, Harry took the pram from the woman and lifted it onto the path.

She didn't look at him, or thank him. Turning back to Veronica he lifted his cap and left.

Veronica stood for a few minutes, watching Harry, the army vehicle and the young mother. She reflected on her reasons for meeting Harry, and feelings to where she was now. Another army vehicle drove slowly by, full of soldiers with the guns pointing at the streets ready for attack, so Veronica didn't stay long in the street. She needed to contact Michael, and he had moved to his new office.

35

'Veronica, would you go to Michael's office? It's 76 Harcourt St. He sent word that he needs somebody to take shorthand and type the letters for him. Be a dear go, my legs are stiff and swollen today,' said Mrs O'Reilly as she rubbed them, hoping to find relief.

'Grand, I'll make you some tea first before I go. It's the least I can do for you.'

Lately, Mrs O'Reilly found it hard to climb the two flights of stairs to the office. In the small kitchen, Veronica made some tea and put it in Mrs O'Reilly's favourite pink cup and saucer. She managed to find her a few biscuits hidden in the cupboard.

She carried the tray back to the office past Michael's old room. The bookshelves had been emptied, the filing cabinet hung open, and three boxes of files were in the middle of the floor. Somebody else was ready to move in. Mrs O'Reilly smiled when Veronica returned with the tea, but Veronica knew it was the biscuits that made her smile.

'Lovely, dear, though you know I probably could lose a few pounds,' she said, spooning three sugars into her tea. 'Don't forget your coat and hat, it's still cold out there.

And take paper; I'm sure Michael will have some but take your own. Always be prepared, Veronica.'

As she left the building, she spotted four soldiers standing opposite the entrance. They never took their eyes off her while they stamped their finished cigarettes into the ground. She ignored their stares but felt their eyes burrowing into the back of her neck. Looking ahead, she walked to Michael's office as if she didn't care about them.

Few people were on the street and the walk to Michael's building only took a few minutes. His office was on the second floor. As she passed the closed doors on the way up the stairs, she heard the low murmur of voices behind them.

The smell of fresh paint lingered in the hallway, and she knocked carefully on Michael's door as she wasn't sure whether it was dry. Michael sat behind a mahogany desk covered in loose sheets of paper. The fire blazed, but the windows were wide open.

'Veronica, it's good to see you.'

To the left and right of Michael's desk were large stacks of papers. The bookcase behind was overflowing with books and files. The smell of fresh paint inside the office was a reminder of how her own office at number 6 had the 'lived in' look. A lovely smell of turf filled the room, and memories of home pulled her away from Dublin for a minute to Cavan.

'Oh, Veronica, take a seat and take notes. I want to write to everyone in business to tell them to stop paying taxes to the Inland Revenue in England. One, it will hurt their tax intake, and two, we will use the money for our government.'

Michael made it sound so simple.

'When they are typed, send them out to as many people as possible. And I'll get it printed in the newspapers.'

When she'd finished taking notes, Veronica tucked her notepad and pencil inside her coat. 'I'll hurry back to the office and Mrs O'Reilly and I will have them typed in no time. Also, Michael, I bumped into the major by accident on the street. He asked me to meet him the last Saturday of this month at the Shelbourne.'

Michael chewed on his pencil, 'I don't know, he hasn't given us much information. Let me think for a minute or two.'

She shivered as a gust of cold air blew into the room, the flames of the fire flickering, fighting against the wind.

'I don't know. I'll get back to you about the major. Hurry back now and keep the notes tight in your coat. Keep a watchful eye on the crowds, you never know where they will seize you. We're all being watched.'

She hurried back to the warmth of her office at number 6 and shook off the cold as she entered the building.

Mrs O'Reilly got up from her desk when Veronica entered the office. 'You look perished, dear. Warm yourself at the fire, and I'll make the tea.'

'Thanks, Mrs O'Reilly, you have no idea how cold his office is. Michael wants these letters typed as soon as possible and sent to as many businesses as we can.'

Mrs O'Reilly's eyes narrowed as she read the letters. She sighed. 'He is such a clever man. And Veronica, did he tell you about the film?'

'No.'

'Oh Veronica,' Mrs O'Reilly was excited. 'Sorry, dear, I have to catch my breath. Michael is going to make a film showing him receiving money from important people in the hope ordinary people will donate money for the new Dáil.'

Veronica frowned. 'That surely wouldn't work.'

Mrs O'Reilly didn't answer. She was typing furiously, returning the carriage on the typewriter without stopping. 'Veronica, come on, we have a lot of letters to type.'

They stayed late to get the letters typed and posted the following day to the farmers and the trade unions advising them not to send money to the English Inland Revenue. It was a success. Money flowed into Harcourt St, and from there it was sent to a safe house for those hiding from the soldiers.

The last Saturday of the month approached, and Veronica had spent the week waiting for Michael's orders, but he was never in the office more than a few minutes.

On Friday evening as Veronica tidied her desk, ready to go home from work, Michael called into the office for paperwork from Mrs O'Reilly.

Before he left, he passed Veronica mouthing, 'Good luck,' and said more loudly, 'I'll see you Monday, Veronica,' and winked.

That evening Veronica sat at the kitchen table with paper, a pen and a pot of ink to write to Susan while Betty darned a sock that had seen better days. The cat pulled the wool, Betty pulling it back from him in a game of tug of war.

'Veronica, are you all right? You look worried.'

'I'm fine,' she said with a smile, hoping to placate Betty's worries. Veronica knew she looked upon her as a daughter; just because Padraig was dead, she hadn't lost her mother's instinct to protect her young.

'Betty, I'm fine. I'm just telling Susan I'm meeting Bridget tomorrow afternoon.' She dropped her eyes in shame. So many lies. She didn't know if Michael's nod and wink were an affirmation to meet the major.

'Have you heard from Eddie?'

Veronica's eyes snapped to Betty. 'No, have you?' she asked, searching her face for some positive news.

'No,' she said sighing as she dropped the sock and needle on the small table beside the fire and took rosary beads from the table. 'Last night, I said an extra decade of the rosary for him.' She rolled her fingers over her beads, her mouth silently moving as she began her first *Hail Mary*. The cat jumped on her lap, knowing he would get at least twenty minutes of peace while Betty was lost in prayer.

Veronica shook her head. All Betty's rosaries hadn't helped Padraig.

She started to write to Bridget, asking about Sam. In Bridget's last letter to Veronica, she had asked her if she met anyone yet? What could she write? Could she write yes, she had, that he was kind, handsome, polite, but the purpose was to get information from him because he was the enemy? Why would she think of words like those to describe him? She should be writing words of disgust and anger. The blank page lay on the table. She was out of her depth. Delivering the parcels for Tom had been so simple.

But this situation could go in any direction. Ink fell from her pen onto the blank paper and was swiftly absorbed, its tributaries spreading in different directions. Veronica folded the paper in the middle of the inkblot, a game she and Eddie had played as children. She opened the paper, and the symmetrical shape looked like a butterfly. She studied it, and then confidence simmered. If something so bland and nondescript could change into something as beautiful as a butterfly, then she could meet the major and improvise to see what direction it took.

36

On the last Saturday of May, just before 4 p.m., Veronica stood outside the Shelbourne. Her cheeks still hurt where she had pinched them. It was something she had learned from Bridget.

'Veronica, pinch your cheeks, my older sister told me boys find red cheeks attractive,' she had said one Saturday afternoon while they sat near the window in O'Shea's tearooms, watching a group of young lads on the opposite side of the street.

It wasn't a boy she was meeting, but a man. Not in the circumstances she had imagined, a man that was the enemy. She still wanted to impress him though, and she had taken care with her choice of clothes, choosing a cream and brown dress that complimented her green eyes, before pinning her unruly hair.

As she walked into the hotel, she didn't make eye contact with the stiff doorman at the entrance. His black tailcoat with gold buttons and cold stare made her quiver, but she held her steel and ignored him. The gold and white marble in the foyer had a soothing calmness that was a stark contrast to the unrest on the streets. The Shelbourne had suffered attacks in the 1916 Rising, but they were quick to restore it to its former splendour.

The silver-haired woman at the front desk was a little less rigid than the doorman. Smiling at Veronica, she said, 'Can I help you, madam?'

Veronica took a steadying breath. 'No, thank you, I'm meeting a friend,' she said, and hurried towards the tearooms, not wanting to engage in a conversation as her accent was a sign that Veronica shouldn't be there.

The tearooms were not as busy as the first time she had been there. She guessed it might have been because of the dangers on the streets. Once men had kept their arms out of sight, now they were openly carrying rifles, slung casually over their shoulders. On the streets of Dublin, an exchange of gunfire between the British soldiers and the Irish had become a daily occurrence.

She waited at the door to be seated, and a gentleman the same age as her Uncle Tom passed her on his way out. But that was where the similarity ended, with his finely oiled moustache and crisp white shirt. He nodded and tipped his hat at Veronica.

Harry sat at the corner table, the waiter pouring his tea. He didn't see her approach, and he spoke to the waiter who laughed as he served him. Harry rose when he saw Veronica and pulled the chair out for her.

As soon as she sat down, he took her hand. He looked at her, his brown eyes dull, without the confident, warm aura he usually radiated. He dropped his head and whispered, 'I'm sorry, I've been keeping something from you.' The words rushed out of his mouth. 'I am engaged.'

She pulled her hand away. This should not be a problem, yet she was experiencing an emotion that she knew she should not have – jealousy.

A heavy silence fell between them; neither tried to break it.

His head hung low. 'I know little happened, but really I wanted it to.' He leant over the table, taking her hand in his. 'Veronica, please believe me, it will be a loveless marriage. My father arranged it. Our family has little money. When my father married my mother, not only was she French, but a French Catholic, and that was frowned upon by his superiors in the army, so he didn't get promoted. Subsequently, my father arranged for me to marry a woman of means. He sprung it on me when I went home, and I didn't feel like I had a reason, one he would accept, to say no. If I told him I was seeing an Irish Catholic woman… I can't imagine it would have gone well.'

Veronica took a sharp breath, trying to control her anger. Why did she feel anger?

'Sir, do you want to order tea for the lady?' the waiter interrupted them, the same waiter who had served them the first day she had met Harry in the Shelbourne.

This revelation was unexpected, but did it matter? Her job was not to question his fidelity. She had to help Ireland and if it meant meeting an English soldier, then she would.

'Are you angry?'

'Harry,' she hesitated and chose her words carefully and in a measured tone. 'I've enjoyed my time with you.' The words did not come easy. She composed herself and looked him straight in his eyes, concentrating on the green fleck in his right eye. 'No, I'm not angry.'

She looked at him carefully, noticing stress lines she hadn't seen before. He had dark shadows underneath his eyes, and his cheekbones were slightly prominent.

'But it's not right. Would it not go against your beliefs, your Catholic beliefs?'

Taking a deep breath, she said, 'No, not at all.' Mystified why she was feeling the way she was, that jealousy hovered. She even felt slightly sad for him.

He held her gaze, and she stared back, putting her feelings aside. This was silly, she told herself. She was with him to do a job, and nothing more.

The rattle of teacups broke their silence. 'Sir, madam, your tea.'

When the waiter left, Harry half-smiled. 'Are you sure, Veronica?' His eyes searched hers.

'I'm not naive,' she said and smiled at him. 'I understand that we could never have a future together.'

He collapsed back into the chair. 'Veronica, I'm so glad. I so wish it could be different. I like the Irish. I met many of them in the trenches, and I felt I had a connection, and the stories from their homes were awful. Many said they had no choice but to join the army, as they needed to feed their families. I think some were from a place called Dingle. They told me about the famine, and I was so ashamed when they told me stories of grain grown in Ireland in 1847, which was sent to England instead of being given to the poor. Many of them said they lost family to hunger, and if not hunger, then it was to the boat. I am English, and I know the role I have played here in Ireland, but it has never really felt like a choice.'

Veronica couldn't speak. She found it hard to reconcile that he had empathy with the Irish during the famine. Guilt washed through her that he gave more thought about the plight of her ancestors than she had. Now she saw poverty flowing on the streets of Dublin, a kind of poverty that she hadn't seen or noticed in Virginia, she realised how selfish her thoughts had been.

The clock chimed 5 p.m.

'Veronica, I've got to go,' he said and drank the last mouthful of tea.

'Oh, so soon? I thought we might go for a walk.'

'Veronica, it has gotten so dangerous, I don't want to put you in danger.' He paused, his eyes and brown hair light in the sun that shone through the large window. 'I fear for your safety. Maybe it would be better if we didn't continue.'

'No,' she said and meant it.

'Maybe the next time we should meet somewhere discreet?'

Did he fear for her safety, or was he hiding her from his superiors?

Her reaction surprised her as there was a tug of sadness that she might never see him again. She pushed this aside. She had a job to do.

She took his hand and a jolt ran through her. Again, a feeling she couldn't explain. 'Harry I'd love to continue meeting you. As I said, it doesn't matter to me that you're engaged.'

He smiled and held her gaze as if memorising her face. 'We'll meet soon. Now I really must go. They are waiting for me back at the barracks,' he said, and motioned the waiter to bring his coat.

He pulled out her chair, and bent so his lips brushed her cheek. 'See you soon, Veronica.' His smell lingered in the air as she watched him pull up his collar and hurry towards the door. He looked back at Veronica, smiled and then hurried on to his destination.

Before Veronica went to work Monday morning, she called at Michael's new office.

Michael sat at his desk with a phone and two piles of papers. His right hand flicked through a pile, while his other held the phone. He nodded at her to sit down in front of him until he'd finished his call. 'Well, Veronica, have you news for me? First, what do you think of this?'

She took the paper he slid across the desk. It had a red wax seal, and she carried it to the window to see it better. The seal she had seen many times before on documents in the office. It was a lion and a horse, standing on two legs, and in the middle was a coat of arms.

'What do you think? Does it look authentic?'

'I'm not sure, what am I looking at?'

'The Royal Seal or, to be more exact, The Great Seal.'

'What are you using it for?' She was confused.

'Well, we could send a letter to General Maxwell that they want him back in the UK, then attack the Castle. Enough about that, what news have you for me?' He poured milk into a teacup, gulped it in one mouthful and wiped his mouth. 'Well?'

Veronica smiled apologetically. She believed the news the major was engaged would be of little significance to Michael, though she had tossed and turned Saturday night ruminating on the news. 'He is engaged to an Englishwoman. I'm sorry I have nothing worthwhile for you.'

Michael clasped his hands. 'That's brilliant, tell him you will meet him.'

'Eh, I already did. But why is that brilliant?'

'Blackmail, that's why that's brilliant.'

'How? I didn't think of that.' She frowned. 'Tell his fiancée?'

Michael shook his head, 'No, he is more afraid of General Maxwell than his wife. The last thing he would want his superiors to know is his liaisons with a Fenian, and a Fenian who works for Sinn Féin. I guess it would mean treason, and you know what that means?'

Veronica shook her head.

'Execution. He'd be seen as a traitor, and the last thing the army wants is someone sleeping with the enemy.'

Veronica gasped. 'I'm not sleeping with him.'

Michael frowned and waved his hand. 'I mean metaphorically, not literally.'

The phone rang. Michael answered it and put his hand over the receiver. 'Veronica, brilliant work, I'll talk to you later this week. I'll think of something. Keep him interested.'

She went to work. Mrs O'Reilly smiled at her and

chatted about the lovely hydrangeas in her garden, telling her they were pink last year, but blue this year. She wasn't listening. Blackmail sounded dangerous, but she would have to trust Michael.

The following day, Veronica and Bridget met in the tearooms in Abbey St.

She crossed the river at the Ha'penny Bridge to Abbey St leading to Mary St, where two soldiers tore posters from the wall in front of the Volta Electric Theatre, laughing as they threw the ripped paper on the ground.

Three young boys sat on the wall opposite the cinema shouting at them. 'Go home, ye English scum.'

She tried to read the next poster before they ripped it from the wall of the cinema. The soldiers ignored Veronica as she walked by. A piece of the poster lay on the ground, and she read it upside down: *Now Showi... Dáil Loan.*

It was the poster for Michael Collins's film, to get money for the Dáil Loan. Bile rose in her throat. She clenched her fists and wanted to shout *stop*, but the soldiers' guns rattled as they pulled and ripped the posters. She was no match for them. Michael would be furious; all his efforts to contact people here and in America, and they were trying to jeopardise it.

The clouds parted, throwing light in her path. Usually, it pleased her to look at the shadows created by the surrounding buildings, but today, all sense of pleasure was lost. When she finally got to the tearoom, Bridget entered at the same time.

'Bridget, you look great! Work must agree with you.' Veronica knew she herself looked drained.

'It's great, V, the girls are so good, but your work must be a lot more exciting. I am so jealous.'

Bridget's eyes danced. 'Veronica, I have some news. Sam asked me to marry him.'

Veronica hugged her instantly. 'I'm so happy for you.'

'I'm nearly twenty, and I don't want to be left on the shelf. Mammy and Daddy have come around to him. They see that he is a hard worker and he doesn't drink at all.'

They drank tea as Veronica listened to Bridget tell her all about Sam. A lump swelled in her throat. They parted with promises to meet again soon, but Veronica knew that was unlikely as married life meant babies, and Bridget's new role as a wife would mean looking after Sam.

37

The nights became shorter, and the days warmer as St Stephen's Green burst into life. With the gentle riot of greens and vibrant colours of the rhododendrons on the Green, memories of the countryside surfaced. Veronica gave into homesickness, and her desire to see the ducklings on the lake of Lough Ramor and walk in the fields surrounding their farm, so went back to Cavan for a few days.

She took the train from Broadstone to Oldcastle, where her father met her. He had finally bought a motorcar. The fresh breeze replaced the stale pungent air of the city. The hedgerows of primroses and thorn bushes replaced the red-brick buildings of the tenements. She had missed the unrestricted freedom of the air in the countryside; only now did she realise how constricted city life was. As she passed through the village of Virginia and over the Blackwater, she relaxed when she saw the entrance to her home. Nearing the house, the donkey brayed, and the chickens clucked in the yard at the back of the house. For once, she missed the simplicity of country life.

When she got out of the car, her mother was waiting at the front door.

'Veronica. Look at you, so thin and your hair in... I don't know what sort of a style that is.' Her mother was flapping around her. 'You look well, though. Richard, bring in her case.'

The smell of freshly baked bread made her mouth water. As much as Betty tried, she couldn't make bread like Mrs Slaney.

They had a light lunch of eggs and lettuce, most of which Veronica pushed around her plate, lost in thought of the letter she would write to Harry. Why was she upset he was engaged? It shouldn't bother her he had another life, or that he had feelings for someone else. Their entire relationship was a lie, after all. Susan convinced Veronica that they should get out of the house for a while, so they packed a small picnic and went to the lakeshore.

'Veronica eat some of these buns, you are so thin. They are delicious.' Susan was lying on her back, twisting the bun above her, trying not to let the glistening cream drop on her face.

'No, I'm not hungry.' Veronica's throat was dry and tight; her head spun.

'What's wrong?' Susan mumbled as she brushed crumbs resting on her chin.

'Nothing, I'm fine. I feel a bit hot.' Veronica didn't like hiding anything from her family, but she could not tell Susan about Harry.

'Veronica, are you listening?' Susan sat up. 'I was telling you about the rooster chasing the chickens, and Daddy had to go in and stop him because he wanted to catch a chicken to kill but...' She looked at Veronica, a frown crossing her forehead. 'Something is wrong.'

'No, I said I'm fine.'

Susan leaned in whispering, 'Eddie...'

'What about Eddie? Has he been home?' She didn't know if he had been back to Virginia or was still in Cork.

Susan started crying. 'No, you know he is in prison. I hate this country. Why couldn't we have stayed the same? Everybody is going away.'

Veronica moved to sit beside Susan and took her hand. Her father had shielded Susan from Eddie's escape. 'Susan, you know Father is passionate about the cause. We need our freedom. It's our right.'

Still whimpering, Susan replied, 'I know.'

Veronica pulled her cardigan tight around her, as the clouds crossed over the sun.

'Veronica, tell me what's wrong. Mother is worried. I'm worried. You're thin. You haven't touched the scones. Mrs Slaney baked them, especially for you.'

'Susan, I'm just tired. I probably need a tonic; that's all.' She took a scone to prove she was feeling fine but spilt the cream and jam on her dress. She watched the spilt red jam seeping down the white cotton.

'Father is away all the time, and poor Eddie is never coming home, and Mother cries all the time alone in her bedroom.'

'Well, these are the times we live in,' Veronica snapped, 'nothing is constant.'

'V, where are you going?'

Her mother shouted something to her as she ran past the drawing-room and into her bedroom, but she couldn't hear her. She lay down on the bed, thinking, trying to rationalise everything. She pulled out the pins in her hair, letting it escape over her pillow to fall asleep. Mrs Slaney fed her, and her mother fussed over her, and after a few days, she was rested and well-fed, and ready to return to Dublin.

In Thomas St, she sat beside Betty at the fire, the dancing flames soothing her. As usual, Betty had the rosary beads in her hand and was at the last bead, her mouth moving to finish the prayer before she spoke to Veronica.

'I'm glad you're home, if this can be called home for you.'

'Of course, it is, even the cat is happy to see me.' That was when she realised the cat had no name.

The sound of boots neared the front door, it opened, and Tom entered.

'Veronica, it's so good to have you back.'

The chair scraped on the wooden floor as he pulled it towards the fire. Once he would have had the strength to lift the table, now he couldn't lift the chair. 'I don't have long left at lifting barrels. Ah, Veronica, don't look so worried, I'm not beaten just yet, I can still flick the reins in the dray, and I'll just get one of the boys to help me lift the barrels of Guinness. Are you going back to the offices tomorrow?'

'Yes, I'm looking forward to it,' she said, thinking about the letter she'd written to Harry. She did as Michael said, and wrote reiterating that it didn't matter he was engaged and hoped they would meet again soon.

The next morning, on her walk to Harcourt St, she saw children waiting outside shops along the quays, to see if the shopkeepers might throw them some sweets or food. As she passed O'Connell Bridge, the women in Sackville St sat at the base of Nelson's Pillar, setting up their baskets of flowers to sell.

At the office, she checked her hair in the window reflection, because the wind had blown her hat off three times.

Mrs O'Reilly sat at her desk, looking flustered. 'Oh, Veronica, thank God you're here. Things have been so busy. We don't know what to do with all the money. I never thought I'd make it here this morning, it's so blustery.'

'Sorry, Mrs O'Reilly, what money?'

'The money. He was right, everybody stopped sending taxes to England, and they sent it here. We are overwhelmed with the amount of money we've got. I know we got some before you left, but a few days later it just kept coming in. And the film Michael made for the Loan worked!'

Veronica cast her eyes over the coins and piles of paper money that lay scattered on the two desks. Veronica had been wrong thinking the soldiers tearing down the posters would destroy the chances of Sinn Féin raising money. The film had been a success and the patriotic farmers bought bonds.

'We have hidden so much of it already in safe houses and shops. The soldiers and DMP keep raiding us hoping to take some of it. Because of the frequency of the raids, we move it out as soon as we get it,' Mrs O'Reilly said. 'Veronica take a pile and start counting it. Put it in a bag and record how much is in each one. Here, take some money bags.' She gave Veronica two bulging brown bags. She looked inside one of them – it was full of copper coins and pound notes, and she counted at least twenty bags on the floor beside Mrs O'Reilly's desk. 'Start counting, and don't forget to write down how much is in each bag.'

At lunchtime, as they ate their sandwiches, Veronica stuck her head out of the window, hoping to catch a breeze. Mothers walked by on the street below, bringing their children to the park to feed the ducks. Michael walked towards her building with the usual confidence, but there was an urgency in his steps. Within minutes he was in the office.

'Veronica, good you're back, there is so much to do. I've records for ye to type for all the money we received. Where's Frank?' Michael asked Mrs O'Reilly. He paced up and down the office. 'Well, where is he? He was supposed to come to meet me and take money to a safe house.'

'He's gone. His wife is in labour, poor woman. It's her seventh child.'

'Or Timmy? Where is he?'

'He's delivering papers but going to see his sick aunt in the hospital after. I think she is dying. His mother died when he was young, and she brought him up and—'

'Christ,' he said, as he opened his jacket letting two packets fall to the ground. He picked them up and put them on the table.

'Is everything all right? Me and Veronica have all the donations in bags.'

'I've just had word the DMP are planning a raid again tomorrow, and I need to get the money delivered to Donnybrook. We have been given a house to hide the money – in fact, a few houses. Is there nobody here?'

'No, all the men are gone out for the afternoon.'

'Jesus.' He paced the room, rubbing his hand through his hair.

He opened his mouth to say something, and Veronica murmured, 'I'll do it.'

Michael slowly turned to Veronica, a surprised look on his face. Nobody, however, felt more astounded than Veronica.

'What did you say?'

'I'll do it. Don't look so worried. It's no problem. I won't get caught, and by now I really have built up nerves of steel. Can it be any more dangerous than walking to work? Just tell me the address.'

Michael scribbled the address down. 'Take two bags and keep them hidden in a coat or something. This is a start. Go when it's dark and be careful, say your sister is having a baby, and you're on the way to help her. And, Veronica, take a bike. It'll be safer.'

At Thomas St, Betty put a plate of eggs and bacon in front of her. 'Your favourite, Veronica. Your father sent it. Tom put down that newspaper and come for your tea.'

Tom threw the paper on the table beside Veronica, the headline: *Alan Bell Dragged from Tram and Shot in Cork.*

She told Betty she was going for a walk after tea.

'I'll walk with you for a bit,' Tom said, giving Veronica a wink.

Outside and with Tom's help, they put the money bags inside Veronica's coat, trying not to make it too bulky.

'Don't look so worried. I'll be all right. I'll take the bike, Tom?'

'Veronica, the bike is gone, someone stole it. You can't leave anything on the streets here before someone goes off with it.'

'I'll have to walk.'

'Be careful, don't talk to anyone and avoid the army,' Tom said.

A wave of emotion came over her; she was so lucky to have so many people in her life who cared for her.

'I'll be fine and thank you so much for everything.'

Tom held Veronica's hand tight. 'Veronica, you're helping us with the cause.' He paused. 'Your arrival into my life – our lives – has been a gift from God. I would despair if anything happened to you now.'

Veronica hugged Tom, 'I'll be fine. I'd better go. Don't be worried, who'll stop me? I'm a woman.'

Night had fallen. The lack of light from the moonless and starless night offered some protection. Thankful of the clouds, she hoped it wouldn't rain. The money wrapped tight around her dug into her waist. The dim lights in the streets got sparse as she covered the distance from the city centre towards Donnybrook. A cat screeched in the distance. Calming herself with the rhythm of her breathing, she counted her footsteps to keep her mind busy. She listened out for the rumble of a patrolling army vehicle. Luckily the night was silent. She didn't notice the group of men in front of her, their dark uniforms concealed in the shadows.

'Well, love, where are you going? All alone?' said a soldier as he moved closer, his face rough and hair unkempt.

She stopped. 'I am on my way to visit my sister; she's having a baby. I know there's a curfew, but it's urgent.'

'Really?'

She couldn't see their faces. Their silhouettes shifted, and there was a rattle, which she assumed was a gun against a belt. Another soldier moved towards her. His baby face hadn't even been graced with a shaving blade yet. He couldn't have been more than sixteen.

'Come on, let's go,' said a nervous voice. This offered her some comfort. He was inexperienced. Veronica knew they would be worried as no protection was provided in the surrounding dark road. There was no light from the lamps, either because they were new or had not been refuelled. If they searched her and found the money, she would be interrogated and maybe even beaten. There must have been a power cut. Sometimes that meant an impending ambush. She hoped not as she didn't want to be caught in the crossfire.

The rumble of a vehicle in the distance approached them. The soldiers turned. This was her opportunity. Veronica quickly opened her coat, ripped out the packets and threw them into the river.

A gruff Cockney accent said, 'Here, what are ye doing?'

He grabbed her, but the money parcels were soon gone with the fast, angry flow of the river.

'Ya' bitch, trying to outsmart us? Here, Derek, hold her.' Another soldier pulled her roughly. 'What the hell was in the parcels?'

'Baby clothes.'

He tightened his grip while sticking a rifle into her side.

'You took me last parcel. It was butter. I wasn't going to let you take them.'

'Lying bitch.'

The vehicle headlights neared and slowed. One soldier stood in the middle of the road and waved it down – it was a patrol truck.

'You're coming with us,' he said, hoisting her up and throwing her into the back of the vehicle.

She fell onto the rough wooden surface, grazing herself, and blood oozed from her knee. Her head hit the side of the truck, and a searing pain went through her body before everything went silent and black.

She woke up groggy. Veronica tried to sit, but her head hurt. She commanded her stiff limbs to give in to her demands and put her hands on the cold dirt floor before heaving herself up. She breathed in deeply, every muscle, every cell screaming in agony. Her eyes slowly adjusted to the darkness. She shivered in the damp air and sat listening. She wasn't in the vehicle anymore, and it was a room that smelled of dust and damp. Faint talking came through the wall.

Now she remembered being pushed into the room and thrown across a dirt floor. Somebody had screamed, 'Where were ya' going?' before a boot had thudded into her side.

She had to get out of the room. Trying to stop herself from fainting again, she crawled across the dirt floor, stopping at a wall. With all her efforts, she stood, ignoring the pain. Veronica ran her hands along the slimy wall, hoping they would guide her to the door. A small rectangular darkness on one side of the wall near the ceiling was a shade lighter indicating it probably was a street window. From that, she guessed the door was on the opposite side across the room. The light was getting brighter, meaning she had been in the basement all night.

The voices started talking again, 'What time ye finish at?'

'The missus is having a baby, so I'll stay awhile.'

Boots moved quickly across the dirt. 'Major.'

'Who is in there?'

It was Harry.

'Some b… It's a woman. I recognised her from our raids on Sinn Féin offices.'

That's why they had captured her. There was silence for a minute.

'Give me the keys.'

Veronica shrank away, fearing how Harry might treat her. Her heart was beating in her ears. Her body shook.

The key scratched in the lock; every scrape of the key against the metal sent shocks through her body.

The door opened, and Harry said, 'It's fine. I'll go in on my own.'

The door slammed shut.

'Veronica, are you all right?' Without saying anything, he took hold of her arm and pulled her to him. 'I heard they had captured a woman – a woman who works for Sinn Féin.' Harry banged on the door. 'Finnegan, open the door.'

A pale soldier stood in front of them. His stance was not confident.

'I'm taking this woman to Kilmainham Jail to interrogate her there.'

'Yes, sir,' he said as he stood aside.

One of the other soldiers slept on the chair in the corner with his feet up on the table.

Harry gripped her arm. She wanted to run. Kilmainham Jail, that was where the leaders of the 1916 Rising had been executed.

They walked in silence along the corridor, Harry bending his head so as not to hit the ceiling. Weak lights hung every few feet along the walls of the stone corridor. They emerged into a yard, the regular yard of Dublin Castle. It was dawn. The cobblestones glistened from rain during the night. Harry guided her to the entrance of the Castle to a waiting car with a soldier in the driver's seat.

'Take this lady home to Thomas St,' he said to the driver of the car.

He knew where she lived. God, he must have had her followed. She shuddered.

He looked at her shocked face. 'Don't you think I had you checked out when I first met you?'

Before she could say anything, even a thank you, he was gone.

Veronica sat in the back of the car. They drove in silence,

and soon the car stopped outside Thomas St. She didn't know whether or not to thank the man. She did.

Veronica watched the car pull away, her emotions in turmoil. She ran up the stairs to Betty and Tom.

Tom met her in the hallway. Hugging her, he said, 'You are so lucky, why did they let you go? Did they hurt you? James Sheridan was here – Michael sent him. His cousin works in Dublin Castle, God you are shaking. Betty take Veronica's coat and make some tea.'

Betty's face was white, but sagged slightly with relief as she hugged Veronica.

'Thank God,' Betty whispered. 'Veronica, are you all right? When James Sheridan called, he told us what happened. We were so worried; we didn't know what we would tell your father if anything happened to you.'

'I'm fine, just tired.'

'Have some tea and go and lie down in your bed for the day.'

'No, I'll go into the office and tell them what happened.' She sat up and stretched the pain away.

'James will have told them, go to bed and rest.'

She shook her head. 'No, I'll go in. It's nine o'clock. I wouldn't be able to sleep.' And she wouldn't. Harry had known all along who she was, but never said. She felt unnerved.

Tom took his coat from the back of the chair. 'If you insist, I'll get the dray ready.'

When she entered the office, Mrs O'Reilly rushed to her, 'Veronica, love. Did the bastards hurt you? Sit by the fire, and I'll get Michael.'

'You're not hurt, are you?' Michael asked after hurrying to her side. 'How did you escape?'

'I'm fine. I'm just sorry I lost the money.'

'Oh, don't worry about that. You're fine, that's all that matters. It's not a disaster; we have so much money coming in, and we can get by without it.'

38

November 1920

Veronica couldn't believe it had been two years since women got the vote. Occasionally, Veronica thought about Harry, but she never let the thoughts linger for more than a second or two, pushing them back into the caverns of her mind. It had been over a year since she had seen him. Most of the time, her thoughts were accompanied by anger. He had deceived her, teasing emotions in her that she didn't know she had, but rescued her.

On Monday, 22 November 1920, Veronica went to work with a heavy heart.

'It's terrible, it's awful,' Mrs O'Reilly said. 'Did you hear, Veronica?' She placed the newspaper on Veronica's desk, white and ashen-faced, and sat down. 'Fourteen innocent men shot in cold blood.'

Earlier that morning on her way to work, at O'Connell Bridge, a paperboy had screamed *Blood Bath in Croke Park, Twelve Dead many Injured*. A group of men had surrounded the young paperboy, throwing money at him and grabbing their papers.

She'd scanned the paper, and run the rest of the way to work.

'My uncle told me yesterday evening. It's all anyone is talking about. So awful, so young, they were just at a football game.'

Over the last year, the war against the English had intensified. The previous March, England sent ex-servicemen called the Black and Tans to help the weakening RIC. The raids by the IRA were showing success, and many of the RIC were abandoning their stations as the Irish gained increasing control of their country. The Black and Tans were former soldiers from the War in Europe who had been sent to Ireland to help the soldiers and RIC control the Irish. They were rougher than the old British soldiers. Many had been in the trenches in Europe, and the scars of warfare left them with little emotions or no empathy. This was evident in the treatment of anyone they thought was an informer or in the IRA: shooting them in cold blood.

Mrs O'Reilly sobbed. 'Veronica look at this, two children killed as well.' She thumped the desk, tears rolling down her cheeks. 'Brutes, those men are nothing more than animals.'

'But, why did they attack innocent people, they were only playing a football match!'

'There had been a raid earlier that morning. Nine British undercover agents had been shot, and this attack on the footballers was in retaliation.'

'But they were innocent people!' Veronica exclaimed. 'God this is awful.'

After lunch, the atmosphere in the building was sorrowful, the building quiet in a mark of respect for the innocent people who had been killed.

Arthur stuck his head of dishevelled hair through the door. 'Ladies, you can go home early.'

The attacks increased on both sides. In December, eighteen Black and Tans were killed in Cork, and in retaliation, the Black and Tans burned half of Cork City.

Christmas arrived and Veronica made the long journey to Cavan to see her parents, glad to be away from the increasingly tense and often violent atmosphere in Dublin. On Christmas morning, the house was full of smells of the festivities. Veronica snuggled deeper into her soft feather mattress. She could get lost for hours in the calmness of her room and lay on her back, looking up to the ceiling. Thoughts of Harry seeped into her mind. Was he with his wife? Did he have children, or was it just the two of them laughing in each other's company? Why did that idea disturb her? The smell of turkey and puddings met her on the landing when she finally got up to go downstairs. Susan had been up for hours helping her mother to prepare the feast. Veronica entered the dining room for breakfast, stopping when she saw Eddie before running to her brother.

'Eddie, it's so good to see you.' She hugged him, feeling the bones of his rib cage. 'Look at you. When did you get home?' She winced a little at his smell.

Mrs Slaney pushed the door open with her back, holding

a tray with a plate of bacon and steaming tea. 'Sit, Eddie. Eat.'

'Does Mammy and Susan know you are here? Does Daddy?'

'Veronica, whist with your questions and let the boy eat. Of course your father knows, he's gone upstairs to tell your mother. You know she'd only faint if she saw him like this.' Mrs Slaney put the tray in front of Eddie, 'I'll have a hot bath ready for you after you eat.'

The door flung open with squeals from Susan, and her mother flapping her arms behind her, 'Eddie, thank God, your safe.'

Eddie wolfed his food, eating bacon and buttered bread in between gulps of hot sweet tea and when he finished, he burped and wiped his mouth. 'Excuse me, sorry, but the food is scarce when you're on the run. You're never sure of your next meal. Me and James left Cork four days ago travelling only at night, and our food only lasted two days.'

'Eddie, have some more tea, I'll go and get Mammy to make more,' said Veronica, but just as she got up, Mrs Slaney brought more food in. A plate of scones with melted butter dripping off them. 'Here Eddie, put some jam on them, you will need your strength before you go.'

Veronica gasped. 'Oh, Eddie, are you not staying for the day?' She sat beside him and took his hand, studying it, before pushing up his sleeve, 'Eddie,' she shrieked, 'look at your arms, they're skin and bone.'

Eddie yanked his arm back, pulling his sleeve down. 'Veronica, I can't wait around much longer. We've got a job to do. The Volunteers – that is, the Irish Republican Army – are getting so close to crushing the English. We have taken over all the RIC stations in Cavan and Monaghan and most of them in Leitrim. In the west, most of the stations have been abandoned, but in Cork and Kerry, it's a different story. We need to push on. At this rate, Veronica, we will be celebrating next Christmas in a different Ireland. But first, we must continue our attacks on the army. They are still putting up a fight, but we are winning more of the battles.'

'Eddie, please stay for the night and get a good rest. Sleeping rough in this weather will give you pleurisy.'

'No, Mammy, I and a few lads have to get going. I know you worry, but we are careful. We have a secure hiding place.'

'All right, let Mrs Slaney get your dinner to take with you, but first, have a bath. And I'll get some clean clothes,' she said, her incessant chatter masking her despair at her son leaving. 'Look, it's so cold outside and damp.'

Eddie took both his mother's hands. 'It's fine. We have somewhere warm and dry. It's better than prison, isn't it?'

'Yes, I know, Eddie, but if you are caught, you might be shot.'

'Ah, the English will never catch us. They aren't tough enough, and we are always one step ahead of them.'

The front door banged open, and their father shouted, 'Eddie, the Black and Tans are up at James Sheridan's house. You'd better leave. James has already left and gone towards Murmod Hill. Hurry, Eddie. You don't want to get caught.'

An ashen-faced Veronica grabbed Eddie's coat. 'Quick,' she said and wrapped the hot buttery scones in a newspaper before stuffing them into the pocket of his jacket.

Eddie hugged his tearful mother. 'Mammy, I've to go, I'll be careful.' He took the clean coat from Veronica.

Susan rushed into the room, crying as she said, 'Eddie, did Daddy say you have to leave? Can you not stay for the day?'

'No, but I'll promise I'll be careful,' he said and hugged everyone.

'Com' on, Eddie I've a horse ready for you. Go across the fields, and follow the stream, you know the way.'

'Eddie, there is food in the Icehouse in the forest. It will keep, so if you need supplies there will be some there.'

Eddie nodded and left. Veronica suppressed her tears, not knowing if it were the last time she would see him.

The Christmas joy was cut short with Eddie's departure, but that was the reality of the times they were in. Veronica knew many households across Ireland had the same experiences.

Veronica left Virginia after a subdued Christmas and returned to Dublin in early January 1921 to a renewed feeling that Ireland could get its freedom. Before Veronica returned to Dublin, her father told her he had read in a British newspaper that the reality was the Irish Republic now exists. The bloodbath in the country continued.

At the end of her first week back in Dublin, she called to see Mrs Sullivan.

When Mrs Sullivan saw Veronica, a smile spread across her face.

'Veronica, I haven't seen you for months. Thank you for your letters. How have you been keeping?'

Veronica loved the soft lilt of Mrs Sullivan's accent. 'How are you and Mr Sullivan?'

'Ah, fine, you know with all the trouble on the streets it's hard. I do love getting your letters. Did Bridget write to you? She's with child and was very sick, but she's fine now and due anytime. Willie, my brother, wrote and said it was terrible in Belfast, trouble of all sorts on the streets. I don't know if it is any worse there or here.' Mrs Sullivan rushed her words, worry on her face.

'Here, I have something for you.' She grunted a little as she bent down behind the counter, 'You know, old age isn't nice, enjoy your youth while you have it,' she said and gave Veronica an envelope with Harry's neat handwriting on the front. 'He left it the other day.'

Veronica stood still for a moment, looking at the envelope. Slowly, she pushed it deep into her bag. 'I'll read it later.'

Veronica stayed in the warm shop, chatting and drinking tea, and left before the streets emptied of the workers returning home. 'I'll go while there are people still on the streets. You never know who is lurking in the shadows.'

On her way home, soldiers stood at the top of Abbey St.

'What's your hurry, love?' they jeered.

Ignoring them, she walked briskly, keeping her head low and not stopping until she reached Thomas St. In the quietness of her bedroom, Veronica opened the letter.

In her room, she kept re-reading the words.

Wednesday, 12 January

Can we meet? I have thought about you a lot in the last year and would so love to see you again.

Please.

Saturday, 4 p.m. at the corner of Abbey St?

Harry.

39

Veronica didn't reply to Harry immediately. They arranged to meet four weeks later on Saturday, 12 February.

That Saturday, Veronica crossed O'Connell Bridge on her way to Abbey St. Harry stood at the corner. From a distance, her heart raced, her mouth dry. 'Veronica,' he said slowly and quietly. 'I didn't know if you would come.'

She didn't speak, her pulse racing. It was hard to ignore the jolt in her stomach as she looked at him, and guilt surged through her that she hadn't confided in anyone she was meeting him. Now she wished she hadn't come. It was so risky; she had no reason to meet him and didn't want to admit that she had wanted to see him.

'I'm delighted you came. Shall we go to O'Shea's for tea?'

She hesitated, then nodded.

'Thank you,' she said, and they walked the short distance in silence. She knew it was risky to be seen with a man in uniform. Harry stood aside to let her enter and chose a corner table away from the street view.

'Tea for two?' a chirpy young waitress asked.

It would have been no surprise to Veronica if she had refused to serve them.

'Please,' Harry replied as if everything was normal.

The tea arrived promptly as the two looked at each other, a little awkwardly. Once their conversation had flowed smoothly, but now, they had little to say.

Veronica broke the silence. 'Harry, I have to thank you for saving me that day. It must have been a risk.'

He shrugged his shoulders. 'It was only by chance I was in the Castle that night. I heard a soldier say they had captured a pretty young woman with green eyes and I knew it was you.' He leaned across the table and looked her directly in the eyes, and her pulse quickened. 'I knew you worked for Sinn Féin. I saw you in the office that day I was there with General Maxwell.'

It unsettled her that a warm glow rose inside as she looked at him, and averted her gaze.

'Veronica. Veronica, please look at me.'

Slowly, she lifted her head; she knew what would happen as soon as their eyes met. She was afraid her eyes would reveal she didn't see anyone else in the tearoom. Now she wished she had told Michael, or even Tom, that she was meeting him.

He took her hand, and her cheeks flushed. 'I miss you so much. I can't eat or sleep. I can't think.'

Their eyes met and locked for a moment before she looked away towards the ringing bell over the door as it opened. Veronica pulled her hand back from his.

Harry whispered as he leaned towards her, 'It is only an accident of birth that I am English. I didn't choose that.

But meeting you was no accident, that was fate. We are meant to be together.'

His hand moved towards her cheek. 'Veronica, my engagement, I told you, it's a loveless one. I was going to go through with it for my father. But the longer I have spent away from you, the clearer it has become that I cannot marry her. I have broken things off with her.'

His eyes locked on hers and she felt lightheaded. His words were too much for her. Surprised she could speak, she said, 'Even so, I am Irish, you are English. A soldier. The enemy! I never told you, but my brother was in prison. Innocent people are being murdered when we only want our freedom.'

Sighing, he spoke more quietly, 'I know your brother was in prison. I met him at Crumlin Prison when I was in Belfast. I recognised him straight away and checked his name. You are so similar. I shouldn't tell you this, but I spoke to the guards, and they weren't too hard on him. I did ask them to look after him, but well, I don't know if they listened to me.'

She couldn't find any words to thank him.

'Veronica,' he spoke more forcefully, 'I am fed up with it. We have lost so many, and we are still losing. It's just so damn hard, Lloyd George won't send any more men.' He sighed and stopped as a woman with a pram passed, trying to quieten a baby.

'Veronica, please can we go out for the day? Please, just one more day, the two of us, and then I'll leave you. Anyway, our time here in Ireland may be coming to an end.'

She didn't reply, thinking, her anger softening the more he spoke. What harm would there be? There was little more she could do for Sinn Féin – why not do something for herself? She was tired, tired of all the fighting – tired of worrying.

She had not drunk her tea, surprised by his words. Not that Lloyd George thought he was losing the war with the Irish, but that Harry had such feelings for her. She was equally surprised to realise that she wasn't playing a game anymore.

40

She couldn't believe what she was doing. She had told Harry she would go to Bray on Saturday, telling Betty and Tom that she would be home late as she was going to see Bridget's new baby. March was not a time to go to Bray, but she thought it would be the only place they would not be seen together.

On Saturday she arrived at Harcourt St train station to meet Harry. She searched the station platform for him, but it was empty apart from the ticket collector and a tall man in a smart winter coat. When the man saw Veronica, he raised his arm. It was Harry. She exhaled with relief that he wasn't wearing a uniform; it was already a dangerous game to be playing meeting him. She sat beside Harry, the rhythmic movement of the train soothing as she stared out the window at the passing countryside, soon replaced by the sea. The sea was angry, and the whites of the waves crashed onto the rocks. The weather was turning from bad to worse.

A cold wind greeted them as they got off the train at Bray. Harry took Veronica's arm, pulling her into him to shield her from the wind. They strolled along the curved beach, oblivious to the few walkers leaving the beach. Thunder rumbled in the distance. The grey-black clouds ominously hung overhead, waiting for another roll of thunder to command them to empty. They walked the arc of the beach, and the waves beat the shoreline and displaced the sand.

Another roll of thunder was followed by the crack of lightning zigzagging across the sky. That was the cue. Icicles of rain fell on the beach, and Veronica's hat blew away with a gust of wind. Harry grabbed her hand and ran to the strand, shielding his eyes from the rain to look for shelter. The trees bent away from the sea as the waves crashed against the shore. Veronica couldn't see, the sheet of rain was like a wall preventing her from lifting her head.

'Veronica, a hotel! Quick, let's run,' he shouted. 'I think I see a light.'

They rushed into the foyer, and Harry had to push the door against the wind to shut it. A fire burned in the large fireplace, and they both sought immediate comfort in front of the blaze. On the piano in the corner, a newly lit candle burned brightly.

'Hello,' Harry shouted into the empty foyer.

A diminutive silver-haired lady appeared from behind a mahogany panel in the wall. She was no more than four and a half feet tall and wore a cardigan that was the most colourful Veronica had ever seen, with every colour of the rainbow – it was also two sizes too big for the lady.

'Look at ye. You're soaked through. Sit down, and I'll bring ye tea,' she commented, and disappeared, returning a few minutes later with a tray of tea and biscuits.

'Get this into ye. It's a bad one out there, trees down everywhere. Pull that sofa closer to the fire,' she said and pointed to the two-seater sofa. 'Make yourself comfortable. I'll take your coats, and dry them in the kitchen by the Aga. It'll be a long night. The roads are blocked by trees, and apparently, a tree just missed a train on its way to Dublin.' She put her hand on her chest. 'Imagine being crushed in a train by a falling tree, perish the thought. So, you live near?'

'No, we're from Dublin, down for the day.'

'Oh, it's an unusual time to visit the sea.' She looked at the door windowpane as it rattled in the wind. 'I don't think you will be going back tonight. Do ye have family ye have to get back to?'

'Oh no, Mr Fairfax and I are just friends,' Veronica said, sticking out her hand, 'I'm Veronica.'

'I'm Mrs Coppinger,' she said and shook Veronica's hand warmly. 'No need to worry, dear. To be honest, I turn the other way. I'm not ignorant to the way of the world and young love.' She sighed, looking dreamily in the distance. 'I remember it well, but that was many moons ago. I'll get two rooms ready.'

How would she get word to her aunt and uncle? What if Tom went to Bridget's house to search for her? She tried to remember if she had ever mentioned where exactly Bridget lived. Her mouth was dry, and her heart raced.

'Dry yourselves, and I'll get some supper ready for you. You're the only guests. We usually only get travelling salesmen at this time of year, but with the weather lately being so bad, we don't get many. It'll be ready at six o'clock. It'll only be soup and bread as I wasn't expecting anyone, and I'll bring it out here to you, the dining room is too cold.' She turned, muttering, 'I won't be long, warm yourselves.'

Veronica laughed. 'She reminds me of Mrs Slaney, our cook, she talked incessantly.' Veronica stood by the fire, rubbing her hands together. With a crack of thunder, the room instantly lit up, and she jumped, knocking the poker and shovel stand.

'What's all that noise, are you all right?' Mrs Coppinger rushed back into the room.

'It's nothing, Mrs Coppinger, the lightning and thunder gave me a fright.'

'Come away from that window. I'm always afraid lightning will come through it. The soup is nearly ready.'

When Mrs Coppinger turned to leave, Veronica realised Harry had his arm around her shoulders and was guiding her back to the couch.

'You're shivering, sit down and wrap this blanket around you.'

He wrapped a tartan blanket around Veronica, and they sat in comfortable silence, watching the flames dance wildly when a gust of wind blew down the chimney.

Soon Mrs Coppinger put a tray onto the table in front of them with two bowls of steaming soup and thick slices of bread smothered in butter. 'Eat while it is hot, and I'll bring you up to your rooms after a while,' said Mrs Coppinger.

After the soup and bread, she joined them for tea. The clock chimed nine.

'God, I can't believe it is so late. I've put bedpans in your beds so I'll show you to your rooms.'

They followed Mrs Coppinger up the stairs along the corridor to the rooms. The hallway lights flickered at another roll of thunder.

'It'll sure be a long night, and I hope you sleep, dear. This is your room,' she said, opening a door. 'I'll show you where everything is, I've left you a few things. Mr Fairfax, there is your room,' she pointed to the door next to Veronica's. 'I put a candle beside your bed in case the lights go out.'

Harry bid the two women good night with a nod.

Veronica had never stayed in a hotel before. The bed was huge, with three white cushions on top of the pillows, and the curtains matched the pink flowery bedspread and pillows.

'I gave you a good room. This is usually where honeymooners stay,' Mrs Coppinger said with pride as she took off the cushions and fluffed the pillows. On the bed lay a white cotton nightdress.

'Thank you,' Veronica said, and Mrs Coppinger chatted as she pulled the curtains tighter to block out the night. The light flickered again and the windows rattled as if the angry wind was shaking its fist. *Traitor.*

'I've left you a candle as well beside the water bowl and jug over there.' She pointed to a small dresser with the holy cross hanging above it on the wall. 'But you should get to bed before the electricity goes completely,' she added before she left the room.

The windows shook as thunder cracked again and the

room lit up with lightning. Immediately immersed in the dark, Veronica tried to remember where Mrs Coppinger had left the candle. She hadn't really listened to her. She had told her where it was but, she hadn't looked; now the room was dark. She inched forward, her foot catching on the rug and steadied herself. If she fell, she could easily hit her head. She imagined lying in a pool of blood – dead, and not found until the morning. She tentatively moved the tip of her foot, hoping to remember where the bed was. It had been to her left, and with caution, she inched toward where she thought it would be, but soon she walked into a wooden door. Her hands glided over the wood. It was the wardrobe. Thinking and visualising the room, she turned around to move again. At this rate, it would be morning before she found the bed. There was a light knock at the door.

'Veronica, are you all right?'

It was Harry.

'No, I can't find the candle.'

The door creaked open, and Veronica saw the flicker of a candle, the light from it highlighting his beautiful face. He waved the candle around the room and moved toward Veronica when it fell on her. He took her hand, guiding her to the bed. The door swung shut. Veronica and Harry sat looking at each other, their faces illuminated by the candle. His eyes travelled over her body. He pulled her towards him and her body trembled as he touched her lips and cheek. He wrapped his arms around her slim waist, his hands lingering on her hips. He kissed her neck, his lips sending shivers through every cell in her body, before he trailed a column of kisses down her neck as soft as a million butterfly wings. She moaned and arched her back.

She melted into him, inviting him to take her. He carefully undid the buttons, and then, as she responded to him, he pushed her onto the bed. As the storm crashed against the windows, their bodies moved with ferocity, a hunger for each other heightened by knowing it would be the last time together. That night she was transported to new heights of desire she'd never imagined possible, refusing any guilt to weave its presence into her morning.

At breakfast, the joy of the previous night was replaced by sadness. The reality of the situation dawned on her. Tom and Betty would be worried, and she was anxious to return to Dublin. She hoped Tom hadn't gone to Bridget's to look for her.

'I'll see if the line is cleared for ye. Did the storm keep ye awake?' asked Mrs Coppinger as she eyed the untouched poached eggs.

'We didn't notice it at all,' said Harry. 'I'll go and see if it looks like the weather will stay calm.'

'Are ye not hungry?'

'No, I'm fine, Mrs Coppinger,' said Veronica. 'Your name is unusual.'

'My grandfather was English and met my grandmother when she was in service in England. They returned here to get married and never went back. He fell in love with the place, loved the sea, as I do.'

Veronica smiled. 'I know the feeling, water has a sense of magic, and an energy, especially in the wind. What about Mr Coppinger, is he about?'

The smile faded from Mrs Coppinger's face, and her eyes watered. 'No, my dear, widowed ten years.'

'I'm so sorry, that was rude of me.' Veronica's face flushed.

'No, no, dear, don't be embarrassed.'

The door to the breakfast room opened.

Harry came in. 'It looks like the rain will stay away. The station master said all the trees on the line are cleared.'

'Great, finish your tea. I've your coats all dry now.'

When they left the hotel, a few stray branches lay on the road, but the cloudless blue sky gave nothing away of the previous night's anger.

The train arrived, and soon they were on their way back to Harcourt St station. They leaned into each other, with nothing but silence, knowing this was the last time they would see each other, their bodies moving in unison with the train as it rattled through the remains of the storm. The countryside was soon replaced by houses, and she braced herself for the departure.

When the train pulled into Harcourt St, they gathered their coats and stood on the platform.

'Veronica, I have to go. They'll be wondering where I am at the barracks, and I need to change back into my uniform. Your aunt and uncle will be...' but before he could finish the sentence, the reality of their situation was thrust upon Veronica. Three soldiers entered the platform, watching the passengers waiting to board with suspicion. The soldiers, young men, looked tired and fearful. One of the soldiers boarded the first carriage of the train, his gun cocked ready to defend himself. The other two soldiers called over the Ticketmaster, and after a few words, the soldiers walked along the platform slowly, looking at the passengers who waited to board the train. Harry kept his head low, and when they passed, he turned to Veronica. 'I have to go,' he said and pulled her to him. 'This is harder than I thought, but it's too dangerous to be seen together.' He whispered into her neck, his breath hot. 'Veronica, I will miss you.' She watched him leave, with no guilt, glad she had never told Michael, or Tom. This was her secret, and she vowed never to tell anyone.

41

Eight weeks later Veronica sat on the bed in Bridget's room with her hands on her stomach.

'Veronica, what's wrong? You're white as a ghost. Here, have my hanky, and please stop crying. Veronica, please tell me what's wrong. I haven't seen you for months. Have you been sacked from your job? When you last wrote, you said everything was great?'

Veronica hugged her legs, rocking lightly, as tears flowed down her cheeks. Bridget moved closer and held her hand gently stroking it. Veronica's body heaved and shuddered against Bridget.

'Veronica, I'm worried now. The only time I saw anyone cry like this was my sister, and that only meant one thing... Jaysus, you're not?'

In between sobs, Veronica said, 'I'm pregnant.'

There was a tap on the door. 'Bridget, are ye all right? I've to go out in a few minutes, and the baby needs feeding.'

'Mam, I'll be down in a minute. Veronica is nearly finished fitting on the dress.' She whispered to Veronica, 'Ma is great to help me out with the baby with Sam having to go to England for work, but Veronica, she would take one look at you, and you'd be straight down to the convent. She knows these things – I don't know how, but she always knows when someone is pregnant. Veronica, I would hate for you to end up in a mother and baby home. The nuns can be so cruel.'

'But, you said they helped Maura.'

Bridget shook her head. 'No, it wasn't help,' she said, bitterness spitting out the words.

'My mam's brothers, uncle Tommy and Sheamie in England sent £100 to the nuns to get her out, and then she took the boat to them in Merseyside. She had to pretend to people her husband had been killed in the war.'

'I don't understand, £100?' Veronica's eyes widened.

'The laundries the nuns run, washing the sheets for the hospital. Girls who have gotten into trouble are sent to the laundries. They work there until they have the baby with two choices.'

Veronica knew what she was going to say.

'If the girls don't pay, they keep the baby and the mother gets it back after working for four years in the laundry. But, most don't. They give them away to families who can't have a family.'

'That's bordering on criminal,' Veronica said.

'Veronica you can't say that about the nuns. You either pay £100 to get your baby back or work doing the laundry for four years – and sometimes, well most of the time the girls don't get them back.' Veronica's eyes widened with shock, and Bridget continued, 'You're so innocent, Veronica, God help you. It's a cruel world for an unmarried woman. Maura was lucky, but her friend Mary, got herself into bother as well, but she had no money. She had a son around the same time as Maura. There had also been no goodbyes to her son. "It's God's wish," the nuns told her. And Mary asked about her rights as a mother. The nuns told her she'd lost her rights when she had taken her knickers off!'

Veronica whimpered, 'Oh God,' drawing her knees to her chest, rocking back and forth. 'Bridget, what in God's name am I going to do?'

'Are ye sure? Ye could be wrong. If it was because your monthly bleed didn't arrive, it happens to me all the time.'

Putting her head in her hands, Veronica said, 'I'm sure. I went to the doctor!'

Bridget gasped, sitting back on the bed. 'How did you explain that? You're not married, how did he see you?'

'I took my Aunt Betty's ring. Since Padraig died, she has become so thin, and she must take it off, or it will fall off when she scrubs the floors. When I started to get sick in the mornings, I never paid much heed to it, but my blouse became tight, and I missed two months.'

'V, I couldn't bear for the same to happen to you like Maura. Will he stand by you?'

'No. He can't.'

'Why? Jaysus, Veronica, he has to.'

She told Bridget everything.

'You have to tell him, V. It will be tough on your own, and the only other solution is to go to a mother and baby home.'

Veronica squeezed up in a ball on the bed, sinking into the feathers. Bridget was still in shock from the revelation.

No words came, but she curled up beside Veronica and rocked her to sleep.

When Veronica woke, Bridget had gone. Veronica thought about what her friend said, she would try to get word to Harry. Gathering herself together she found Bridget in the kitchen feeding her baby and said her goodbyes.

Bridget held her tight. 'Veronica, tell him, you never know what he will say.'

'I'll think about it. I don't know if he is still here. It looks like the British army is already leaving. Dáil Eireann and the British government are negotiating their leaving. I should be thrilled that we are finally on the road to our independence, but now...' Veronica began to cry again. Bridget got a handkerchief for her friend. 'Now look at the mess I have got myself into.'

'Bridget, are you home?'

'It's my mother, Veronica. Put your coat on, or she'll know.'

'I'm going,' she said and left by the back door before Bridget's mother entered the kitchen.

On the bus on her way home, she felt numb and stared out the window to avoid contact with anyone. A family sat a few seats in front of her. She stared at the mother as a child slept in her arms. The child woke as the bus suddenly jolted to a stop.

'Hooligan,' shouted the driver out of his window at a young boy on his bicycle that was far too big for him.

The mother rocked the crying child, trying and failing to get her to sleep with a soothing song. The baby girl stretched her arms out for her father, who sat next to them. He had the same mass of curly brown hair as the baby. She wrapped her tiny arms around his neck and fell asleep. Veronica put her hand on her stomach while she watched them, rubbing her tummy gently. Her blouse was now tight over her swelling breasts. She was lost in thought for most of the journey as the bus passed by a familiar street. The glow of the lights of the Shelbourne Hotel was ahead. Her heart quickened, and her pulse raced. Without giving it a second thought, she pulled the rope. The bell rang, and the bus slowed to a stop. Veronica gathered her coat and bag and rushed past the conductor not replying to him as he said goodnight.

Standing in front of the Shelbourne, she put on her coat and fixed her hair and looked in the dining room window; a group of men laughed and joked over dinner. She took a deep breath and pushed the doors open. The doorman leaned on the desk, talking to the desk clerk. Few guests would be expected this late. Neither saw her enter, and she turned left to the dining room and scanned the room full of diners. The smell of cigar smoke reminded her of her last meeting with Harry. Murphy, the waiter who had always served them, leaned over the table, pouring wine for a young couple whose eyes and hands were locked in love.

He walked towards the kitchen door but dropped his towel. As he bent to pick it up, he saw Veronica standing in the shadows of the entrance to the room.

He looked around the room and walked to her.

'Yes, ma'am, can I help?'

'Please, Harry. Major Fairfax? Do you know if he has gone back to England? Or do you know his address?'

'I have an address to forward on his things.'

She took paper and pen out of her bag, and scribbled a note, folding it in three. 'Could you give this to him?'

He stood still and silent, for what seemed like an eternity. Eventually, he slowly put out his hand for the note. Mouthing thanks, she left to go home. At Thomas St, Veronica ignored Betty's questions about Bridget, saying she had a headache, and went straight to her room. She lay thinking about the letter to England. She wasn't sure how long it would take to reach Harry, but if she heard nothing in a few weeks, then she would go home to Cavan.

The following Friday morning before she left for work, Veronica tried to eat breakfast but then pushed the bowl away. Her stomach heaved at the smell of food.

'Who's that at the door, at this time of night?' said Betty.

Veronica hadn't heard a knock, but she heard Tom thanking someone.

Tom entered with something in his hand. 'Veronica, some man left a letter for you,' he said, holding a white envelope. 'A posh fella, with a black moustache and grey hair.'

Murphy, she thought. 'Eh, that's Mrs O'Reilly's husband.'

'Grand. I've got to go to work,' he said, and he left.

She took the letter and pushed back the chair, and Betty had to catch it before it hit the ground.

In her bedroom, she ripped the letter open.

Can we meet on Saturday? The Shelbourne at 5 p.m. I am back in Dublin finishing off business, and I got your note that you wanted to see me. I have to leave on Sunday.

H.

42

On Saturday, the doorman at the Shelbourne opened the door for Veronica. In the foyer, she fixed her hat as one of the blue orchids had come loose. The yellow primroses on it reminded her of the hedgerows at home, always the first signs of spring, the beginning of new life.

The previous night she had practised her speech. It was short. She would tell him she was pregnant. She daydreamed he would grab her hand saying he would leave his wife, he had already, and she was sure he meant it. They would leave the hotel hand in hand. Everything would be all right.

The tearoom was nearly emptied now of the afternoon tea people. There was a sense of calmness about the room, the dim lighting creating a sombre atmosphere which was some comfort to Veronica. She took it as a good sign.

A poker straight grey-haired man in the black regulation uniform of the Shelbourne approached her, 'Yes, ma'am, can I help?'

'I'm meeting Major Fairfax.'

'He's expecting you. I'll take your coat and hat.' He gave them to the cloakroom boy before bringing her over to Harry, who was wearing a shiny blue jacket with a matching tie.

She sat down, twisted her pearls, ready to speak, but Harry talked first.

'I have to leave tomorrow.' He squeezed her hand. 'I'm sorry, Veronica.' He looked up at her. 'You know, they found out I helped.'

She gasped. 'Harry, I—'

'They told me I had to leave the army at the end of the year. Which is fine, I wanted to, anyway. They will give me a small army pension. My father arranged my engagement to Felicity because I couldn't live on my wages. Then I met you.' Sighing, he continued, 'I do love Ireland, but you were right, it would be impossible. No one would ever accept us.'

She couldn't think. She wanted to cry.

There was a cough. The waiter had a cheery smile, his bright waistcoat in contrast to the atmosphere. 'Excuse me, sir, your car is here.'

Harry nodded to the waiter. 'Just another few minutes.'

Veronica stood up, abruptly pushing the chair aside.

'Wait, Veronica, sit down.' Harry tried to grab her hand.

'No, Harry, goodbye.' She ran to the cloakroom. The boy had her coat and hat in his hand. She grabbed her coat as Harry chased after her.

Harry shouted after Veronica, 'Your hat!'

Now all that was left for her was the mother and baby home.

43

On Tuesday morning, a loud, impatient knock on the door put Veronica and Betty on edge. Few, if any, visitors called to Thomas St. The streets were alive with fighting – rebels against the DMP and soldiers. The DMP raided houses looking for rebels. Betty didn't answer, but as the knock grew louder, she put aside the clothes that she was washing to answer the door.

'Is Veronica there?'

It was James Sheridan.

Veronica followed Betty to the door. James was a little thinner than she remembered, and his eyes more sunken.

'James, come in and warm yourself.' She closed the door after a quick furtive look out into the hall.

He stood in front of the fire, opening his jacket to warm himself. It was then she saw the pistol.

Betty pulled a chair out from the table, motioning James to sit.

'I'll get both of you some tea,' Betty said and left the two to talk.

James sat down and rubbed his hands through his hair. 'Oh, Veronica, it's all such a mess. First, I have to say,

355

I'm sorry. Sorry for being horrible to you when we were teenagers, and secondly, well, sorry again, when I tried to kiss you that night.'

'No, I'm not mad at you, I know you only wanted to help our country. It was childish of me; I was jealous Eddie was spending so much time with you.'

The tea arrived with bread, and he took a few mouthfuls and gulps of tea before taking some papers from inside his coat. 'Here, I need to get a message to Michael. Eddie and I—'

'Eddie – how is he? Why didn't he come?'

James gulped more tea and finished the bread. He wiped his mouth with the back of his hand. 'Eddie is fine. He couldn't come here because there are English spies everywhere, and he didn't want to put you in any danger. If they catch him, he will be shot. Those bastard Black and Tans have no mercy. I'm not known to them, well, not really. They know my name, but don't know what I look like.'

She stood up and wiped away crumbs from her skirt. 'I'll just get the brush; I don't want to encourage the mice.'

Betty poked the fire and put the kettle back on it to boil.

James followed Veronica into the kitchen. 'Do you know the lads at the bank asked about you, and why you had no man? They thought you might be having an affair with Michael Collins. They said the two of you were always in the office together.'

'That's ridiculous.'

'Why, what's so funny about that? You're an attractive woman, and we never saw you with anyone.'

'Who is we?'

'Well, when I came to Dublin to work in the bank, I pointed you out to some of the lads when I saw you. They said they didn't hear you were with anyone.'

She glared at him. 'I didn't know you were checking up on me.'

'Ah, Veronica, don't be mad, just saying. Anyway, we have more important things to worry about.'

James stopped talking as they heard footsteps on the stairs. They approached the door, and then a baby cried.

'That's Sheila Flaherty. She lives upstairs.'

'All right.' James stood, gathering his cap and closing his jacket.

Suddenly, he groaned and fell forward, hitting the table before slumping to the floor. His empty cup shattered when it hit the floorboards.

'James, what happened?' He lifted his right arm, and a pool of blood was on the floor under him. Veronica took off her cardigan, pressing it to his arm. James cried out.

'That's too hard.' Through pained words, he said, 'I've been shot, Veronica.'

'What's wrong with James?' asked Betty, rushing into the room. 'God, the blood.'

'Help me, Betty, James is bleeding. Please get some clean cloths and hot water. He's been shot.'

Betty got hot water and clean cloths and helped Veronica wrap his arm. The blood slowed when she tied the knot on the cloth tightly and, after a few minutes, stopped altogether.

'Betty, help me get him into the armchair.'

He's heavier than he looks,' Betty said as they heaved him over.

'I can't go to work now.'

James fell asleep or passed out, full of fits and shakes. Throughout the day, Betty sat on the ground beside him, gently wiping every new bead of sweat that appeared on his forehead. She knew Betty was thinking of Padraig's final moments, hoping someone might have cared for him the same way.

'The blood has stopped, but what about the bullet?' Betty asked Veronica.

'I don't know, maybe it passed through him. I think the good thing is it's stopped bleeding. We can only hope that it is.'

When Tom came home, Betty gave him buttered bread for his tea, and they explained about James. After tea, Tom knelt beside Betty. 'I think you should go to bed. I'll sit with him for a while. Veronica, you get some sleep too.'

James had stopped shaking and was in a deep sleep. The next morning both women were up before the whistle blew at the brewery. James was awake and talking to Tom.

Kneeling beside him, Veronica said, 'Thank God, James, you gave us a fright.'

'How are you feeling, James?'

'I'm fine now. Would you take this letter to Michael? It's to tell him the Black and Tans have a list of spies' names, and they are going to arrest them. I fear they will murder them! They know their time is limited here. They are thugs and want one last reign of terror before they leave.'

'Will you be able to go?' He looked at Tom. 'Can you take her?'

Tom shook his head. 'The horse is sick, and we don't have any to spare.'

Without hesitation, Veronica said, 'Don't worry, James, I'll be fine, I'll walk. Betty, don't look so worried,' she said and laughed. 'I've been in worse situations.' And she had little to lose now as it couldn't get any worse.

'We'll have breakfast, and then you can get on your way.'

Tom stood. 'James, stay here and rest. When you're better, I'll get you to a safe house after it's dark.'

After breakfast, Betty cleaned the table and busied herself sweeping the floor, all the time keeping an eye on James as he dozed.

'Betty, I'd better go to the office and see if I can get word to Michael.'

'I'm so worried about you. It's a terrible situation.'

'It's fine, honestly, don't look so worried. I'll be fine.' Before she left the house, she checked herself in the mirror on the hallstand and put her hand on her stomach. She didn't feel anything.

She buttoned up her coat, the letter safely in the inside pocket. Betty had left Veronica's new hat for her, the hat her mother had got her for her birthday.

Outside she passed night workers on their way home from work, and men on their way to work. Her heart beat fast. She knew she should have been cold, spring was late this year, but the adrenaline surged through her body, keeping her warm. Soon she saw Harcourt St and relaxed.

She didn't hear the army vehicle pull up beside her.

'Where are ya going?'

It was the Black and Tans.

'I'm going to my office to work.'

'What's your name?' The man stood directly in front of her.

She tried not to wince at his stale cigarette breath mixed with alcohol. He was the soldier who had questioned her in the raid looking for Michael Collins.

'Where are you going, a pretty little thing like you, all out on your own.'

She couldn't let her guard slip. 'Excuse me, I have to go to my aunt, she's expecting me at work.'

'What's going on here, lads? Never mind her. We've word Michael Collins is around here somewhere.'

'Go on then.'

Veronica breathed slow and long.

'Wait,' he said, 'what did ya say your name was?'

'Patricia,' she replied.

'Patricia, what?' he growled, shoving a gun in her ribs. He took out a piece of paper from his jacket pocket. He looked at her showing his black teeth, 'Patricia what?'

'Sweeny.'

'That's not Patricia Sweeny.'

Christ. It was the sergeant that had raided Harcourt St looking for Michael Collins. He remembered her. 'Her name is on the list,' he said as he grabbed it from the Black and Tan. 'Look there, it says Veronica McDermott.' He pointed his finger at her. 'That's her. She works for that Fenian. Where is he now?'

Again, he prodded her ribs, this time more forcibly.

My baby.

'Oh Christ, a Cryer. It's bad enough to have to listen to my wife. Lads just get the truck and bring her to Kilmainham Jail.'

She was thrown into the back of a vehicle. Immediately they moved, and she was thrown from side to side as it navigated through the streets. Eventually, it stopped, and the doors opened.

'Com' on. Follow me.'

Veronica didn't move.

'Did ya hear me?' he snarled. He got in and yanked her hair, pulling her outside.

She inhaled deeply as the Black and Tans pushed her towards the doors.

The doors opened as they approached. Inside rows of dim lights hung on the walls. Veronica's eyes adjusted to the low light, and there was a long staircase in front of her, but she was shoved into a cell to the left of the stairs and fell on the dusty dirt floor. After a few minutes, she stood to shake the dust from her skirt. The cell was only four feet by eight feet, containing a narrow bed. Iron bars guarded a small window high up on the wall. This was the second time she was looking out a barred window, and there was no Harry to rescue her now.

The bed was hard, but she was emotionally and physically exhausted, so succumbed to sleep. She only woke when a key scratched the lock, and the door opened.

A soldier towered over her bed. 'Up. Now.'

A narrow shadow of moonlight fell into the middle of

the cell floor, but it soon disappeared as clouds covered it.

'Get up now, stand in front of me.'

'I'm not deaf. There's no need to shout at me.'

'Don't give me any of your gruff, put your hands out in front of you,' he said, and he tied them together. She noticed it was a knot that her father had taught her to tie the parcels of meat in the shop. He pushed her outside into a bright yard. 'Go on, keep moving.'

A deafening noise like a continuous flow of gunfire sounded directly above her. She looked up to a domed ceiling that was made of glass, rain pounding on it.

'My coat.'

'You won't be needing that where you're going.'

He pushed her forward past the spiral metal staircase up to the next level. She counted three levels all in a circular shape. Looking down, all the wooden doors were identical. Was this where the leaders of the 1916 rebellion were held before they were executed?

'Forward, through that door,' he said, pointing straight ahead of them.

It brought her to a narrow corridor. One side was a continuous line of cells while the other was a stone wall with a few small windows high up, letting in a little light.

At the end of the corridor stood a soldier and he opened the door as they approached. She halted at the sound of gunfire.

'Move, no time for dilly-dallying,' he said, pushing her out of the corridor into a courtyard.

The rain had stopped, the clouds retreated and by the light of the stars and the full moon she saw a single upright stake at the wall at the end of the courtyard. The soldier pushed her forward with the butt of his rifle. She lost her balance on the wet pebbles and stumbled forwards. Two soldiers dragged a man past her. His once white shirt was grey, torn and covered in blood. His skinny body gave the impression he may not have reached adulthood.

'He's not dead,' said the soldier with a Dublin accent and dropped him like a bag of coal. The taller of the two soldiers aimed his rifle at the man's head and pulled the trigger. Blood splattered Veronica's clothes and face. The man crumbled on the stones.

Veronica screamed. Her thumping heart hurt her chest.

'Turn away. Here put this on.' A young soldier handed Veronica a single backcloth. 'For your eyes, miss.'

Veronica looked at the dead young man, her mouth dry, and standing tall, she stared directly into the soldier's eyes. 'I don't want that.'

He raised his eyebrows. 'You sure? Orders, ma'am. Sorry, I have to put it on everyone.' He pulled it tight around her head, so everything was black.

He pulled her to a stake and tied her hands behind it. As he tied the rope, he whispered into her right ear, 'I really am sorry, miss. I have never shot a woman.'

Bleakly, she thought that at least now her family would be spared the shame her pregnancy would have brought them. Tears streamed down her face, not for her, but for her unborn child. There was no hope for her now.

'Aim, ready.'

She took a breath and stood up straight.

'Stop!'

It was Harry.

Everything was quiet, then boots scraped on the stone yard coming towards her.

'Yes, sir. Great news, sir.'

Veronica didn't know what they were talking about. Again she heard, 'Yes, sir. Of course.'

Somebody now stood beside her. She could hear him breathing, smell his familiar scent. It was Harry. He pulled her blindfold down. It took a few seconds to adjust her sight. Harry stood in front of her. He pulled her into his embrace, holding her tight.

'Veronica, there is a truce. You are safe.'

A chaos of noise ensued in the courtyard, but Veronica thought about her family. She pulled back and looked at Harry. It was the second time he saved her life, her guardian angel. *What would they say?*

'Veronica, I know about the baby. I realised I'd made a mistake and went to find you. I called into the shop, and your Mrs Sullivan's niece was there. She told me everything. I'm so sorry, Veronica.' He hugged her once more, and then pulled away. 'First, we must get you back to your uncle and aunt. Everyone is safe now, including your brother.'

Veronica was silent, unable to process his words. He led her to a waiting car, opening the door for her before slipping in beside her.

'I'm sorry, Veronica, for doing that to you,' he said, taking her hand. 'I kept thinking about you and how I left you there at the Shelbourne. I promise I will never leave you again.'

'But how, Harry?' Veronica asked, her eyes desperate.

'How can we be together? You said it yourself that it would be impossible.'

'I have thought about nothing else for the last month. I'll speak to your family. But we have to be together. I need you.'

'But—'

'Please just think about it, Veronica,' Harry said gently. 'I don't want to be parted from you again. First, let me take you back to your family.'

44

20 Years Later

Gabrielle entered St Mary's Church in Virginia, in the same white linen dress that Veronica had got married in. They had taken it in together.

Gabrielle's primrose headdress rested like a halo on her golden-brown curls. She stood at the entrance of the church, waiting for the harpist to announce her arrival. The rays of the morning sun squeezed through the bell entrance of the church surrounding Gabrielle. Harry stood beside Gabrielle looking down at his eldest daughter. Arm in arm, they walked slowly, one step at a time up the aisle in step to the wedding march. Harry was unsteady, his limp never having fully recovered from the war, and the damp weather in Ireland didn't help.

Life had been trying in Cavan for Harry and Veronica at first because of the hostilities towards the English. But, when Harry steadfastly attended Mass every Sunday with Veronica and their expanding family, they gradually softened towards him.

The small stone church crowded with family and friends,

and all eyes on the bride. Veronica's mother and father sat at the top pew, too frail to stand. Eddie and his wife Helen smiled at their niece, tears of pride in their eyes, watching the happy couple.

Veronica wiped away a tear. At the altar, her daughter Gabrielle exchanged vows with Joe, her fiancé. Veronica held the notebook Harry gave her on her wedding day. It was the notebook Harry had with him on their days in Kingstown. She opened it. A young, naive girl of eighteen sat on a bench with her eyes closed, and if you looked closely at the pencil drawing, the corners of her mouth were slightly turned up into a smile. She closed her eyes, and she saw herself wearing the jade green shirt and cream blouse and could taste the sea on her lips.

Acknowledgements

Thanks to my husband John, who encouraged me to continue to write after our daughter Ciara passed away in 2016.

I also want to give my thanks to my family and friends for their unwavering support through our time of grief. And thanks to my agent Kate Nash for her belief in this book. Finally, thanks to my editors Rhea Kurien, and Hannah Smith from Head of Zeus and Aria.

About the Author

EIMEAR LAWLOR was born in Co. Cavan and now lives in the medieval city of Kilkenny with her husband John and two sons. She met John in London while she was studying for a BSc. Unfortunately, her middle child Ciara passed away in 2016, who was the inspiration of her writing career. Eimear worked as a teacher for a few years and became a stay-at-home mum after the birth of Ciara when Eimear was diagnosed with Multiple Sclerosis. When Ciara was twelve, she told Eimear to do something with her life other than drinking coffee with her friends. She did the NUI Maynooth Creative Writing course in 2014. Her writing has been on *The Ryan Tubridy Show*, and *The Ray D'Arcy Show* on RTÉ Radio 1 and her short stories have been published in two anthologies.

This is her debut novel and a work of fiction which was inspired when she read her aunt's Bureau of Military Statement. Her aunt worked in Dublin for the political party in 1917 that was trying to gain independence from England. Her aunt worked with Michael Collins and Éamon De Valera who she continued to work for after the Civil War as his private secretary.

Hello from Aria

We hope you enjoyed this book! If you did let us know, we'd love to hear from you.

We are Aria, a dynamic digital-first fiction imprint from award-winning independent publishers Head of Zeus. At heart, we're committed to publishing fantastic commercial fiction – from romance and sagas to crime, thrillers and historical fiction. Visit us online and discover a community of like-minded fiction fans!

We're also on the look out for tomorrow's superstar authors. So, if you're a budding writer looking for a publisher, we'd love to hear from you. You can submit your book online at ariafiction.com/ we-want-read-your-book

You can find us at:
Email: aria@headofzeus.com
Website: www.ariafiction.com
Submissions: www.ariafiction.com/
we-want-read-your-book

f @ariafiction
🐦 @Aria_Fiction
📷 @ariafiction